FRINGE CITY
NIGHTFALL

Hamish Spiers

ISBN: 978-0-6485479-4-5

First published: 2013
This edition published: 2020

6 5 4 3 2 1

Books by Hamish Spiers:

Star Frontier
Star Frontier: Beyond the Veil
Star Frontier: Dangerous Games
Star Frontier: Descent
Star Frontier: Intrepid

The Sentinel
Fringe City Nightfall

The Sun Always Sets

The Martian Archaeologist

The Veya Child

hamishspiers.com

As usual, this book is dedicated to, among others, my wife Erin, my son Jason, and my brother Rob who has given me so much advice and feedback on my novels over the years. I also want to thank Geof, who first suggested that I pen a sequel to *The Sentinel*, and Steve for all the feedback he's given me.

Eight years ago, Jason Harding turned away from his life as the Sentinel for good.

Or so he believed…

HERE COMES THE NIGHT

CATACLYSM

"*W*HEN MY PATIENT DEREK BRADLEY WAS* moonlighting as the vigilante Orion, there were several other prominent figures on the scene who had also taken the law into their own hands but Derek was the only one who was brought in. From my understanding, and he knows this too, he crossed a line the others hadn't. He had killed, although that wasn't all. Those he killed weren't exactly upstanding citizens as he tells it. But when he intervened in a hostage situation, his actions resulted in the death of a nurse, Danielle Sutherland, just twenty four years old.*

Some say my involvement in Derek's rehabilitation is a conflict of interest due to the coincidence surrounding this fact, that for a year or so I provided counseling to Danielle's family members. However, I personally never saw my involvement with these truly courageous people and Derek Bradley as a conflict of interest. I provide my help to those who need it. Danielle's family needed it for a time. Believe me, they needed it. And so has Derek Bradley, although I believe that time has now come to an end.

It probably goes without saying that Derek is resentful of

3

the way he's been treated. Charles Faulkner, the District Attorney of Fringe City argued hard in court for clemency on my patient's behalf and although Derek Bradley was considered by police and psychologists to be too dangerous to be released at the time of his arrest, he never went to a conventional prison but to a secure psychiatric institution. He was not thrilled about that, I can tell you, but it was a much better environment for him than prison would have been. A while after that, with good behavior, he was moved to a more relaxed institution.

To be perfectly honest, if he so wished, Derek Bradley could easily have escaped custody at any point during the past five years. He has remained where he is by choice and that is my opinion both as a professional in my field and simply as an observer with two eyes.

However, Derek has never forgiven the law enforcement agencies of the city for singling him out while allowing others who took the law into their own hands to go free. And he has never forgiven them for the fact that they, as he sees it, prevented him from carrying out his duty.

This is one point on which Derek cannot be persuaded. There is another one that is even more problematic for me. And saddening too, I have to admit.

I want to help Derek Bradley but the truth of the matter is that there's really nothing left I can do for him. He is the one patient I've completely failed. And that is why I've ended my sessions with him. I last saw him this morning..."

. . .

It was pleasant in the outdoor gardens of the Palmdale Mental Health Institute. Dr. John Carter sat down at the table across from his patient. At his request, Derek Bradley was unaccompanied by any guards and not restrained in any way.

If Derek wanted to, he could kill him. If Derek wanted to, he could also kill the guards and break out of the institute.

But Derek restrained himself these days. It was something that John had observed some time ago, although it wasn't until two years before this meeting that he had managed to persuade the necessary people to give Derek some space. That hadn't been easy but John had believed it was worth it. Now though, he had his doubts about that.

"I wonder about you," he said to his patient. "You could leave here any time you want really. But you don't. I wonder why."

"Why don't you just ask the question straight?" Derek suggested.

"Because you've been evasive before when I've raised it. You don't give me straight answers."

"Maybe today, I will."

"Any particular reason?"

Derek shrugged. "You deserve it. You've been meeting me for over six years now. That's a long time.

I've rarely seen such dedication to a single goal."

"A goal?"

Derek smiled. "My so-called rehabilitation."

John looked a little disappointed. "The way you say it doesn't exactly fill me with any hope for today's session. So you're going to start off by telling me that we're at the same impasse we've been sitting at for the past few years?" He tried a little humor. "You won't give me anything? For an old friend? You said I was dedicated."

Derek didn't budge. "You are. But I'm even more dedicated. If you release me, then Orion will return and I'll finish what I started. I'd like nothing better. And I've been keeping myself in good condition."

John eyed some notes in a folder he had lying open on the table. "Yes. The staff have mentioned that."

He frowned and turned back to his patient. "Why do you tell me things like that? You don't want to escape for whatever reason. I assume it's to do with pride—"

"Partially correct."

"—but if you want to return to being Orion once more, then you must know that telling me your plan prevents you from ever carrying it out. As long as we believe there's some possibility you may revert to—"

"Revert?" Derek asked, raising an eyebrow. "I've never *changed*."

"Okay," John said, trying not to let Derek get under his skin. He knew the man did that deliberately sometimes. Usually just for the fun of it. "I mean as long as we believe your attitude remains unchanged as far as Orion's concerned, then you know you will never be released."

"True enough," Derek conceded. "However, I said I'd be straight with you today and I mean it. So this is on the house. I'd like to help Fringe City but I won't until the city proves that it deserves my help. And until I'm released without conditions, I'll just stay here thank you very much. Anyway, why should you care? I'm out of harm's way as far as the law enforcement agencies are concerned and I've got no intention of leaving here. As far as I can tell, everyone should be happy."

"Well, I'm not happy, Derek," John replied. "I want to help you."

"You want to change me," Derek told him. "And I don't want to change." He smiled. "Besides I'm in love with one of the nurses here."

John nodded. "Can I ask which one?"

Derek's smile remained in place. "You can ask but I'd like to keep it to myself if it's all the same to you. However, she's not the one you'd think. Although that girl *is* rather easy on the eyes."

John watched him for a few moments. "You're

serious, aren't you?"

Derek stopped smiling. "Perfectly serious. I'm still a man like any other. If there were a chance this girl could marry me, I might well tell you everything you want me to say."

John shook his head. "Then I wish there was a chance. I wish you'd ask her to marry you right now."

"Not today," Derek said. "I have to be patient and let her get to know me better."

"Okay," John told him. "Then let's get back to business. Why do you still want to wage your one man war on crime when it's gone down so much? Fringe City isn't the place it was eight years ago. We've got people coming to live here *by choice* now. We get visitors. Grand Central's been torn down and replaced with a park. Parents are okay with letting their kids play there."

Derek shook his head. "There's still crime though. There's always crime."

"I know that," John said, "but it's manageable now. The police can handle it these days. We don't have big crime syndicates acting like they own the place. The street gangs have largely disappeared thanks to the wonderful work by Outreach. The National Guard never has to visit. Fringe City doesn't *need* Orion. Surely, you can see that."

Derek extended a hand palm upward. "Let's see

about that, shall we? Do you have my papers?"

John sighed. He reached down into his bag, which was sitting beside him, and pulled out two newspapers, the *Fringe City Times* and *Sun Central*. He slid them across the table.

Derek picked up the first of them, opened it up, skipped through the pages, stopped on an item and then showed it to John. "There. Young woman, aged eighteen. Left to die in a gutter."

John looked at the article. "I know," he said, his tone sympathetic. "But—"

"You have a daughter her age," Derek told him. "If this had been *your* daughter, you wouldn't be talking to me about how much crime has gone down. If this had been your daughter, then you would wish the city had let me do what needs to be done."

"However," he added before John could reply, "the people of Fringe City have made it clear they don't need me. *You* have made it clear you don't need me. Besides, believe it or not, I'm actually happy here."

John frowned. "I don't believe that for a second."

"Well, you should, Dr. Carter," Derek replied. "John. I've told you before. I'm an honest man. And I'm in love with that nurse."

John sighed and stood up to leave. "I'm sorry, Derek. I really am. I do hope though that you can find some form of contentment one day."

"Like this city, you mean?" Derek asked him, with just a hint of something in his voice.

John stopped. "What's that?" he asked, turning around.

"You can't turn your back on this city, Dr. Carter," Derek said. "And I don't mean that in vague terms. I mean right now, you should tell the dedicated people in the law enforcement community that something is happening out there and that they need to be ready."

John frowned. "Do you know something, Derek?"

"People always repeat the mistakes of the past," Derek said. "History shows us that in painful detail. An endless silly cycle. But I'm not talking to you about vague feelings of uneasiness. I'm talking about something concrete that is happening right now. I shouldn't tell you, god knows. It's a blow to my pride. But the fact is that whether Fringe City deserves my help or not, I *do* care about the people here. And right now, they're in danger."

"All right," John said. "What do you know?"

"That copy of the *Fringe City Times* you just gave me? In the finance section on page thirty-seven, it mentioned that the stocks for a company called CR Edwards dropped by over a dollar-sixty."

"You couldn't possibly have noticed that in the time you were flipping through that," John said, reaching for the paper.

"Have a look."

John did. Then he shook his head and put the paper back down. "That's unbelievable."

Derek shrugged. "I've always been observant."

"However, I still don't see what that has to do with anything."

"In and of itself, it probably wouldn't have meant anything to me either," Derek said. "However, it reminded me of an article I read in the *Sun Central* paper you gave me last week. An economics article about how theft is basically ingrained in the overhead running costs of your average business these days. It cited several examples of corporations that had been hit over recent months and one of them was CR Edwards. Then when I saw the name just before, it clicked in my head. I know what CR Edwards does. It's a demolition company."

"I don't know if we can ever help Derek Bradley," Dr. John Carter finished, speaking into his handheld recorder, "but I think, if we're willing to listen to him, Derek Bradley might be able to help *us*."

He turned the recorder off and picked up the file he had just faxed to the police headquarters. CR Edwards was a local company, he had found out. So if Derek's hunch was right, then it was indeed a Fringe City problem, rather than something that the people of, say, Delaware had to worry about.

He looked at the file with a heavy sense of apprehension. There were probably several things that people could steal from a demolition company of course. But only one of them came to mind.

"Well, the past participles of *regular* verbs are the same as the past simple forms," Jason Harding said to the young woman standing next to him. "Some of them have non '-ed' ending options like 'proved' and 'proven'. But you'll naturally pick up on those things later. But really, you only need to worry about the irregular forms."

Kaori Tanaka nodded. "Okay."

She was a pretty girl, Jason thought to himself. It wasn't the most professional thought, he knew, but it was a fairly natural one. However, as long as he kept such thoughts to himself and didn't fudge progress test results for his more attractive students, it wasn't too much of a problem. But he liked Kaori. She was really nice natured and she had a great attitude towards the course.

It was nice, he had to admit, teaching English to adult students from around the globe. A welcome change from teaching high schoolers. He and Angie had been at this place for five years now and not once had they looked back.

They didn't make as much money as they had while working at East Somerset High but they were a lot happier. Also, it just so happened that this particular international language school was attached to the university where Jason's old friend Geoffrey used to work; and he occasionally stopped by his friend's old science department and caught up with the guys who were still working there. But all in all, work was all right. And that meant a lot to him.

"Don't try to learn them all at once though," he said to Kaori. "Just learn them as you need them. If you actually need to use a part of the language, you're more likely to remember it. But if you learn things out of context, your brain probably won't see the point of it and so it might throw it out."

He mimicked the action of discarding trash and Kaori laughed. "Ah. I get it. You forget it if you don't need it. Um… Use it or lose it."

"Exactly."

"Thank you, Jason."

Jason smiled. "Not a problem."

Another girl came in with a broad smile. "Oh, sorry, Jason. I didn't realize you and Kaori were still talking."

"That's all right, Ji Eun. We're just discussing past participles a little more. It's okay." He turned back to

Kaori. "So you understand all that? All the past participles for regular verbs are…"

"The same as the past simple forms," Kaori said, nodding. "So I only need to remember the irregular ones."

"That's it."

"Thank you so much for helping me," she said as she put her books away. "I'm sorry to take up your time."

"No, it's fine," Jason told her. "I'm glad you asked me. It's better to ask than to pretend you understand something when you don't."

"Yes. I think so too. Well, thanks again," Kaori said, joining her friend. "See you, Jason."

"Bye, Jason," Ji Eun joined in.

"Bye, Kaori. Bye, Ji Eun."

Once the two girls had left, Jason put his own books away and headed down to his staffroom. Angie was there already.

"Has anyone seen the class set of *Agendas in Text*?" she asked the room at large.

One of the other teachers slapped his thigh. "Damn. Sorry. I left it in my classroom last week. I'll run up and get it for you."

Angie gave a dismissive wave of her hand. "No, don't worry. I can pick it up in the morning. I just wanted to know where it was."

"Oh, all right," the other teacher said. "Anyway, sorry about that."

Angie shrugged. "No problem." Then she turned around and saw her husband. "Hey, Jason. Have a good afternoon?"

"Yeah," Jason told her. "What about you?"

"Yeah, fine."

Jason turned to one of the other teachers there. "Hey, Mike. Where's your guitar today?"

"At home," Mike said with a shrug. "Amanda said she only wants to see it on Fridays for the afternoon activity classes."

"Ah, she's a hard taskmaster, isn't she?"

"Yeah," Angie joined in. "Just the other day when I was suddenly sick, she took my class herself and gave me the day off."

Jason shook his head. "The heartless woman. That's exactly what I'm talking about."

He smiled at his co-workers. "Well, I think we're off. Are we still on for dinner on Friday night?"

"Yeah," another teacher joined in, a rather tall fellow called Johnson. Presumably, he had a first name as well but no one knew it, possibly Johnson included. "That's going ahead. We found a new place."

"Really? Where is it?"

"Don't remember exactly," Johnson said. "But we'll find it. Anyway, you'll love it. Mike and I went the other week."

Jason nodded. "I look forward to it."

Angie slapped him on the arm. "Come on, Jason. Ethan will be waiting."

"Right." Jason gave the room a group wave. "All right, guys. See you tomorrow then."

"See you, guys," Angie said, waving as well.

The handsome dark man dragged his younger companion through the doorway by the scruff of his shirt. He caught the eye of the woman standing behind the desk and shook his head. "He's on the stuff again."

Gwendolyn Fletcher looked at the kid. "Aidan? Are you messing with us?"

The kid avoided looking her in the eye. "No, Miss Fletcher."

"Should we call your mother again this time, do you think? Or should we just save ourselves the trouble and call the cops?"

"I'm sorry."

"Sorry?" Gwendolyn asked. "That's not going to cut it."

The other man shook Aidan's collar. "Hey. Wake up, Aidan. Who should we call this time? Your mother or the cops? Miss Fletcher asked you a question."

The kid began to cry. "Don't call them. I'll be good

this time. I promise. I just... You know, it's hard coming off."

"Hey, George," Gwendolyn said to the other man. "Maybe we ought to ease off a little."

George smiled at her. "Don't worry, Gwendolyn. I won't be too rough with him. But I think Aidan and I ought to have a chat up back."

Just then, another woman came out from said back, saw the scene before her, shook her head and turned to Gwendolyn. "I think you ought to let George handle it his way. Aidan needs some tough brotherly love right now." She smiled at George. "Hey, George."

George returned the smile. "Hey, honey."

Gwendolyn turned to the other woman. "You heard all that, did you, Sonya?"

Sonya shrugged, turning her gaze to the rather pitiful sight of Aidan blubbering. "Enough to know that Aidan's gotten himself in trouble. Again."

"Where did he get the stuff, George?" Gwendolyn asked.

"There's some kid on the corner of Adams and West," George said. "White kid, whiter than you two. Peroxide hair. Stupid piercings. Ugly face. Couldn't miss him."

"You *saw* him?"

George smiled. "Oh, yeah. I saw him all right. Aidan says he was there the same time last week too.

I'll check in with my liaison on the force after I have a chat with Aidan here. I don't think it should be too difficult to pick this guy up."

"Not too bright, is he?" Sonya asked her husband.

"Not too bright," George said. "And far too cocky."

Sonya smiled. "Good job."

George shrugged. "Hey, this neighborhood practically patrols itself these days." He patted Aidan on the shoulder. "Come on, Aidan. I'm not going to bust you or call your mother. Let's go out the back and have a chat. I'll make you a coffee if you like."

"I don't drink coffee," Aidan said. His tone was meek but he was no longer crying.

George grinned. "Sure you do. Come on."

Once they were gone, Sonya turned to Gwendolyn. "Well, George has things under control here and Mike and Dan are coming in in about an hour or two. Why don't you go home and have a rest?"

"I'm okay," Gwendolyn said, brushing her hands up along her cheeks and dragging her fingers through her hair, teasing it out. "I thought Claudia and Kathy were going to stop by here tonight and we were going to have a little catch-up. Or have I got the day wrong?"

"No, you were right," Sonya said. "But they had to cancel. Claudia's found some people who are interested in running that new center we've got down in Gainsborough West and she and Kathy are interviewing this week."

Gwendolyn nodded. "Ah, well. That's a shame but it's great they've found some people already. I had no idea we'd get so many Outreach centers up and running. Considering we were originally thinking of just one or two, fourteen's unbelievable."

"Yeah. It is," Sonya said. "Anyway, we'll get together and have a girls' night out soon. But since there's nothing else going on, why don't you go home and spend some time with that nice man of yours?"

"Assuming Charles has let him have the night off today. They work long hours in the D.A's office."

"They appear to," Sonya agreed.

Gwendolyn picked up her bag and headed for the door. "Well, I'll see you tomorrow then, Sonya. Say goodnight to George for me as well, will you?"

Sonya smiled. "Will do. See you, Gwendolyn."

Charles Faulkner, District Attorney for Fringe City, smiled at the younger man beside him as they walked along the corridor back to their offices. "You did well in there."

Devan Fletcher shrugged. "There wasn't much to it really. I figured out all the loopholes in environmental law they might try to use before we started today's session and already had the counter-arguments ready to go." He shook his head. "I reckon a lawyer's in trouble when the only things he's got going for his case are loopholes."

Charles inhaled a sharp breath. "Yeah, that should be a given but it never ceases to amaze me how many things without a shred of merit get through the system based on exploiting the wording of the law while willfully ignoring the spirit in which it was written."

"You know, before you came along," he went on, "it was all mob bosses, murderers, narcotics rings and a whole lot of other things I'd just call urban terrorism—"

"Sounds exciting," Devan said, in jest of course.

"It wasn't," Charles said, shaking his head. "It really wasn't. It was monotonous. Real soul destroying stuff. And for years, it stopped me from doing more worthwhile things. You know, getting corporations like the Alliance Bank to sort out its environmental track record, banning the production of that pesticide Escar was pushing all those years... *This* is the exciting stuff. This is making a difference."

"True," Devan agreed. "Hey, you left out that rather dubious character who was running that property scam."

"Which one?" Charles asked. "There have been a few."

"The guy who gave loans to purchase property he owned under a subsidiary. You know, he deliberately looked for clients he thought would default on their loans. Then he could evict them, rake in the interest and re-sell his property over and over again."

Charles grimaced. "Yeah, I remember that guy. What a nasty piece of work. Although you should give *yourself* some credit for that case, Devan. As I recall, you helped me a lot."

"Oh, I suppose I helped a little," Devan admitted. "Hey, that was around the time you showed me the work you were doing with Outreach, wasn't it?"

Charles smiled. "Yeah, I think that was when you first met Gwendolyn."

"Best day of my life."

"I would have thought the wedding might have topped it," Charles said, getting a little laugh from Devan.

"Yeah, good point," the younger man agreed.

They walked in silence for another moment or two.

"Anyway, I think I interrupted you back there," Devan said. "What were you saying?"

"About the mob bosses and all that stuff I had to deal with before you came along?"

"Yeah. That stuff."

Charles nodded. "I was just going to say that even though we're not fighting those guys any more, we're still fighting their lawyers and they're still every bit as down and dirty in the courtroom as they were before.

They may have different employers now but they themselves haven't changed a bit. They follow the scent of the money and exploit every vulnerability in the law they can to win their cases. So never drop your guard in there. Not for a second."

Police Commissioner Eric Hutchens looked at the new file in his in-tray, a fax from one Dr. John Carter. He knew John well. He was a good psychiatrist. A good man too. However, he probably wouldn't be a natural police officer.

It was good of him to send the fax though, Hutchens thought after he'd read it. It was the civic thing to do. However, all it did for him was to make him more anxious than he already was.

He'd known about the CR Edwards incident the moment the theft had been reported. He'd known about it for two weeks now and for the entire time, he'd been sending officers left, right and center looking for any leads they could find on the missing explosives, all the while trying to maintain the veneer of calm to prevent any unnecessary panic.

Mayor St. Claire had been adamant about that. She was, if anything, more anxious about the whole thing than he was but she didn't want him bringing any public attention to the investigation.

And that made sense, Hutchens knew. Anything that got into the media could also let the culprits know where his officers were in their investigations at any given moment. Not that those officers were right on their trail or anything like that but it was still good policy.

He put the file down and shook his head. He hadn't felt this impotent since he'd set out to track down the Bandit. For eight years, Fringe City had been free of the kind of deranged lunatics who would gun down twelve people in a cafe or blow up a metropolitan police station. It had been a good eight years. Hutchens didn't want the city going back to the way it used to be.

Most likely, the culprits of the CR Edwards robbery weren't psychotic mercenaries like the Bandit or calculating killers like the Specter. For all he knew, they were a couple of teenagers who thought stealing high powered blasting explosives was a bit of a laugh. Unfortunately, that really didn't make any difference in the grand scheme of things.

Ken Doyle was adjusting his tie as his secretary came into the office.

"Hello, Samantha," he said, smiling. "You're working late."

"It's only five-thirty," Samantha replied, putting a bundle of papers in his in-tray. "I was on a roll and I thought I may as well finish this lot before I head off. It means less work for me in the morning."

"Makes sense," Doyle agreed. "But if you keep getting everything done so efficiently, you're going to leave me with no choice but to give you another raise."

Samantha smiled. "I couldn't ask for another one so soon."

"By the way, there's nothing scary in that pile of papers, is there?"

"Not unless you count speaking at that high school and hosting next week's charity drive," Samantha told him. "The charity drive's probably fine but you know what high schoolers can be like."

Doyle laughed as he arranged some folders on his desk. "Don't I just?"

Samantha hesitated. "Uh... Alec called earlier."

"Oh, yes?" Doyle replied, without looking up. "What did he say?"

"He wanted to know why you insist on these meetings with Simon Mercer. He doesn't think it's a valuable use of your time."

"Perhaps I should call Alec," Doyle said, putting some papers away, "and tell him to let *me* worry about what I do with my time."

"Well, you do pay him to consult you," Samantha

reminded him, smiling. "That's what consultants do. You know? Consult?"

Doyle laughed again and shook his head. "I know. You're quite right."

"But anyway, Alec just doesn't see why your organization should be interested in doing business with Citisafe Security Systems. What about the inner city school computer lab initiatives or working with the local universities to extend their scholarship programs?"

"You're right," Doyle said. "And Alec too. But Simon and I are old friends and I do have a personal interest in how he's getting on. And I'm also somewhat curious about the work Citisafe Security Systems does. They *do* care about public safety and that's certainly something we can get behind."

"Public safety, yes. But Alec thinks they're driven by profit rather than any altruistic concerns."

Doyle sighed. "Yes, I'm aware of Alec's opinion on them."

Samantha shrugged. "I'm just passing on the message."

"I know," Doyle replied. "All right, Samantha. Why don't we call it a day?"

. . .

As she stepped through the door, Diane Felding was almost knocked to the ground by her oldest daughter, Caroline. Five, sweet-natured, bright and boisterous.

"Mommy!" the little girl shouted, wrapping her arms around her waist.

Diane smiled, knelt down and gave her a big hug. "Hello, Caroline!"

Another little girl was right on Caroline's heels, Elizabeth, the younger of Diane's daughters at two. She looked a *little* like Caroline but with a darker complexion and not as much hair. But she embraced her mother in a perfect imitation of her older sister.

"Mommy home!" she exclaimed with an earnest expression on her sweet little face.

Diane laughed and kissed her on the cheek. "Mommy's home, Elizabeth. Did you have a good day at day care? Yes?"

Elizabeth gave an emphatic nod. "Yes!"

Diane ruffled her hair and smiled at her husband, who was standing behind the children. "Hello, Mark."

"Hey, honey." Mark laughed a little. "She cried a lot when I dropped her off this morning but the teacher said she settled down after I left."

Diane nodded as she climbed back to her feet. "Ah well, that's good."

"You're a little late," Mark told her. "You're still only working part-time, right?"

"Oh yeah," Diane said, waving her hand when she saw his expression of concern. "I don't want to go back to full-time policing. However, Hutchens is a little worried about…"

She trailed off, glancing at her two daughters who were now playing with each other in the corner of the room. She'd decided when Caroline was born that she wasn't going to bring her work home with her when she had a young child in the house. And now she had two of them. Also, Caroline was good at picking things up from tiny snippets of a conversation and Diane didn't want her imagination getting carried away.

"Um…" she tried again. "That stuff from CR Edwards is still missing. We're not turning up any leads."

Mark nodded, his concern evident in his expression only. "Ah, well," he said, his voice not giving any of it away. "That explains it."

"What about your day?" Diane asked him.

Mark shrugged. "Oh, you know. Same old, same old. Old being the operative word. These sweet old dears are pretty fond of their routines." He looked down for a moment. "Although, Mrs. Gonzales passed away last night."

"Oh," Diane said. "I really liked her."

"Yeah, me too," Mark said. "And she had a really great sense of humor too. But, well, she was almost ninety-seven. She wasn't going to be around forever."

"Yeah, I know. Still though, are you all right?"

Mark sighed. "Yeah, I'm fine. It was just a bit of a blow. You know how it is."

"I'm sure," Diane told him.

Her husband gave her a smile. "Anyway, the kids are home, you're home and I've got a Uzbekistan chicken dish sitting next to the stove ready to put on the table."

"Wow," Diane exclaimed. "Sounds great. I'll just go and get changed quickly and then I'll be right back."

"No problem," Mark said. He turned to the girls. "Caroline? Elizabeth? Are you hungry?"

Jason and Angie Harding were also sitting down to dinner at that very moment, to Jason's own homemade variation of tandoori chicken, with some plain chicken, lettuce and mash potatoes for their seven year old son, Ethan.

Ethan beamed at them from his end of the table. "And the spaceship went whoosh..." Feeling that 'whoosh' didn't demonstrate just how spectacular this was, he waved his hand through the air to drive it home. "And the other one couldn't go as fast and it hit the asteroid and crashed and the..." He took a moment to catch his breath. "And the other ship escaped!"

Jason nodded. "Is that right?"

"Yeah!"

Jason grinned at his boy. He loved him more than words could express and he also found he could listen to his stories all day.

Angie could too, of course, and she loved him just as much as Jason did. However, being more pragmatic about certain aspects of the whole parenting business than her husband, she knew when to interrupt as well.

"Okay, Ethan," she told him. "Now eat your chicken before it gets cold, okay?"

Ethan smiled. "Okay, Mom." He put a forkful of meat in his mouth. "And the ship—"

"And don't talk with your mouth full," Angie reminded him.

"Okay, Mom."

Sergeants Myers and Walsh watched the traffic heading over the West Avenue Bridge from below. There wasn't much to see really from that angle. In daylight, the tops of the cars would probably be visible. At night, all they could see were the yellow glows of headlights, the red glows from tail-lights and the occasional truck if it was large enough.

In front of them, there was a largely empty parking lot and an entirely empty area where weekend markets were held sometimes. The view to the sides and in the rear-view mirror was a little more lively with the shops and restaurants about the place but after watching it all for two hours, the novelty had well and truly worn off.

Then Walsh sat up and pointed through the windshield. "Myers, do you see those kids?"

Two youths were climbing down the brickwork of the nearest bridge pylon.

Myers frowned. "Where the hell did *they* come from? Were they on the walkway or something?"

Walsh shook his head. "They weren't on the walkway. They came out from under it."

"What the hell were they doing up there then?"

Walsh pulled out his radio. "That's what I want to know." He switched it on and made a call. "This is Sergeant Walsh. I'm with Myers by the east end of the West Avenue Bridge. We've just seen two young men come out from under the road and they're climbing down the pylon. I reckon they're up to no good and I want to climb up there and see what they were doing."

"There are two of them?"

"Yeah. I know. Myers and I could try to get them both but someone ought to have a look at what they were up to."

"We'll send someone right away but you stay with Myers and bring those two men in."

"Okay then. It's your call but I'm worried."

"I understand," the lady on the other end replied. "But Sergeants Tate and Delgado are half a block away. You stay with the suspects."

"Got it," Walsh replied. "Over and out."

He turned to Myers. "Well. You heard her. Let's get these guys."

He turned the key in the ignition and unlatched his door. Myers unlatched his own.

Leaving the headlights off, Walsh let the handbrake off, put the car in drive and let it roll forward, hardly tapping the accelerator at all. He steered it behind the handful of cars in the parking lot, hoping the two youths couldn't see him. So far, they hadn't but they were now just thirty yards in front of the car and three yards off the ground.

Walsh put the car in neutral, pulled on the handbrake, switched off the motor and took out the keys. He nodded to Myers and they both gently gripped the door handles.

Then the two youths jumped the remaining yard to the ground, and Walsh and Myers leapt out of the vehicle.

"Hold it right there!" Walsh shouted.

The young men turned only long enough to get a look at them and then shot off, legging it around the pylon and down the street.

"Shit," Myers muttered, pulling out his gun.

Walsh did the same as they took off after the men but he felt uneasy about it. Pulling guns on suspects was very much old school Fringe City policing and Mayor St. Claire was not ambivalent in her opinion on it. However, Walsh was even less keen on the idea of charging after possibly armed suspects without a weapon of his own.

As they ran, Walsh flicked on his radio. "Suspects are running south. They're on the river drive but there are a lot of buildings 'cross the street. We're in pursuit on foot."

"Got it," the same lady from before replied. "Back up's on the way."

Sergeant Tate leapt out of the vehicle and slapped the hood of the patrol car. "All right."

It shot away, sirens blaring.

"Go get them, Delgado," Tate muttered and then he jogged over to the bridge pylon and started climbing, remembering the rule not to look down.

"Tate, you're under the bridge?"

Tate glanced at the radio clipped to his front pocket. "I'm climbing."

"You don't have any safety gear, Tate. Remember that. We've got a special team en route so just see what you can from your vantage point."

"From this vantage point?" Tate asked, shaking his head and pulling himself up onto the next foothold. "From here, I can't see shit."

Then he frowned and a bead of sweat trickled down his brow. "Hang on."

The sound was deafening. Truly deafening. A tremendous crack that sheered through everything. The sounds of people talking, the music coming from a nearby bar, the noise of engines and the wailing of Sergeant Delgado's siren.

The ground shook and people fell down, hands out to brace themselves and then immediately planting those same hands on their ears.

For a moment afterwards, despite the odd scream here and there and the sounds of sobbing, it was deathly quiet. Then there was a cacophony of groans and cracks followed by a deafening crash.

Slowly, the people sprawled about the street turned back to watch as half the West Avenue bridge slid into the river, pouring dozens of vehicles into the water and onto the banks to its side. Several people screamed in horror. Others watched in stunned silence.

Walsh pushed himself to his feet and brushed at his forehead. His hand was smudged with thick blood and gravel.

He set off after his target again, not realizing that Myers was down with a broken ankle behind him.

Fortunately, Delgado in the car saw it, along with Myers' man darting off down a side street.

Throwing the rules to the curb, Delgado swerved the car around, sliding across the road and bringing it to a sudden stop beside the street.

He leapt out and shouted at the running man. "Stop right there, you son of a bitch!"

The man was just about to disappear into an alleyway. Delgado pulled his gun and jogged after him. "Stop or I *will* fire!"

The man darted forward, turning in his stride as he reached the corner, then his leg slid out from under him and he landed painfully on the sidewalk with Delgado's bullet in his thigh.

Delgado ran over to him and before the man could even think about putting up a fight, he cuffed his hands behind his back and rolled him onto his front.

Sweating and breathing heavily, he flicked on his radio. "Delgado. I've got suspect one here." He stopped to take a deep breath. "Myers is down. Looked like an ankle injury with the explosion..." He trailed off as another fact hit him hard.

Dropping his weapon and the radio, he knelt down and pressed his palms against the footpath.

"Delgado!" the lady on the other end called out.

"Just stay there. *Everyone* will be there in a few minutes, you got that? Just wait."

Delgado nodded, unable to vocalize a reply.

"Where's Walsh?"

"Still running," Delgado muttered, his voice breaking into a sob.

"Okay," the lady said. "Thanks, Delgado. Just keep it together a little longer, okay? Back up's on the way."

Walsh was now running as hard as he could and he wasn't gaining any ground on his target. The man veered to his left, darting across the road. Walsh stayed with him.

He veered to his right, running up along a boardwalk and leaping over a low chain fence into a closed parking lot by a private jetty. Walsh stayed with him.

His heart was pounding in his ears and he had a painful stitch in his side but he stayed with him.

The man veered again. Walsh matched him.

The man turned into a side street. Walsh followed.

Then the man turned once more and three officers leapt, seemingly from out of nowhere, and tackled him to the ground, cuffing his wrists behind his back and shouting at him.

Only then did Walsh stop. Wheezing heavily, he

planted his palms against his thighs and stood there in a daze. Dizzy, exhausted, angry and confused.

One of the other officers came over and put a hand on his shoulder. "Well done. You ran that son of a bitch down like a bloodhound."

Walsh nodded an acknowledgement to the other officer but he couldn't speak. Not yet. It was too painful just trying to breathe.

Then he looked at the man lying handcuffed on the ground. He was a kid. And if he was over twenty, then Walsh would have been very surprised.

In that moment, he found his voice again and it was loud. He lunged forward and turned the kid onto his back, holding him by the collar of his shirt.

"You stupid little shit!" he cried, tears streaming down his cheeks. "Why did you do that?" He shoved the kid back onto the sidewalk and collapsed, resting his head in one hand and bracing himself with the other.

There was a lot of confusion and grief all around. It wasn't long before a flood of patrol cars arrived. Commissioner Eric Hutchens was on the scene in almost no time and so was the head of the fire and rescue department, along with numerous fire engines and ambulances. Naturally, the press were there in droves as well, like vultures hovering over the carnage.

Hutchens nodded to the yellow lines of police tape that were being dragged across the area, while the sturdier barricades were put in place.

"Yeah, keep all these people back," he said to the nearest officer as he paced back and forth, deciding what he ought to do next. Unfortunately, there really wasn't much else he could do but secure the area and keep everyone away from the edge of the river so the fire department could do their work, clearing the rubble and looking for survivors.

Hutchens had divers in the river already. They had found a few people who had managed to survive falling in their cars but for the most part, it was a morbid business of retrieving dead bodies and recording the plates of the cars they'd been dragged from to aid faster identification. So far, the death toll was in the forties. Most likely, the actual toll would be two or three times higher.

Then in the haze of still burning fires, thick smoke, mist from the fire hoses and the dappled red and blue light all around him, he made out Alison St. Claire coming towards him.

"Ms. Mayor," he said.

"You sound tired, Commissioner," St. Claire told him.

"You don't sound much better yourself."

St. Claire shook her head. "I'm not."

She looked much older now than when he had first met her, Hutchens thought. The stress of the job had given her a number of premature grey hairs and lines around her eyes. There were dry blotches of tears there now as well. She didn't look well.

"So you've found your missing explosives then, I take it?" she asked.

"So it would seem," Hutchens told her. "However, we're checking out the residences of the culprits just in case." He nodded to the rubble that was all that remained of the nearest bridge pylon. "And I've got a team of people combing through that mess who should be able to work out how many of the explosives were used." His voice wavered. "I'm so sorry, Ms. Mayor."

"No, no," St. Claire told him. "You worked around the clock for two weeks trying to track down the missing explosives. There was nothing else you could have done."

"But it was two weeks' wasted."

"Listen to me, Eric," St. Claire said, looking him in the eye. "What happened here tonight was not your fault. All right?"

Hutchens nodded. "Yeah. Yeah, I know."

"Now, I've talked to Chief Roberts already. And we're bringing in some cranes to help clear the debris and reach anyone else who's trapped. But is there anything my office can do for *you*?"

Hutchens shook his head. "No, Ms. Mayor. I think we're probably covered. Find the survivors, clear the debris, mourn the dead and lock away the culprits."

"At least you've found *them*," St. Claire said.

Hutchens shrugged. He couldn't find much comfort in that. "For what it's worth."

"And he smiled happily," Jason said, turning the page. "'I've done it!' he cried. And all the other animals cheered. 'Hooray! Hooray!' The little sparrow was delighted. Now he realized that being small was not so bad after all. Being small made him *very* special. And from that day on, the little sparrow never worried about being small again."

Ethan smiled and Jason leaned over and kissed him on the cheek. "Okay. And now, I think it's time you went to sleep."

Ethan smiled back and shuffled under the sheets to make himself more comfortable. "Okay."

"And say goodnight to Mom."

Ethan hugged Angie. "Goodnight, Mom."

Angie kissed him on the cheek as well. "Goodnight, Ethan." She turned her head and tapped a finger on her own cheek. "Do I get a kiss as well?"

Ethan smiled again and gave her a big kiss. Then he

leaned back on his pillow. Angie tussled his hair and wishing him goodnight, she and Jason switched off the light and left the room.

"What do you want to do tonight?" Jason asked, stretching out on the sofa.

Angie shrugged. "I don't know. Have we missed our show?"

"Not sure." Jason glanced at the digital clock on the side table next to him. "Um... no. I think it's probably only just started."

"Ah ha," Angie exclaimed, nudging up beside him. "We got him to bed earlier than I thought."

She picked up the remote, switched it on and frowned. Then she clamped her hand over her mouth in horror as she watched the special news bulletin. "Oh, my god. Jason! That's the West Avenue Bridge."

Jason stared at the TV in disbelief.

"Turn it up a little," he told her.

"Mariane," a news anchor was saying, "what can you tell us about the situation at the moment? We understand the death toll has already passed the hundred mark."

"Yes," the woman replied. Mariane O'Hara, the

chief reporter for Fringe City Central. "The police divers have located all the vehicles in the river now. They've been working very hard all night, doing what must be an extremely difficult and emotionally wrenching job, pulling the victims out of cars and trucks and bringing them back to the riverside where they can be identified. At the moment, a hundred and six people are confirmed dead, with forty-three injured. However, as you can see, emergency services are still working behind me to clear the rubble there and we don't know whether there are any more people trapped underneath it."

"Now, has the police commissioner made any statement about the culprits of this crime?"

Mariane was quiet for a moment due to the audio delay. "The police commissioner is obviously still very busy," she said, "and he hasn't said a lot. However, he did confirm to journalists half an hour ago that the culprits have been caught. The two men who planted the explosives under the bridge were seen leaving the scene of the crime by two officers on patrol in the area and they were apprehended shortly afterwards. The commissioner stated that police know where the men responsible acquired the explosives and that all the explosives that the men had in their possession were used in this attack tonight. He also assures us that the men acted without any further assistance from outside parties."

"Well, that's fast work," the anchor started. "But—"

"It is," Mariane cut him off, her tone abrupt.

"All right," the man said. "We're going to cross over soon to our live panel discussion on this frankly devastating event but you're the one on the scene there. Is there anything else you'd like to tell our viewers before you go?"

Mariane nodded. "Obviously, this is, as you say, a devastating event. It's a horrible tragedy and right now, there is a lot of confusion, anger and immense sadness over this senseless violence. People are very upset and it's also hard to come to terms with because it's been so long since anything remotely similar to this has happened in our city. I think I speak for most of us when I say we thought we'd left this kind of stuff behind nearly a decade ago. However, I think it's important that we don't lose perspective on this either. It's a terrible tragedy but it shouldn't mark the beginning of a slippery slope back into this city's violent past. As the commissioner said, the culprits are in police custody and there were no further accomplices. So we need to rebuild and keep going. This city deserves a bright future and we've been steadily working towards that. And there's no reason why we should let a pointless act of violence by two callous individuals ruin that. In moments like this, I think it's important that we come together and help one another. We can and we will get through this."

"Okay, Mariane," the news anchor said. "We'll have to stop there. We'll see you again for another update in an hour."

Mariane nodded. "See you then."

The next morning, Jason sat on his desk and looked at his class.

"All right," he told the students. "You obviously want to talk about it." He slid his lesson plans to the other side of the desk. "So let's talk then."

"Was it a terrorist attack?" one of the students asked. Chen. A bright guy under normal circumstances, this morning he looked like the proverbial deer in headlights.

"Yes and no," Jason said. "Any indiscriminate killing like that is basically terrorism. But on the other hand, it doesn't sound as though the perpetrators were motivated by any political reason."

"Perpetrators?" Chen asked.

"The people who did it," one of the other students, Ricardo, chimed in before Jason could explain.

"Do you think there'll be more attacks like this now?" Ji Eun asked, looking rather worried. "Copycat attacks, perhaps?"

Jason sighed. "I don't think so."

The conversation went on like that all morning. The students were clearly in shock over it all, having come from all over the world to study in Fringe City and now finding themselves in a situation like this. Some of them had commuted over the West Avenue Bridge before the attack as well. Jason didn't know how they'd gotten to the classroom this morning but they must have seen the mess by the river. On the news, it looked like a scene from a war zone.

When he got home, things weren't a whole lot better. In fact, as far as Jason was concerned, they were worse.

Ethan looked at him with glassy eyes when he was putting him to bed. "Daddy?"

Jason smiled as he patted the blanket in place. "Yeah, Ethan?"

"The other kids said there was an explosion."

He was trembling.

Jason grimaced inside. These other kids clearly had parents who didn't understand they were supposed to protect them from things like that.

"Did they?"

"Was there?" Ethan asked.

Jason looked at his little boy, watching him from over the covers. It was obvious he more or less knew

44

what had happened, despite his efforts to make sure he didn't. So he went for the truth, but giving as few of the terrible details as he could.

"Yeah," he said, his voice soft. "There was. And some people were hurt."

"How can that happen?"

It was a good question. "I don't know," Jason admitted.

"But you know everything."

Jason laughed a little and brushed a strand of his son's hair. "Who told you that?"

"But you do, don't you?" Ethan asked.

Jason shrugged. "I know some things. A lot of things. But nobody knows everything."

"What about Mommy?"

Jason smiled. "*She* might. Anyway, why don't you try to go to sleep? Think of spaceships and other planets. Or dolphins. Puppies. Happy things."

"But what if there's another explosion?"

"I don't think there'll be another one," Jason told him.

But Ethan still didn't look happy.

"Daddy?" he asked.

"Yeah, Ethan?"

"Can you read me a story?"

Jason gave him another smile. "Sure. I can do that."

. . .

The clean up was still going on a fortnight later and Fringe City was still very much in shock. At the behest of Mayor St. Claire though, work on repairing the West Avenue Bridge had already commenced as, in her eyes, it was important to get the city back to normal again so the senseless crime wouldn't leave it in a perpetual state of fear.

This was a sentiment echoed by Charles Faulkner, along with his protégé Devan Fletcher, and Police Commissioner Eric Hutchens, who addressed the issue in a televised statement to a room full of reporters from every network in the city, and a number from outside.

Sitting in his office, Charles Faulkner watched and listened.

"The culprits have already been tried and convicted," Hutchens said. *"Each of them has received life sentences —"*

"Why didn't they receive the death penalty?" one of the journalists cut in.

Hutchens leveled the man with a scowl. *"Because this isn't Texas. If you bothered to find out anything about this state before dropping by, you'd know that the vast majority of the population here are opposed to that, something that's reflected in our laws."*

The man didn't have a reply.

"So while you're enjoying your stay here," Hutchens

suggested, *"why don't you visit one of our wonderful public libraries and read up on it?"*

This got a few chuckles around the room and the man sat down, looking humiliated.

"Besides, a lifetime of solitary confinement should give these men plenty of opportunity to reflect on what they've done," Hutchens added. He shuffled the papers in front of him. *"Now, if I may continue, we are aware that a quantity of explosives was stolen from a local demolitions company and that quantity matches that of the explosives that were placed under the West Avenue Bridge on the night of the tragedy. So the culprits are in custody, they have no known associates and all the explosives they stole in order to carry out their attack have been accounted for. And, ladies and gentlemen of the press, as far as my department is concerned—and the mayor and the D.A. see eye to eye with us on this as well—this concludes the affair. Yes?"*

"Are the police not concerned about the reasons behind this act?" another journalist asked, not the man from earlier.

"We are concerned," Hutchens told her. *"Of course we are. Understanding why this happened is invaluable in our efforts to prevent this from happening again. And we have a wonderful team of criminologists who are working on this. However, it is our considered opinion that, whatever the motive of these two men, making it public won't serve anyone's interests. We don't need the media ascribing some*

kind of social cause to these murderers or otherwise turning them into martyrs or role models for other deranged lunatics."

Before anyone else could say anything, Hutchens promptly ended the conference and left the room.

As he watched, Charles smiled in approval.

"He did well," he told the younger man beside him.

"He was as blunt as hell about it though," Devan Fletcher said. "I wish we could be that direct sometimes."

"Oh, well," Charles said. "He's the commissioner. He can get away with it. Anyway, I'm glad to see the media hasn't turned this into the circus frenzy it could have been. Considering how dreadful this thing was, the fallout could have been a lot uglier."

"Well, you contacted several of the networks as well," Devan reminded him.

"True. I think it was mostly Ms. O'Hara's work though. Fringe City Central holds a lot of sway over the other networks, even its biggest rivals. But once I talked to her about it, she completely understood. Then she talked to some of her network executives as well and got them to contact their counterparts."

Devan stifled a yawn. "Well, anyway. It was a good job all round."

Charles flicked the television onto another channel and almost did a double-take.

"But we can learn from this tragedy," a youngish man was saying. A striking man actually, with a strong jaw and bright clear eyes. *"Clearly, we have become too relaxed in our attitudes towards safety and have made assumptions. Dangerous assumptions."*

The man shuffled some notes in front of him and paused for effect.

"He looks familiar," Devan said.

"That's Ken Doyle," Charles said. "That's who he is."

Devan nodded. "Ah. I thought I recognized him from somewhere."

"While recognizing the progress that we have made in our fine city," Doyle said, *"we need to understand that we are not in the clear. Not by a long shot. It is obvious that we still have very dangerous elements in our community, and in the wake of this incident, you can be sure that these other elements will be aching to try their own hand at shaking the foundations of our community."*

Ken Doyle shook his head. *"And it would be extremely naive to assume that these elements would be scared off simply because the perpetrators of* this *crime were brought to justice. Because the truth is that no criminal believes they'll be caught. If they did, they'd never become criminals in the first place. No, you can be certain that these people will make their own attempts to undermine the collective goodwill of the community. And we need to be prepared for that. We need tighter security laws. We need increased on-the-ground surveillance and more extensive use of CCTV, following the examples of cities like London."*

He paused before he continued. *"This will not be easy. It will require sacrifices and the willingness to give away some of the personal freedoms we hold dear. But we cannot flinch in the face of this duty. Because, as the saying goes, vigilance is the price of freedom. Thank you."*

There was a tremendous round of applause, while in the midst of it all, the speaker stood silent.

Charles muted the television and put the remote down.

"I don't understand it," he said. "I thought all the networks were behind us on this. Because whichever network *this* is has basically just undermined the efforts of the rest of them, along with my own efforts and those of the mayor and Commissioner Hutchens."

He shook his head. "And why are they getting the opinion of a former congressman almost no one would remember in the first place?"

Devan thought it over.

"It's a good question," he said at last. "But I wonder if perhaps they *didn't* seek him out. Perhaps he sought *them* out."

THE ONSLAUGHT

THE DAPPLED LIGHT OF THE MORNING sunshine penetrated the canopies of the trees, casting everything in a bright and cheerful aesthetic.

Dr. John Carter felt strange as he looked around the gardens of the Palmdale Mental Health Institute for his patient. One day, one hundred and thirty-six people are killed in a horrific act of indiscriminate violence. Then, barely two weeks later, he was in a garden enjoying the pleasant morning sun.

He knew a lot about survivor's guilt. He'd diagnosed it often enough and had devised numerous strategies to help patients cope with it. Right then however, he was having to use some of those strategies on himself.

Then he saw his patient. The man had changed their usual table. There would be a deliberate purpose to that, John knew. He wondered what it was.

"Hello again," he said as he sat down.

Derek Bradley smiled. "I'm surprised to see you again, Dr. Carter. I understood you had terminated these sessions."

John gave him a blank look. "What made you say that? I've just been busy these past two weeks."

"Of course," Derek said, although he didn't appear to believe that was the sole reason for his absence.

"You changed the table, I see," John said.

"A new start, Dr. Carter," Derek told him.

"And perhaps a new leaf?"

"You know," Derek said, "you often ask me questions you already know the answer to."

"I do," John agreed. "I have my reasons."

"Incidentally," Derek said, flicking a fly beside him so hard he instantly killed it, "I understand you've been involved in interviewing the perpetrators of the West Avenue Bridge incident. The murderers of one hundred and thirty-six people. How's that working out for you?"

"You know about doctor-patient confidentiality, Derek."

Derek smiled again. "True. I just wonder as a concerned citizen whether the work you and the team of criminologists are doing there is paying off. In general terms."

John read between the lines and decided that, given the fresh start, he would indulge him. "What do you think, Derek?"

"I think it's probably been a frustrating waste of

time all round. Those two men? *They* won't know why they did it. So how could you?"

"Well, I pride myself on my insights," John replied. "I've had a lot of experience with people who don't understand themselves. It's a large part of my trade. Why are you concerned anyway?"

"I'm concerned for your well-being, Dr. Carter. Anyway, I think those two men are simply idiots and, while I'm sure you'd cover the fact with a whole lot of technical words and a psychiatric smokescreen, I think you agree with me."

John smiled. "You mentioned earlier that I ask questions I already know the answer to."

Derek smiled back. "I know. I do it too. Like you, I also have my reasons. But by and large, they're less manipulative than your own. I just like making chitchat." The smile faded. "I'm sorry my information wasn't any use."

"Well," John told him, "that's partly why I'm here today. You're no good in here, Derek. You know that. You have a gifted intellect. If you had been outside working with the members of our law enforcement community, perhaps this tragedy could have been averted."

"Perhaps," Derek said.

"Does it have to be on your terms, Derek?" John asked him. "You'd make an outstanding police officer."

"I *wanted* to be an outstanding police officer once," Derek reminded him. "I failed my psych examination. You know that."

"Yes, I do," John told him and his voice was now hard. "But this, Derek... What you're doing now is wallowing in self-pity. You want the city to come crawling on its hands and knees to you for help. And when you give it, it's got to be your terms or nothing." John paused for a moment. "You're familiar with Achilles, I'm sure."

"I am," Derek said. "I've read *The Iliad* in English, French and both modern and ancient Greek."

"Then you'll know he was a very mighty warrior," John said. "And you'll also know that for a lot of the story, he was about as useful to his comrades as a hole in the head since he spent the time moping over the sleights against him while his comrades fought on without him. Perhaps now, Achilles would be a more appropriate name for you than Orion."

Derek didn't reply immediately, which was unusual. John was starting to wonder what to make of it when his patient brushed his hands over his eyes, sighed and held out one hand in an open palm position. "Did you bring my papers today, Dr. Carter?"

John nodded and pulled them out of his bag. "Yes, Derek. I have them here."

• • •

"Which station put that idiot on last night?

Charles Faulkner glanced at Mayor St. Claire before turning back to the commissioner. St. Claire didn't look very happy herself but Eric Hutchens looked ready to tear someone to pieces.

"It was FCBN," Charles told him.

"Can I arrest the network execs for deliberately stirring panic? Behavior likely to result in widespread idiocy?"

Charles shook his head. "I wish you could. This is the downside of democracy, I'm afraid. Everyone gets a voice."

"Yeah," Hutchens muttered. "And some of them don't know when to shut it."

St. Claire extended a hand in a gesture for calm. "All right, Eric. We're all a bit upset about this."

"You're damn right," Hutchens said. "I spent a lot of time thinking about the best way to handle this and then this Ken Doyle upstart comes completely out of the blue and screws it all up. Well, he'd better watch his back because if he slips up in his own affairs just one little bit, I'm going to throw the book at him. A parking violation. A discrepancy in his tax records. Just give me one little reason."

"Well, that's all well and good," St. Claire said with

a sigh of exasperation, "but it's hardly productive. We need to think about how to keep things in check and stop everyone from getting carried away."

Hutchens looked uneasy. "Are you thinking of a press release in response to this guy?"

Charles sat up too. "I think Eric's right to worry about that, Ms. Mayor. I don't think you should engage this man in a public debate. You'll give him a false sense of legitimacy and the perfect opportunity to make another statement of his own. He wants to challenge you."

St. Claire looked at him in disbelief. Even Hutchens looked surprised.

"Challenge me? For Mayor?"

Charles nodded. "I believe so, yes. I've been doing a little bit of background research on the man. I haven't got very far—I only started last night—but he's been doing a bit of work around the place to generate some goodwill for himself. And I'm sorry if that sounds like a cynical interpretation of some of the actual useful work he's been doing but it's an interpretation based on a lot of years' experience and observation of people in general. I've seen his type and I think he's a rather ambitious son of a…"

Hutchens chuckled. "It's all right, Charles. You're in like-minded company."

"Son of a gun," Charles finished, settling for

something a little bit closer to his usual manner of speech.

"You're late," Gwendolyn remarked, a little surprised.

"Charles had an emergency meeting with the mayor," Devan replied as he sat across the table from her. "He wanted to talk to me about it afterwards. You know, I've got to know about these things if I'm ever D.A. myself and all that."

"True."

"So," Devan said, looking at his copy of the menu, "have you ordered yet?"

"No. I wanted to wait for you."

"That's kind of you. What looks good?"

Gwendolyn looked at her copy, running her finger over the names. "I think I'm going to try the... ah... Coq au Vin... if that's what it's called. It's a chicken dish. But I imagine that Beef Burgundy dish would be your kind of thing."

Devan had a look. "It does sound pretty nice. And what about the wine? Would it break the bank if we bought a bottle?"

"Not if we got something from the top of the list," Gwendolyn said. "What are we celebrating?"

They weren't celebrating of course. They were giving themselves a break from all the exhausting work they'd been caught up in since the tragedy at the bridge.

"There's not much to celebrate at the moment really, is there?" Devan said. "But I think coming here's a nice idea. We've both been overworked lately, haven't we? And I've been so caught up in my own work, I haven't noticed how busy you and everyone else at Outreach have been organizing aid for the West Avenue Bridge victims. Hospital care. Counseling. Donations to help with the clean-up operations." He shook his head. "You and your friends are amazing, Gwendolyn."

Gwendolyn smiled. "Well, it's the same kind of work we always do. It's just on a larger scale, that's all. And we've got the funding for it and the means to get people and funds where they're needed. But how are you doing? Because it sounds like Charles' meeting with the mayor's gotten you a little worried. Do you want to talk about it?"

"Maybe after we order."

Gwendolyn nodded. "Sure."

She caught the eye of a waiter as he came past and they ordered two mains and a bottle of wine.

When the waiter left, Gwendolyn turned back to her husband. "So let me guess. It was something to do with this Ken Doyle character, right?"

Devan nodded. "Yeah. Charles, the mayor and the commissioner were discussing how to respond to his stunt on the television last night."

"And what did they decide?"

"They're going for the 'ignore him and he'll go away' approach. Because if they make any reply or public acknowledgement of his statements, then they'll be declaring an open debate with the man."

"Well, that makes sense, doesn't it?"

"Yeah, it does," Devan said.

"So what's bothering you?" Gwendolyn asked.

Devan sighed. "Well, if there's no response, then Ken Doyle is also effectively getting the last word. So it's a catch twenty-two situation. Damned if you do, damned if you don't. Those things he said are out there now. The damage is done."

Gwendolyn reached out and held his hand. For a moment, neither of them spoke.

Then Gwendolyn smiled. "Do you hear that?"

Devan smiled back. There was a gentle tapping on the windowpane. "Why, I do believe it's raining."

And it was raining. And in a matter of minutes, it was proverbially and literally pouring. It fell heavily, hammering on anything metal, overflowing from the roofs and rushing out of the drainpipes in a torrential flow that turned the street level gutters into swift flowing streams. The only thing that was lacking was the gondolas.

However, this didn't stop the city's movers and shakers from, well, moving and shaking, and right then a large number of them started to gather in the grand function room of one of Fringe City's finest hotels.

And it was grand. High-ceilinged with an elaborate domed skylight, chandeliers, indoor plants, several fountains and an artificial waterfall that flowed down the tiled wall behind the jazz band.

In the middle of it all was a large desk where the various guests stopped, wrote checks and handed them to the staff who were manning it. For the frivolities had a more charitable bent than it would at first appear. It was in fact a fundraiser for victims of the West Avenue Bridge tragedy.

Before long, there was a good sized crowd in the room and the party had begun. There were people chatting, dancing, drinking and generally having a good time.

And then the music stopped. And the conversation stopped. And the various guests looked around to see what was going on. Every entry and exit was blocked.

Evocatively dressed women, holding slender firearms had the guests surrounded. And three more women entered, with two of them flanking the last one.

These three were dressed along the same lines as the

women by the doors, meaning dressed along the lines of corsets, lace and leather. However, the woman in the middle of the group differed by carrying a riding crop instead of a firearm and she had noticeably exquisite—and noticeably sharp—fingernails.

Accompanied by her two companions, she strode into the middle of the room, hips swinging, and came to a stop.

The guests at the party fanned out, creating a circle around her, some of them fanning far enough away from her that they were almost brushing up against her friends by the doors. Oddly enough, while those women were more obviously armed, they were less frightening to the guests than their leader.

The woman turned, surveying the little groups of huddled guests, and smiled. "Good evening, ladies and gentlemen. It is nice to be back."

No one said a word.

"Quiet lot, aren't they?" she said to her companions. She walked to the proceeds desk.

"Commendable," she said to the assembled guests. "You're all pitching in after this shocking tragedy at the bridge."

"A terrible tragedy," she said perusing the checks for a few moments. "Such *indiscriminate* killing. Such amateur work. And this, ladies and gentlemen, is something I do not stand for. And in fact, I am here tonight partly to warn the criminal fraternity of Fringe City."

She searched the sea of faces before her. "I do believe we have some representatives from the city's television networks here tonight. Why don't you come forward?"

When no one did so, she pressed her lips together and a cruel expression came over her aquiline features. Her eyes narrowed as they fell on one particular man. Then she strode forward, putting the riding crop in her left hand to free her right. She stopped in front of him and, without warning, lashed out.

The guests beside him barely had time to see what happened and for an instant, it felt like some dark magic. One moment, the man was standing there. The next, he fell to the floor, blood pooling beside him. And as the witnesses' eyes turned back to the woman, they saw that the nails on her right hand were tipped with that same blood.

She crouched and wiped them clean on the jacket of her victim before standing up again.

"It looks like Five's Late Edition will need a new anchorman," she said. "Now, would the *remaining* media representatives here tonight please come forward?"

There was a shuffling in the crowd and eleven men and women stepped into the center of the room. Those whose job it was to appear in front of cameras knew they didn't have a chance of hiding in the crowd. And those who worked behind the scenes now knew better than to *take* that chance.

"That's better," the woman said. "Now, take note, members of the press and let me remind you who you're dealing with. I am Lady Vice and I have a message for those who live in the shadows. Shoving some explosives under a bridge in the dark and running away like little wimps seriously lacks style. If any wannabes out there don't know how to work the limelight, then they should *stay* in the shadows. Because if they don't, then they'd better pray that the police find them before I do."

The assembled guests remained quiet.

"And now I have a message for all of *you*," Lady Vice said to the room at large. "Give generously and you might just make it out of here alive."

"Eight years ago, Lady Vice held a group of citizens hostage in the grand ballroom of the Sapphire Hotel. The siege ended when she and her associates made their way to the basement level of the building and escaped into the stormwater drains. Despite an immediate and extensive search by the police, they were never found and since that time, no one has seen or heard anything about this woman and her gang again.

That is, until last night.

Barely a fortnight after the West Avenue Bridge tragedy, with work crews still clearing the debris, Lady Vice has returned, breaking into a charity event that was raising money for the victims. According to reports, Lady Vice issued a challenge, oddly enough, to the perpetrators of the West Avenue Bridge incident and other criminals of the city who could possibly be like-minded, deriding them for a lack of style. It's difficult to fathom her possible motives for this but police believe her statement may provide some explanation as to why now, of all times, Lady Vice has chosen to come out of hiding.

Her return is obviously a concern to us all and if it is not dealt with, it may even see a return to the rampaging crime that once saw Fringe City effectively written off by the rest of the nation. And looking just at the problem this woman and her gang pose in themselves, there is another concern. And that is that for all the threats she made leading up to her mysterious disappearance eight years ago, neither she nor any of her gang ever murdered anyone in any of her heists. However, this changed last night with the brutal killing of one of the guests at the fundraiser.

At a time like this, with the city grieving over a dreadful tragedy, the last thing we need is someone like Lady Vice in our midst but this is the stark reality of the situation. Lady Vice is back and she is more dangerous than before.

For Fringe City Central, this is Mariane O'Hara."

. . .

For a while, Jason appeared to be in a state of suspended animation.

Angie prodded him in the side. "Hey. Are you alive?"

Jason blinked and shook his head, coming back from wherever he'd gone off to. "Uh... yeah."

Angie suppressed a sigh. "I can't believe it."

"Me neither," Jason said. "It's not Gwendolyn though. You know that, right?"

Angie nodded. "Yeah, I know that. That's not the issue. I mean obviously someone else has decided to adopt the persona for their own ends but... why?"

Jason shrugged. "Well, copycat crime is not unheard of."

"I suppose," Angie conceded. Then something hit her. "Oh no. If this woman's really taking on the persona because she was inspired by the original, how are Gwendolyn and the others going to take it?"

"Not well, I guess."

Angie got up. "Hang on a moment." She tiptoed down what she and Jason so generously referred to as the hall and, as quietly as she could, she opened Ethan's bedroom door and had a look inside. She closed it again and came back to the sofa.

"What was that about?" Jason asked.

"I wanted to make sure Ethan was sleeping," Angie told him. "Because there's something we need to talk about and I don't want him listening in, if you catch my drift."

"The Sentinel?"

Angie nodded. "The Sentinel."

"I told you, I retired him."

"I know you did," Angie said. "But with something like this, I can't help thinking that you might want to break out the suit again and bring your old alter-ego back into action."

Jason shook his head. "No, no. I'm sure the police can handle this."

Angie's gaze flicked down momentarily. "That's not what I wanted to hear, Jason."

Her husband frowned. "What do you mean?"

"I mean I thought the Sentinel was retired because neither of us wants you putting your life on the line day in and day out."

"Well, yeah... but—"

"But what you just basically told me then was that the Sentinel's only retired as long as the police can handle whatever crimes are happening at the moment. And that implies that if they *can't* handle something for whatever reason, you might well put the suit on again and jump back into action."

Jason nodded. "Okay. I'm sorry. I didn't mean it

that way."

"Good."

"I just mean that—"

"Because you're not my live-in boyfriend any more. And you're not just my husband either. You're a father, Jason. And I want you to be there for Ethan for as long as you can. Now what you did as the Sentinel is incredible. I still find myself wondering how one person could do so much but both you and I also know that a lot of the work was smoke and mirrors. Putting on the suit didn't turn you into a superhero then and it won't now. If anything, putting it on again will turn you into a target. And I'm sure you'd agree that you, Ethan and I could live without that."

Jason sighed. "You're right. I know that. And I agree with everything you said there. But I'm not planning on bringing the Sentinel back."

Eric Hutchens picked up the handset and dialed. He didn't have to wait long.

"Charles Faulkner."

"It's me, Charles."

"Eric? What's up?"

"I want to ask you for a favor," Hutchens said. "I need some warrants."

"All right."

"I want to put wire taps on the phones in Ken Doyle's office and I want to put him under surveillance."

There was a slight pause before Charles replied. "I see. Is there any reason why?"

"Because I'm suspicious of the bastard, that's why. One minute he's on TV telling us that we've all got to be alert because a new crime wave is coming our way and then, viola! Five minutes later, we've got one. Come on. Tell me that doesn't seem dodgy."

"No, I'm with you on that. I think I can make a justification for the wire tapping and the surveillance that should hold up but as far as the latter's concerned, I don't think I can give you a warrant to investigate any personal property or his home. So your surveillance will just have to be on the street."

"What if I can find, shall we say, more 'justification'?" Hutchens tried.

"If you do, I'll be all ears, Commissioner."

The next day, Jason watched the rain splashing against the windows. It hadn't let up since the other night, when the new Lady Vice had made her debut appearance.

"Dad?"

He turned away and smiled at his son. "Hey, Ethan.

What's up?"

"Can I watch a DVD?"

Jason shrugged. "I don't know. Maybe. But you know Mom's rule. No more than one hour of TV a day or one movie on special days."

"I haven't watched any TV today," Ethan told him.

"I know, but wouldn't you rather watch a movie after dinner? Saturday night. Special treat."

Ethan paused. "Okay, Dad. I'll think about it."

He went off and Jason cocked his head as he watched him go. The way Ethan had spoken then had sounded like he was mimicking his mother.

Then the sound of the phone ringing intruded on his thoughts. He picked it up. "Hello?"

"Hi, Jason. It's Diane."

"Oh. Hey, Diane. How's it going?"

"Okay. What about you?"

"Can't complain," Jason said.

"Well, that's good to hear. Are you busy today?"

"Not really."

"I'd like to meet up," Diane said. "Do you think you can come over for lunch?"

Jason glanced at his son but he was happily playing with his toys and wasn't paying him any attention.

"Um, do you mean just by myself?"

"Just you," Diane told him. "And Gwendolyn too if I can reach her. I'm going to call her in a minute."

"Uh huh. And Mark and the kids are out, are they?"

"Not yet but they're going to the aquarium later on."

Jason nodded to himself. "Well, Angie's in the shower so I'll have to wait until she's out before I can check it with her. But I think it should be okay. But... do we really need to talk about this? Angie and I had a chat about it last night."

"Well, we don't *need* to do anything but just for my own peace of mind, if nothing else, I'd like to talk to you and Gwendolyn face to face, just to make sure we're all on the same page."

"Um..."

"Lamb souvlaki and pita bread for lunch. The souvlaki's my own recipe."

Jason loved Diane's homemade souvlaki and she knew it.

"Well, I'm sure Angie wouldn't mind taking care of Ethan for a few hours."

"All right," Gwendolyn said. "See you then."

She hung up and frowned.

"Anything wrong?" Devan asked.

Gwendolyn took a breath. For years, she had wondered whether or not to tell her husband about this but she knew she couldn't keep it secret from him any longer. And after all, his boss knew about it so why shouldn't he?"

"That was Diane. She wants to talk to me about this thing in the news with Lady Vice."

Now Devan was frowning too. "Why would she want to talk to *you* about that?"

The problem, Gwendolyn knew, was that telling him wasn't going to be easy. After taking another breath, she decided she'd just tell it straight. No conversational detours and no cushioning the blows.

"The original Lady Vice was a hoax," she said. "She never existed."

"What do you mean?"

"She was a creation, a myth that I, along with the other founding members of Outreach created as part of a long-term strategy to cripple the criminal syndicates that were strangling the city."

"Wait. Hang on a minute," Devan started. "The robberies..."

"All real. The illusion had to be complete," Gwendolyn told him. "Don't interrupt. I just need you to listen to me for a moment. The robberies were designed to build Lady Vice's reputation. Then when Lamont's organization splintered, we used Lady Vice to make deals with the other groups in the city to consolidate the funds, stockpiling them for the Outreach program and driving the groups into bankruptcy. It wasn't all clean. One mobster tried to put the Bandit on us. So—"

"So you were the ones who brought him down?" Devan asked.

"Yes. We didn't kill him, as you know, but we incapacitated him so he'd never pose a threat again. But as you see, things definitely got ugly."

Amazingly, Devan was still standing under the torrent of surprises but he was clearly stunned. "Gwendolyn, I don't know what to say."

"Don't say anything yet," she told him, "because I'm not quite finished. There are a couple of other things. First, after we had succeeded in our operation to clean up the city, we worked with the mayor, Commissioner Hutchens, your boss Charles Faulkner and the Sentinel to set a trap for Orion."

"The Sapphire Hotel? So *that* was what all that was about."

"That's right."

"And Charles was in on it?"

"*Everyone* was in on it."

Devan shook his head. "Okay then... But what about the money and everything?"

"Well, if by everything, you mean the proceeds from the public robberies, everything we took from innocent citizens in order to establish the Lady Vice persona was quietly returned, with the police contacting people individually so no one would ever know that the entire collection of stolen goods and cash had been found. That would have raised awkward questions. And as for the funds we acquired from the syndicates, we built Outreach with them. And Charles helped us make it all look proper and legal."

"I can't believe it," Devan told her. "Why haven't you ever told me this before?"

"How would I go about it, honey?" Gwendolyn asked him. "And when? Before the wedding or on the honeymoon? Believe me, I've wanted to tell you for years. I just didn't know how. Are you all right?"

"I'm all right," Devan said. "I'm just having a hard time reconciling you and your friends with Lady Vice and her gang and the idea that you all pulled off something as dangerous as that. And I can't *believe* Charles was involved. Charles! Straight and narrow. By the book. It doesn't sound like him at all."

Gwendolyn smiled. "Well, you should be grateful he *was* involved. Because if it wasn't for his assistance with the operation to trap Orion and his subsequent involvement with Outreach, you would never have met me."

"And the mayor and the commissioner know all about you too. And the Sentinel. How did *he* get involved?"

Gwendolyn shrugged. "I worked out who he was

and asked him to help."

"One of these days, Gwendolyn," Devan said, "I'm going to have to hear the long version of all this. However, I think I'm going to need a year or two to digest the short one first."

"Talk to George," Gwendolyn suggested.

"Sonya's husband?"

"Yeah. He's been through all this already so he's had more time to deal with it. And it might be good to have someone else you can relate to. Another husband of the Lady Vice gang."

Devan nodded. "That sounds like a good idea. And I think I'd like to talk to Charles about this sometime as well."

Gwendolyn gave him an understanding smile. "Yeah, I thought you might."

"So," Devan said, trying his best to keep up and doing an incredible job, "does Diane think this woman in the news is a straight-up copycat?"

"I imagine so. *I* think she's a straight-up copycat and so do the rest of the girls."

"So why does Diane want to see you, do you think?"

Gwendolyn shrugged. "I guess she's going to tell me that I shouldn't feel responsible for this woman. And she's probably going to warn me off taking matters in my own hands. Not that I've got any *inclination* to do that but I guess she wants to be sure."

Finally, Devan decided that he *did* want to sit down for a moment. And for a little while, he was quiet. When he spoke again, his voice was little more than a whisper. "Wow."

An hour later, Jason and Gwendolyn were at Diane's place. Sonya was there too. True to her word, Diane had cooked up lamb souvlaki and, as always, it was delicious. Jason then leapt into action, cleaning the dishes while Gwendolyn persuaded Diane to relax and leave making the coffee to her. Then, sitting around Diane's kitchen table, they talked.

"Well, Angie and I had a good chat it about it last night," Jason said. "And you know, I'm married and I'm a father. And the situation with the police is hardly the same now either. All the guys like Sergeant Hemming and Commissioner Levings are gone and so are the mobs that were paying them off. So there's no real need for vigilantes any more anyway. But to cut a long story short, I'm not going to go dressing up in a Kevlar suit every time some nut job shows up like Pavlov's dog and a bell."

"I didn't think I had to worry," Diane told him, "but it's good to hear it from you directly."

"And we were done with the whole Lady Vice thing

eight years ago," Sonya joined in, speaking for Gwendolyn and herself. "And we're not losing any sleep over the fact that this woman's using the name. She's nothing to do with us. As far as we're concerned, this is a police matter."

She frowned. "Were you put up to this?"

Diane's gaze flicked down for a moment and she looked a little embarrassed. "Well, the mayor and Commissioner Hutchens thought it might be good just to make sure we all kept a level head." She smiled. "And don't worry. They know you guys weren't involved."

"Well, that's good to know," Sonya said. "But anyway, getting back to whether we'd try anything stupid, what could we really *do*? Challenge this lady as an imposter and draw her out or something? I mean, I'm sure it'd be a fun PR stunt and it'd be interesting to see if my corset still fit but that'd be about it. None of us would be any good if it came to a straight fight with this woman. Or anyone really. We dealt with the mob of course, but always on our terms."

She reflected on it all for a moment. "Anyway, we were all smoke, mirrors and subterfuge when we were running that show. And corsets, I guess."

"And as for Jason," she added, "what would he do?" She turned to him. "Do you think you could find the new Lady Vice with nothing to go on?"

Jason looked at Diane. "*Is* there anything to go on?"

"There's not a lot," Diane said. "These ladies left the scene of the crime in an armored van which turned out to be a stolen S.W.A.T. van. It was found a few blocks away and they had wiped it clean of fingerprints before they left it."

"Professional job," Jason said.

"Yes, it wasn't a spur of the moment thing."

"Well, given that," Jason said, turning to Sonya, "I wouldn't know where to start, frankly. If this were some late nineteenth century novel with a line-up of ten suspects, I might be able to have a crack at it. But not in a city like this."

There was a pensive look in Diane's eyes. "Jason, do you still keep in touch with Sophia Garcia?"

"A bit," Jason said, "generally to see how she's holding up."

"She's still here in Fringe City?" Diane asked, a little surprised.

"Yeah, she's still here. Hell, I'm still here and I thought I'd be living in San Diego by now. Or Canada."

"Well, Angie says it's too cold there," Gwendolyn reminded him.

Jason smiled. "True." He turned back to Diane. "But yeah, Sophia's still here. But you'd hardly recognize her now. The luxury apartment's gone, along with all the expensive dresses and the fine champagne. She's living quite a modest life these days."

Sonya started nodding. "Yeah, she's one of our biggest contributors."

For Diane, it was yet another surprise. "Is that right? I didn't know that. So you two see her regularly as well?"

Sonya exchanged glances with Gwendolyn and they both looked back and nodded.

"Yeah, we might well see her more often than Jason does," Gwendolyn told her. "However, if you were going to ask Jason whether Sophia might know anything about this new Lady Vice, I'm pretty sure the answer would be a no."

"So she's got nothing in the way of underworld contacts then?"

"What underworld contacts?" Gwendolyn said. "Any contacts she had in the past would want nothing to do with her now. And most of them would be in jail anyway."

Sonya gave Diane a cheeky grin. "And aren't you supposed to be dissuading Jason from getting involved here?"

Diane laughed, draining some of the tension she had been feeling. "You're right, Sonya. I guess I was falling back on bad habits."

Sonya shrugged. "It's all right. They're the best

kind."

"By the way," Jason asked Diane, intervening, "are you involved with the investigation at all?"

"Not officially," Diane told him. "Not unofficially either really."

"You're a commander now though."

"True, but I'm only a police officer part-time these days," Diane pointed out, "and Hutchens keeps me out of harm's way because he knows I've got a young family and he feels he owes me."

"He's right there," Jason said. "The whole city owes you."

Diane smiled. "Sweet of you to say, Jason."

Hutchens dragged his fingers through his thinning hair, massaging his scalp. He was not having a good day.

"Go on," he said, knowing what he was going to hear while hoping like hell he was wrong.

The officer standing in the doorway hesitated. "The missing S.W.A.T. team turned up," he said, handing him a file. "Um…"

"Dead?"

The officer nodded, looking at the floor. "Yes, sir." He then looked the commissioner in the eye. "I'm sorry, sir."

"It's all right, Owens," Hutchens told him. "You didn't kill them."

Owens nodded. "Yes, sir. Ah... sir?"

"Yes, Owens?"

"There's more, sir. In the report. The men's weapons were missing."

Hutchens closed his eyes for a moment and sighed. "Don't worry, Owens. I figured that would be the case."

He sat up and forced a smile. "You've been working all day on this, Owens. Why don't you go home and have a rest?"

The young officer hesitated again and held out another folder. "Well, um, actually... there's more, sir."

Frowning, Hutchens took it and flipped through its contents. "What's this? *This* isn't related to the case, is it?"

"No, sir," Owens said. "But Palmer said you'd want to see it."

Hutchens looked at the file again. Really looked at it. Then he frowned. "'Hypovolemic shock'," he read aloud, "'due to severe blood loss. No stains on bed sheets or the victim herself. Minute...'" He shook his head. "What? 'Minute puncture wounds on the neck. Sharp incisions'?"

"What the hell is this?" he asked Owens. "Is Palmer making this up?"

Owens was a little worried. He knew Hutchens was not a shoot-the-messenger type but it was hard to convince his nerves of this fact.

"No, sir. He said he saw this firsthand on the way over here."

"But this has got to be some kind of prank. Surely."

"I don't know *what* it is," Owens admitted. "Except it's pretty damn sick."

"But this reads like a gothic horror novel," Hutchens said, holding up the offending file.

Owens didn't say anything.

"All right, all right," Hutchens said, forcing himself to calm down. "So, this isn't some office prank."

"Well, frankly speaking, sir," Owens told him, "I don't think anyone here would be stupid enough to pull a stunt like that on you,"

"No, you're right," Hutchens said. "And I've known Palmer for years. He'd never make up something like this."

"So, what should I tell him?" Owens asked.

"Tell him I'm going to head over there and have a look at this myself," Hutchens told him, getting up. "Actually, wait. I'll tell him."

Ken Doyle walked out of the store and put his groceries in the trunk of the car. Soon, he was on his way home.

He glanced in his rear-view mirror and checked it again a few moments later. Frowning, he looked ahead, found a place to pull over and came to a stop.

He got out and watched as the grey car that had been trailing him cruised past and went around the corner.

Shaking his head, he got back inside his own car and continued on the way home.

Hutchens looked at the door as he stepped inside the little apartment. Palmer was waiting for him.

"How old was this girl?" he asked.

"Twenty-three," Palmer said.

Hutchens shook his head. "Man." He took a moment to pull himself together. He wasn't ready for this sudden crime wave.

"Was that door forced?" he asked.

"Not when we got here," Palmer told him. "We opened it to get in."

"And how did the intruder get in? And out?"

"Through the girl's bedroom window."

Hutchens sighed. "All right. Let's go in there and have a look."

Palmer frowned. "Are you sure you want to go in, sir? You look exhausted."

"Well, if this is the work of another neurotic psycho like Lady Vice, then I should probably know about it."

Palmer nodded and opened the bedroom door.

Hutchens walked in slowly, passing the Forensics officers who were going over the whole place with a fine tooth comb.

When he saw the girl lying on the bed, drained of all color, tears slid down his cheek.

"Poor kid," he murmured.

Palmer put on surgical gloves and gently turned the girl's head. "Here are the puncture wounds from the report."

When Hutchens looked at them, he felt numb to the core. He had seen wounds like those ones before but only on television and in movies.

He nodded to Palmer to put the girl's head back on her pillow.

"All right, Palmer. Let's go."

"This is a prank, Palmer."

They were now driving back to headquarters.

"Probably," Palmer said.

"Probably?" Hutchens asked. "Listen, I'm willing to believe in a lot of weird stuff. This city's certainly thrown enough of it our way. But vampires? That's a load of shit."

"Sorry, sir," Palmer said. "I misunderstood. I thought you meant this crime was committed as some kind of sick joke."

Hutchens frowned. "Actually, I kind of doubt that. I reckon there's a highly calculated motive behind this. A crime like this would require a lot of careful planning. A lot of work. I mean, you tell me there are no fingerprints anywhere. No sign of a struggle. No bloodstains despite the fact that the victim died from severe blood loss—"

"I'd say it was collected in stages and washed down the drain," Palmer said.

Hutchens shrugged. "That'd probably be the simplest way of disposing of it, sure, but that's still a lot of effort. And stemming the bleeding after all that blood was taken out? We're probably dealing with syringes, pumps, swabs and so on and this tells me that we're looking at a highly skilled and very well-prepared culprit."

"What I want to know is why he or she went to so much trouble to do this," Palmer said. "Pretending to be a vampire? What's the point?"

"That's the question," Hutchens said. "And the only thing I can think of is that someone wants the city to feel uneasy. *Very* uneasy. And believe me, with the West Avenue Bridge tragedy and this business with Lady Vice, it wouldn't take much to turn the citizens of

Fringe City into a collective paranoid mess. A real 'lock your doors and bar your windows' kind of town." Hutchens frowned. "And I think that means we'd better keep this under wraps. Not a word to the press."

Palmer glanced at his superior and hesitated. The string of vicious crimes that had just hit them out of nowhere was taking its toll on the commissioner and Palmer was worried how he'd take this.

"Uh, it might be a little late for that, sir."

"What?" Hutchens whirled around, taking his eyes off the road.

Which was another reason for Palmer's hesitation. Hutchens was driving.

"Who told them?" Hutchens demanded.

"Not sure," Palmer said. "FCBN said they'd received a note from a concerned citizen. They told *us*."

"FCBN, you said?"

"Yeah."

"Those guys are the same shitheads who put Ken Doyle on the TV and let him completely undermine our efforts to keep everyone calm," Hutchens muttered.

"That's true," Palmer pointed out, "but still, they're the ones who alerted us. We wouldn't have known about the crime otherwise."

Hutchens sighed. "I see."

"Also—"

"Oh yeah, and ten bucks that 'concerned citizen' was the perpetrator." Hutchens shook his head. "He's a clever prick. Looks like he's going to get his publicity after all."

"It looks that way," Palmer agreed. He opened his mouth to say something but Hutchens was still on a roll.

"And I can see why this guy chose FCBN," the commissioner said, plowing on. "Any station that would give some nut job like Ken Doyle free airtime would give *anyone* a slot."

"Sir, there's something else," Palmer said, rushing in before Hutchens could cut him off again. "It's interesting that you've mentioned Ken Doyle twice now."

"Well, it's a bit convenient that his new crime wave's cropped up right after he went on air warning us all about it, isn't it?" Hutchens asked.

"I doubt *he'd* think there was anything convenient about it, sir."

"Why's that?"

"The girl back there? Didn't you see the name on the report?"

Hutchens blinked a bit and flicked on the wipers as rain started splashing against the windshield. "I read it, yeah. I just don't remember it right now."

"Her name was Alicia Doyle," Palmer told him.

"She was Ken Doyle's niece."

Hutchens glanced sideways then watched the road again. He flicked the wipers onto a higher setting as the rain got heavier. He opened his mouth to say something and closed it again.

"What the hell is going on, Palmer?" he asked instead. "What the hell is going *on*?"

Ken Doyle frowned at the rain that was smothering his windshield.

"Can't see a thing," he muttered to himself. He checked the wipers. They were going as fast as they could. Shaking his head, he pulled over and turned off the engine.

He would wait it out.

Judging by the tail lights he could make out in the washy blur, other drivers had the same idea.

He put his seat back and made himself comfortable, although he had hardly settled when his cell phone rang. He picked it up.

"Doyle."

"Ken? It's Samantha."

Doyle sat up. "Samantha? What's going on?"

"Where are you?" Samantha asked, sounding distressed.

"I'm heading home."

"You're not *driving* in this weather, are you?"

"No, I'm sitting it out for a while," Doyle replied. "Samantha, what's wrong?"

"Your brother called. He was trying to reach you at home but you weren't there." She hesitated. "Um, Ken. You need to call him." Now she was crying.

"Samantha? What's wrong? Samantha?"

It was late when Commissioner Hutchens got home.

"Eric?"

Hutchens looked up as his wife appeared, her expression radiating concern and the same weariness he seemed to have been carrying everywhere since the West Avenue Bridge incident. If it wasn't easy being a police commissioner in a place like Fringe City, it wasn't easy being married to one either.

"Hi, Sandra."

"Long day?"

Hutchens shook his head. "You have no idea. What time is it?"

He had a watch but he was so exhausted that this didn't register.

"Almost ten," Sandra told him.

"But not quite?"

"No."

Hutchens pried his sodden feet out of his soaking

shoes and wrenched his leaden socks off before the osmosis process between cotton and skin made things any worse than they were. Then he wriggled his toes and massaged his feet on the carpet.

"That's better," he said to himself. He turned back to Sandra. "I've just got to watch something. *Then* the day will be over."

Sandra frowned. "What do you want to see?"

"I want to know how bad the damage is."

He walked into his living room, flicked on the TV and searched through the channels with the remote until he reached FCBN.

"Perfect timing," he said to himself as the news logo showed up. "All right, Mike Evans. Let's hear it, you monkey in a suit."

"Good evening," the news broadcaster on the screen greeted his viewers. *"I'm Mike Evans. Our top story tonight, a shocking murder that has added to the overnight rise in crime here in Fringe City. First, it was the West Avenue Bridge disaster just over a fortnight ago. Next, it was Lady Vice's reappearance after an absence of almost a decade. Now, it appears there is a new criminal in our midst who may be even worse, a figure seemingly straight out of myth and nightmares."*

"Way to cool the fire, Mike," Hutchens muttered.

"Earlier today, FCBN received anonymous information which led police to the discovery of a disturbing crime scene.

In a small inner city apartment, a young woman lay dead. No fingerprints in the apartment. No apparent point of entry."

"Stop trying to sound like a detective. You're *not*."

"—face of it, no apparent evidence of foul play at all. However, this was no case of illness or illicit drug use. This was a young, healthy woman with no known vices. And the cause of death? Hypovolemic shock brought on by severe blood loss through two tiny incisions in the woman's neck. The similarities to certain details in well-known folklore, stories, novels and movies are unmistakable, and one can imagine it won't be long before Fringe City residents start calling this killer the Vampire."

"It won't be now, you idiot," Hutchens told the TV. "And that's exactly what this guy *wants* you to call him."

He shook his head and turned to Sandra. "These media clowns are indulging these lunatics for ratings."

Sandra nodded. "I know. They don't think about the big picture. So is that what you were worried about?"

"Yeah, except 'worrying' generally implies that you think something *might* happen whereas I *knew* these idiots were going to do this. I just wanted to be wrong."

Sandra nodded to the TV. "Hang on. You might be interested in this."

Hutchens turned back to watch it.

"—given Mr. Doyle's cautionary words and his argument for more vigilant measures to protect public safety here, one can't help but wonder if this murder could have been politically motivated. Mr. Doyle had this to say."

The live feed cut to pre-recorded footage of Ken Doyle leaning over a podium. His face was puffy. His eyes were red from crying but he spoke with a gentle dignity.

"I can't speculate on the motives of this killer," he said to a group of assembled journalists. "I don't know why my niece was targeted. Whether she was targeted because of the things I said or if she was targeted randomly... I don't know. But one thing I do know is this. If her death was meant to frighten me, to dissuade me from speaking out about the things I believe in, then this killer is going to be disappointed. Because this hasn't weakened my resolve. It has only made it stronger. Because if there's any good that can be gained from this horrible tragedy..." He trailed off for a moment. He looked down and took a few breaths to compose himself. When he looked back at his audience, fresh tears glistened in his eyes.

"If there's any good to be gained from it," he said loudly, his voice wavering with emotion but losing none of its strength for it, "it's that we can learn from it. We can put in the measures that we need to keep the city under constant watch. Under constant vigil. And we can prevent what happened to Alicia from happening to anyone *else."*

He took another deep breath, his lips quivering.

"Thank you," he finished. Then he turned and left the podium.

Hutchens turned the TV off and sat where he was.

"The poor man," Sandra said at last. "I know you don't agree with his ideas, and I don't either, but still…"

Hutchens nodded. "Yeah." He sighed. "I don't know *what* to think of all this. Right now, I wish Palmer was in charge and I could be a lieutenant or something. Hell, I'd rather be a rookie right now."

Sandra gave him a little smile and kissed him on the cheek. "Sleep on it. Things always look clearer in the morning."

"Hey Ricardo. Where's your writing piece?"

Ricardo looked a little embarrassed. "Ah, I'm sorry, Jason. I'm lazy. I know. I'll remember next time."

Jason sighed. "Ah, you don't have to apologize to *me*. But it does mean I can't give you any feedback so you're missing out. And *you* know you need the practice."

Ricardo nodded. "Yeah, I know. I just don't like writing much."

"But if you want to do the Academic English

bridging course and move over to faculty, you're going to need to do some writing eventually," Jason pointed out. "When you're studying your major, do you think you'll be able to get out of doing *any* writing?"

Ricardo laughed and shook his head. "No, you're right. I'll do some practice tonight. And I can get my friend to check it."

"Well, that's a start," Jason conceded. "Okay, Ricardo."

Ricardo stepped aside and Kaori and Ji Eun stepped up, smiling brightly and holding their exercise books out open for Jason to see.

"Here you are, Jason," Kaori said.

"We wrote about the Lady Vice incident," Ji Eun added.

Jason nodded, reaching for the books. "Uh huh. Well, I look forward to reading about it."

"We even did some extra research," Ji Eun said. "We went to the main campus library and checked out news reports about her previous crimes eight years ago and earlier."

"Um… good job," Jason said.

Kaori frowned. "Is there anything wrong, Jason?"

Jason had been drawn to a paragraph near the bottom of the first page of Kaori's piece and some of the words within it. *The Sapphire Hotel. Mayor St. Claire. Orion. The Sentinel.*

He looked up at Kaori's concerned gaze and shook his head. "No. Nothing's wrong." He smiled. "You did a lot of work. I'm impressed."

"Wait until you read mine," Ji Eun said with a big grin. "It's better."

Jason grinned too, playing along with the mock contest the two students had set up. "We'll see. I'll let you know on Thursday."

Ji Eun feigned disappointment. "Thursday? Why can't we find out tomorrow?"

"Because these writing tasks are long, there are fifteen of you and I've got a seven year old boy to take care of," Jason told her, his smile still in place.

Ji Eun laughed. "You're funny, Jason."

"Who said I was being funny?" Jason asked.

When Jason stepped into the office, Johnson and Mike were deep in discussion.

"But why would this guy appear right after Lady Vice did?" Mike asked.

"It's classic mob mentality," Johnson said.

One of the other teachers, Melissa, turned around at her desk. "What the hell are you on about, Johnson? Mob mentality? Where did *that* come from?"

"No, no. It makes sense," Johnson told her. "It's like this, you see. You know how when there's a riot or something like that, you get a whole lot of ordinary people doing things they'd never do under normal circumstances, right?"

Mike nodded. "Yeah, yeah. I get it. Safety in numbers. Anonymity and all that."

Johnson nodded and gestured to him with an open palm. "Exactly." He turned back to Melissa. "With Lady Vice back in the limelight, actually *deliberately* trying to be public enemy number one, it provides other nut jobs out there with some form of cover."

"Yeah," Mike joined in. "If everyone's trying to track down Lady Vice, that means there's less attention on them."

Jason joined in. "That's a possibility. But also, don't forget the fact that Lady Vice is getting away with it too. That might make the other nut jobs out there a little bolder."

"But she hasn't been getting away with it for long," Melissa pointed out. "She only got started a few days ago."

Jason shrugged. "Depends on how you look at it."

Then Johnson shook his head. "No, no. The vampire must have been planning his crime for a while. It sounds too complicated to have been a spontaneous idea."

"Yeah, I can see that," Jason conceded. Then he frowned and shook his head. "Man, I'm worried about the news being filled with this stuff. Parents are telling their kids about it for sure."

"Yeah?" Mike asked.

"Well, Ethan found out about the West Avenue Bridge incident," Jason said. "And I didn't tell him. I wonder if I should write a letter to his principal and ask her if she can request parents not to discuss these things with their kids. It's pretty inappropriate for kids under the age of ten."

Mike shook his head. "I wouldn't write a letter. You can't really stop parents from doing that. I mean, I'm with you and all. Parents *shouldn't* share that kind of stuff with a six year old but it's not illegal."

"It should be," Jason said. "Taking a five year old to see a horror movie's illegal. How's this any more responsible?"

Mike shrugged. "Ah, I wouldn't worry too much. Chances are Ethan wouldn't understand what the kids are going on about anyway."

Just then, Angie came in. "Hey, Jason."

Jason turned around. "Hey, Angie."

His wife put a pile of books on her desk. "I'm with Mike. Don't write that letter. Ms. Sullivan wouldn't listen to you anyway."

"Ethan? Have you brushed your teeth?"

Ethan smiled at his mother, showing his teeth so she could see them for herself.

Angie smiled back and gave him a big hug. "Good boy!"

"I brushed them the way they told me to at school last week," Ethan told her.

Angie looked at him in surprise. "They taught you how to brush your teeth at school?"

Ethan nodded and pointed to his teeth. "They gave us this red stuff. It sticks to your teeth. When it's all gone, your teeth are clean!"

"I remember that when I was a kid," Jason said, coming into the room. "That was cool." He kissed Angie then knelt down and gave Ethan a hug. "Sleep well, Ethan."

"You too," his son said, embracing him in return.

"I love you."

"I love you too, Dad."

Ethan repeated the routine with Angie. Then, when he was in bed, she and Jason both said goodnight, turned off his light and closed the door.

They then went into the living room, Jason stopping by the kitchen en route to put the pot on to boil.

"Is there anything good on tonight?" he called out as Angie settled down on the sofa.

"No idea," she told him, picking up the remote. "Let's see."

When she turned the television on, she had stumbled onto the middle of a news report.

"*Only days after hitting headlines around the country, the Vampire has struck again.*"

THE DARK

"WHEN DEREK BRADLEY OPERATED UNDER THE name of Orion, he was formidable. I have discussed his extreme views, his brutality and the unfortunate recklessness that led to the tragedy at the Graceville Hospital. The death of twenty-four year old nurse Danielle Sutherland.

However, these facts only tell half the story of this remarkable man. He also exhibited an incredible intellect, which was possibly best demonstrated by the Specter case.

The Specter, for those who may have forgotten—if there are such people—was a serial killer who announced all his crimes in advance. Despite his warnings and the subsequent efforts by the Fringe City police to prevent him carrying out his threats, he still succeeded.

The Specter used a variety of methods, killed fourteen prominent citizens and yet, the police repeatedly failed to find and apprehend him.

Then, almost an entire year after his last killing, the man who donned the mantle of the Specter was dumped outside the Fringe City police headquarters. A corpse. And the man who had found him and put an end to his spree was my *patient, Derek Bradley. Orion.*

On occasions, I have asked him about this case. But at best, his responses to my questions have been sketchy. However, I suspect that he quite enjoys talking about his crime-solving methods. He's highly intelligent and I believe he appreciates a bit of mental stimulation from time to time. And so, in light of this recent development with the Vampire, I thought it would be interesting to ask Derek Bradley about the Specter case again."

"Is this about the Vampire?"

Dr. John Carter's face remained impassive. "Maybe. Would it matter if it were?"

Derek Bradley shrugged. "It wouldn't matter to me. However, I should tell you that this is unlikely to help the police if that's your ulterior motive in asking me about it. There are some general principles that one can apply to a range of investigations but, in my experience, each investigation has its own unique peculiarities. This 'Vampire' sounds like a very different beast from the Specter."

"I'm sure he is," John said. "However, I don't want to talk about the Vampire."

"Or Lady Vice?" Derek asked.

"Or Lady Vice."

"Because you know she's not the same woman—or

should I say *women*—who originally used that pseudonym."

John frowned. "What do you mean?"

"It's fairly straightforward," Derek said. "*This* Lady Vice is not the previous Lady Vice."

"Do you think the police know this?"

Derek smiled. "Well, those who need to know would, certainly. Are you all right, Dr. Carter? You look a little uncomfortable."

"I'm fine," John said, working to hide whatever signs of agitation his patient had detected.

"Don't worry about Lady Vice, Dr. Carter."

"I won't."

Derek leaned back a little. "So, you want to know about the Specter. It'll rather spoil the illusion I built when I brought that case to a close though. There is after all a reason why magicians rarely share their secrets."

"Well, consider me a student of the craft then rather than a member of the audience."

Derek smiled again. This time with a little more warmth. "The truth is that it was a long and tedious process. I didn't solve the Specter murders as a series of cold cases. I worked on the last murder when the trail was still hot and I kept at it until I hunted that son of a bitch down and killed him."

"You're trying to get under my skin a bit today,

Derek," John said. "What's wrong?"

Derek shrugged. "Why do you think I'm trying to provoke you?"

"You know I don't like hearing you talk about killing people."

"Sorry."

"You don't have to apologize. I'm just curious as to why you're doing it. Is something on your mind?"

Derek said nothing.

"Lady Vice?" John prompted. "The Vampire?"

Derek didn't react to either name. "What will you say about this when you write up your notes later?" he asked instead.

"Why do you think I'll write anything?" John asked in return.

"Your mind is always ticking, Dr. Carter. You don't switch off. I watch you every time you come here. Always ticking away. Analyzing everything I say, turning every word over and over in your head. You remind me of myself in many ways."

"Would that be a compliment?" John asked, trying a little smile.

"You know, it might very well be."

"Well, I'll be straight with you then," John said. "I suspected that either the subject of Lady Vice or the Vampire brings about unpleasant mental associations for you. And while you didn't react to either name when I asked you about them, I suspect that Lady Vice is the subject that bothers you. It reminds you of the day you were captured. And you tell me the woman using the Lady Vice persona is not the same Lady Vice who held the mayor hostage eight years ago. So I've formulated a theory. The siege that night was staged. It was an entrapment operation, designed for you."

It was rare to see Derek impressed but he was then. "That's pretty good, Dr. Carter."

"I think I understand you more now, Derek."

Derek leant forward. "Don't go to anyone with this, Dr. Carter. It was off the record. And it'd be more than your career's worth to try to bring it up."

"You care about my career?"

"Sure I do," Derek said. "I don't hate you, Dr. Carter. Far from it. You're about the only friend I've got."

For a moment, John was taken aback. "Well, um… Thank you, Derek."

For a moment, neither of them spoke.

"Well," John continued, "we certainly got a bit side-tracked there. Why don't we go back to the Specter again?"

Derek shrugged. "Sure. Why not? Firstly, I used a range of techniques to find my man. In one of his murders, he used a substance that could be manufactured by anyone with the know-how and the component substances it required... except one of those component substances was itself a complex substance of many parts.

"Now, *that* substance could be purchased from industrial manufacturers but if not, an individual could mix it themselves. So firstly, I checked out official transaction records involving the shipping of the substance. But it quickly became clear that all shipments of the stuff were accounted for. So I then investigated the shipping of the various substances that would be required to make it."

"That sounds tedious," John said.

"It *was* tedious," Derek said. "And as it turned out, it was a complete dead-end. I also tried to create a suspect pool by ascertaining patterns in the Specter's killings and possible motivations and that was a long road to nowhere as well. However, when he committed his last murder, I was able to break into the crime scene when the police weren't there and find enough evidence in the form of clay particles from his footwear to track him to a subway platform where he boarded a train."

"A little while after that, I broke into the Fringe City Metro's security archives and was able to get my first look at the man. Not much of a look really but it was a start. I worked out where he got off and found out where he was staying and what name he had stayed under."

"And that's when you got him?" John asked.

"He had already cleared out," Derek replied. "However, I then had a vague idea of what he looked like. I also knew he lived off the grid and I knew one of the aliases he used. After that, it was a matter of keeping an eye on suspicious residence records, while trying to work out how he had gotten the forged documents he needed to adopt the one alias I knew he had used. And eventually, I found him."

"And brought him in," John said with a nod.

"And brought him, yes."

John stirred. "Do you miss the thrill of the chase sometimes?"

Derek shook his head. "No."

"No?"

"No," Derek said. "I miss the satisfaction of the catch."

Devan Fletcher took a sip of his drink, while Charles Faulkner loosened his tie and poured himself one as well.

"They were different days, Devan, as you know."

"I'm not judging anyone here," Devan told him. He sighed. "I know what it was like. Aside from a handful of officers, the police were effectively working for the mob and people like Martin Lamont had a stranglehold over all our legal institutions as well."

"We were still trying to play it straight then though," Charles pointed out. "It was Orion that prompted us to make our secret deal with Lady Vice. Well, those dedicated women who had created the persona back *then*, I mean. Your lovely Gwendolyn among them. But basically, Orion was a loose cannon. He may have cleaned up every last bit of crime in Fringe City if we had left him to it but the collateral damage would have gone through the roof. Who knows how many Danielle Sutherlands would have been killed along the way if we hadn't intervened?"

Devan put his glass down. "He's a rather angry man, isn't he? This Derek Bradley."

Charles shrugged. "He's got his reasons to be. There was plenty in this city to be angry about." He paused for a moment. "And there still is," he amended. "Also, I doubt he'd have any love for *us*."

"Do you think this Dr.... um... Carter could bring him around?"

"I'd like to think so," Charles said, frowning. "However, there seems to be another question in that."

"And you appear to already disapprove of the idea," Devan said. "And given what you, the mayor and the police commissioner agreed to eight years ago, I hope you'll forgive me if I say I find that a little hypocritical. Why shouldn't I contemplate whether or not we might let Orion loose again?"

Charles took a long sip of his drink and put the glass down. He thought about it for a moment before he replied.

"Well, first of all, our deal was made with people who were trustworthy. And not to mention sane. Now, I'm not saying that Derek Bradley is incapable of rational thought or anything like that. In many ways, he's saner than you or I am. However, he has violent tendencies which we saw played out time and time again. And he also suffered from a dangerous level of obsession. And don't forget, Devan, that one of the women we worked with back then was your wife."

"I know," Devan replied. "But also, don't forget that I never said I disapproved of what you did either. Or what Gwendolyn did. I've had some time to think about it and I can tell you without any doubt that I'm proud of her. What she and her friends did—and what they're still doing now—is incredible."

Charles nodded. "I know. And I didn't forget that. You want to know why I differentiate between bending the law to work with your wife and her friends eight years ago and bending the law to let Orion loose now."

"The time is also significant then?"

"Not the time so much," Charles said. "The

circumstances then and now. I know things don't look good right at the moment. Someone out there has resurrected the Lady Vice persona for reasons that are obviously no good and this Vampire, whoever he or she is, has already killed twice in under a week. However, we need to keep our heads about this. These people have only just appeared and the police are working hard to track them down. We just need to give them some time. Things haven't spiraled out of control."

Devan nodded. "And what happens when they do?"

"We just deal with things as best as we can," Charles said, frowning again. "What's come over you, Devan? I've never seen you like this before."

"It's a hunch," Devan told him. "I think things are about to head south in Fringe City. Maybe not on the scale of what happened at the West Avenue Bridge but if this new Lady Vice and the Vampire have free reign of the place and the police can't bring them in soon, then things will start to fall apart really quickly. Public confidence will be a thing of the past. That's one thing. And if syndicates around the country see that you can run rings around the police and the legal institutions of Fringe City, we'll effectively be rolling out the welcome mat for them. But in the Palmdale Mental Health Institute, we've got a man who could stop this before it gets any further out of hand. Right now. So really, we'd be crazy not to consider him as an option, wouldn't we?"

Charles sighed. "You may be right, Devan, but I'd rather exhaust every other option available to us first. Because to me, Derek Bradley is the textbook *definition* of a two-edged sword."

Mariane O'Hara walked up the hallway to her apartment, turned the key to her lock, opened the door and stepped inside.

It felt a little chilly inside. Admittedly, it was a chilly day outside as well with the wind and the rain but she remembered leaving the windows closed before she left. Now, it seemed as if every last one of them was wide open and she heard bits of paper blowing around in the living room.

For a moment, she wondered whether the kids had left the things open but she knew that couldn't be right because they were with their father in Florida.

A sense of dread stole over her; the Vampire entered his victims' bedrooms through the windows.

Her heart racing, she flicked on the light switch beside the door and saw several things—but not for long. The main window in the living room was shattered and standing in front of it were three women in corsets. Then one of them threw something at her feet and its contents exploded on impact.

And that was all she saw. She had enough time to let out one brief scream before she was overcome by the gas that poured out and then she slumped to the floor in an heap. One of the three women picked her up and strapped her to her waist. Then they all walked backwards, pressed down on small devices attached to their belts and disappeared through the window, hoisted out of sight by thin cables.

Mariane awoke in a strange room, though well-lit and far from the type of dark unpleasant place she expected. She was reclining on a quite comfortable sofa and sitting across from her, her legs folded elegantly with one thigh emerging bare from the slit in her dress was a woman offering her a glass of champagne. A woman who was both familiar and yet, at the same time, not.

After her previous encounter with Lady Vice eight years earlier, Mariane had sought counseling and read up on literature related to dealing with hostage and kidnap situations. Unanimity of opinion was something that was lacking in all those books, in reverse proportion to the large degree of ambiguity, but one thing she had latched onto was the idea of taking control of these types of situations as best as one could.

"You look different," she told the woman, declining to accept the drink.

"I imagine I do," the woman confessed. "Eight years is a long time and, while I'd like to imagine I'm well preserved, I'm older than I was when we last met. And I tend to change my make-up a lot."

"Why have you brought me here?"

"I want the people of Fringe City to have a chance to get to know me better," the woman replied. "When we last met, I asked you if you would provide me with the appropriate media coverage and you didn't even run the story yourself. This time, I thought we might make things a little more... intimate."

She gestured to her right and her left. Two women emerged, similarly dressed, and stood behind cameras mounted on tripods.

"An evening with Lady Vice would make a nice name for the segment," the woman continued. "And you, being the golden girl of Fringe City's news networks would be the perfect host."

"What if I decide not to run this?"

Lady Vice smiled. "Oh, don't worry. We'll find someone to run it if you manage to talk your own network executives out of it. We'll find several if we have to. And if no one agrees, we can always run it ourselves."

"I find it hard to see how," Mariane said.

Lady Vice's smile remained but it now had a cruel edge to it. "Oh, we have our ways."

Jason hesitated before he rang the doorbell but his urge to talk to Diane as soon as he could overrode any doubts as to whether this was the best time. He rang it.

About twenty seconds later, Diane appeared.

"Jason. This is a bit of a surprise. Why didn't you call?"

Jason shook his head. "I don't know. I'm sorry if this is a bad time and all that."

Diane frowned. "Are you all right?"

"I think I'm onto something."

"What do you mean?"

Jason glanced over her shoulder. "Um, I need to talk to you somewhere privately. Look, there's a cafe down the road. It's got enough space and background noise for the job."

"Like old times, Jason?" Diane asked. But her frown remained. "You're not moonlighting, are you?"

"Nothing of the kind," Jason told her. "But something's come up and I think you should see it."

• • •

"What's this?" Diane asked as Jason passed the open exercise book over.

"I got this from one of my students," Jason said. "As for her information, it's all public record. All she's done is drawn her own conclusions from it."

"Which are?" Diane asked, skim-reading.

"That the Lady Vice out there now is not the Lady Vice who terrorized the city before. And that the previous Lady Vice may not have been what she appeared. She cites discrepancies in official reports and what she perceives to be the gaps in the story." Jason pointed to part of the page. "See? Here." He shook his head. "Damn *Agendas in Text*. I basically taught these students to do *just that*. Although, these students were already pretty damn bright to begin with."

"I see what you mean," Diane said, reading the part Jason had pointed out. She slid the book back. "But there's nothing incriminating in there."

"That's not what I'm worried about," Jason told her. "But if international students who haven't even been in the country for six months can work that out, then surely long-term Fringe City residents can too. And I think we may have to consider the fact that the people who are running this new Lady Vice scheme know what really happened. And that could put a new spin on things."

"You think they're trying to call us all out?" Diane

asked. "But what would that get them?"

"Do they need a reason? It could just be a bit of fun for them. But it's also possible that they're planning to blackmail people, using the information as leverage."

Diane nodded. "That's a possibility. But why haven't they come to us with their demands yet?"

"I don't know," Jason said. "Maybe they're afraid we can still bring them in. They might be waiting until they're in a position where they know we can't touch them."

Diane was quiet for a moment.

"Thanks, Jason," she said at last.

"Just like old times?"

"Yes," Diane said. "Those days were *such* fun."

After she and Jason left the cafe, Diane called her husband to tell him she'd be out a little longer and then she drove straight to police headquarters and saw Hutchens.

"Commander Felding," Hutchens greeted her. "This is a bit of a surprise. Don't you usually have Wednesday's off?"

"I do but I have a little time today. And there's something I need to talk to you about."

Hutchens nodded. "It's not about the Vampire, is it?"

"Lady Vice."

"Ah," Hutchens said. "Running second place to public enemy number one and still vying for first prize. I wonder what the score will be at the end of the week."

"Hard to tell," Diane said.

Hutchens sighed. "All right, Diane. Let's go into my office and talk there."

Diane followed Hutchens, declining the offer of a coffee and going straight into explaining Jason's theory.

Hutchens frowned when she had finished. "So Jason thought this up after he read this student's paper, did he?"

"That's what he said," Diane told him. "He showed me the student's work as well. It was just a simple homework assignment."

"Well, I suppose that makes sense," Hutchens said but he didn't seem entirely convinced. "But even the fact that he picked up on the implications—"

"First of all, I'd say he's got valid reasons to have a personal interest in this investigation," Diane said. "If this lady using the Lady Vice persona now intends to blackmail us, he could be exposed too."

"I doubt it," Hutchens said. "Only a handful of us know he was the Sentinel. He doesn't have as much to lose as you or I do. Or Charles or the mayor."

"Maybe," Diane said. "But we can't be certain. But the second point I wanted to make is that I've talked to Jason about this twice. The first time when you asked me to talk to him, along with Gwendolyn and Sonya. And I also talked to him about it today when he told me his theory. He's not running any off-the-record investigations or dressing up in that suit of his. This is something he more or less figured out inadvertently."

"I hope you're right," Hutchens said. "Because if he brings the Sentinel back and gets himself in the papers, I don't know if we could turn an official blind eye to him again. The city's not the same as it was eight years ago. People were a little more inclined to let things slide back then but these days, they tend to notice a bit more when things don't seem quite right. I mean, take Jason's student for instance. And he raises a good point there. If someone from overseas who is still learning the language can pick up on these discrepancies, then you can bet a few of our long-term residents can as well."

"Well, the brighter ones, certainly," Diane said.

Hutchens smiled. "Right. We probably don't have to worry too much about the ones watching reality TV programs." The smile faded. "But anyway, that's the first thing. The second thing is that if this new Lady Vice *is* actually trying to gain leverage over us, then we definitely couldn't turn a blind eye to Jason if he brought the Sentinel back."

Diane nodded. "I know."

"Well, since you're his friend, you should really make sure he knows too."

"I will."

"And there's another thing I need to mention as well," Hutchens said. "Mariane O'Hara was kidnapped last night."

"Oh my god," Diane said. "Have you tried looking—?"

Hutchens waved his hand. "No, no. It's all right. She's safe and sound. The whole thing lasted about six hours and for four of them, she was unconscious."

"She was injured?"

"No," Hutchens said. "And this is where it gets interesting. Our new Lady Vice kidnapped her, you see, to have her conduct an interview. When Mariane was released, she had a tape of the interview with her."

"Her network's not going to air it, are they?"

"They're not," Hutchens said. "They sent it to us."

"Have you seen it yet?" Diane asked.

Hutchens shrugged. "I'll watch it later. I thought it'd be better to let the specialists watch it first to see if there's anything on it that might help us find this bitch."

"Fair enough."

"However, as for Fringe City Central not airing it, I

think it's fairly certain this woman will send copies of the tapes to the other networks. And I don't know if they'll show as much forethought."

"You know, you might be able to file injunctions against them if they air something like that," Diane pointed out. "You should talk to Charles."

"Not a bad idea," Hutchens said.

"Now somehow this all relates to Jason, right?"

"Right," Hutchens nodded, glad of the reminder. "When Mariane was kidnapped from her home, she was rendered unconscious by some kind of stun gas before being taken to another location. I think you can see where I'm going with this."

Diane frowned. "I think I do. And I don't think I like it."

"I don't think I like it either," Hutchens said. "Forensics analyzed trace elements left behind in the apartment and they match those left behind by the stun gas Jason used in his Sentinel days. So his theory that this new Lady Vice knows practically everything that went on back then may well be right on the money."

"I don't suppose someone else could reverse engineer the gas, using the trace elements that remain afterwards?" Diane asked.

"That might be a possibility," Hutchens said. "But I don't think that would invalidate the theory that this woman intends to blackmail the lot of us."

"No," Diane agreed. "But it might well help us track her down. Now, I imagine these trace elements don't remain behind very long. When did Forensics investigate Mariane's apartment? After she was released or right after she disappeared?"

Hutchens looked impressed. "Right after she disappeared. The neighbors heard her scream and called us right away. Forensics was on the scene fifteen minutes after she disappeared. The trace elements you're asking about dissipated about ten minutes after that."

"So if she did reverse engineer the gas, she might have an associate who worked in Forensics eight years ago."

"What a comforting thought."

"Or his friend who supplied him with the gas may have been compromised."

"Well," Hutchens said, leaning back in his seat, "since Jason's already thinking about all of this, you may as well tell him about the stun gas too."

"I think I have to," Diane said.

A couple of hours later, Hutchens looked up from the photos on his desk. Photos he had been staring at, that hadn't offered up a single useful clue.

"Palmer. What's up?"

"I thought you'd better see FCBN's evening news bulletin," Palmer told him.

"Why? Is Mike Evans going to choke on his tie?"

"Possibly," Palmer said. "But I just saw an ad for the program and they're going to air the interview with Lady Vice."

Hutchens nodded. "Right. The one that both Mariane O'Hara and all the executives at Fringe City Central are refusing to air because it was conducted under duress. Well, I suppose we might as well watch it now."

"The team downstairs haven't finished with the tape?"

"Not yet."

Palmer nodded. "Ah, well. I thought you probably hadn't seen it yet. However, there's also something else. Someone's sent FCBN footage of the Vampire as well. They're going to air it after the interview."

"Footage of the Vampire? Where did that come from?"

"It was taken after the last murder."

"Who took it?"

Palmer shook his head. "They didn't say. But I've got a unit ready outside. The minute we see the footage, I can determine where it was taken from. Well, assuming that it's genuine and shows the Vampire leaving the last crime scene. But anyway, if it *is* the real article, then I can take that unit around to investigate it right away. FCBN can go on about informant confidentiality if they wish but we never agreed to any such thing."

"Right, good thinking," Hutchens said, getting up. "Now, when's this thing starting?"

Palmer glanced at his watch. "In about five minutes."

Hutchens nodded. "Let's go then. Even if it doesn't help us with either of our investigations, I'm pretty sure FCBN is about to give me a reason to file an injunction against them."

"We received the tape this morning from Lady Vice," Mike Evans said. *"While Fringe City Central has refused to air the footage, we believe the viewers at home have the right to see this. Sensitive viewers however are advised that Mariane O'Hara conducted this interview under duress and the footage may be disturbing."*

The screen cut to a familiar corseted figure, reclining in a chair, twirling a strand of her hair in one hand and playing with a riding crop with her other.

"Lady Vice, thank you for joining me here tonight."

The voice was one that would be familiar to most viewers but the tone of that voice, along with the strain that tainted its edges, was different.

The woman inclined her head, smiling. *"Thank you for having me."*

"My first question is this. And I'm sure many of our viewers at home are wondering the same thing. Why, after all these years, have you come back now?"

The woman's smile remained. *"Who says I have come back?"*

"Would you care to elaborate on what you mean by that?"

"Why don't we let the viewers form their own conclusions on the subject, my dear?"

"Then why have you chosen to announce your presence to Fringe City now of all times?"

"I am a woman who knows which way the wind is blowing," Lady Vice replied. *"And right now, in Fringe City, it's blowing hard to the south. Let's just say that things in Fringe City are about to get a lot more interesting."* She turned to the camera. *"And to everyone watching out there, if you were worried that Fringe City isn't as lively as it used to be, then I've got news for you. The good times are back."*

"All right then," Mariane said. *"Let's just get to the next question."*

There was an uncomfortable pause and a sharp intake of breath.

In the silence, another woman's voice was heard. *"Stick to the cards."*

There was an audible gasp, followed by another pause, shorter this time, and Mariane resumed speaking. *"Next question. What is your opinion of the Vampire?"*

"So far, so good," Lady Vice said. *"He's not an amateur. He's innovative. But I'd like to challenge him to lift his game."*

"Oh, great," Hutchens muttered as he watched it. "Extra incitement for that psychotic. Did these idiots actually *watch* the tape before they decided to air this?"

"I want to make it clear that I welcome a bit of friendly underworld rivalry," Lady Vice continued. *"But, as I've said before, there's no room for mediocrity here. If you want to work Fringe City, you've got to know how to put on a show. Something that a few small timers out there have been finding out the hard way."* She nodded over her shoulder. *"Like my friend here."*

"What friend is that?"

Lady Vice climbed out of her seat. Behind her, two of her associates had dragged in a half-sedated young man, with peroxide dyed hair and multiple piercings, handcuffed with his arms behind his back. He looked frightened and confused.

Lady Vice walked over to him. *"This pathetic vermin you see before you here, Ms. O'Hara, whose only party trick is selling industrially negligible quantities of illicit drugs to kids too stupid to know better than to buy them."* She looked at the young man with open disdain. *"Unimaginative. Unoriginal."* She raised one hand, her nails glittering in carefully positioned lights. *"And just plain, unforgivably—"* Then she struck, slashing the man across the side of his neck. *"—bland."*

Mariane screamed as the man collapsed on the floor out of sight behind Lady Vice's vacated chair.

"I've got those stupid sons of bitches now," Hutchens said, pointing to the screen. "Broadcasting a real murder. That's a damn snuff film." He nodded to one of the other officers beside him. "Jackson. Get on the phone to the D.A.'s office."

"Got it," the officer replied, springing to his feet.

"You're gone, Evans," Hutchens muttered.

In another part of the city, George and Sonya Hines were watching the same program but not really out of choice. It was more a case of being frozen to the sofa in horror. George then got up and dragged his hands through his thick hair.

"What's wrong, honey?" Sonya asked.

"That guy," George said, pointing at the screen where Lady Vice's victim had been standing moments before. "He's the dealer who was selling that stuff to Aidan and his friends."

Sonya frowned. "But I thought you said the police were all set to take him in."

"They were," George said. "But then the West Avenue Bridge disaster happened and they never got around to it."

"But Lady Vice was probably just after the dealers, right?" Sonya said. "Not the kids who were buying from them."

But George was already heading for the door. "Wait here, honey. I've got to go."

"However, I'm a reasonable woman," Lady Vice continued, nodding to her associates to remove the late drug dealer from the room and resuming her seat.

She turned back to Mariane. *"In fact, I would welcome more newcomers to the scene. They just have to be up to standard. It's been a while since we've had serious showmen like the Bandit and the Specter. If there's anyone out there who thinks they've got what it takes, then I welcome you with open arms."* She turned to the camera again. *"And who knows?"* she asked with a wink. *"An open bedroom door might be on the cards as well."*

"And on the subject of open arms and bedroom doors," she continued, *"let me finish by saying one last thing. Tonight, I'm officially declaring open season in Fringe City. Step up if you've got what it takes. Stay out of sight if you don't. And if you don't want to play at all, then stay inside and bolt your doors."* She gave one last wicked smile to the camera. *"Let the fun begin."*

The video ended and Mike Evans appeared once more, looking flustered.

Hutchens noticed right away.

"They didn't watch the tape first," he murmured to Palmer. "I knew it."

Palmer nodded, his gaze still glued to the screen.

"So, there you have it, ladies and gentlemen," Mike said, his voice a little shaky. *"Lady Vice has officially declared war on the city. Under any other circumstances, one would imagine that would make her public enemy number one right there. But as we're all aware, another underworld figure is now menacing our streets. One who has so far remained silent on his motivations, who has so far remained entirely in the shadows. But this evening, here on the Fringe City Broadcasting Network, we invite you to join us in*

witnessing an exclusive piece of footage we received today that will shed some light on this mysterious killer. Once again, we advise sensitive viewers that this footage may be disturbing. This, ladies and gentlemen, is the Vampire."

A block of apartments appeared on the screen, twenty or thirty yards from wherever the footage was taken. Soft orange glows were visible in some of the windows but most of them were dark.

In the shadows of one of the latter, a small red glow appeared and a strange apparition appeared on the ledge. A figure draped in some type of cape. Streaks of red appeared as it shuffled position but the impression it gave was largely one of black and flashes of silver. And where its eyes should have appeared were two dull red glowing lights.

The figure lunged from the window, falling then gliding straight for the camera. Then it swooped up, disappearing from sight.

When the footage cut back to the news desk, Mike Evans looked sick. Clearly, he hadn't previewed that footage either.

Palmer got up.

"You think you can find the place?" Hutchens asked.

"I think so," Palmer replied, pulling out his radio

and heading for the door. "At least, I think my people can."

"Let me know what you find," Hutchens called after him.

"Will do," Palmer called over his shoulder.

Hutchens then swung himself off the desk he was sitting on and headed back to his office. He left the TV on as there were a handful of officers in the room still watching but he'd seen all he needed to.

He locked his door after he closed it, picked up the phone and dialed.

"Eric?"

"Yeah," he said. "It's me, Charles. Did Jackson tell you what our friends at FCBN have done now?"

"He did. Although, I saw the whole thing myself," Charles Faulkner replied. "I had a feeling you'd call." There was a slight pause on the other end of the line. "I can't believe they'd be that stupid."

"Oh, I can," Hutchens said. "First, that business with Ken Doyle. Then giving the Vampire his first dose of free publicity, very likely giving him the encouragement that led to that second girl getting murdered—"

"You may be right, Eric," Charles said. "But we've got to be careful about saying things like that. You know how it is."

"Yeah, I know," Hutchens muttered. "But I'm not

telling the whole world here. I'm just telling you."

"I know that. But I also know you're probably pretty strung out right now. We've got to keep our heads level about all this."

"Yeah, I know."

"But FCBN has seriously crossed the line tonight. Actually, I'm like you. I saw something like this coming too, for the same reasons you did, and so I've already been giving an injunction some thought. But I'm not planning a cease and desist order for you now. I'm going to be pressing charges against these people."

"Good."

"Yes, well... First of all, the fact that they didn't send their copy of the tapes to the police, knowing full well what they were, and then proceeded to air them could be interpreted as tampering with evidence."

"You could charge them with that?"

"It'd be tricky," Charles said. "But I'd argue that it was highly possible that you may have wanted to keep that footage off the air for the purposes of your investigations. So by their actions, FCBN could well have undermined those same investigations. They should have consulted your people about those tapes. Also, there's the recklessness in airing footage likely to incite not only widespread panic but also a string of other crimes. Add that to the fact that they aired a snuff film, on prime time when young children were probably watching, and they're in a lot of trouble."

"Good," Hutchens said. "That's good. Trouble's exactly what I want to send their way. However, we've got some other problems now, don't we?"

There was *definitely* a long pause this time. "We do. Yes."

"What are we going to do, Charles?"

"Aside from me asking you to bring this woman in and you telling me that you're already doing everything you can?" Charles asked. "I'm not sure. Although I *am* sure the mayor's going to want to know what we've got."

"I don't think she's going to want to *hear* what we've got."

"No," Charles agreed. "I don't think she will either."

Meanwhile, Sonya picked up her own phone. "Honey?"

"Yeah, it's me," George replied.

His voice said it all, Sonya knew, but she asked anyway. "Is Aidan all right?"

"Aidan's dead."

Sonya sniffed a little and brushed some tears from her eyes. "I'm sorry, honey."

"Yeah," George replied. "Me too."

. . .

A little later back at the police headquarters, Hutchens answered a phone call too.

"It's Palmer."

Hutchens sighed. It was going to be more bad news and he was getting really tired of it.

"All right," he said. "Hit me. The witness who sent the footage is dead?"

"Well, the owner of the apartment is dead," Palmer replied. "But whether this guy sent the footage or not... I can't really tell at the moment. We haven't found the camera, that's for sure. And the place is ransacked."

"The Vampire saw him taking the footage perhaps?" Hutchens asked.

"Beats me. That may be what it's supposed to look like but for all we know, the Vampire paid this guy to take the footage and send it in and then cleaned up the evidence afterwards."

"Yeah, that would fit," Hutchens said. "All right. I'm on the way over there now."

"I can't believe they showed that."

Jason nodded. Chen had it right there.

"I can't believe you guys watched it," Ricardo

joined in.

Jason listened in silence. While it wasn't exactly what he had planned for the morning, a task-based learning lesson based around an article on climate change, the news was generating a lot of discussion. He just had to make sure it didn't get out of hand.

"You didn't watch it, did you, Jason?" Ricardo asked him.

"No," Jason replied. "No, I didn't."

Ricardo turned to Chen. "See?"

"Did you know it was on, Jason?" Ji Eun asked.

Jason shook his head. "No. I didn't know anything about it until I came to work this morning. The other teachers were talking about it. But even if I had known about it beforehand, I wouldn't have watched it."

"It's not good for the mind," Ricardo said.

"I wish I hadn't watched it either," Ji Eun admitted.

Beside her, Kaori shook her head. "That gave me nightmares."

One of the other students, Patrick, spoke up. "I think the Vampire's costume was designed to unsettle viewers. And I think he wanted the costume to seen."

" 'Be' seen," Ji Eun corrected.

Patrick smiled. "Be seen. Sorry."

"Or you could omit 'to be' entirely," Jason suggested, "and say he wanted the costume seen. 'To be' would still be there but it would be implied rather than explicit."

"How come in the lower level, you said we couldn't do that?" Ricardo asked. He was smiling though. Now he was in a higher level class, an elite club that was allowed to bend the grammatical rules of English a bit like native speakers did. It was kind of fun.

"Advanced speakers of the language know what they're omitting when they do that," Jason said. "But pre-intermediate speakers—and even intermediate speakers—*don't* always know. That's why it's important for students to learn the full grammatical forms first so they understand how the language works. Also, that helps them understand what other speakers mean when *they* omit things."

Jason decided to take advantage of the fact that the conversation had moved on from the footage FCBN had aired the night before. "All right, everybody. It's time for me to return your homework tasks."

He pulled out a pile of exercise books from his bag and put them on the desk beside him. "Come and get them. Read the comments carefully and ask me if you don't understand any of them."

The students came over and collected their books. When Kaori picked hers up, Jason thought a bit of praise was in order.

"That was very good, Kaori," he told her. "I was really impressed by your theory."

"Thanks, Jason." There was a pensive expression in Kaori's eyes. "Actually, is it okay if I write some more about this topic for next week as well? I want to... um... add newer information..."

"You mean you want to update it?" Jason asked.

Kaori smiled and nodded. "Yes. Can I?"

Jason shrugged. "I think that's fine. As long as you're getting the necessary writing practice. And it's obviously a subject you're really interested in. Go for it."

"Thanks, Jason."

Gwendolyn studied the brochure. "Well, I think these look all right. They're all close to shops and public transport and there's a park just a block away. Four million dollars and we've found homes for twenty families. That's a *very* good deal."

"We're only trying to house twelve families at the moment though," Sonya pointed out. "We don't need to buy *all* these units up."

Gwendolyn shrugged. "We don't need to, sure. But these are better offers than anything we've seen for quite a while. And you know we'll need places to house families down the line somewhere."

"What about the property taxes though?" Sonya asked, frowning.

Gwendolyn regarded her friend for a moment. "We can cover them by leasing the spare places. You know that." She frowned. "Are you all right?"

Sonya tried to smile. For a moment, she managed it. Then she burst into tears. The attack lasted a moment and she brushed the tears away quickly, looking embarrassed. "You know, I remember a few years ago when *I'd* be the one asking that question."

"George told me about Aidan," Gwendolyn said. "I know you two knew him better than I did. You must be upset. *I'm* upset."

"We worked hard with Aidan," Sonya told her. "And he was making progress too."

"I know."

"And then there's this thing with Lady Vice."

Gwendolyn eyed the door, making sure no one was about to walk into the place and listen in on their conversation.

As it turned out, there was someone out there. Her husband.

"Devan," she said as he came inside. "This is a surprise. Are you done for the day?"

Devan loosened his tie. "Well, I was going to talk to Charles about this business with FCBN last night but he got called in to have a chat with the mayor."

"About Lady Vice?"

"I guess so."

"Any idea what she's playing at?" Sonya asked. "Is she after *us*? Does she want to blackmail us and drain all our funds or something?"

Devan shrugged. "I suppose she could be after Outreach's funds. Your little charity isn't exactly a corner thrift store. But I'd say she's more likely after the mayor, and maybe Charles and Eric Hutchens."

"Based on?"

"Well, let's call it a hunch."

Sonya smiled. "Are you even *allowed* to have hunches in your profession?"

"Hunches?" Devan asked. "Sure. I've often gone fishing in the courtroom. It's amazing what you catch sometimes."

"Go fishing," Gwendolyn murmured.

"What's that?" Devan asked.

"It seems to me that with this new Lady Vice, we're waiting for her to make her moves and then reacting. Everything we're doing, we're doing on her terms. What we need to do is catch her before she can get us."

Devan frowned. "Well, that goes without saying. But how?"

"I'm not sure yet," Gwendolyn replied. "I've got a vague idea where to start but there are a few things I need to think over first."

. . .

When Jason finished class for the day, he packed up his books and switched his cell phone back on; he always turned it off before class. As the phone came back to life, it vibrated.

Jason looked at the screen and saw there was a text there from Diane. He clicked on it and read the message: *"Call me when you get off work."*

Jason pressed down the speed dial number, held the phone up and waited.

"Jason? You got my message?"

"That's why I'm calling," he said. "What's going on?"

"Can you meet me this afternoon?" Diane asked.

Jason glanced at his watch. "Maybe. Angie and I are about to go and pick up Ethan but maybe afterwards, we can go to that place we went the other day."

"Okay. Thanks, Jason."

"No problem. I'll call you back in an hour or so."

They met at the cafe they had last used, ordered drinks and waited. Then after the drinks had arrived and Diane knew they weren't going to be disturbed, she got into it.

"I don't know if you watch FCBN much," she started.

"I try not to," Jason said. "And I missed last night's

fiasco."

Diane nodded. "I did too, luckily. However, I was filled in today. What about you? Are you up to speed on everything?"

Jason leaned back in his chair. "Well, let's see. Mariane O'Hara was kidnapped the night before yesterday by the new Lady Vice and forced to conduct an interview with her. FCBN aired the tape last night, despite the fact that Mariane's own network had decided to send the tape straight to the police. They didn't preview it and so they ended up televising a real life murder on prime time, like a bunch of morons. Then they aired footage of the Vampire as well. Oh, and in the Lady Vice interview, she was inciting others to come and join in the new crime wave. Did I miss anything?"

"No," Diane said. "That was pretty good. Did your co-workers fill you in?"

"Actually, it was my students."

Diane shook her head. "I'm sorry to hear that actually. Those poor kids of yours have traveled from halfway around the world to get here in some cases, expecting an experience that will enrich their lives in a positive way and instead, they've ended up being confronted with almost daily horrors on the news. I wouldn't be surprised if international students stop coming here."

Jason nodded. "Yeah. That's a real worry actually. Because if that happens, then Angie and I are either going to have to go back to public school teaching or move out of Fringe City."

Diane smiled. "That's not exactly the most difficult dilemma I've ever come across."

Jason smiled too. "No. Perhaps not. But actually, since things have been looking up for the past few years, I haven't minded living here so much anymore. It's only now I'm having those second thoughts." He looked out the window for a moment. "I wonder if I can take the family to San Francisco and stay at my parents' place."

"Why wouldn't you move in with your sister Cassie in Vancouver?" Diane asked. "It's a lovely city."

"Angie thinks it'd be too cold."

"She's never heard of central heating?"

Jason smiled again. "She's heard of it. But she doesn't like the idea of weather that *requires* it."

"Fair enough."

They were quiet for a moment, the brief levity over.

"But you were going to tell me something I didn't know, weren't you?" Jason asked.

Diane nodded. "Not everything about the new Lady Vice's stunt is public knowledge. And part of what isn't public knowledge may concern *you*."

Jason sighed. "All right. Anyway, I thought that'd

probably be the case. So what do the police know that the brain dead idiots at FCBN don't?"

"Mariane O'Hara was knocked unconscious by some form of stun gas before she was taken from her apartment," Diane told him. "Forensics analyzed trace elements shortly afterwards. It's the same stun gas you used when you were the Sentinel."

"One of the varieties I used, anyway."

"What?"

"I used different types of stun gas," Jason reminded her. "For knocking people out for varying lengths of time. Remember my twenty-four hour variety?"

Diane nodded. "Yeah, I remember. Although, if I remember correctly, that wasn't *your* variety at all, nor were any of the others. I seem to remember you telling me once that your friend at the university manufactured the stuff before he moved to Boston. And if I were you, I would talk to that friend of yours."

"You don't know him," Jason said. "He'd never do anything that could compromise me. He used to have a real casual manner that a lot of people misunderstood but when it came to anything that was really important, there was no one in the world you could trust more."

"But shouldn't you just make sure?" Diane asked.

Jason frowned. "And just how well do you think that would go down? 'Hey, Geoff. Back when you were helping me out with that really top secret project of mine, did you by any chance blab about it to any less discriminating friends or colleagues?'" He shook his head. "Whatever happened, it didn't happen at the university."

Diane sighed. "Look, Jason, I know this is difficult but this is serious. Obviously, don't put it in those words. Just explain the situation to him and ask him if he's got any ideas."

"All right," Jason said, relenting. "Although, I reckon someone probably analyzed trace elements of the gas at a crime scene like your Forensics people did in this case and then reverse-engineered the stuff. Either an amateur who had the skills, the experience and the equipment or someone actually from Forensics."

"And don't forget," he added, "that basically half the police force back then worked for the mob."

"I remember it well," Diane told him. "It's impossible not to."

Jason hesitated a moment and sighed. "I'm sorry, Diane. I didn't mean to stir up bad memories."

Diane shook her head. "No, it's all right. It's true. And we'll have to check out some of your old cases and see who was working on them."

She decided to change the focus of the conversation. "Now, there's another thing I wanted to talk to you about. Hutchens told me yesterday and I said I'd tell you. If this new Lady Vice is threatening to expose what we all did eight years ago, then we all have to avoid doing anything that could make this all worse. We think that most likely, she's after the mayor and possibly Charles Faulkner and Eric Hutchens. But she might want Gwendolyn, Sonya and the others as well. And she might also be after you. So that makes it even more important for the lot of us to play things very carefully."

Jason nodded. "Don't worry. I've told you. The last thing I want is to bring back the Sentinel."

"I know," Diane said. "But Hutchens really wanted me to make sure you understand just how serious the situation is. Because if you ever do bring the Sentinel back, there's no way we could turn an official blind eye to it. Fringe City's going to be watching us all very closely and we have no idea when this new Lady Vice is going to drop the hammer on us."

Rather than heading straight home after seeing Diane, Jason found a nearby park with a bit of space and privacy and called Geoffrey, a friend from his university days who had played a critical role in assisting him as the Sentinel. They weren't as close now as they had once been, as time and distance does this to a friendship. But if they didn't see each other for twenty years, they'd still be friends.

"Geoff?"

"Hey, Jason. Long time, no see."

"Yeah," Jason agreed. "It's been a while."

"Is everything all right?" his friend asked. "Charlotte and I have been seeing all this stuff on the news about what's been happening down there since the West Avenue Bridge incident. It almost looks worse than when I left."

"It could be a close contest, that's for sure."

"You're not thinking of..." Geoffrey hesitated. "You know."

"No. Diane's just told me in no uncertain terms that that would be a seriously bad idea. You see, it's possible the new Lady Vice knows about the unofficial deals we all made back then."

"Ah ha." The bitterness in Geoffrey's voice wasn't difficult to understand. He and Charlotte had witnessed one of the heists Gwendolyn and the others had carried out in order to build the original Lady Vice persona and, not being in on the scheme, it had left a mark on them. Jason had explained the situation to Geoffrey later of course but he was still pretty sore about it.

"Anyway," Jason said, "the thing is she might have something on me directly. When she and her girls kidnapped that reporter the night before yesterday, they knocked her unconscious with stun gas exactly like one of the varieties you made for me."

"I see."

"Personally, I think the most likely explanation is that it was reverse engineered from trace elements left somewhere when I used it on the job but I thought I'd better consider every possibility."

"I understand," Geoffrey said. Thankfully, he didn't sound offended.

"Any ideas?"

"I wish I could help. But everyone in the lab then was rock solid. You could trust them to the moon and back."

"Oh, I don't think the problem's one of trust. I just wonder whether it might have been a bit of minor negligence somewhere. You know, a gas canister left lying around somewhere or something. Because while they were all bright people, it was a pretty casual group. When I first met them, the big project they were all working on was something related to brewing beer."

Geoffrey chuckled. "Our one great failure. But you know those guys. Casual, sure. But negligent? Never."

"Don't forget I had to remind you what the day was sometimes," Jason pointed out.

"Yeah, sure," Geoffrey replied. "But I never forgot

important things."

"Yeah, you're right. Sorry, Geoff. I'm just trying to go through all the possibilities here."

"I know. But in the meantime, why don't you just do yourself and your family a favor and keep a low profile?"

Jason sighed. "That's the plan."

When he hung up, Jason sat down on a bench and looked around at his surroundings for a few minutes. Even though there wasn't much left in the afternoon and the evening was waiting in the wings, it was quite a nice day, the wet weather having cleared up the air a bit. He just wished he was in a mood to enjoy it.

Sighing, he stood up and went home, calling Angie on the way to ask whether he should pick up anything for dinner. Apparently however, there were leftovers to take care of.

Leftover food. A nice reminder of the leftover evidence that could possibly incriminate him and tear his family apart. He wondered whether he should tell Angie the great news. He'd have to, he knew. If she found out after the fact, she'd never forgive him.

"Sorry we didn't get a chance to play in the park

today," Jason said to Ethan, brushing his hand through his son's hair. "Maybe we can go tomorrow. All right?"

Ethan smiled. "All right, Dad."

Jason kissed him on the forehead. "Good boy. Okay. Now, time to sleep."

"Okay."

"Goodnight, Ethan."

"Goodnight, Dad," Ethan said, closing his eyes and rolling over in his bed sheet, tucked up for the night.

Jason turned the light off and closed the door.

Angie was waiting for him in the kitchen. She'd made coffee.

"So what did you want to tell me earlier?"

"This new Lady Vice," Jason said. "She kidnapped Mariane O'Hara by knocking her out with one of the same types of stun gas Geoff made for me back when I was... you know."

Angie took a long sip of her drink and put her cup down. Not a moment too soon probably. Her hands were shaking. "Jesus."

"It might not mean anything though," Jason pointed out. "It's possible she's just doing these things to unnerve all of us. You know. And it's probably really intended for Alison St. Claire, Charles Faulkner and Eric Hutchens."

"But still."

"Yeah," Jason agreed. "I can't say I'm happy about

it, that's for sure." He sighed. "She probably reverse engineered the stuff or arrived at it by coincidence. And who knows? It might have nothing to do with unnerving people at all. It might just be that she believes it's an effective weapon and that's all there is to it."

Angie was quiet for a bit. "Maybe we should get out of Fringe City. Get out of the country even. Want to move to Australia?"

Jason shrugged. "It's pretty nice. Geoff and I had a great time when we stayed at the Gold Coast back in university. Saw *a lot* of hot... ah... weather. But I have a friend there and he says it's pretty expensive these days."

Angie shrugged. "Or we could move to Mexico."

Jason chuckled. "Yeah. It always seems to work in the movies." He took a sip of his coffee and put it down again. "No, we should be all right, honey. I talked to Diane about it and she just said to stay low until things settle down."

"And when will that be?" Angie asked, looking serious again. "When they bring this woman into custody? Because so far, they haven't been having a lot of success with that."

"It's only been about a week or so since she's shown up, hasn't it?"

"Yeah. You're probably right," Angie said. "It feels

a lot longer though." She sighed. "Ah, Jason. Do we really want to raise Ethan in a place like this?"

"But how long can all this stuff go on for?"

"I don't know," Angie said. "But I'm afraid to find out."

The next day, Jason's class was noticeably quiet. Ji Eun and Kaori were away, which was unusual, and some of the students who shared the same nationalities would occasionally break away from the tasks the rest of the students were working on and have short hushed conversations in their own languages.

Patrick and Ricardo would tell them to use English and the students would switch back but although Patrick and Ricardo did this in their usual playful manner, it was quieter today and Jason knew their hearts weren't really in it.

And when the students did switch back to English, it was fairly obvious to him that they weren't talking about the same things any more. It was an act. They were all acting as if everything was normal and it wasn't.

He wondered about asking them what was going on but he was nervous about it. Besides, they were all adults. If they wanted to tell him, they would. So he didn't say anything.

. . .

When he was back in the office, he tried to act as though everything were normal but the somber mood of the class had affected him too and he couldn't really do it.

Then, while the other teachers were talking about something, the door opened and the director of the institute stepped in.

"Oh, hey Amanda," Johnson said.

Amanda smiled. "Hi, Johnson. Hi everybody." Her smile was forced though and her voice came across a little soft. She came over to Jason.

"Um, Jason, can I see you for a minute?"

Jason nodded and got up. "Yeah. Sure."

He followed her out of the room to her office. Amanda gestured for him to have a seat and then she shut the door. Rather than sitting across from him on the other side of his desk, she pulled her chair around and sat next to him instead.

"So what's going on?" Jason asked.

Amanda hesitated. "Um, I've got some bad news for you. The police department called the school today. This morning actually, but I didn't think it'd be good to tell you in the middle of class. But I think it's better if you hear it from me now rather than see it on the six o'clock news."

Jason frowned. "What's happened?"

Amanda's voice wavered. "One of your students, Jason. Kaori Tanaka?"

"Yeah, she's one of the top students in the class."

"She's dead, Jason," Amanda told him. "The police found her this morning. She was murdered by the Vampire."

Jason didn't reply. He felt sick and he had a trembling sensation in his throat. Then he realized he was crying and he brushed the tears away.

"I'm so sorry, Jason," Amanda told him. She grabbed some tissues from her desk. "Here."

Gratefully, Jason took them and wiped his tears away. He exhaled a breath of air and took a moment to compose himself.

"Ji Eun knows about it already too," Amanda said. "She was the one who notified the police."

"She and Kaori were very close," Jason stammered.

Amanda nodded. "I know. I know that. Jenny went out to her place today to see if she was okay. We're giving her some time off. And Jenny and Ekiko are talking to immigration so she won't get penalized or lose her student visa or anything like that. That should be fine."

"I want to write something to Kaori's parents," Jason said. "Do you think Ekiko could translate it for me?"

Amanda gave him a smile. "I'm sure she'd be happy

to do that for you, Jason. Now, what about you? Are you going to be okay? Because if you want some time off as well, that's fine. We can do that."

Jason sighed. "I don't know. We're preparing for the next level test and all that and…"

"We can handle it, Jason," Amanda told him. "It's all right. If you need to take some time off, then you should do it. This is not a typical situation and I know you really like all your students. You may *need* some time."

Jason nodded. "I'll sleep on it. See how I feel in the morning."

Amanda didn't look convinced but she agreed. "All right."

When he left Amanda's office, Jason said goodbye to the other teachers without discussing what had happened. Then he and Angie left.

They went home first before they picked up Ethan. When they got inside, Jason told Angie what had happened.

"Oh, I'm so sorry, Jason," she cried, holding him close to her. Home at last, with the person who knew him better than anyone, he didn't need to try to keep things together anymore and so he let himself cry, sobbing on Angie's shoulders until he was too tired and numb to do it anymore.

Then they had a coffee and sat down on the sofa in silence.

After a while, Angie stirred. "Jason. I'll have to go and pick up Ethan now. You stay here. I'll go."

Jason was quiet throughout dinner. Ethan asked him if there was anything wrong but Jason did his best not to worry him, assuring him with false smiles that everything was fine.

Angie read Ethan his favorite books that night before he went to bed, something Jason usually looked forward to every day. However, he knew he'd be no good this time.

Jason didn't watch the news that night. He couldn't face it. There was something so impersonal about the news. People all over Fringe City would hear about what happened and they'd be saddened to hear it of course... but to them Kaori Tanaka was just a name. A victim. A statistic. They didn't *know* her.

Jason did. He knew how bright she was. How generous to others she was. He knew she'd had a great sense of humor and a real zest for life. He knew her friend Ji Eun was going to be traumatized by her loss for the rest of her life and while he had a fair idea of what she was going through right then, he also knew he couldn't really imagine it.

And he couldn't shake the horrible thoughts from his mind. How Kaori's life, all her potential, all the things she might have done and the people she might have met, had been taken away. And the tragedy of that was immeasurable.

Briefly, he wondered how many people suffered this emotional torment after the West Avenue Bridge tragedy. He'd been upset by the tragedy, as everyone had. Very much. But now that he was personally affected by the deliberate murder of someone he knew, he realized he hadn't been upset *enough* back then.

However, that was the past, and this was the present. And right then, he was enveloped in darkness, knowing that a young girl's life had been cut short and that her last waking moments had been ones of terror.

In a daze, he got up from the sofa and walked over to his computer.

"Jason?" Angie asked. "Where are you going?"

"I need to see something."

After the computer started up, he opened his browser and did a short search. Not surprisingly, he had plenty of results to choose from.

Hesitating, reluctant but doing it anyway, he clicked on one and watched what half of Fringe City had seen on FCBN the night before. The footage of the Vampire.

"Honey," Angie said, trying to pull him away from

the monitor. "Don't watch that. Please."

Jason's eyes were moist with new tears. "This is the last thing Kaori ever saw, honey. It's not right."

"Come on," Angie said, closing down the browser and shutting off the computer. "This isn't doing you any good. Let's go and watch something light-hearted on TV. Okay?"

It worked for a little bit. They watched a couple of episodes of a comedy Jason had on DVD. And for a while, he felt a bit better. But he didn't sleep at all well and the next day, he felt very down.

The classroom was somber once again with pockets of hushed conversation throughout the morning. The difference from the previous day was that now, everyone knew what was going on and they knew that everyone else did too.

Then Monica, generally a good-natured and mature student, decided to stop pretending everything was normal.

"Hang on, shouldn't we talk about what happened?"

Everyone looked her way. Jason too.

The room was very quiet.

"I don't know if we're all ready to talk about it, Monica," Jason said. "I think we were all pretty close to

Kaori."

The students were all watching him as if something was very wrong, Jason noticed. Then he realized that he was having a breakdown in front of his class.

"Jason, I'm sorry," Monica said, getting up and coming out to hold his arm. "Do you want to sit down?"

Jason shook his head. "I'm sorry, everyone. Can you excuse me?"

Monica wanted to go with him but he told her he'd manage. Then he went down to his office, collapsed in his seat and closed his eyes, tears trailing down his cheeks.

He was aware, after a while, of light and silhouettes. Then he realized Angie and Amanda were looking at him.

"Jason?" Amanda asked. "Can you hear me?"

He sat up. "Yeah, I can hear you. I'm sorry I left the class. I just needed to take a minute."

"You blanked out for an hour," Amanda told him. "Monica came to see me because she was worried about you." She frowned. "You didn't know you were out for an hour?"

Jason looked at the director in confusion. "No."

Amanda sighed and turned to Angie. "Why don't you take him home? There's only the afternoon lesson left anyway. And you and Jason teach the same level so

I'll just combine your classes. And I can bring in a substitute tomorrow to cover Jason's classes for the next little while. Really. It'll be fine. We're planning to expand the programs two sessions from now anyway so this might be a good chance to bring in some new teachers. And no one's being replaced so there's nothing to worry about." She turned to Jason. "But you really need to take some time off."

Jason nodded and climbed to his feet. "I'm sorry, Amanda."

"Don't be," Amanda told him. "Now go and get some sleep."

It was good advice and Jason slept through the afternoon, dinner and Ethan's bedtime. Ethan asked his mother what was wrong but Angie just told him Jason was feeling sick.

Jason later woke in the middle of the night and switched the light on. He rummaged through his bedroom cupboard, eventually pulling out a large bag which he threw on the floor and opened up.

Inside it was an assortment of things, including Kevlar body armor, a rather fancy looking helmet, gas powered grappling hooks and numerous small canisters.

Reaching into a pocket stitched into the side of the bag, Jason pulled out a CD.

He then went into the living room. Angie was there.

"Jason. What are you doing?"

"I can't sleep," Jason told her. "I just want to have a look at something."

Angie nodded. "All right."

Jason went to the computer on the far side of the room, booted it up and put in the CD.

His friend Geoffrey had given it to him before he had left Fringe City and settled down in Boston. And although Jason had never had a need to look at it until now, he more or less remembered what was on it. How to manufacture some of the bits and pieces of equipment he'd used as the Sentinel. Where to get certain items that weren't available in his local supermarket. And finally, the contact details of several people who Geoffrey believed could help him if he ever needed it. People who not only had the expertise but people Geoffrey trusted.

He found the list of names and looked over it. There were four names there. However, Jason still kept in touch with the guys at Geoff's old lab and he knew that of those four people, only one of the people on the list still worked there. A guy called Scott Wilson.

Jason looked at the details on the screen and copied one of the numbers he saw onto his cell phone. He then ejected the CD and shut down the computer. "I'll be back in a bit," he told Angie and then he went to the bedroom, sat down on the end of the bed and dialed the number.

"Scott Wilson," came a voice on the other end.

"Hi, Scott. It's Jason. You know? Geoff's friend?"

"Yeah, sure. You came to that New Year's Eve get-together of ours. What's up?"

"Geoff said if I ever needed help with… a certain project of mine, I could talk to you."

"I see. Yeah, I remember Geoff talking to me about that. Don't worry. You can trust me on whatever it is. Geoff made me promise that I'd help you out if you ever needed it. No strings attached. Are you planning on going hunting?"

"Yes."

"So what exactly do you need?"

"I don't need any new gear," Jason said. "But if I come and see you tomorrow, could you check the equipment I've got? It's been in a cupboard for eight years gathering dust. I just want to make sure it's all fine before taking any of it out into the field."

"That's all?"

"Yeah. That's all."

"That shouldn't be a problem."

"Thanks, Scott. What time's good with you?"

"Is one o'clock all right? In front of the lab?"

Jason nodded, vaguely aware of the fact that body language was inherently useless in phone conversations. "That'd be fine."

"And once you show me what you want me to look over, we can decide on a time for you to pick it up again."

"Thanks, Scott."

"All right, Jason. See you tomorrow then."

When Jason hung up, he reached down into the bag on the floor and pulled out the helmet, turning it over in his hands.

FOOTSTEPS

Derek Bradley turned the newspaper around, looking at the picture from different angles.

"It was a calculated move on the Vampire's part," he said to Dr. Carter. "He either paid the owner of that apartment to take the footage and then killed him after he sent it in…"

He paused, putting the newspaper down on the table. "… or he broke into the man's apartment, killed him then set up a camera to take the footage himself. Personally, that's the theory I'd lean more closely towards."

"A hunch?" John Carter asked.

Derek made a disapproving clicking noise. "Dr. Carter. Dr. Carter. You've actually *seen* the footage. I've only had it described to me. But I know that in the footage, the Vampire swoops down first and then up." He paused again. "Although, of course, he'd *have to* do that."

"Why's that?"

"Because if he didn't," Derek explained, "then what

I suspect was a folding glider or whatever it was he was using would pick up too much speed and he would smash himself to pieces on impact with the first thing he hit," Derek explained. "Climbing up is the only way he could safely land."

He smiled. "You didn't think this guy could actually fly, did you?"

John frowned. "I don't know *what* he did exactly. It's hard to tell from the footage. It gives you impressions, rather than details. Enlarging it past a certain point makes the image too pixilated and motion blur obscures a lot of vital detail too."

"That would also add weight to the theory that the Vampire set the camera up himself," Derek added. "He wants people to be confused by what they see. To let their imaginations run wild a bit. And he wouldn't want anyone to be able to figure out for certain what his tricks are."

He pointed at part of the picture. "Now, I don't know what his glider looks like exactly or how it must fold and unfold. I can only guess. Because you see here that a lot of the trails and loose threads of his rather theatrical cape obscure anything that could be hiding beneath it."

John nodded, looking where Derek was pointing. "Yeah. That makes sense." He looked back at his patient. "But what were you going to say earlier about your theory?"

Derek smiled. "Yes, I got a little side-tracked there. All right. I said he swooped up to land safely. And if we're going to assume he can't fly—and that's what I'm doing—then he must have landed on top of the building where that footage was taken from. I'd imagine he then climbed down the building from outside, picked up his camera and then he climbed down to the street and disappeared. He would have had everything planned to the last detail before he carried out the plan."

John nodded. "I want to bring this to the police."

Derek sighed. "I'm *telling* you, Dr. Carter, so you can bring it the police."

John was quiet for a moment. This was a significant breakthrough.

"Thank you, Derek," he said.

Derek shrugged. "Don't mention it."

At a quiet spot on the university campus, Jason met Scott Wilson. He was a bit older than Jason and he was somewhat more serious than Geoffrey was when he'd worked at the university. Although since Geoffrey was hardly his old self either these days, perhaps that didn't mean much.

Scott handed the bag over to Jason. "I'm glad you're

taking this off my hands. It's not the easiest thing to lug around. How do you manage it?"

Jason shrugged. "I don't know. I'm no gym junkie. I guess you get used to it. But anyway, how is everything?"

"Everything's in perfect working condition," Scott said. "As good as new."

Jason smiled. "That's a relief. I guess Geoff built these things to last."

Scott smiled too. "Yeah, I'd say so. By the way, who are you after? The Vampire?"

Jason frowned. "Yeah. How did you guess?"

"Well, it was either that or Lady Vice. I just picked one. So how exactly are you planning to find him?"

"I don't know," Jason said. "The hard way, I guess."

"Well, if there's anything else I can do to help you out, let me know."

"Thanks, Scott."

The next port of call on the way home was Diane's place. Jason took the line of reasoning that if Ethan was still in school, then Diane's kids wouldn't be home either. What he didn't consider due to his distracted frame of mind was that Diane might not have been home either. Yes, she worked part-time but that didn't mean she was free all week. And as it turned out,

Diane wasn't home.

Jason called her.

"Hi, Jason."

"Have you got a minute, Diane?" he asked.

"I'm at headquarters at the moment. We're looking into the latest Vampire killing."

Jason swallowed. "That's what I want to talk to you about."

"Hang on, Jason..." Diane's voice grew quiet and Jason heard a door close on the other end of the line.

"I thought we'd talked about this," she said.

"We did," Jason said. "But I'm afraid I can't keep our agreement. The Vampire's latest victim? Kaori Tanaka?"

"Yes?"

"She was my student."

There was a pause.

"Oh, Jason. I'm sorry."

"Thanks, Diane."

"But—"

"Diane," Jason interrupted. "I need to do this now. Not only for Kaori. But for myself."

"What's that?"

"Look, can you give me a call when you finish work? I really need to talk to you. And anything you can give me about the Vampire to get me started, I want it."

"Have you talked to Angie about this?"

Jason hesitated then sighed. "No."

"Well, I'm not giving you anything, Jason, until you talk this over with your wife first. Because I think she's got a right to know what you're up to if you're going to go ahead with this. Don't you?"

Jason nodded to himself. "All right."

Jason waited for Angie in the living room. He'd called her and asked her if she could stop home first before picking Ethan up.

When she came through the door, she found Jason sitting on the sofa, his Sentinel gear visible in the open bag in the middle of the floor.

"What's going on?" she asked.

"I can't deal with this, Angie," he told her. "This isn't like losing someone to old age or a wasting disease or a car accident. There's a monster out there who killed Kaori. And he killed two other girls as well. And he did this in the space of a week."

Angie didn't say anything. She knew her husband well and there was another thing on his mind as well.

"There's something else," Jason added, sensing that Angie was waiting for him to say what it was. "I'm scared of this man, Angie. I woke up in a cold sweat five times last night because of him."

Jason took a moment to pull himself together before continuing. "I know he's not a real vampire. I know he can't fly. That was a trick of some sort. And I'm sure the glowing eyes are a trick too. And I know this probably sounds strange to you... but even though I know all these things, I can't actually convince myself. You know, it's like the head and the heart or something. But if I can find this guy... If I can catch him and bring him in and see with my own eyes that he's just a coward in a mask, then I think I might be able to sleep a little better at night."

Angie sat down beside him and held his hands. "I understand what you're saying. I do. But..." She trailed off for a moment, her voice wavering. "But you're a father now. Do you want Ethan to grow up without his dad?"

"No, of course not," Jason said. "But I'm not doing this for a laugh. I'm doing this because I think I have to. Besides, do you want Ethan growing up in a town where monsters murder people in their beds? Because I sure as hell don't."

Angie sighed. "I'm not in the exact same situation as you are, Jason, so I don't know if it's my place to say. But I really hope you know what you're doing here. Also, you tell me you're going after the Vampire but we've seen this before. When you went after Sergeant Hemming all those years ago, it didn't stop there, did it?"

Jason sighed too. "Yeah, I know."

"I'm worried this might get out of hand."

Jason looked at her. "It *will* get out of hand. That's pretty much a guarantee. But I think things will be better afterwards."

Angie got up and headed for the door. "All right. But pack that stuff away before Ethan gets home."

Jason knew the conversation had probably gone as well as it could have, given the circumstances. But he wished Angie had been more openly understanding.

"I love you, honey," he called out, hoping to get maybe a small sign of support in return.

"I love you too, Jason," Angie said as she reached for the door handle. "That's why I worry."

"I'd love to see Mike Evans in the stand too," Charles Faulkner said. "That'd wipe that silly smirk off his face. But that'd be shooting the messenger. No, we're just going to concentrate on Edmund Peterson. It's his station. It was his call." He gave Derek Fletcher a smile. "But don't worry. If we play this right and get him sweating, he'll name others for sure."

Devan nodded. "That makes sense."

The two of them were waiting in the police headquarters to talk to Commissioner Hutchens about the incident. However, there was a slight delay.

"Do you know what's going on?" Devan asked, glancing to the door.

"It's to do with the Vampire case," Charles said, frowning. "It might be interesting to know exactly what it is. That's Doctor John Carter in there. He's been in charge of Derek Bradley's rehabilitation since the day he was brought in. At a guess, I'd say Derek's given him some information about the case."

There was a distant look in Devan's eyes. "That's Derek Bradley's doctor?"

"Yes."

The door opened and John Carter emerged, veering away in the opposite direction from Charles and Devan.

They got up and Charles headed to Hutchens' office. But Devan turned to follow Dr. Carter. "Can you excuse me, Charles?" he asked.

Charles frowned. "Where are you going?"

"I just need to stop by the men's room," Devan told him. "I'll see you in a little bit."

"All right then." Charles turned away and entered Hutchens' office.

Devan quickened his pace and caught up with the man who had just come out of the room.

"Dr. Carter?"

The man turned around and Devan extended a

hand in greeting, which John Carter accepted.

"Devan Fletcher. It's nice to meet you."

"Devan Fletcher," John replied, reviewing the name in his head. "I understand you're working closely with Charles Faulkner. You're very much his protégé if I'm not mistaken."

"People say so, yes," Devan said. "And I understand you're working closely with Derek Bradley in his rehabilitation."

John's gaze drifted down for a moment before he looked back at Devan. "Ah, yes. But you must also understand of course that I'm not at liberty to discuss certain matters related to that. Even if it weren't law, I'd still be a firm believer in doctor-patient confidentiality. There has to be a certain level of trust in my profession, as I'm sure you can well imagine."

"Of course," Devan said. "And in my own profession, we're quite well aware of the law in this regard and the reasons for it. But anyway, I still very much want to talk to you."

"What about?"

Devan shook his head and indicated the various police officers around the place. "Not here. It's a little too public. But could we perhaps exchange numbers so I can get in touch with you? It *is* important."

"Well, if you say so."

• • •

Jason met Diane in the cafe again. She didn't look any happier to see him than Angie had been.

She handed him a file, barely making eye contact. "This is what you wanted."

"Thanks, Diane," Jason said, taking it and flipping it open for a moment to peruse its contents.

Diane closed her eyes and exhaled. "For god's sake, don't look at it *now*."

Jason closed it and put it into the bag he had brought along with him. "Sorry."

He could have told her he had made sure no one was nearby before he'd looked but he knew better than to make a big deal out of it.

Angie was worried that he was going to get himself arrested or killed. Diane thought he was throwing caution to the wind, and potentially throwing her, Mayor St. Claire, Charles Faulkner and Commissioner Hutchens to the lions at the same time.

"Hey," he started. He hesitated but not for long. If he could explain things to Diane better, it'd be good practice for talking to Angie later. "I'm not planning on getting into brawls here or deliberately trying to get myself into the paper. I'm going to conduct my own independent investigation. Quietly. I don't know if I'll have any more luck than the police but if I don't do anything, I know this is just going to get to me more and more. And if everything goes to plan, no one's going to even know I'm out there. This isn't the grand comeback of the Sentinel or anything like that. The suit's useful for scrambling around the rooftops. It'll protect me if anyone takes a stray shot at me and finally, if anyone sees me, the suit gives me anonymity. That's all."

"That's all for now," Diane said. "But what happens when it escalates out of control? And you know it will."

Jason sighed. "Isn't anyone on my side here? I'm trying to deal with what happened in the only way I know that might possibly work. And I'm trying to protect people. Last night, I lay awake for hours thinking about what Kaori must have felt in her last waking moments. I don't want any more people to suffer that. Surely, you can understand that, can't you? I can't handle this, Diane. I've *got* to do something."

Diane sighed. "All right, Jason. God knows what Hutchens would say if he found out but if you're going to go ahead with this, then you can at least count on me."

"Thanks, Diane."

Diane smiled. "Hey, we're friends, right? And after everything we've been together, I couldn't sell you up the river. And I tell you what. I'll even have a chat to Angie for you as well. Woman to woman. Maybe I can convince her to cut you a bit of slack."

"I'd like a bit of slack," Jason said.

Jason read Ethan's bedtime stories again that night and he hugged his son longer than he usually did.

"What's wrong, Dad?" Ethan asked when he let him go.

Jason realized there were tears in his eyes. He smiled and brushed them away. "Ah, it's nothing, Ethan. I just got something in my eye. Anyway, sleep well."

"You too, Dad."

Jason smiled a bit more, chuckled and ruffled Ethan's hair. "Hey. My little guy."

When he left the room, Angie was waiting for him by the door. She'd gotten his bag ready for him.

She sighed. She'd been crying while he'd been putting Ethan to bed, Jason realized.

"Don't worry, honey," he said. "I'm not planning on staying out too late."

"Shut up," she blurted, more tears sliding down her cheeks. She held him close and didn't let go for a few long moments. "You take care of yourself out there, all right?"

"I will," Jason promised. He picked up his bag and slung it over his shoulder. "I love you, honey."

Angie nodded. "I love you too, Jason."

• • •

Jason slumped down in the seat on the train, staring at the reflections of fluorescent lights in the windows and the people on the platforms as he passed the various subway stations on the way to his destination.

When he got off the train, he walked as though he were in a daze, heading up the stairs onto the sidewalk and moving slowly in the direction of the apartment where the footage of the Vampire had been taken. The one where, if the theories in Diane's report were right, he set a camera up to film himself.

The Vampire had killed *two* people that night, Jason reflected as he reached the place. The girl in the first building and the man who lived in the apartment where the footage had been taken from.

Putting the thought aside, Jason climbed up the fire escape on the side of the building. But as he got closer to the roof, he felt something was wrong. And when he realized what it was, he felt very annoyed. There were people up there but they weren't criminals and they weren't police either.

He went up to have a look and found four men and a woman. A couple of the guys had binoculars and the woman was asking one of them if she could borrow his.

Jason looked at the nearest man. "Um, what are you

guys all doing up here?"

The man smiled. "Looking for the Vampire."

Jason worked hard to keep any of the various emotions the man brought out in him from showing in his expression. The goddamn amateurs thought this was a bit of fun or something, watching out for the Vampire as if they were sitting on the hood of a car watching the sky for a comet. And never mind the fact that there was no way in hell the Vampire was going to revisit the crime scene after the police had combed it.

And then there was the fact that the man was standing around grinning like a twit, close by to where two people had been killed and showing no respect for either of them.

Jason wanted nothing more than to punch the guy's daylights out. However, he knew that aside from the fact that it'd be a pretty underwhelming way for the Sentinel to return, it wasn't exactly the smartest thing to do if he wanted to keep off the police radar and out of the papers. But this was *not* how he had planned the night's expedition.

Still…

"Have you seen anything?" he asked.

"Not yet," the man said. He held up an impressive looking camera. An *expensive* looking camera. "Still though, if we can get some more footage of the guy, FCBN will pay five grand for it."

Jason frowned. "FCBN?"

The shocks of the evening were quickly grating on his nerves. He'd rather been under the impression that FCBN were in so much trouble right now that they'd be working very hard to keep a low profile. Clearly, they weren't. Jason could only hope that Charles Faulkner would take them to the cleaners when their court date rolled round.

However, for the moment, what he really needed to do was to get these morons off the roof so he could investigate the crime scene in peace. An idea came to mind.

"Yeah, FCBN," the man replied. "You didn't hear about it? There's an ad on the TV and there were ads in the papers too. Five grand for high quality footage of the Vampire."

Jason smiled. "That would be pretty sweet." He then gave the man and his companions an apologetic look. "But anyway, I hate to spoil your fun but I've got to fix two air conditioning units and a couple of other things while I'm up here as well so I'm afraid I'm going to have to ask you to clear the roof for a while. You're welcome to set up over the street if you want."

"We're happy *here,*" the man said with a tone of insolence that brought Jason right back to East Somerset High and some of the aggravating bastards he had used to teach there. And for all he knew, this guy might have been one of them. The urge to beat his head in came back stronger than ever but Jason suppressed it.

"Well, I really hate to be a prick about this, guys," he said, "but you *are* technically trespassing here. I don't want to have to call the cops on you but if you don't clear off, then I'm afraid I'll have to."

"We live here," one of the other men said.

Jason gave him an odd look. "On the roof? I kind of doubt that. But the landlord didn't mention anything about people being in the way up here."

"Come on," the first man said. "Give us a break."

"I can't work with you guys in the way," Jason told them. "And it's late for Christ's sake. I'd really like to finish up and go home."

The man relented. "Oh. Sorry, buddy." He nodded to his friends. "Come on, guys. We can go vampire hunting tomorrow night." He made a gesture to mimic staking a vampire and the others laughed.

"Thanks, guys," Jason told them as they climbed onto the fire escape. "I appreciate it."

A few moments later, he had the roof to himself.

"Dickheads," he muttered when he was sure they were out of earshot.

He then had a look around the roof. He didn't know what he expected to find but, whatever it was, he didn't find it.

He sighed. "Well, so much for that." He looked across to the adjacent apartment and the room where the Vampire had launched himself from.

"All right," he said to himself. "So he swoops down and then comes up again to avoid splattering himself on the street. Then what?"

He walked along the edge of the roof, looking down until he was standing above where he judged the footage had been taken from. Then he looked down at the vacant lot between the two buildings.

If the theories in Diane's report were right, then the Vampire had climbed down from the spot where he was now standing and then he'd retrieved the camera on which his footage had been filmed.

With the show over though, there'd be no reason for the Vampire to climb back up again after retrieving the camera. Most likely, he would have gone down. And since it was unlikely he could lug around his cape, his glider and whatever else made up his costume without a lot of people seeing him, he might well have had a car below. He could climb inside in the dark, get changed and then drive slowly away.

Jason opened up his bag and pulled out his gear. It was pretty dark down behind the building but it was still possible that someone might see him. In his Sentinel gear though, they wouldn't recognize him.

However, he then realized there was a drawback to

this plan. If those idiots he had just kicked off the roof saw him in his Sentinel gear, they might mistake him for the Vampire, snap a picture and then he'd be in the papers on day one. Not a very good start if he wanted to keep a low profile. And he could only imagine the trouble he'd be in with Angie and Diane.

With a sigh, he put the suit away and closed the bag. "Damn it."

There was no helping it.

However, now he had some idea how he might start his investigation so the evening hadn't been a total waste. Tracking a wraith-like monster that flew in on beams of moonlight and then vanished in a cloud of bats was probably impossible. Finding a car on the other hand was another story.

WAR ZONE

CUPID'S BOW

The sudden thunderclap and the clear shattering of glass that accompanied it sent officers diving to the floor.

Paper flew everywhere, coffee cups were shattered as they were dropped and someone screamed.

On his hands and knees, Hutchens waved at the officers in the room. "Stay down!" he ordered.

He crawled over to Palmer, who was crouched up against his office's door frame and loading a weapon.

"Is anyone hurt?" Hutchens called out as he pulled himself up beside his friend.

No one answered at first.

"We're all right, Commissioner," someone then called out, realizing a bit more was needed.

"All right," Hutchens said, projecting as much confidence as he could to keep everyone calm. He even smiled. "I'm glad to hear it. Where did the bullet come from? Did anyone see?"

It was pretty dark out there though, he knew. And since everyone had hit the floor more or less at once, no one would have had time to see anything anyway.

"Never mind," he said. "Where did it come through?"

There was some hesitation again but not because no one knew.

"Uh... three inches from your head, Commissioner."

Hutchens kept up his charade, still smiling. "Ah well. I must be doing something right then. I guess I've got either Lady Vice or the Vampire running scared."

He turned to Palmer. "Don't do anything silly, Palmer. Whoever's out there has all the advantages. Just wait."

He crawled across the floor to his desk and yanked the phone down, expecting the unknown assailant to try to blow his hand away at any moment. However, no second shot came.

He dialed and waited but not for long.

"Commander Harris. Get a team on the roof."

"We heard the shot, sir. We're already on the move."

"Glad to hear it," Hutchens told him. "Stay on the line and tell me what you see up there."

It wasn't a long wait.

"There's some equipment or something on the roof of the building across the street. Hang on..."

"This guy left his gun?"

"Ah… sort of, I think. But not exactly."

"Damn it, Harris," Hutchens said. "Then what *are* you looking at up there?"

Hutchens, Palmer and Commander Harris looked at the dead man, propped up in a kneeling position with a rifle in his hand. Looking down from where the man was positioned, they saw the break in the window where the bullet had just missed Hutchens' head.

"We'll need to make sure," Hutchens said, "but it does look as though the bullet was fired from up here."

He frowned and looked at the corpse with the gun again. "Although probably not by this guy here. He looks pretty cold and stiff."

"I wonder who he is," Harris said.

"I know him," Palmer volunteered.

Hutchens and Harris both turned to him.

"You do?" Hutchens asked.

"He's a drug dealer. He was out on parole. Not a major crook but he's been in and out of prison quite a few times."

"Well, he won't be going through the revolving door any more now," Hutchens said. "And I'm guessing that it wasn't his parole officer who did this to him."

"No," Palmer agreed. "Still, this guy was clearly left

here to get our attention."

Just then, some of Commander Harris' S.W.A.T. team reappeared after reconnoitering the roof.

"Anything?" Hutchens asked them.

"No. All clear, sir," one of them said.

Hutchens turned back to the late drug dealer. "So whoever did this took the shot then shoved the rifle in this guy's hands... or he took the shot with another gun and this rifle is nothing more than a prop. But either way, he fired on us to get our attention and then he used this poor bastard to lure us over here. Gentlemen, I'd say this is a message of some kind."

Palmer shook his head. "I'd rather they phone or send an e-mail."

"Yeah," Hutchens agreed in an absentminded manner as he looked over the dead man for any sign of the message. "Me too."

Then he saw something. "There. A USB on his belt. Get it checked to make sure it's not a bomb or anything. Then bring it in to the station, plug it in a spare computer that's not on the network and see what you can find."

Palmer nodded. "I'll get right on it."

In under an hour, the USB had been checked for explosives, poisons and computer viruses and was ready for inspection.

Hutchens came into the room with the computer it was plugged into.

"All right," he said to Palmer and the technician there. "I'm ready. Open it up."

The technician clicked on the USB's icon, revealing one lone icon inside.

He shrugged. "It's an audio file."

"Well, I suppose we should play it," Hutchens said. "And hope it's not too disturbing."

The technician winced. "Yeah. Well. Here goes."

He clicked on it and they listened.

A man spoke in a strong voice, with warm tones. *"I aimed to miss, Commissioner. Believe me, you have enough trouble as it is without having to worry about me. I have but four targets, Commissioner Hutchens, and I will reveal these people to you in good time. Rest assured however, they'll receive due warning.*

"I know that you will probably wish to conceal this message from the press and I promise you, I'll bear no grudge against you if you do. The people of Fringe City will know of me soon enough. I am Cupid, Commissioner Hutchens, and I am coming."

The recording stopped.

"That's it," the technician said.

Hutchens nodded. "All right. Thank you, Romero."

"No problem."

Romero climbed out of his seat and left the room, leaving just Hutchens and Palmer.

"Well?" Palmer asked.

Hutchens shrugged. "I'd say we've got more problems. Obviously, we should comb that roof across the road and see if there's anything else this guy left behind but it may well be that we'll have to play things his way to start with."

"Do you want to suppress that message?" Palmer asked, nodding to the computer beside him.

Hutchens frowned. "You don't?"

"Well, if we release it, we may be able to ask if anyone's got any information that could help us out with our investigations," Palmer pointed out. "Besides, it sounds fairly certain that he's going to get himself on air anyway."

"Hijack the airwaves?" Hutchens said.

"Or the digital... ah... waves. Broadcast a powerful signal at the right transmission near the point of origin of one of the TV networks' stations or mess around with their cables, planting secondary cables. Doing a bit of both. Covering the airwaves and digital TV at the same time perhaps."

Hutchens raised his eyebrows in mild surprise. "You've given this a lot of thought, haven't you?"

Palmer shrugged. "I saw it happen in a few movies when I was a kid and I wondered whether it was possible or not. It's happened a few times in real life too."

"Yeah, Captain Midnight," Hutchens said. "And a few more incidents come to mind. Actually, now that I think about it, it's a lot more common than I thought."

"True."

"And I suppose we've only got ourselves to blame," Hutchens added. "Clearly, this guy is planning to work around the fact that we're trying to stop idiot television networks from airing every damn piece of footage that gets sent their way."

Palmer nodded. "Yeah, I'd say that's the case."

Hutchens then shook his head. "And... Cupid? Why do these guys always have to have a stupid pseudonym? Why can't they call themselves Dennis or something?"

"I don't know," Palmer said. "But 'Dennis' just doesn't have the same ring to it."

"But Cupid? This guy doesn't sound like a friendly little cherub to me."

"No," Palmer agreed. "Me neither."

"Ah well," Hutchens said, getting back to the job at hand. "At least we've got somewhere to start our investigations. Let's see if we can arrange for a few people to keep an eye on the neighborhoods around our various television and radio stations."

Palmer hesitated. "Uh, we might be undermanned

pretty shortly, sir. As well as regular patrols, we're running two major investigations at the moment."

"I know that, Palmer," Hutchens told him. "Believe me."

Diane listened as Jason recounted the events of the night before.

"Well," she said, "I'm glad to hear you kept a level head about everything and avoided bringing any more attention to yourself than you had to. It's good to know you're not being reckless about this."

"I told you I'd be sensible," Jason reminded her.

"So far, you've done all right."

Jason glanced downwards. "Still, it's kind of annoying that there are all these people who think looking for the Vampire is some kind of game or something."

Diane nodded. "It's a problem. And those people you saw aren't the only ones."

Jason sighed. "They're not all over the city, are they?"

"They're all over the city," Diane told him. "You won't have the rooftops to yourself until they get bored and find a new hobby."

"I guess I need some longer grappling hook cables. Then I can get onto the higher rooftops they can't reach."

"I suppose that's one way of looking at it," Diane conceded. "Although a rather Jason Harding way of looking at it."

"I know," Jason said. "But with all these amateurs around, it's going to make it that much harder to stay under the radar."

Diane smiled. "Ah, well. Far be it from me to try to talk you out of whatever you've got in mind. What can I do to help?"

"I'm sure the Vampire had a car in that vacant lot and that he just drove away after he made that footage of himself. And I'm pretty sure that on the main street, I saw one of those large apartment complexes with all the security cameras and whatnot that go along with them. I'd like you to get a look at anything they've got that shows a view of the street."

"Was this place across the road from the vacant lot?"

"Not directly across," Jason said. "But further along, yeah."

Diane nodded. "All right. I'll check it out and get back to you." She started to climb out of her chair and stopped. "However, just one thing. Whatever I find, I'm also passing on to the police as well. Just so you know."

"I know," Jason told her. "This isn't a contest."

Diane smiled again. "Just making sure."

Devan Fletcher dialed and waited.

"Dr. Carter."

"Dr. Carter," he said. "Devan Fletcher. We met at the police headquarters yesterday."

"Ah, Mr. Fletcher. Hi."

"Just call me Devan, Dr. Carter."

"Then by the same token, just call me John," came the reply.

Devan smiled. "All right, John."

"So what can I do for you?"

"I want to meet you in person, John. There's something I'd like to discuss."

"Involving my patient?"

"Better if I tell you in person," Devan said. "Are you free now?"

"Yes."

"Can I come and see you at your office?" Devan asked.

"I suppose. Where are you?"

"In a car. Outside."

There was a slight pause on the other end and a sigh. "Well, come on in."

. . .

"Would you like some coffee, Devan?" John asked him as he came through the door. "I just brewed a pot."

"Yeah, thanks," Devan said, sitting down. "Sounds good."

John poured two cups. "Do you take milk or sugar?"

"Milk and one sugar."

John passed him his cup and sat down across from him, taking a sip from his own. "Well then, Devan. It's clear you've got something on your mind. Let's talk."

"Well, as you know, Lady Vice and the Vampire are running rings around the police," Devan said. "They're having no luck finding them. However, at the Palmdale Mental Health Institute, you've got a man who brought in the Specter."

John nodded. "You want Derek Bradley."

"Yes, John. I want him."

"He's made a lot of progress over the years," John said, his tone non-committal. "But he's not ready to be reintegrated in society yet."

"I'm not asking for him to be reintegrated, John," Devan said. "You know what I'm asking."

John sighed. "You're asking me to let Orion out on the street. Do you have any idea how dangerous that would be?"

Devan shrugged. "Do you have any idea how desperate I am?"

"If you give him the chance, Derek Bradley will pick up exactly where he left off. Self-appointed judge, jury and executioner. Is that what you want, counselor?"

"Put a leash on him."

"Not an easy thing to do," John said, "keeping a leash on someone as resourceful as Derek Bradley."

Devan thought for a moment, glancing down. He looked back at John. "Are you absolutely sure he'd revert to killing everyone with an unpaid parking fine or are you projecting your own ideas here?"

"Devan…" John started.

Devan reached into his briefcase, pulled out some papers and handed them to the doctor.

"What's all this?" John asked, frowning and perusing the sheets he'd just been given.

"I've done my homework, John," Devan said. "You moved Derek Bradley into an institution with absolutely minimum security, knowing full well he could break out of there any time he wanted to."

John frowned. "If you're intending to blackmail me here, Mr. Fletcher, you'll find that I only did so when I was absolutely certain that Derek Bradley wouldn't *try* to break out. The fact that he's been there for five years now without making so much as a single attempt would support my hypothesis, wouldn't you say?"

Devan chuckled and shook his head. "I'm not trying to blackmail you, John. That's the last thing in the world I'd want to do. What I'm trying to say here is that I think you're not giving Derek Bradley *enough* trust." He smiled. "And the fact that he's been at Palmdale for five years and hasn't tried to escape once would support *my* hypothesis."

John sighed. "All right, Devan. Let's say you're right and I'm wrong. How would you propose we go about this?"

"Officially," Devan told him. "Sign a release form. Let him go."

"No conditions?"

"None. Just tell him the city needs him before you let him go. Give him something to think about."

John got up. "I believe Derek Bradley's already got more than enough to think about for the moment. And you'll forgive me if I don't take your suggestion up but I've been working on this man's rehabilitation for eight years. It's been a quite painstaking process and I'm not going to waste all that effort by rushing the last few critical steps."

"I could try to get him out my way," Devan pointed out, getting up as well. "I've got plenty of court tricks."

"And do you think the D.A. would sit idly by and let you do that?"

Devan smiled. "I don't think you know the D.A. the way I do."

"Perhaps you're right, Mr. Fletcher," John said.

"Maybe I should take the time to *get* to know Charles Faulkner better. Perhaps a discussion about our conversation today might be a good place to start."

Devan sighed. "Look, John. I'm not trying to tread on your toes here. I'm trying to do whatever I can to help the city."

"And I'm trying to do whatever I can to help my patient," John countered. He looked at his watch. "I'm afraid I have to leave now, Mr. Fletcher."

The crate doors swung open and the men looked inside.

"Jesus Christ," one of them said, looking at the stacks of packages that filled the entire thing. "How the hell are we supposed to move *this*?"

"We've *got to* move it," one of the others replied. "Mr. Caldwell's orders. Clear this crate by Friday and there's a new one coming on Monday."

"I already know where we'll find a few of the local dealers," another joined in.

"But they're running scared of Lady Vice now," the first man pointed out.

The other smiled. "Well, that's where we get another advantage. What other supplier can offer *protection* as well as the goods?"

"Yeah," the second man beamed. "Mr. Caldwell's

right. We can corner Fringe City's market by the end of the week."

"I hope so," the first man said, "because we're going to have a hell of a time getting back into the game in Detroit if we have to bail out here."

"Come on, lighten up," the second man chided him. "This is our big opportunity. Anyway, we can't leave this stuff here. Let's load up the truck."

Charles Faulkner opened the door to his office. "Ah. Devan. Come on in."

Devan closed the door behind him and followed Charles into the room, sitting in front of the desk, while the D.A. sat behind it.

Charles leant forward, clasping his hands. "Devan, I just had a rather interesting conversation with Dr. John Carter."

"I'm sure you did," Devan said. "However—"

"Devan, do you respect me?" Charles cut him off, his tone abrupt.

Devan paused, taken aback. "Of course I respect you, Charles. I just—"

"Because it sure doesn't seem like it to *me*," Charles told him. "You think it hasn't occurred to me that Derek Bradley might be useful in locating Lady Vice or the Vampire? Aside from the fact that we've already discussed this, remember that I was there when he was active as Orion. I've met the man. I argued for clemency on his behalf and I've liaised closely with Dr. Carter on his progress during the past eight years. And then you come along, a young hotshot lawyer and like a cocky kid straight out of high school, you try to sneak this man out of custody behind my back."

Devan hesitated before answering. The reproach had hit him hard. "Look, Charles, you bent the law when you thought it was necessary. I didn't judge you. But—"

"We've *had* this conversation," Charles reminded him. "And when you asked me about letting Derek Bradley loose on the city, my answer was no. Then, instead of waiting or talking to me about it, you went behind my back and met up with Dr. Carter. What am I supposed to make from that?" He shook his head. "You've let me down, Devan. I had high hopes for you. I thought you could be the chief prosecutor in the Edmund Peterson case. But now, I don't know any more."

Devan waited a moment before answering. "I'm sorry, sir."

Charles sighed and stood up. "Go home and see your wife, Devan. You'd better apologize to her too."

"Gwendolyn?" Devan asked, standing up as well.

Charles looked at him in surprise. "Or did you

forget that she and her friends put themselves on the line to help us catch Orion?"

"Charles, I—"

"Save it, Devan," Charles told him. He nodded to the door. "Go on. Go home. I'll see you tomorrow."

Devan saw himself out.

"Dad?"

Jason smiled. "Yeah, Ethan?"

"Can I stay up late tonight?"

Jason frowned. "What? Why do you want to stay up late?"

"Brendan's parents let him stay up to ten-thirty every night," Ethan pointed out.

Because they're a pair of irresponsible idiots, Jason thought to himself. He'd met them a couple of times too and this had only reinforced his opinion.

"Yes, well, your *mother and I* want you to get plenty of sleep," he said instead, glancing at Angie and giving her a little wink.

She gave him a subtle raised eyebrow expression that suggested she'd interpreted the wink as something more suggestive than it really was.

Jason turned back to their son. "You want to grow up big and strong, right?"

"Yes!" Ethan said, rocking back and forth in his seat

and beaming.

"Well, then you've got to do two things," Jason said. "Eat well and get lots of sleep."

Ethan sighed. "Okay, Dad."

For a few moments, the table was quiet.

"But, Dad, can I watch a movie tonight?" Ethan tried again. "Just one night."

So that was what it was about, Jason thought.

"Don't worry, Ethan," Angie said. "I'm sure Daddy can tape it for you."

"I sure can," Jason agreed.

"They're not tapes," Ethan said. "They're DVDs."

"You know the difference?" Angie asked.

"You know what tapes *are*?" Jason asked.

"Yes," Ethan said. He paused, a smile spreading across his face. "Mrs. Henderson uses them in the library sometimes for old shows."

"Uh huh."

"But Brendan's parents say she's a dinosaur."

"Brendan's parents say too much by the sounds of things," Jason muttered.

"Jason," Angie said, giving him a mild look.

Jason shook his head and turned to Ethan. "Um, Ethan. Brendan's parents shouldn't really say that. It's not a nice thing to say."

"What's wrong with dinosaurs?" Ethan asked.

"Nothing's wrong with them," Jason said. "It's just

that the expression…"

"Well, go on," Angie told him.

"Dinosaurs are old, right?" Jason asked his son.

"Yes."

Jason nodded. "All right. So when someone calls someone a dinosaur, what they're really saying is that they're old-fashioned."

Ethan looked puzzled. "But tapes *are* old-fashioned."

Angie laughed. "He's got a point, Jason."

"But don't worry," Ethan said. "I'm not mean to Mrs. Henderson. I like her."

"You do?"

"Yes," Ethan said. "She always helps me find books. I found one today about dinosaurs!"

"Wow," Jason said. "And we were just *talking* about dinosaurs."

"Do you want to see it?"

"Sure. Maybe you can show it to me after dinner."

"Brendan wanted one about vampires," his son added, turning back to his half-finished dinner. "But the other kids took them all."

When Devan opened the door, he expected to find Gwendolyn looking pretty angry. He didn't expect to find her sitting down with a glass of cold water just looking tired.

"Honey," he began.

Gwendolyn waved her hand. "Don't worry. Charles told me already."

Devan closed the door. "Yes, I know. But before you judge me too, just remember that I'm trying to do the right thing here. I want to stop the Vampire and this new Lady Vice. Help the city get back on its feet."

"I know what you're trying to do, honey," Gwendolyn told him. "You're trying to be a hero. You're trying to effect an overnight solution to a tough problem."

"But this could really work."

"That's not the issue here, honey," Gwendolyn told him. "And you know it. Sure, Orion could probably bring in Lady Vice and the Vampire. And for a night, the city would celebrate. But the next day, he'd bring in a kid like Aidan."

Devan frowned. "Who's Aidan? You and Sonya were talking about him when I came in the other day."

"He was just a kid," Gwendolyn said. "A nice enough kid who made a few dumb choices. Outreach tried hard to provide him with a second chance. Orion on the other hand would never do that. Oh, and that's another thing. If Orion had had his way eight years ago, Outreach wouldn't exist at all. I'd be dead. Sonya would be dead. Cathy and Claudia would be dead. All of us. That's something else I think you forgot."

"Well, hang on a minute," Devan said. "You mentioned second chances. Don't you think it'd be a little hypocritical to deny that to Derek Bradley?"

"I don't believe *anyone's* denying him a second chance," Gwendolyn said. "I think everyone's been quite understanding, given the circumstances. And as far as I'm aware from what you and Charles have told me, the only thing that's really keeping Derek Bradley in custody now is himself. If he's willing to show that he can be trusted, then he's free. That's *all* he has to do. And that, honey, is something that will happen when he's ready and not before. Because while I may be no psychologist, I'm pretty sure you shouldn't try to speed up the schedule here."

Devan sighed and raised his hands in a gesture of defeat. "All right. All right. I give in." He slumped down in the chair next to Gwendolyn's and sighed. "Isn't *anyone* on my side?"

Then Gwendolyn smiled. "I never said I wasn't on your side, honey. And I know you might not believe me but I've actually given your ideas a lot of thought."

"But you just condemned them pretty thoroughly," Devan pointed out.

"Yeah, well, letting Orion loose on the city is a pretty dumb idea," Gwendolyn replied. "However, that doesn't mean we can't use Derek Bradley *at all*."

. . .

*"Good evening. I'm Mike Evans and this is FCBN news, live
at six. Our first story tonight. Former congressman Mr. Ken
Doyle, whose niece was the first victim of the Vampire, has
returned to the public spotlight to spearhead a campaign to
bring the dangerous killer into custody, donating one
hundred thousand dollars to the city's police department for
the purchase of additional resources and equipment. This is
but the start of a campaign that Mr. Doyle hopes will bring
in many more contributors."*

The image cut to a conference. Ken Doyle stood at a
podium, addressing a small crowd.

"Ladies and gentlemen," he said. *"The Vampire
epitomizes everything that is wrong with our city right now.
He breeds fear, despair and grief. He is a creature of
nightmares. But this is a nightmare I believe we can wake up
from. If we can bring him in, take off his mask and expose
him to the world for the coward he is, we can in effect
destroy the monster and take away his power. To that end—"*

For a moment, the screen went blank. Then a new
image appeared. A stylized glowing blue bow, with an
arrow on its string, set against a plain black
background.

. . .

"This one's FCBN," Palmer said.

Hutchens frowned. "Hold on a second." He picked up the remote beside him and flicked the channel. Then he flicked it again.

He put the remote back down. "Clever man. He's hijacking *all* the major networks."

"Good evening, Fringe City."

The symbol on the screen remained where it was. There was only the voice.

"I am Cupid. There are some among you no doubt who will compare me to the Specter. And given the manner in which I act, I understand that I invite such comparisons. However, I am not the Specter. I am far more sporting. I do not use poisons. I do not use bombs. Just one bullet. One shot. And if I miss, then I don't take another. Those are my rules."

There was a pause.

"I have but four targets, ladies and gentlemen. And tomorrow night, I will take my shot at target number one. It appears that Edmund Peterson, head of the Fringe City Broadcasting Network, is facing a serious lawsuit for broadcasting harmful footage that could create needless panic and incite others to violence. I applaud the move, even though I deplore the delay in making it. However, Mr. Mike

Evans, it appears, is not facing any consequences for his own small role in the affair.

"Mr. Evans, if you are listening to this and I know you are, then hear me now. You are a spineless coward for your complicit involvement. The great journalists of history have always commanded the conviction to do what's right, even when doing so has brought down heavy penalties upon them. But you are not among their ranks. You lack this conviction, Mr. Evans, and if my shot rings true, you're going to lack even more than that. Tomorrow night, Mr. Evans. Live at six. I will see you then."

The image on the screen faded and cut back to the newsroom, where Mike Evans looked pale enough to be sick.

"Ah..." he hesitated, looking for some guidance from his producer behind the camera. "We apologize for the interruption and we should have everything back to normal shortly. For the moment however, we'll be taking a brief commercial break."

"Great," Hutchens muttered, swinging himself out of his seat. "Now everyone's going to think that *I'm* Cupid."

"Right," he said to the assembled officers in the room. "You heard what our friend with the bow said. Tomorrow. Six p.m. Just a gun and one shot. As long as we keep Evans in an enclosed environment, away from any windows, we're fine." He smiled. "And in fact, I think we'll tell FCBN to go ahead with the news as normal. We can get all non-essential staff out of the room, do weapons checks on anyone remaining and guard the perimeter."

He took a measure of the room and nodded. "All right, everyone. Let's plan the specifics."

"Here," Diane said, passing Jason another file.

Jason glanced around to check there were no staff members or anyone else around and then he had a look at the photos. "All right."

Diane nodded. "Yeah, just the one vehicle. It doesn't appear coming from the other direction on *this* camera," she said, pointing to one photo, "but it shows up *here*. It had to have come out of your vacant lot."

Jason looked at her. "Well, you know what we've got here then?"

Diane gave him a small smile. "A lead."

Jason looked at the photo as though it were a prized possession. "A lead. Has anyone in the department followed up on it yet?"

Diane shook her head. "We will. But this Cupid business has really thrown a wrench in the works."

Jason sighed. "I can imagine. I think we could really

live without Cupid right now."

"Yeah."

"Six o'clock tonight?" Jason asked, looking at the photos again.

"That's what the man said," Diane replied, taking a sip of coffee and glancing over the rim of the cup. "Now, put those away. There are normal people coming."

Jason dialed and waited.

"Charlie's Parts and Spares."

"Yeah, hello," Jason said. "I'm Sergeant Gardner calling on behalf of the Fringe City Police Department. How are you today, sir?"

"I've got no complaints, Sergeant. How can I help you?"

Jason looked at the paper in his hand. "We're trying to locate a missing vehicle and we're checking with wreckers and impounds to see if it's turned up anywhere. You're both, right?"

"That's right. Registered impound since 1967. Second oldest in the city."

"Is that right?" Jason said. "Well, there might be a good chance the vehicle could have turned up there. If the license plates were still attached, the number was GLM 2159."

"GLM 2…?"

"159."

"Hold on."

"Sure," Jason said. He waited while the man on the other end of the line did a search of his records.

"Yeah. We've got it," the man said. "No one's come to claim it. Do the police want to take it off our hands?"

"No idea," Jason said. "I'm just the message boy. But we'll see. At the moment, I just want to check when the car was found or brought in. And if it was found, where."

"Yep. Got all that right here. Have you got a pen?"

Angie watched Jason, taking a sip of coffee. "Well?"

"The Vampire dumped the car at this address," Jason told her, looking at the piece of paper in his hand. "Tomorrow, I'll go and talk to some people in the neighborhood."

"And why would they talk to you?" Angie asked. "You're not the police. And I assume you're not going to shake them down Sentinel style."

Jason smiled. "Don't worry. They're not going to be talking to Jason Harding *or* the Sentinel. Until the police can sort out this Cupid nonsense and get their other investigations back on track, private detective Gregory Fuller is going to be handling the case."

Angie smiled and shook her head. "Is he registered?"

Jason shrugged. "Not exactly. But who's going to care?"

"And who's going to find out once you're done?"

Jason smiled back. "Something like that."

Diane kissed Mark. "Sorry about this, honey. Almost all the part-timers are being called in."

Mark frowned. "Are you covering staff at the station or are you going to be at the scene?"

Diane glanced over his shoulder, looking through the door to the adjacent room where Caroline and Elizabeth were playing.

She turned back to her husband. "I'm not going to be in the FCBN newsroom with Evans or even in the building. But I am going to be in one of the groups watching the perimeter."

Mark sighed. "Be careful, honey."

Diane kissed him again and brushed her hand down his cheek. "I will, honey."

Inside the newsroom at FCBN, Hutchens eyed the assembled group. The producer was present, as was one lone camera operator and a gaffer. Mike Evans himself was setting up along with the other newscaster and the weatherman, who—much to Hutchens' total lack of surprise—had no background in meteorology.

He had officers in every corner of the room. And… one of the station managers was trying to come in, despite the fact he'd been told to stay out.

With a sigh, Hutchens walked over to the man, thinking how he could put things diplomatically.

"Excuse me just a moment, will you?" the man demanded, leaning past one of his officers to shout at him. "I have to be in the room to oversee everything. I'm *always* in the room!"

"Not tonight, boy-o," Hutchens muttered to himself as he got closer. He smiled at his officer. "It's all right, Delaney. I'll handle this."

The officer nodded and stepped aside, leaving Hutchens face to face with the station master.

"I told you to stay out of the room," Hutchens told him. "Now get out or I'll haul you to the station myself."

"But—" the man started.

"On second thought," Hutchens said, cutting him off and turning back to Delaney. "Sergeant?"

"Yes, sir?" Delaney asked.

"This man is under arrest. Take him downstairs but not to the station." He glared at the man. "He can wait in the car until we're finished here."

"Now, wait a—" the man started.

"Be quiet if you know what's good for you," Hutchens told him as Delaney cuffed him. "Remember? Anything you say can and will and all of that?"

The man glared back but Hutchens paid him no mind. He gave Delaney a nod. "Get him out of here. Read him his rights downstairs."

"Right, sir."

Hutchens looked at his watch. It read 5.56 p.m.

"All right, Eric," he muttered to himself. "He can't get in here. And no bombs or poisons, remember. One shot. His rules."

Then there was a loud crash. The lights went out and a fire alarm sounded.

"Clear the building!" someone shouted.

Hutchens stumbled over to where Evans was sitting. "Mr. Evans. Wait there. Officers, to me!"

He heard them come over.

"How could he have cut the power to the lights but not the fire alarms?" he asked them.

"Are the lights off in the whole building, sir, or just on this floor?" someone asked.

"All right," Hutchens said. "I see your point. Watch your fingers, Mr. Evans." He pushed himself onto the news desk and tentatively reached up to where the nearest light fitting was. "The lights have shattered.

Now, you'd *really* better watch your fingers, Mr. Evans."

"Yes, sir," came Evans' weak reply.

"He's trying to herd us out, sir," one of the officers suggested. "Maybe we should stay put."

"Maybe," Hutchens replied, reaching for his radio. "But it depends on whether or not there's a real fire."

He switched the radio on and held it up. "Palmer. We've got a fire alarm going here. Is—"

Hutchens didn't get the rest of the sentence out as just then, there was a muffled explosion and the floor gave out at one end of the room, sending everyone sliding to the level below in a cloud of dust and debris.

And in the midst of it all rang the clear sound of a single gunshot.

Hutchens climbed to his feet, coughing up dust. He turned around, not knowing where to look in the dark. "Damn it. Anyone got a flashlight?"

"Yeah, one moment," one of the officers replied.

When the flashlight came on, Hutchens looked behind him to see Mike Evans lying dead in the rubble, a bleeding wound in the side of his head. With a sigh, Hutchens had another look at his watch. 6.01 p.m.

"Son of a bitch," he muttered. "No bombs, he said. He only meant he didn't *kill* with the things."

Switching on the radio again, even though he knew the order he was about to give would probably be an exercise in futility, he called Palmer. "You there?"

"What happened?" Palmer asked.

"Tell you soon," Hutchens said. "But Evans is dead and Cupid might still be in here. You know what to do."

"Right," Palmer said with a weary sigh of his own. "I'll seal the building then."

ADVERSARIES

"*Despite the extensive efforts of the Fringe City Police to prevent the killing, Cupid succeeded in carrying out his threat to assassinate Mike Evans. The similarities to the Specter are unmistakable and yet—*"

Hutchens switched off the TV and turned to the others in the room. "Not exactly an unqualified success, is it?" He held up a file. "And here's tonight's news story. Vampire victim number four. Found the poor kid this morning."

He sat back down, slumping into the chair.

Mayor Alison St. Claire was quiet for a while. "Well," she said at last, "I don't know what to do but I'm open to any suggestions and I'm willing to spend, pull strings or anything else either of you think might help."

She turned to the other person present. "Charles? How's the Edmund Peterson prosecution going?"

"The trial is slated to begin in a few days," Charles replied. "I don't think it should drag on too long but one never can tell with these things. If I wrapped it up sooner rather than later, do you think it would make any difference where Cupid, Lady Vice and the Vampire are concerned?"

"I don't know," St. Claire said, "but I think we can all agree that we can do without any distractions right now. We're tied up enough as it is." She turned to Hutchens. "Do we have any more news on the Lady Vice case?"

"Not at the moment," Hutchens said.

"All right," St. Claire said, leaning back in her chair and thinking over her options. "If I call in Federal agents, would that help you?"

Hutchens shrugged. "It probably wouldn't hurt. If nothing else, we could do with the extra manpower. But I don't see what they could do with the useless and non-existent leads we've got."

"There's nothing on *any* of these people?" St. Claire asked.

"That's the long and short of it," Hutchens said. "We may have *one* lead on the Vampire but it doesn't sound like much. It's a car he used to get away from one of the crime scenes. But if he's smart, I doubt he would have used his own vehicle. But we'll see."

"Okay," St. Claire replied.

"The only other thing your office might be able to do is put up rewards," Hutchens told her.

Charles shook his head. "No, no, no."

Hutchens glanced at him. "Why the hell not, Charles? We've tried everything else."

"Because it'd start a massive witch hunt, that's why. And all our resources, which are already twisted in knots, would be tied up even more trying to determine whether or not there are sufficient grounds for the countless citizens' arrests that are going to be made."

"Come on," Hutchens said. "How many idiots do you really think are out there?"

Charles raised his eyebrows in mild surprise. "Do you really want me to answer that?"

Hutchens sighed. "Then we're screwed, Charles. And I may as well hand in my resignation. Let Palmer handle everything."

"Eric!" St. Claire exclaimed.

"Why not?" Hutchens countered. "Why not quit while I'm still only marginally behind?"

"Give it a month," St. Claire told him. "If you still feel that way at the end of it, I'll accept your resignation then. But give it a cooling off period first."

Hutchens sighed. "All right." He pushed himself up from his chair. "Well, if you'll excuse me, I'm going to go and see which hopeless case takes my fancy today."

He paused, turning to the district attorney. "By the way, Charles, I was talking about rewards for information, not citizens' arrests."

Charles nodded. "I know."

• • •

Jason sighed. So far, it had been a very disappointing morning. He hadn't known what he had expected but he now knew what he *should* have expected. After all, it wasn't as though he were any smarter or more resourceful than the best detectives on the police force; and they hadn't had any more luck than he had. No. Nothing was what he should have expected and nothing was exactly what he was getting.

He opened the door to the last place, a little bakery.

"Good morning," the sole occupant of the place said, a well-built man who may have been quite intimidating if it weren't for his big friendly smile.

At a glance, he seemed like such a gentle person that Jason felt a little bit bad about dragging him into the ugly affair that was his business of the day.

"Morning," Jason said, walking over to him. "I'm Gregory Fuller. I'm working on the Vampire case."

"Is that right?" the man asked, frowning.

"Independently," Jason said with a slight smile. "I was hired by the family of one of the victims." He continued before the man had any time to form suspicions, reaching into his pocket to pull out a photograph. "I've, ah, been looking into the matter of a car that was seen leaving one of the crime scenes." He passed the photograph to the man, who brushed flour off on his apron before taking it and having a look.

"The car was towed away from here five nights ago. The man I suspect is the Vampire abandoned it."

At this, the man rolled his eyes. "Ah, that thing. Yeah, I remember. Blocked the road for a few days. I was the one who reported it."

"Uh huh," Jason said. "I wonder... Is there any chance you saw the man who left it across the road?"

The man shook his head. "No."

Jason put the photo away. That was that. His lead had dried up.

"Ah well," he said, forcing a smile with some effort. "Thanks, anyway."

"Don't mention it," the man said. "Do you want anything before you leave?"

Jason shrugged. "What are those things?"

The baker smiled proudly. "Norwegian cardamom buns. Made them this morning."

"They sound good. I'll try one."

The man got out a paper bag to put the bun in and Jason looked around the little store while he waited. Then his gaze came to rest on a camera on the back wall.

He nodded to it. "That camera of yours... Would it cover the street?"

The man glanced back at it. "I'm not sure, come to mention it. I've never watched the tapes. Or the DVDs,

I should say. It's just there for the insurance company."

"You've got the DVDs here in the shop?" Jason asked.

"Yeah," the man replied, pointing a thumb over his shoulder. "In the kitchen there. Do you want to have a look?"

"What's this?" Devan asked, looking at the files Charles had just dumped on his desk.

"I haven't told the mayor yet, or those vultures in the press," Charles told him. "But you'll be the lead prosecutor when the trial opens next week."

"But I thought you said I was off it."

"I said I didn't know whether to let you take it or not," Charles said. "However, I've worked hard to teach you everything I know and I don't have a second choice. I don't have a back-up plan."

Devan frowned. "But what about *you*? Why don't you lead the prosecution? You're the D.A., remember, not me."

Charles hesitated as if he were going to say something else but he stopped himself. "I think this is important, Devan. For you. I'm going to have to hand the reins over *someday*."

Before Devan had a chance to reply, Charles left the office, leaving him with every single file on the

Edmund Peterson case he had.

Jason left the bakery with a newfound sense of optimism and a Norwegian cardamom bun. He took a bite out of it as he walked.

"That *is* good," he said to himself. Then putting it back in the bag for a moment, he got out his cell phone and dialed.

"Diane? It's Jason. Have you got a minute?"

"Yeah. At the moment," his friend replied. "What's up?"

"I've got something to go on but I'll need your help again for the next stage."

"All right," Diane replied. "What do you need?"

After she hung up, Diane checked her watch. She probably had enough time to arrange a copy of the relevant surveillance footage to be sent over. Then, even if she didn't get a look at it then, it would at least be ready for her tomorrow.

She checked her watch again and relaxed. It wasn't that bad. She could take her time, do it properly, and still be on time to meet Gwendolyn at five. She wondered what her friend wanted to talk to her about.

Putting it off for the time-being, she made her calls

and arranged for the footage to be sent over, both through electronic transfer and on a disk in the mail.

With that done, she headed over to Outreach to meet Gwendolyn.

"Jason?"

Jason stopped. He recognized the voice, although it was heartbreaking to hear how flat it sounded, as though Ji Eun barely had the energy to speak. When he turned around and saw her, it was obvious she had been crying earlier and she had a hollow weary look to her eyes.

"Oh, Ji Eun," he said. "I'm so sorry about Kaori."

Ji Eun burst into tears again.

Having worked at a high school for some time, Jason had had the rules about appropriate teacher-student interaction drilled into his very bones. And he'd carried all that stuff with him into the language institute where we worked now—or rather, where he'd worked until Amanda had given him this down time to get over his nervous breakdown. However, right then, seeing Ji Eun all alone crying her heart out on the sidewalk, he had only one thought on those rules and guidelines. To hell with them. He put his arms around Ji Eun and let her sob on his shoulder till she felt a little better.

"I'm sorry," she said at last, brushing a few remaining tears away.

"It's all right, Ji Eun," Jason told her. "There's nothing wrong with crying at a time like this. Believe me. Are you all right? Is the school looking after you? Are some of the other students coming to see how you're doing?"

"Ricardo and Monica visit every day after school," Ji Eun said. "And Abdul's organized a nice dinner for me and the rest of the class tonight." She looked at him. "Do you want to come?"

Jason smiled. "I think that should be a night for you and your friends. And actually, I'm a bit busy anyway."

Ji Eun's eyes widened. "You're looking for the Vampire, aren't you?"

Jason shook his head. "No. I'm not looking for him. I'm sure the police will bring him in."

"But why were you asking questions to the people in those shops across the street?"

Jason was surprised. "You saw that?"

"I was watching you," Ji Eun said. "You want to catch him."

Jason sighed. "I want to help, Ji Eun."

She nodded, gazing down at the sidewalk. Then she looked up again. "Can I help?"

Jason put a hand on her shoulder. "Sure. You can

help me by keeping safe so I don't have to worry about you too. Oh, and don't tell everyone what I'm doing. I'm trying to keep this quiet."

"I understand," Ji Eun told him. "Jason?"

"Yeah, Ji Eun?"

She gave him a little smile. "Good luck."

George came through the door, embraced Sonya and gave her a kiss. "Hey, honey."

He turned to Gwendolyn. "Hey, Gwendolyn."

She smiled. "Hey, George. Is everything all right?"

George sighed. "Is it that obvious? I was trying to keep it cool."

"It's in your eyes, George," Gwendolyn told him.

"Yeah," Sonya said, looking at him and joining in. "What's wrong?"

George sighed and held up his hands in a placating manner. "All right. All right. I've got some news." He pulled out a camera and sat down across from where Gwendolyn was standing.

Turning it on and browsing through the images, he selected one to show Gwendolyn and Sonya. "Here. Have a look at this. Five blocks away. Leadensway."

Sonya looked first and then Gwendolyn.

It was a photograph of a drug deal.

"Leadensway's been clean for eighteen months,"

George told them. "Not a single deal in the whole area."

When Gwendolyn glanced at him, he returned the look with a steady gaze. "Believe me, I'd know if anything went down. I've got a lot of contacts working on the ground there now."

Gwendolyn nodded and looked back at the picture. "I believe you."

"Did you get in for a closer look?" Sonya asked her husband.

George shook his head. "No. Too dangerous. I have no idea who that dealer is and he might have been armed."

Sonya gave a sigh of relief. "You did the right thing."

Gwendolyn turned the camera off and turned it around in her hands. "George, would you mind if Sonya and I hung onto this for a little bit?"

George shrugged. "No problem. Why?"

"We're meeting Diane this afternoon to talk to her about another matter," Gwendolyn said. "But while we've got her, we might show her this as well."

Diane looked at the image carefully and handed the camera back.

"Gwendolyn, can you e-mail that to me later?"

"Sure," Gwendolyn replied, giving the camera to Sonya, who put it in her bag.

Diane brushed her hands over her temples, running them back through her hair.

"Are you all right?" Sonya asked her.

"Yeah," she said with a sigh. "It's just been a busy day. With Cupid, getting stuff for Jason and liaising with the officers in charge of the official investigation into the Vampire... and now this. It feels like a full-time job again."

"That's too bad."

Diane smiled. "Ah well. Could be worse. Anyway, what did you two really want to talk to me about tonight?"

"We want to explore another option that might help us deal with Lady Vice," Gwendolyn told her. "And possibly Cupid and the Vampire as well. We think we can enlist some help."

"So you two want to start your own investigation into Lady Vice to run alongside Jason's one man war against the Vampire." Diane shook her head.

"Not exactly," Gwendolyn said. "We're talking about enlisting the help of someone else entirely."

"Why are we watching this?" Jason asked Angie, slinging himself down in the sofa. "It's bad for my health."

"Then go for a walk or something," Angie told him. "Because there's nothing else on. However, if you wait a few minutes, Fringe City's daily dose of depression should be over."

"God, I hope so," Jason said, sitting back, watching and waiting it out.

"Citisafe Security Systems representatives said they were disappointed by Mayor St. Claire's decision," a news anchor was in the middle of saying, *"stating that they believe it was motivated by budgetary rather than ethical concerns."*

"What's next?" Jason muttered. "The suits from Wall Street wetting themselves over the excitement of the Dow Jones index?"

"Citisafe wants to cover the entire city in surveillance cameras," Angie told him. "I'm glad the mayor's shot that idea down."

"Well, for now anyway," Jason said. "But she's not going to be mayor forever. And then what?"

"We move to a place where they don't treat the lot of us like criminals," Angie said. "Hang on. I want to hear this."

She turned the volume up a little.

The mayor was now on the screen, speaking at a press conference. *"There are budgetary issues at stake here. Taking out a contract with Citisafe Security Systems to cover the entire city with CCTV cameras would be phenomenally expensive. And spending on other essential public services would have to be drastically cut to cover the costs. Or taxes would have to be raised. And I'm sure most residents of Fringe City would be opposed to that."*

"You've got *that* right," Jason said.

"However, there's more to the decision made by the council and myself on this matter. And that is that neither we nor any of the members of our constituency who took the time to share their views with the council want to see Fringe City turned into a surveillance state."

The scene cut back to the newsroom. *"And in other news,"* the anchor said, *"it appears that in the midst of last night's violence, another tragedy took place. Yet another victim has fallen victim to the Vampire."*

Jason sat up in his seat, now looking intently at the screen.

"Twenty-four year old —"

The screen went blank and the now familiar image of a glowing bow against a black background appeared.

"Citizens of Fringe City. I have eliminated the first of my targets. Tomorrow evening, I will take my shot at my second. I said that the effort to prosecute Edmund Peterson started too late for my liking but I did not say why. Now I will.

"The small minded fools of FCBN have attempted to stir

hysteria for ratings time and time again. The ill-conceived comments shortly after the West Avenue Bridge tragedy by former mediocre congressman, now mediocre citizen, Ken Doyle may have directly or otherwise brought on the crime wave that has taken this city back to the Dark Ages. And it was FCBN that put this man on the air.

"That was the time to take action but none was taken. And it is for this reason that I have chosen Charles Faulkner as my second target."

"Oh my god," Angie murmured.

"Tomorrow night at eight-thirty," Cupid finished. *"You know my terms."*

The screen went blank again and the news resumed but Angie muted it and turned to her husband. "Jason?"

"I'm bringing the Sentinel back, Angie," he told her, his voice firm. "I have to."

This time, there was no argument.

"Charles, this is serious."

Charles Faulkner nodded to himself as he listened to the mayor on the other end of the line. He understood the gravity of the situation. He had reflected on it since the moment he knew he was targeted... when Cupid had left the deliberate hint about the second target while he was threatening his first. He applauded the move to prosecute Edmund Peterson of the Fringe City Broadcasting Network, *even though he deplored the delay in making it.*

When he heard the words, Charles had known he was next. That he was marked. And from the message Cupid had left last night, he knew that Ken Doyle was the next target after *him.*

"Charles?"

He blinked, coming back to the present.

"I know it's serious, Ms. Mayor. Alison. But I'm not leaving the city. Whoever Cupid is, you can be certain he'll be watching my movements throughout the day. If I try to get out of the city, he'll follow me. Eric agrees with me on this as well. He says the best option is to stay put in a secure position."

"He said the same thing when Cupid targeted Mike Evans," St. Claire pointed out.

"True," Charles said. "However, he's also had time to reflect on what went wrong that night. He wasn't looking for pre-planted explosives. He wasn't expecting them. But now he knows about the trick, he's not going to be taken by it twice."

"And Cupid would know that too," St. Claire said, "so you and Eric shouldn't assume he'll *try* it twice."

"Trust me. Eric and his officers are doing everything possible to secure the premises. In an hour or so, I'll be moving up to a room on the top floor with a group of hand-picked officers, some of them from S.W.A.T. teams as well. And there are no windows and the walls are concrete."

"In an hour?" St. Claire asked, despair evident in her voice. There was a pause. "It's six o'clock already?"

"Ten past," Charles said.

"Oh, Charles!" St. Claire exclaimed and Charles knew she was crying.

He tried to reassure her. "I've had a good run, Alison. If this is to be my last night, I can live with that."

"Charles, don't talk that way."

"It'll be all right, Alison."

"Can't we go in and see him?"

Diane looked tearfully at Gwendolyn and shook her head. "No one else is allowed inside the upper levels. Eric wouldn't even let Devan see him."

"Oh my god," Gwendolyn cried.

"Can't we get in?" a new voice called out.

Sonya, standing beside Gwendolyn, turned around and saw Claudia rushing up from the curb, where she'd just leapt out of a taxi.

Sonya had tears in her eyes as well but she kept her voice firm. "Hutchens has already sealed off the upper levels. He's playing this close to the chest." She looked around for a moment. "Where's George?"

Another taxi pulled up and her husband climbed out and walked over.

"It's good to see you," Sonya said, embracing him.

"Hey, honey," George said. "I'm sorry I couldn't get here any sooner."

"It's all right," Sonya said, brushing a tear away. "I'm glad you're here."

While this was going on, Gwendolyn walked over to Diane. "Where's Jason?" she murmured.

"He's on one of the rooftops behind us," Diane said. "But he's lying low. The S.W.A.T. teams and sharp shooters have no idea what Cupid looks like and if they spot Jason, they might shoot him by mistake."

Gwendolyn frowned. "The rest of the cops are still in the dark about him being here?"

"The department can't turn a blind eye any more, remember?" Diane reminded her.

"Still?" Gwendolyn asked, looking up at the roof of Charles' office complex. "I thought we were past that now."

Diane gave her a puzzled look. "Why's that?"

"With everything that's happening at the moment," Gwendolyn said, "I doubt anyone would give a damn about the new Lady Vice's blackmail scheme. If you want my opinion, then I'd say that right now all bets are off."

. . .

Jason crouched by the ledge of a fifteen storey building, looking at the scene below. There was a slightly taller building to his left, with another fifteen or sixteen storey one below it, another taller tower behind the building he was on, a ten storey one immediately below him and across from that, the six level office complex where Charles Faulkner was now secured, surrounded by a handpicked guard of Hutchens' best officers.

And here *he* was, after eight years, in the Sentinel suit once more. He'd be lying to himself if he said he didn't get a thrill out of it but he wished the circumstances were almost anything else than what they were.

He'd tried to save people marked for assassination before. He'd saved Sofia Garcia from Orion. Admittedly, it was mostly by talking Orion out of killing her but he had still succeeded. He had also dealt with failure. He had been too late to save Diane's partner in that alley. And when he had warned the police that Orion was heading for the Graceville Hospital, Orion had still broken into the place and that nurse, Danielle Sutherland—whose name Jason had never forgotten—had been killed.

However, none of these experiences compared to the present. When the time came to act, he would get one chance to save Charles Faulkner and that would be it.

He glanced up at the building behind him, wondering if Cupid was on *that*. Tweaking the controls on the side of his visor, he found the binocular function and zoomed in on the ledge. There were two police sharp shooters stationed there, which effectively ruled out any possibility of Cupid using it as a vantage point from which to take his shot.

It also meant that Jason didn't have to go up there to check it out himself, which was another added blessing.

For one thing, he didn't have any grappling hook cables long enough for him to get up in one single ascent. And for another, he had what he liked to think of as a healthy fear of heights. While masked crime fighters standing atop of skyscrapers was all well and good in the movies, real life was a different story, what with things like vertigo and gale force winds to contend with.

He'd always tried to avoid taller buildings during his last stint as the Sentinel. When he'd made his network of flying foxes across town, he'd picked buildings under ten storeys wherever he could.

He didn't particularly enjoy being on the building

where he was at the moment either. The only reason he could handle it was the fact that he had all his assorted grappling hooks that he had learned to trust.

Although... looking at the taller buildings around, as much as he had no desire to go up any of them either inside or out, having longer grappling hook cables could be handy. He made a mental note to talk to Scott about it later.

Then he slammed the brakes on his train of thoughts. He had to concentrate on the job at hand.

"There's concrete on the other side of these walls, isn't there?" Commissioner Hutchens asked, tapping the nearest one.

"They're concrete, Eric," Charles said.

"I just want to be sure."

Charles looked around him. The other police officers were standing a small distance away, giving him and Hutchens a few moments alone.

"Eric," he said. "You've asked me that five times in the past hour."

"I want to be absolutely certain that Cupid can't reach you," Hutchens replied, pacing back and forth. Then he paused. "Five times?"

Charles smiled. "I'm afraid so."

Hutchens shook his head. "I'm losing it, Charles."

He looked at him again. "And you're not helping me. Couldn't you at least *try* to look a little worried? Cupid's gunning for you and you seem to be the only person in town keeping their cool."

"Eric. Would worrying accomplish anything now?"

"It's natural."

"So's resignation."

Hutchens grabbed Charles' shoulder. "Damn it, Charles," he said, tears in his eyes. "You're not going to die on my watch."

Charles gently pushed his hand down. "Eric. You may be right. He might not get me. But if he does, I'm ready. I've had plenty of time to think it over. I'm not a young man, Eric. I've had a full and eventful life. Eventful enough for several, I'd say. And I've already planned for this. I'm not going to leave a vacuum in the city. I've taught Devan Fletcher everything I know and—"

"We're not talking about your job here, Charles," Hutchens interrupted. "We're talking about you. You're more than just the D.A., you know. You're a friend."

Charles' smile remained. "Well, you can remember me as that. I'm glad to *be* your friend, Eric."

From his vantage point, Jason tried to see the other

police snipers. There were four on the roof of Charles' office complex, looking in all directions. That brought the total up to six but he knew there'd be more.

He took another look at the building below him. There didn't seem to be anyone there at first. Then he saw them. Three officers, partially shielded by some large turbine roof vents, bringing his running total up to nine.

He turned to the larger building to his left and zoomed in with his visor controls to have a look at the roof.

He paused.

Two officers, slumped over on the edge. He zoomed in as far as he could, amazed by how much he could magnify the image thanks to Geoffrey's ingenuity eight years ago. He saw a dart in one of the men's necks.

He thought about it for a moment. A high-powered dart gun wasn't stipulated in Cupid's rules but then again, as everyone now knew, his rules seemed to only apply to the actual assassination of his selected targets. Killing Mike Evans with a bomb blast would have been against his rules but blowing the floor out from under him before killing him with a bullet to the head wasn't.

Cupid's rules were not all that restrictive.

Jason pulled out the untraceable cell phone that Geoffrey had made for him after that episode with the Black Bandit during his last stint as the Sentinel. He called Diane.

She answered a moment later. "What's happening up there?"

"Cupid's taken out two of your sharp shooters," Jason said, looking at the building for a name or some kind of distinguishing characteristic. "Top of the building behind you with the large antennae on the roof."

"Dead?"

"Don't know," Jason said. "The one I saw had a dart in his neck. Warn the others. I'm looking around."

"I'll use the police radio," Diane told him. "Don't hang up."

"Got it," Jason replied. He looked around, listening absently while Diane contacted the officers on the perimeter. He checked the building behind him where two men had been positioned five storeys above him. They'd been taken out too.

"Twenty storey building to the north of the last one," he told Diane. "Both men down."

"Then where's Cupid?"

"Believe me, I'm looking," Jason said, scanning his surroundings.

"We're getting all the snipers to report in," Diane told him. "So don't worry about them. Just look for Cupid."

"Right."

Jason kept looking. Then he heard the sounds of helicopters and he saw two of the things circling the area with their search lights swinging back and forth across the buildings.

"Quite the party we've got up here," he muttered to himself.

"What was that?"

"It's crowded up here," Jason told her. "This is going to give Cupid a whole lot of confusion to mask his movements."

"Well, I don't think anyone's going to send the choppers away," Diane said. "If Cupid's taking out our men on the roofs, we're going to need all the extra eyes we can get."

"Yeah, I hear you," Jason told her. "Although, you might want to tell them I'm one of yours just in case a trigger happy S.W.A.T. officer takes a shot at me. Tell them I'm part of a special unit or something."

"All right," Diane sighed. "For what it's worth."

Jason heard her making the calls.

"Come on, Cupid," he muttered to himself. "Where are you?"

A shot then rang out, echoing between the buildings.

Jason whirled to his left to see where it had come from; one of the helicopters, swinging south on the near side of Charles' office complex moved erratically for a moment and then quickly shot off, losing altitude at an alarming rate. Jason zoomed in on it with his visor and switched to infra-red view for a moment; the vehicle was leaking fuel.

It lined up with the street running alongside Charles' office complex and Jason watched as it made a shaky descent.

"Did you see that?" he asked Diane.

It was a stupid question he realized as he watched cars moving out of the way and a crowd of onlookers breaking through police barricades for a better view. By the looks of things, several hundred people had seen it.

"Yeah, I saw it," Diane replied, not bothering to point that out. "The other chopper's moving in on the shot's point of origin now."

Jason looked back up. Sure enough, the second helicopter was coming in fast, its rotor blades beating furiously. It was almost on top of him.

"Are they idiots?" he shouted into his untraceable, trying to be heard over the noise. "Cupid'll take them out too!"

"I don't know *what's* going on," Diane said. "But—"

There was another shot.

Jason heard the impact and looked back to see the second helicopter whirling out of control. The groaning vehicle, fire and smoke pouring out of a breach behind the cockpit, smashed into the side of the building behind him, tearing metal, shattering glass and spraying the debris on everything below.

For a moment, it looked as though all the debris was going to come right down on top of him.

Jason ran to the north side of the building, trying to get clear. But as he looked back, he saw that most of it missed the building, falling to the street along with the stricken vehicle. He heard the crash and the cries of panic below.

"Jesus Christ," he muttered. He glanced at his watch. Not a specialized part of his gear. Just a watch. It was 8.23 p.m.

"What's happening out there?" Hutchens asked.

"The other chopper's down," came the reply. "Cupid shot it out of the air."

Hutchens knew the voice well. "Diane?"

Charles moved over to Hutchens to listen in on the conversation.

"Yeah, it's me," Diane replied.

"So this prick's just killed five of my officers," Hutchens said. "And now we've got no-one in the air or on the roofs. Is that about it?"

Diane hesitated but only for a moment. "Not entirely, Eric. Jason's out there."

A few days ago, Hutchens would have taken issue with that. But now...

He sighed. "Well, that's something."

Jason knew it was all on him now and he had no more than seven minutes left. Cupid had already proven his split second timing.

However, in taking out those helicopters, Cupid had—even if only temporarily—given away his position.

Jason hooked his untraceable into a holder and got out two grappling hooks, holding one in each hand. He fired the right one at the top of the building behind him, tested the weight and held down the recoil trigger, shooting up towards the roof. Thankfully, a myriad of other anxieties were able to mask the terror of being so far outside his comfort zone height-wise. As he soared to the roof where his right grappling hook was lodged, he fired the left one at a protrusion to slow his forward momentum. Then he released the right hook and hoisted himself on top of the building, using the left one.

Then he looked around.

To his left was one of the police officers he'd seen earlier. He took a second to check on him and saw he was still breathing. The darts weren't lethal.

He then looked east. That was where the shots that had brought down the helicopters had come from. There was another building of similar height to the one he was now standing on and there was that other building immediately to his south... and there was a wire running between the two of them, with a flying fox mechanism and a harness swinging in the air; it had been used only moments ago.

Jason grabbed the untraceable again. "Cupid's moving in from the east. He's using flying fox wires to get around."

He looked at the building to the south. But Cupid wasn't there; he'd rappelled four storeys down and crossed another flying fox wire to the next building over. And as Jason watched, the assassin pulled out two weapons that were strapped to his back.

The obvious sniper's rifle was put aside however in favor of something a little more obscure.

"Cupid's setting up on the KST center," Jason said, keeping up his running commentary on the untraceable. "Is there anyone else up here?"

He could hear the anguish in Diane's reply. "Just you, Jason."

"Move Charles to the western side of the building," Jason told her. "Or down or something. I'm moving in."

He fired a grappling hook at the taller of the

buildings to the south and swung across. He looked down to the roof of the KST center.

"Where the hell did he go?" he exclaimed. He looked at the building to the south-west of the KST center, right across from where Charles was. In the time it'd taken him to swing across to his current position, Cupid had packed up his gear, slid across another wire to the next building over and set up again.

Cupid must have seen him.

Or had he?

Still dangling by his grappling hook, Jason looked back at Charles' office complex. There were a handful of odd looking things on the upper eastern walls. Then he saw Cupid firing more of the things at the southern ones.

Jason rappelled down to the KST center, released his grappling hook and grabbed the untraceable again.

"He's firing plastic explosives at the walls!" he shouted at Diane. "Get Charles out of there! I'm on Cupid now!"

"Got it," Hutchens replied after Diane had relayed the message. He grabbed Charles. "You heard the lady."

"No argument from me," Charles replied. Even now, with the odds stacking up against him the way they were, he kept the cool and level head that had distinguished him over the years.

"We'll head for the street," Hutchens said. "See if we can get out the western side. We only have to keep out of his sight until eight-thirty ticks over and then we're clear."

He forced a smile he really didn't feel. "They're the rules, right?"

Jason flicked off the untraceable and, running, clipped it to its holder mid-stride. He raised his grappling hook again to fire at the building Cupid was on. Then, with a rush of air, he was smashed to the roof.

He rolled on his back and looked up at a masked visage with glowing red eyes. The glow really came from *around* the eyes through colored lights but he only noticed this on a subconscious level. On the conscious level, he was just bewildered.

He'd wanted to track this monster down more than anything but he wasn't ready to deal with him. Not right then. Not tonight.

There was a sound like a thunderclap. The eastern and the southern sides of the top few floors of Charles' office complex blew away. However, the support struts remained, holding the roof and the ceilings intact. And when the dust cleared barely moments later, the floors and all their occupants were exposed. Then a shot echoed between the buildings and the air was filled with shouts and cries.

The time was 8.30 p.m.

Eric Hutchens supported his friend by his shoulders with one hand, cradling his head in the other and lowered him to the floor.

"Charles," he murmured in farewell.

Then standing up, he stepped aside as the medics knelt down, checked for vital signs and attempted to revive his friend.

Hutchens had to admire them for trying.

Diane was helping two of her officers assist the one survivor of the first helicopter crash when it happened, trying to move the badly injured man out of the burning wreckage in the middle of the street.

Smoke billowed over the gathered crowds and the patrol cars on the other side of the police barriers with their red and blue lights distorted in the haze.

Diane then heard the explosion above and saw the debris tumbling down onto the sidewalk and across the road. Scores of people fell to the ground, some of them badly injured.

She saw Gwendolyn and the others scrambling back to their feet, surrounded by the shattered glass and mortar. Devan was there too.

And then they heard the shot.

Diane closed her eyes and lowered her head with a sigh.

Then she turned back to her men.

"Commander Felding?" one of them asked.

Tears came to her eyes but she brushed them away. She nodded to the bloodied and battered survivor from the crash. "Let's just get this man to safety, Michaels."

She scanned the crowds for some of the medics who'd been stationed outside the building, her gaze coming to rest at last on an ambulance inside the cordoned off area.

Jason pushed the Vampire away from him with all his strength and kicked him in the chest as hard as he could. His assailant buckled from the blow but only slightly; he was wearing a light armored vest under the tattered red and black robes that covered him.

Even up close, Jason saw he was still mostly an impression. There was very little to focus on. A whirl of red and black and flashes of silver.

Flashes of silver!

Jason rolled out from under his assailant just in time as the Vampire slashed at him with metal claws built into his glove.

"You're quite the showman, aren't you?" he said, scrambling to his feet and keeping back. "Do you really need claws to terrorize young girls?"

"Is that what you are?" the Vampire asked, his tone mocking and… not quite right.

It was theatrical, Jason thought, but something about the voice—or the words themselves—didn't seem to fit with something. But didn't seem to fit with what?

There was no time to think about it. The Vampire slashed at him again. Jason leapt back and tried to kick him, noticing for the first time the strange folded apparatus strapped to his assailant's back. A folding glider. Derek Bradley, the man who had once been Orion, had theorized that the Vampire must have had a piece of equipment like this. And that theory had been passed onto the police and then, through Diane's agency, Jason had read it as well.

The theory was correct and if Jason could damage the glider, then the Vampire would be trapped on the roof with no escape route. The Vampire must have guessed his intentions though because he circled Jason warily, keeping his folding glider behind him.

Jason then noticed something else. In the midst of this scuffle, Cupid had vanished.

Then, feeling the weight of all his anguish and anger crashing through, Jason raised a grappling hook and fired it at the Vampire's wrist. He recoiled it as it caught, dragging his assailant stumbling over.

The Vampire swung at him but he was off balance. Jason kicked him behind the knee, dropping him and coming at him again. For a moment, he felt like killing the Vampire then and there.

The Vampire pried off the glove that Jason's grappling hook was latched onto, freeing his hand, then scrambled to his feet and ran several yards before whirling around.

"You slippery little bitch!" Jason shouted. "Why the hell did you come here tonight? Are you working with Cupid?"

"Working with Cupid?" The Vampire all but laughed.

On that subconscious level again, Jason saw that his assailant had been wearing a glove of black cloth under the metal one he'd just pried off. Which meant the latter wouldn't likely yield any fingerprints.

"Cupid's no friend of mine," the Vampire said. "He's ruining everything. Apparently." Then he shrugged. "But he sure is fun."

The Vampire ran for the eastern side of the roof and

as he did, Jason observed the mechanism of his glider. As the Vampire ran, he reached back, grabbing two rigid struts and pulling them outward. He strapped one to his left wrist and the other to his right with an expertise borne from lots of practice. Jason also glimpsed small handles attached to the Vampire's wrist straps. Already now, a partial wing of fabric stretched behind the Vampire's back, with trails of red and black cloth billowing around it to obscure the struts. Then the Vampire pulled down on the handles and the struts divided, fanning out, stretching fabric and creating a glider five or six yards from edge to edge. Then he leapt out into the air, sixteen storeys above the street.

Jason was hot on his heels, slamming against the roof ledge and watching his opponent, not even registering the dizzying drop below. He saw the Vampire in silhouette gliding over the lights from the street and he saw the crowds watching from below.

He readied another grappling hook. The Vampire began to climb, gaining height. He was gliding between the two larger buildings to the east, aiming for a lower building just past them. As Jason fired the grappling hook, he had a fleeting thought. If he didn't fall to his death, Angie was going to kill him for this. But the hook latched onto the Vampire's foot, much to Jason's surprise, and he launched off the building, swinging underneath the Vampire and dragging him down. It was terrifying but exhilarating at the same time.

Jason felt the air rushing past. Then he looked up at the visage of glass and metal that was rushing to greet him and, momentarily, he forgot everything else.

"Holy *shit*!" was all he managed to get out before, turning his back to it and huddling into a crash position, he smashed through a window and swung back out into the open air.

Dizzy, but alive and surprisingly intact all things considered, he looked up to see how the Vampire had fared and saw the figure draped in red and black trying to pull himself up on the roof of whatever building this was, no easy feat with his hands strapped to the struts of his glider.

Search lights swung across the building, trying to focus on them both. Jason ignored them.

Pulling out another grappling hook with his left hand, he fired it at another section of the roof. If he could yank the son of a bitch off his perch and get him below him, then he could uncoil the cable from both grappling hooks, lowering the Vampire almost to the level of the street. Then he could drop him the rest of the way and let the police could take care of him.

But the Vampire wouldn't budge.

Then Jason heard a grating sound and he figured it

out. The prick had lodged the steel claws on his left glove into the roof. He was also *very* strong, a man of athletic strength and prowess.

And again, Jason got the feeling that he was missing something. He couldn't figure it out right then and dangling two hundred feet off the street probably wasn't the ideal place to think it over anyway.

There was a tug on the cable.

"What's that bastard up to now?" he muttered, looking back up and wondering why he was swinging back and forth.

The reason was immediately apparent. That was exactly what the Vampire was doing. Then the gliding showman launched himself through a window and into the building.

"Got you now, asshole," Jason grunted. He recoiled the left grappling hook, bringing himself up to the roof about forty feet to the Vampire's left, while at the same time he recoiled the right cable—the one wrapped around the Vampire. With a crash, the Vampire was flung back out of the building and Jason saw him falling below.

But as he watched, he saw that the Vampire's hands were now free from his folded glider and mid-fall, the man pried the grappling hook from his foot, strapped his hands back into the glider holds, reopened the thing and got enough lift to crash land through a fourth floor window of the building across the street.

Jason couldn't believe his eyes. "Son of a *bitch*!"

He hoisted himself onto the roof and turned around. He'd have to get across to the other building but the swinging grappling hook cable wasn't the tool for the job. Not unless he wanted to relive the excitement, and mortal uncertainty, of smashing through another set of windows.

Briefly, he wondered whether Diane would send him a bill for the damage when he was done. Between him, Cupid and the Vampire, they'd thoroughly trashed the central business district of Fringe City.

Clipping his other grappling hooks onto his belt, Jason got out a double-ended one, fired one hook onto the edge of the building he was on and then another onto the edge of the one across the street.

Then, retracting the cable from one end, while unwinding the cable from the other, he soared over the street and scrambled onto firmer footing. With that done, he released both hooks and retracted the remaining length of cable. He latched the double-ended grappling hook on his belt with the others.

The way he figured it, the Vampire would take an elevator up to the roof and then try to make a fresh escape.

Then he heard another crash of smashing glass but it was very faint.

Sighing, he looked down and saw the Vampire launching himself from the building with his glider again. This time from the seventh floor.

Jason watched as the Vampire glided down then up, steering himself around another building and landing on a six storey affair behind it. Then he disappeared from sight and Jason was exhausted.

Charles was dead. Cupid was still at large and, after so thoroughly ruining everything, the Vampire had escaped.

It was time to call it a night.

Rappelling down and moving between the buildings in easy stages, Jason made one last errand and retrieved the Vampire's glove.

Then he set off again, sliding up, rappelling down and crossing streets until he reached the roof where his bag was safely hidden away. Then he got changed and headed home.

RETREAT AND REGROUP

MAYOR ALISON ST. CLAIRE DID NOT WANT TO see former congressman Ken Doyle that morning but she had agreed to meet him. And while she spoke to him, she tried her best to be gracious about it.

She waited as the young man who had brought them coffee left the office and then turned to her guest.

"Some time ago, Mr. Doyle," she said, picking up her cup, "a man attempted to blow up an airplane by smuggling a bomb on board in one of his shoes. Since that incident, passengers traveling on airlines all around the world have had to put up with the nuisance of removing their footwear before boarding their aircraft, not to mention being treated like criminal suspects. Guilty until proven innocent, as opposed to the traditional convention in many countries."

She took a sip of her coffee and continued. "In my eyes, when everyone is punished because of the actions of a handful of individuals, then we've lost. And *they've* won. Because where does it end, Mr. Doyle? When we're all huddled behind barred, bullet-proof windows, with bright search lights swinging back and forth outside? When we take an armed escort every time we go to the shops or take the kids to the park, is that going to be any way to live? We'd be safe, yes, but at the cost of living like prisoners in our own homes."

Ken Doyle frowned. "That's a rather extreme prediction, Ms. Mayor."

St. Claire smiled. "Oh, of course. It's *reductio ad absurdum*, a reduction to absurdity. I know that well-meaning people such as yourself don't intend to deliberately turn countries into police states. But the fact of the matter is that all these little rules and regulations add up. They pile on top of each other and none of them are ever retracted. Usually, this is because bureaucrats are generally more skilled in making matters worse than improving them but sometimes, it's just too hard to change something once you've fully committed yourself to it. And I can well imagine that after forking out the cash to install several million CCTV cameras across Fringe City, they'll be here to stay."

"You don't leave me with much room to move here, Ms. Mayor," Doyle said. "What about the events of last night? Don't they mean anything to you?"

St. Claire took a moment before she replied. She needed it.

"More than you could possibly know, Mr. Doyle."

If Doyle saw the warning, he didn't take any notice.

"If we had had the surveillance network in place last night—" he started.

"Charles Faulkner would still be dead and you might have got a fuzzy picture of the man who killed him."

"We could track his movements."

St. Claire measured Doyle with a searching glaze. "And how many cameras exactly do you think you would have needed to cover every possible route this man may have taken? Rooftops. Streets. Third storey balconies. Twenty-fifth floor windows. How many cameras, Mr. Doyle? Could you perhaps enlighten me with a conservative estimate?"

"Well, I'm not sure," Doyle said. "But—"

"If you don't know, Mr. Doyle, that's fine," St. Claire told him. "But if you wish to pursue this matter further, then perhaps you should find out. Just how many cameras do you want? And where do you want them?"

Doyle nodded and stood up. His coffee was untouched. "All right, Ms. Mayor."

As he walked to the door, he paused and turned to her once more. "I know you must be very upset at the moment. But I understand. I've suffered a terrible loss as well, as you know."

St. Claire nodded. "I do. And believe me, Mr. Doyle,

you have my most sincere sympathies for the death of your niece."

When Doyle had left, Devan Fletcher came through the door.

"Ms. Mayor," he said.

"Mr. Fletcher," she replied, crossing the room and clasping his hand. "Devan. I'm sorry about Charles."

"Me too," Devan replied.

"How did your wife take it?" St. Claire asked. "I understand she and Charles were very close."

This was something of an understatement. Charles had worked with Gwendolyn tirelessly for at least two years to help her and her friends set up Outreach without bringing any undue attention to the noble but somewhat *extra-legal* manner in which it was initially funded.

"She's very upset about the whole thing," Devan said, his delivery stiff. "But she's holding up pretty well all things being equal."

"And you?"

"I'm all right."

St. Claire frowned. It seemed to her that Devan was upset about more than just the fact he had lost his friend and mentor.

"Charles always spoke most highly of you," she

said, trying to help Devan feel more at ease.

"Did he?"

There was no mistaking it this time. Tears had come to his eyes.

St. Claire made a stab in the dark. "You didn't part on the best of terms?"

Devan shook his head. "Not exactly. We had a minor falling out."

St. Claire nodded. "Believe me, Devan. These things happen. But if Charles were still alive, you two would sort it out eventually, wouldn't you?"

"I suppose."

"Then don't think about the end. Think about the many years of friendship you've shared. Trust me. It's better that way."

Devan nodded. "I'll try."

"There will have to be another election for the position of district attorney," St. Claire told him, changing the subject and motioning him to have a seat. "However, as I'm sure you know even better than I do, in situations such as this, the laws of our state require me to appoint an acting chief public prosecutor in the interim. In accordance with Charles' wishes, I'm appointing you."

Devan nodded but didn't reply.

"I know you probably hoped to become D.A. under happier circumstances, of course," St. Claire continued.

"But, all the same, I'd like to congratulate you on your appointment and wish you the best of luck in your new position. Starting with the Edmund Peterson trial next week. Are you ready for it?"

"I'll do my best, Ms. Mayor."

"*The dizzying aerial skirmish with the Vampire was witnessed by hundreds of citizens. However, despite his repeated valiant efforts, the Vampire escaped, eluding capture and so, for now, he still remains at large.*

"*One thing is certain and that is that if it weren't for the Vampire's sudden appearance on the scene, the Sentinel would clearly have stopped Cupid and things would have turned out quite differently. But whether he was aiding Cupid or acting on motives of his own is not clear. Regardless, the need to bring this monster to justice is greater than ever.*

"*However, despite the terrible tragedies—multiple tragedies—of last night, we can take some comfort in the return of the Sentinel, whose courage and commitment to protecting this city are an inspiration to us all. Welcome back, old friend. The city needs you.*

"*For Fringe City Central, this is Mariane O'Hara. Goodnight.*"

Angie switched off the television and snuggled close to Jason.

"I know I haven't been as supportive of you in all of this as I was the last time," she said. "But I want you to know that, right now, I'm very proud of you."

Jason smiled. "Thanks, honey."

Angie shook her head. "No, I really mean it. And there's another thing too."

Jason turned to her. "What's that?"

"I think you've thrown a pretty big wrench in the works for the new Lady Vice and her blackmail scheme. If she wants to incriminate the mayor or the police for working with you, it's not exactly going to create a major public backlash against them. Right now, the city loves you."

Jason smiled. "Ah well, it's nice to be loved."

"So as far as big returns to the spotlight go, that was pretty good."

"Well, I'm glad you think so," Jason said. He was quiet for a moment, gazing down. "I just had a thought. The new Lady Vice's blackmail scheme won't be as effective now anyway since Charles is dead. Exposing a conspiracy involving the police and the mayor wouldn't be as dramatic as exposing one involving the mayor, the police and the D.A." Then he frowned. "Hang on a second."

"What is it?"

"'Cupid's ruining everything... apparently'." Jason started speaking faster. "That's what the Vampire said to me."

"You mean..." Angie started. "Lady Vice's blackmail scheme?"

Jason nodded. "That's *exactly* what I mean."

He got up, walking over to the phone. "I've got to talk to Diane."

"Um, it's nine o'clock at night," Angie said. "She might be busy putting the kids to bed or something. And Charles' funeral is tomorrow as well. Don't forget that."

Jason stopped and put the phone down. He sighed. "You're right. It can wait a little bit."

Then he noticed a message on his cell phone. He checked it.

"What's that?" Angie asked.

Jason frowned. "It's from Sophia Garcia. She wants me to call her."

"Tonight?"

"As soon as possible," he said, reading the text. "She said she'll wait up."

Angie glanced in the direction of Ethan's bedroom. "I wonder... She probably saw your TV advertisement just before. The one about the Sentinel being back in business. And if that's what she wants to talk about, maybe it'd be better if you talk at her place. She's only three blocks away now."

Jason nodded. "Yeah, good idea."

. . .

Sophia Garcia wasn't the woman she'd been when Jason had first met her. In the eight years he'd known her, she had made a conscious decision to move away from the glamorous life, live modestly and age gracefully. And she looked very well for it. An attractive, vibrant woman of almost sixty. And she was happy.

She also spent a lot of time working with Gwendolyn and her Outreach friends, occasionally working in the local center. Looking at her these days, it was hard to believe that at one point in time, she'd been living large as the sister of Fringe City's most prominent mob boss.

"I hope you don't mind," Jason told her. "But you said in your message that you'd wait up."

"It's fine, it's fine," Sophia said. "Come on in. Sit down. Can I get you a coffee?"

"Ah, I've just had one," Jason told her. "Although... it wouldn't kill me to have one more."

Sophia smiled as she put the pot on. "The way you were swinging around skyscrapers last night—and through them too, by the looks of things—I doubt a bit too much caffeine would have much effect on you."

Jason chuckled. "True." He pretended to stretch his shoulders. "Oh, and don't remind me of crashing through windows. That was *not* fun."

Sophia came and sat down by him, passing him a cup of fresh coffee. "Here you are."

"Thanks," Jason said, taking a sip. "Nice." He then turned to his friend. "So, what did you want to talk to me about?"

"Distractions."

"Distractions?"

Sophia nodded. "There's another problem building up out there and with Cupid, Lady Vice and the Vampire to contend with, I think we could all really live without more problems. It's just regular everyday crime, simple at heart and profit driven, but it could end up being a real nuisance down the line if we don't put a stop to it now."

Jason nodded as he got it. "A distraction."

"Right."

"A new syndicate starting up?"

"You guessed it," Sophia said. "A group from Detroit. I think they're taking advantage of the general chaos here to set up a new market."

"Drug dealing?"

"Yeah."

Jason took another sip of his coffee and leaned back against the sofa. "Actually, after last night's debacle, I think I could really go for kicking somebody's ass. Let off some steam. It could be therapeutic. So what do you know about it?"

"Well, a few weeks ago, I got a tip from a friend of mine," Sophia started. "She's a little bit like myself. Stuck in the mob business more by bad luck than design. Anyway, she told me a man named Bobby Caldwell was apparently coming to Fringe City and suggested I lie low because he was a friend of my brother's. At the time, I thought she meant he was just coming for a visit. And who knows? That probably *was* the original plan. But anyway, I didn't really think about it for a while.

"Then I heard from Gwendolyn and Sonya that George had discovered new drug deals going down in neighborhoods that had been clean for years and I got suspicious. I know Bobby Caldwell, sadly. I've had the displeasure of meeting him on a few occasions in the past and I can say without any reservations that if there's any new drug distribution going down in Fringe City, then Bobby Caldwell would be my prime suspect."

She handed Jason a piece of paper.

"What's this?" he asked, unfolding it.

"His address in Fringe City," Sophia told him. "I called my friend back and got it off her." She took a sip of coffee and put her cup down. "If this is like your typical drug smuggling operation," she said, "then the channels of distribution won't be particularly sophisticated yet. That kind of thing takes time. So for the moment, exposing the operation shouldn't be too difficult. Also, if Caldwell's just trying to get a feel for the market here, then he probably hasn't invested a huge amount of effort into starting his operation up yet. Most likely, he only has a handful of men moving his goods to middlemen."

Jason put the address away. "All right. Thanks, Sophia."

When he got home, Jason looked through the various pieces of equipment that Geoffrey had made for him during his original stint as the Sentinel and smiled as he found what he was looking for. Remote tracking devices.

The next day, he went to the neighborhood where Caldwell was staying. It wasn't a particularly uptown area, which surprised him at first. But on reflection, it made sense; if Caldwell was just getting a feel for Fringe City and hadn't decided yet whether he wanted to reside there permanently, a low-key neighborhood allowed him to do so without anyone noticing him.

From a concealed vantage point, Jason watched the apartment complex throughout the day. He knew that

Diane and Gwendolyn would be at Charles' funeral right then but he hadn't been close enough to the man personally to attend himself. Also, if he went along, people might wonder why a relative nobody was there, which could lead to problems down the line.

Yes, he appeared to have gotten away with getting his alter-ego plastered all over TV screens across the country and the Sentinel was very popular again. But there was no sense in deliberately pushing his luck.

Jason's stakeout was a rather boring affair, really, and his only comfort were the sandwiches and snacks he bought from the nearby convenience store to help him through it. But by two o'clock in the afternoon, he knew what Bobby Caldwell looked like. He knew what car he drove and when he left the neighborhood, he had a tracking device in place underneath it.

He checked the whereabouts of the car throughout the day on his remote tracker. On the subway home. While he was waiting to pick up Ethan from school. After dinner. And Bobby Caldwell had made several trips to the docks area, going to the same part of it each time.

As Sophia had predicted, the operation wasn't very sophisticated yet.

Jason smiled as he packed his Sentinel gear for another outing. Tonight, he wasn't going to be repeatedly frustrated, thrown about and smashed into buildings. Tonight, he was going to kick some ass.

A breeze was blowing a mist of sea spray over the wharf. Nearby the water, a man in a scarf and a cap sat on a pile of wooden crates beside a container. Then, seeing a group of men arrive, he swung himself down and walked over to them.

"All right, guys. You've got my money?"

"You know the rules, Briggs," the nearest of the newcomers replied. "Not until we've seen the merchandise."

Briggs sighed theatrically. "Where's the trust, eh?" He nodded for the men to follow him. "All right. Come on and have a look."

He unlatched the container he'd been waiting next to and slung open the doors.

"There you go, Briggs," the other man said, handing him a package. "Not so hard, is it?"

Briggs shrugged. "Not so hard but how long has Caldwell known me?"

The other man smiled. "You don't get to reach Caldwell's position without taking a few precautions." Then he turned to his companions. "All right. Get to work." As the others went about their jobs, he pulled out a cell phone and made a call. "All clear."

A couple of minutes later, two small trucks arrived.

The drivers hopped out and helped the men on the wharf load the packages from the container into the back of them.

Then several canisters hit the ground, shattering and releasing a gas that spread over the area.

Briggs, the drivers and the rest of the men collapsed, unconscious.

Bobby Caldwell got out of his car and walked over to the entrance to his apartment. As he reached the steps, something caught around his ankle and he was yanked off his feet.

Terrified, he watched as the ground fell away from him at dizzying speed. Then a gloved hand gripped him by the collar and he was turned around, face to face with a masked apparition.

"Bobby Caldwell."

"Who the hell are you?" Caldwell demanded.

"Just a citizen doing his part for Fringe City," the Sentinel told him. "We don't need you, Caldwell. We've got far more important things to deal with than little parasites like yourself."

"What do you want?" Caldwell asked, his defiance from a moment earlier now forgotten.

"From you, Mr. Caldwell?" the Sentinel asked. "Not much. But you really should have stayed in Detroit."

Then the Sentinel moved back, something shattered near Caldwell's face and everything went black.

Commissioner Eric Hutchens stepped into his office and poured himself a cup of coffee. He sat down, took a sip, leaned back and shut his eyes.

With Charles Faulkner's funeral and everything else the day had thrown his way, he was very tired. However, the day wasn't quite over yet.

He frowned at his cell phone but then he saw it was Diane calling. And if it was Diane, it was probably important.

"Hey, Diane," he said. "What's going on?"

"I thought you'd like to know that while we were dealing with the fallout from the other night, Jason stopped a crime syndicate from Detroit from setting up here."

Hutchens would have believed anything right then. The way things were going, if Diane had called to tell him she'd discovered an interdimensional rift with giant monsters pouring out of it, he probably wouldn't have blinked.

"Is that right?"

"I've e-mailed the footage Jason took for us. And Palmer and I are picking up everyone involved in the conspiracy."

"Jeez."

"Jason thought it'd be better to stop this thing straightaway before it got out of hand."

Hutchens nodded. "He got that right."

"You sound tired, Commissioner," Diane said. "You don't have to worry about this now. Palmer and I have got it all under control. You just let Devan know about it so we can get these guys processed and locked away as soon as possible." She paused for a moment. "Oh, and you don't have to, of course, but if I were you I'd see about arranging a short press conference to warn off any other mob bosses who might be thinking of taking advantage of the situation here."

Hutchens nodded. "Good idea. And thanks, Diane."

"Don't thank me," she replied. "Thank Jason."

"Tell him for me, will you?"

"Will do. Goodnight, Commissioner."

"Goodnight, Diane."

Hutchens hung up and dragged his hands over his eyes, his temples and then through his hair, trying to massage some semblance of life back into himself.

Then he switched on his computer and looked for the e-mail Diane mentioned. It was not hard to find.

He watched the footage of men at the docks unloading drugs, in which Caldwell was mentioned by name several times. Then he saw a few photos showing Caldwell and his car. And a few more of the car in several places, including the docks.

Hutchens was impressed. Their friend had learned a bit since his last big drug bust. It had been quite a dramatic affair by all accounts but at the time, Jason had been a bit negligent in the area of evidence. In fact, it would be more accurate to say that he had thoroughly trashed any evidence he might have been able to use. But this was as clean and straightforward as anyone could hope for.

Hutchens smiled. Getting this gang of upstarts who thought they could take advantage of his strained police force gave him a much needed morale boost. Yes, Cupid, Lady Vice and the Vampire were still out there but with this Caldwell prick, they'd had a nice quick and decisive victory.

The next morning, Jason met Diane at her home.

"It's been a busy couple of days, hasn't it?" Diane remarked. "I can't believe we haven't had a chance to chat about the other night until now."

"Me neither," Jason said.

"I want to say thank you for everything you've done, Jason. Stopping Caldwell in his tracks last night. And all you did to save Charles."

Jason sighed. "I *could have* saved him if it weren't for the Vampire."

"I know," Diane told him. "Believe me, when we catch him we're going to throw away the key."

"I sure hope so. Could you get anything from the glove I sent you?"

Diane shook her head. "No. Unfortunately."

"Never mind."

"Um," Diane said, "when you called me, you told me you had some news. What was that?"

"The Vampire's an illusion."

Diane frowned. "In what way? Because I thought everyone had already agreed this was an elaborate prank."

"When I ran into him the other night, I think I got a feel for the kind of guy he was," Jason said. "Athletic. Highly skilled. Someone who thrives on adrenaline. A bit of a thrill-seeker. A show-off. But if this guy could murder those girls and leave a sterile crime scene each time, then I'm the U.N. secretary general."

Diane didn't reply. She was thinking it all over.

"And there's something else," Jason continued. "I asked him if he was working with Cupid and he told me, and these were his words, that Cupid was *apparently* ruining everything but he was fun."

Diane nodded. "Ruining everything... but not for him."

"No."

"Do you think he meant Lady Vice?"

"It's a theory," Jason said. "Lady Vice killed those girls and our Vampire was just some dumb stuntman hired to dress up and put on a bit of a show. To add some color to the whole thing. In fact, I wouldn't be surprised if the assumption that these women died from blood loss—hypovolemic shock—wasn't right either."

"But they *had* lost lots of blood," Diane said. "Enough to cause hypovolemic shock."

"And they didn't struggle when they were attacked?"

Diane frowned.

"What if these women had their blood drained from them *after* they died?" Jason asked. "That way, Forensics would assume that was how they died and they wouldn't look for the real cause. Think about it. Lady Vice figured out how to replicate the stun gas I use to render people unconscious. And I'd say now that she probably arrived at the formula by herself. And—"

"That's what we think too."

"So it wouldn't be a stretch to imagine she could make a stronger substance. A *lethal* variety."

"But what would be the point?"

"If the victims died instantly without putting up a struggle, then Lady Vice could rearrange the crime scene at her leisure. Making those unusual wounds, draining and disposing of the blood and then sterilizing everything to leave no evidence of her even being there."

Diane nodded, impressed. "Well, I can't fault any of your reasoning. You know, you would have made a good police officer."

Jason smiled. "No. You know how it is. If you turn your hobby into a job, then you'll take all the fun out of it."

Diane smiled too. "Or you could get paid for doing what you love."

"Hm. Good point."

Diane was quiet for a moment. "Pity we couldn't follow your original lead much further."

Jason frowned. "Oh. I'd forgotten about that. What happened?"

"We couldn't find any subway footage with a high enough resolution to identify the man," Diane said. "And we don't know where he went after he got off at the next station."

"Never mind," Jason said. "Anyway, it wasn't a total waste of time. I did discover cardamom buns."

Diane gave him a puzzled look, her lips twitching into a little smile. "What are cardamom buns?"

"They're delicious, that's what they are," Jason told her. "You should try one someday."

Diane chuckled. "All right. I will."

"Anyway," Jason said, "I'm sure you get your fair share of wasted effort and dead ends in the force, right?"

"We do," Diane agreed. "But we get paid for it."

"I suppose that makes a bit of a difference," Jason conceded. "By the way, is there any chance now of checking whether the cause of death of the Vampire victims may have been something else other than blood loss?"

Diane frowned. "Are you asking for the purposes of the investigations or is this about Kaori Tanaka?"

"A bit of both," Jason confessed. "If she never saw the man I met the other night... if she died in her sleep, I might be able to rest a little better at night."

"Well... we returned the victim's bodies to their families. We didn't want to do any more testing on them than absolutely necessary. God knows those girls went through enough. However, we *did* take blood samples from the little blood they had left. They might help us find the answers you're asking about."

"Why did you take blood samples?"

"For DNA analysis," Diane explained. "However, if Forensics still have the samples... I think you're right. We all just assumed blood loss was the cause of death and once we saw evidence that appeared to support our theory, we stopped there and filed our reports." She shook her head. "You really *could* have been a detective on the force."

They both leaned back on the sofa for a while, thinking it over and Diane took a sip of coffee.

"So our showman," she said. "The man responsible for the Vampire's public image, even if he didn't personally murder those girls. He wasn't working with Cupid. And he said Cupid was ruining everything, which we're assuming here means he wrecked Lady Vice's scheme to blackmail the mayor, the commissioner and the D.A. by murdering Charles. So it sounds as though he was there that night to stop Cupid. To kill him most likely."

"Because he's fast, agile and damn creative with a folding glider that most people would be too terrified to even *think* of using," Jason said. "He was the guy for the job."

Diane looked at him for a moment and nodded to herself. "Yeah, you're right of course. But the interesting thing here is that if he was *supposed* to kill Cupid but didn't, then why didn't he?"

"He *told* me why he didn't," Jason said. "Because for him, Cupid's fun. I'd say after getting his costume and that glider and then getting a taste of the limelight with his recent television appearance, he's decided to have a bit of fun of his own. And extrapolating on that, I'd say Lady Vice's scheme—assuming she's the orchestrator and not a pawn herself—would appear to be unraveling. I think the Vampire's gone rogue."

Diane contemplated this. "An interesting thought. I suppose if this puts an end to the blackmail scheme and helps us bring in this new Lady Vice sooner rather than later, it could be a good thing. But on the other hand, if he really has gone rogue with all that gear of his, then there's no telling what he might do next. Especially now that he's got a taste for publicity."

"So what do we do now?" Jason asked.

"We do nothing," Diane told him. "You go home and spend some more time with your lovely wife and your gorgeous little boy. And I understand that your school's summer vacation is starting next week, so you're going to get a nice little extension to your leave of absence. I think it might do you some good if you tried to enjoy it."

"Fair enough. But if any of the big three make a move again, I'll be waiting for them."

Diane shrugged. "That seems fair to me. But don't go throwing yourself in harm's way just for the fun of it."

"I wouldn't dream of it," Jason said. "But what about you? What are you going to do?"

"There's something Gwendolyn and I were going to do before Cupid targeted Charles," Diane replied. "I think that now we've got a bit of a reprieve, it's as good a time as any to do it."

Jason frowned. "So what are you two up to exactly?"

Diane hesitated. "I'm not sure if you'll like this. But I think you deserve a straight answer. You remember..."

"In other news, police have shut down a crime syndicate that has attempted to create a drug dealing network here in Fringe City. Apparently, the head of this syndicate, one Robert 'Bobby' Caldwell, was hoping to take advantage of the perceived 'state of lawlessness' that many around the country believe exists here at the moment. However, as Police Commissioner Eric Hutchens has stated, any criminals from other parts of the country who believe they can come here and have free run of our city are sorely mistaken."

The screen cut to a press conference, with Hutchens standing at the podium.

"A few weeks ago, Lady Vice gave an open invitation to the criminals of the nation to come to Fringe City and make themselves at home," he said. *"Maybe Mr. Caldwell and his friends got that invitation and decided to accept. Maybe they just saw the near constant carnage we're dealing with at the moment and thought they could come here and go wild. Perhaps they thought we're not prepared to deal with people like them. But whatever they thought, they were wrong.*

"And I have a message now for those people around the nation who choose to break the laws that are in place to keep the collective community safe. We don't have time for mobs, drug runners and the mafia. We've got far more important things to deal with. So if you come here and try to screw around with us, then we'll throw everything in the book at you and then some. If you want to spend the rest of your miserable lives looking at a cell wall, then come and give us a visit. If not, then stay the hell out."

Jason smiled at Angie. "He may not be Shakespeare but he's got style, don't you think?"

Angie smiled too. "It's amazing he gets away with it. But it sure makes a nice change from politicians reading from a teleprompter." She put an arm around her husband. "I notice that you didn't worry about trying to get credit for the fact that you were the one who stopped this group from getting their hooks into the city."

"Well, Sophia did the groundwork," Jason pointed out. "I just finished it up. But yeah, I'm happy for the police to take the credit. It's better that way. It reinforces the message that they're still able to deal with this type of crime. That they're not a powerless group you can run rings around."

"A bit of an illusion at the moment though,

wouldn't you say?"

Jason shrugged. "At the moment, yes. But sometimes, we need a good illusion."

Devan Fletcher took a deep breath and turned to face the court.

"I believe no one in this room today would argue that the defendant's actions were *intended* to cause harm, although the logical counter argument is that Edmund Peterson *should* have known what some of the possible negative outcomes of airing the footage may have been."

He paused to take a measure of the room, and to let his words sink in, before continuing.

"However, as I shall now explain to you, while Edmund Peterson could not know with any certainty that airing the interview with Lady Vice and the Vampire footage he received could have harmful effects, there is no doubt that he suspected it. Strongly suspected it, as you shall see. If he did not, then why did he not view the footage before airing it?"

The room was silent. In the box, Edmund Peterson, the chief executive of the Fringe City Broadcasting Network, looked pale.

"Because," Devan continued, "he wanted to air the footage regardless of what it contained. And by not checking the content beforehand, it was Mr. Peterson's intention to indemnify himself against any charges that he willfully showed harmful and inappropriate footage on prime time television. But ladies and gentlemen, far from indemnifying him, this proves that he was fully aware of the wrongful nature of his actions. He wanted to air footage that would shock the public. To increase the ratings of his network and, subsequently, make more profits from advertisers. These were the only considerations that passed through Edmund Peterson's thoughts when he decided what to do with the footage he had received. Right and wrong did not enter the equation."

When the trial was over, a much older man approached Devan, extending a hand.

"Devan Fletcher," he said, smiling. "I'm Tony McIntyre. I was a friend of Charles Faulkner."

"I know who you are, sir," Devan replied, shaking his hand. "Charles mentioned you once or twice. And I saw you at the funeral."

"I used to work in law, myself," McIntyre told him. "Never a D.A. of course. But Charles and I go way back. Anyway, I just wanted to tell you that I thought you handled yourself admirably today and wherever he is right now, I think Charles would be proud of you."

"Thank you, sir," Devan replied through stiff lips.

Diane and Gwendolyn looked at the sign.

"Palmdale Mental Health Institute," Gwendolyn read aloud. She shrugged. "Well, it seems to be the right place. Not quite what you'd expect."

"Not when one of the most dangerous men in Fringe City is inside," Diane agreed. "However, if he hasn't made any attempt to escape in the five years or so he's been here, then we can probably take it that Dr. Carter knew what he was doing. Still, I'm glad it's so open and cheerful, especially if we have to stay here a while."

They entered the place and Diane went over to the woman at the front desk. "Hi, I'm Diane Felding and this is Gwendolyn Fletcher."

The woman smiled. "I thought as much. I recognized you from the TV, Commander Felding."

Diane smiled. "Is that right?"

"You're quite the celebrity cop," the woman said, passing her a form. "Here. All visitors have to sign in. I'll give you your name tags in just a moment."

"Thanks."

Diane signed the form and passed it to Gwendolyn, who did the same.

"Now, if you'll just wait here a moment," the woman said after she had handed them their name tags, "I'll find Dr. Carter for you."

Diane watched as she left and turned to Gwendolyn. "By the way, does Dr. Carter know you're married to Devan?"

"Probably," Gwendolyn said. "Devan's not exactly a man with a low profile. And the surname's a bit of a giveaway as well."

Diane sighed. "Ah, well. It can't be helped, I suppose. Still though, I wish Devan hadn't gone off all half-cocked, trying to run that scheme of his behind everyone else's back."

"He's sorry he did that."

"I know," Diane said. "And I'm sure he meant well. But still... Well, we'll see. Anyway, Dr. Carter's coming."

Dr. Carter shook their hands. "Commander Felding. Mrs. Fletcher. It's very nice to meet you both."

Diane smiled. "Just call me Diane."

Gwendolyn chimed in too. "And just Gwendolyn for me too."

"Then by that same token," Dr. Carter replied, "feel free to call me John. Now, I take it you want to see Derek Bradley right away?"

"Well, as soon as it's convenient," Diane said. "I hope we haven't come at a bad time but we did make an appointment."

"Oh, no, it's not a bad time," John replied. "In fact, right now's an ideal time to see him. He's out the back in the garden. Good for you two as well." He smiled. "Come on. I'll introduce you."

Diane and Gwendolyn followed him through a series of corridors and then they were outside.

"This is better than how the rest of us live," Diane said, looking around at what was pretty much a small park, with the trees on the edges blocking out the urban surroundings so well, she could easily pretend the city wasn't there at all.

John smiled. "Yes. Perhaps this may be the real reason my client hasn't made any escape attempts."

They found Derek Bradley seated at a table in the middle of the grounds.

"Visitors, Dr. Carter?" he asked.

"Yes," John replied, motioning for Diane and Gwendolyn to make themselves comfortable across the table from him. "And they're ladies too."

Derek gave John a smile. "Then you can rest assured I'll be on my best behavior." He turned to his visitors, extending a hand. "Derek Bradley."

Diane glanced at John before accepting the proffered hand but he nodded his assurance and so she accepted. "Commander Diane Felding," she introduced herself. "Fringe City Police."

"A pleasure," Derek said. He turned to Gwendolyn. "And you are?"

"Gwendolyn Fletcher," she told him, shaking his hand as well.

"Of the Outreach organization," Derek said with a small nod. "Well, this is also a pleasure. And you make an interesting pair. I suppose the reason for you *both* coming here will become apparent soon enough."

"It will," Diane told him.

Derek leaned back, studying his visitors for a moment. "Now let me guess. You're here to ask me to help you with your investigations into either Cupid, Lady Vice, the Vampire or all three. Yes?"

"Something like that," Diane said.

"You know," Derek told her, sitting up again, "not too long ago, if you had asked for my help, I would have laughed in your face. However, I'm not certain my feelings are quite the same now."

Diane and Gwendolyn said nothing. It was obvious that Derek wanted to say more.

"I think we can talk now," he continued. "But before we do, I'd like a straight answer. I think after all this time, I deserve it. And you can trust me. If you tell me anything in confidence, it *remains* confidential. Right, Dr. Carter?"

John nodded. "I can vouch for Derek's integrity on that score. However, as to what you wish to discuss,

I'll leave that to your own discretion."

"I understand," Diane replied, her gaze still on the man across the table. "But I think you deserve a straight answer as well, Derek." She turned to John. "Gwendolyn and I would like to talk to Derek in private. Is that permissible?"

John stood up. "Perfectly. I'll be over there." He pointed to a bench at the far side of the garden. "Give me a nod when you're ready for me to come back."

"We will," Diane assured him. She watched until he was out of earshot and turned back to Derek. "So, you want to know what happened eight years ago."

"I do."

"Well, first of all, I should explain something to you," Diane began. "You were good in your Orion days. Very good. However, you had a fatal weakness."

"My solution to crime?" Derek asked.

Diane shook her head. "That's a different subject. I'm talking here about your investigative method. You brought in the Specter when no one else could. That tells me that you were very good at solving the trickier mysteries. However, it appears to me that you only exercised those skills when you had no preconceptions about a perceived crime."

"Preconceptions?"

"Yes, Derek. Preconceptions. Assumptions. Your tendency towards these things is the weakness I was referring to. If you thought you knew who the culprit of a crime was, then you didn't bother with your investigative technique. You just pursued them. And this was why Gwendolyn here decided you had to be stopped."

Derek frowned. "Gwendolyn decided to stop me?"

"Yes," Diane said. "Gwendolyn and her companions. The original perpetrators of the Lady Vice myth."

She watched and waited as the words sunk in and then continued. "You assumed, like most of us, that Lady Vice was exactly what she appeared to be. However, Lady Vice was a creation, Derek. The crimes she committed were all designed with the sole purpose of building up the credibility of the persona so that Gwendolyn and her associates could infiltrate syndicate circles and systematically shut them down. The money and goods stolen from guiltless victims were later returned quietly in such a way as not to arouse suspicion. And the considerable funds that the group acquired from the syndicates were used to set up the Outreach organization, a charity that helps thousands of families and individuals in need every year and has helped to reduce crime in the city as well. Considerably.

"And you, Derek Bradley, with your assumptions, didn't question your conclusions or exercise your investigative technique. If you had, I'd have no doubt that you would have worked out what was going on fairly quickly. But you didn't and so you simply decided that Gwendolyn and her companions had to die."

Derek looked pale but Diane pressed on, while Gwendolyn sat in silence. "So they contacted us. And they contacted the Sentinel. And together, we arranged one last Lady Vice show to draw you in and, predictably, you came running. And the rest, of course, you know. But if we hadn't trapped you, if you had hunted down Gwendolyn and her companions in your one man crusade, what would have happened then? Several good women would be dead. Women who were fiercely dedicated to helping the city and improving the lives of people in need. There'd be no Gwendolyn Fletcher. No Outreach. The thousands of families that have benefitted from their assistance would still be living with poverty and crime and the crime rate across the city would be much greater overall. So tell me, Derek, if you had been in our position, would you have done things any differently?"

Derek hung his head. "No."

"I'm sorry if I upset you, Derek," Diane told him. "But you said you wanted to know the truth. Now, you do."

Derek looked up. "So what now? Is this a second chance?"

Diane shrugged. "It depends on you. We could really do with your help right now, Derek. But Dr. Carter says that you're not ready to be released yet. He didn't say why though. You know how it is. Patient confidentiality and all that. Do you want to enlighten me?"

"Sure," Derek said. "You gave me a straight answer. It seems only fair that I give you one in return. I told Dr. Carter in no ambiguous terms that if he authorized my release, I would return to being Orion and resume my one man war."

Diane blinked. "Well. I'd say that would probably do it. Do you still feel that way?"

"Now?" Derek asked. He shook his head. "Not anymore."

"Then you should tell Dr. Carter," Diane said. "But wait until you're ready."

She got up and so did Gwendolyn.

"And when you do, Derek," Diane added, "we'll be waiting for you."

"Do you think you were too hard on him?" Gwendolyn asked as they climbed into the car.

"I think he needed a bit of a push," Diane replied.

"His rehabilitation progress ground to a halt years ago and has stayed there ever since. Now, I'm no psychologist but I think that he's probably felt a mixture of anger, confusion and betrayal all these years over what happened back at the Sapphire Hotel when we laid that trap for him. But I think now that the mist has cleared, he'll be able to put all that behind him. And I got to him, didn't I?"

Gwendolyn shook her head. "You sure did. But why didn't you explain all that years ago?"

"It's incriminating stuff if he decides to spout his mouth off about it," Diane pointed out.

"All right then," Gwendolyn said. "So why is it okay now?"

Diane looked at her and frowned. "Hey, this was *your* idea, remember?"

"I know that," Gwendolyn said. "I'm just wondering why you decided to go along with it."

"Well, there were two reasons," Diane said. "First of all, now I know more about Derek Bradley, I'm confident he won't tell anyone else what I told him today. Not even Dr. Carter."

Gwendolyn nodded. "Makes sense. And what was the other reason?"

"Well, it's as you said the other night," Diane said. "The night Charles died. Right now, all bets are off."

. . .

"I want to go on the swing!"

Jason turned in the direction of said swing. "I think those other kids are still using it, Ethan. You'll just have to wait."

"All right. I'll play on the slide," Ethan replied and cheerfully ran off.

Jason smiled. Diane had been right. Taking a break and spending some time with his family was doing him a world of good. And it was a nice day too, which always helped.

Then his cell phone started vibrating. He took it out and checked the caller. It was Diane.

With a little smile, he answered it. "Hello, Diane. I was just thinking of you."

"Were you now?" Diane asked. "Gwendolyn and I have just got back from our visit to Palmdale."

"Oh yeah. And how did that go?"

"Quite well, I think. However, that's not why I'm calling. I had some news from the station and I thought you might want to know."

"About Kaori and the others?"

"Yeah. Do you want to hear it now?"

Jason sighed. "I might as well."

"Well, the testing I authorized has come back. All the girls died of blood poisoning, most likely through a substance they absorbed through the lungs. The team from Forensics say they would have died in their sleep. The blood loss came later and it was, as you suggested in your theory, a distraction intended to create a bit of alarm and throw the police off track."

Jason nodded. He was quiet for a couple of moments, unable to find his voice. Then he wiped a couple of tears away.

"Jason? Are you all right?"

"She died in her sleep then?" he asked, just making sure.

"Yeah," Diane said. "I know that won't bring her back or the other girls but it's something at least. I thought you'd want to know."

"I did. Thanks, Diane. It's something, as you say."

"No problem, Jason. Anyway, that's everything for the moment. Why don't you go back to what you were doing? Are you in the park?"

"Yeah. Can you hear the other kids?"

"I can," Diane replied. "Well, I'll leave you to it. Go and enjoy your time with Ethan."

"I will," Jason said. "Thanks, Diane."

When Devan Fletcher came home, Gwendolyn was waiting for him and she gave him a big hug as he came through the door.

"I heard about your win today," she told him. "You did well, honey. If you keep it up, I'm sure when the election to appoint a permanent D.A. rolls round again, you'll have it in the bag."

Devan laughed. "Maybe. But I shouldn't get a big head. I'm just doing the job I've been trained to do, that's all. What about you? How did your visit to Palmdale with Diane go?"

"Good," Gwendolyn replied. "I think Diane really got through to him."

"So what did Derek say?"

"Nothing yet," Gwendolyn said. "At the moment, Derek Bradley's got quite a few things to think about but when he's had a bit of time to process it all, I imagine we'll be looking at a new man."

"And will we able to use that new man?" Devan asked.

"That's the plan."

Mariane O'Hara took her seat behind the news desk, double-checked the news scripts in front of her and waited for the cue from her producer.

"Good evening," she said, "and welcome to the news hour at Fringe City Central. I'm Mariane O'Hara..."

The other anchor turned to the camera with a smile.

"… and I'm Richard Henderson."

"And *I*," a third voice cut in, "am Lady Vice."

Everyone in the room froze.

Mariane glanced at her producer. The woman was staring at her wide-eyed in fear, with another woman behind her pressing a gun against the small of her back.

Mariane trembled. There was someone behind *her* too. She turned to her left and there was Lady Vice herself, sliding her sharpened fingernails across the news desk with a malicious smile on her lips.

"Hello Mariane," she said. She glanced at the other anchor. "And whatever the hell your name is."

She looked across the room at the camera.

Mariane turned that way as well and saw that Lady Vice's associates blocked all the exits and had their weapons trained on everyone in the vicinity.

She swallowed.

Lady Vice in the meantime began her address. "Ladies and gentlemen. Our viewers at home. I'm afraid I don't quite know how to hijack the air waves in the manner of our friend Cupid. So we're doing this in the old-fashioned way.

"Commissioner Hutchens has laid down a challenge to my girls and myself. I made an open invitation to Fringe City for anyone in the country who's got what it takes to set this city on fire. The commissioner has tried to scare everyone away. He *says* that if any underworld figures want to try their luck here, he'll have them locked up before they know what hit them.

"He says this, ladies and gentlemen, because for some strange reason, he thinks he runs this city. Well, he is mistaken. This is *my* city. And tonight, I'm going to make sure Commissioner Hutchens knows this. At this very moment, I imagine he and the boys in blue are on their way here to arrest me. Well, let's just see how that goes."

One of Lady Vice's associates smashed the camera with the butt of a rifle, while Lady Vice grabbed Mariane by her arms and hoisted her to her feet. "Come on, dear."

Richard, the other anchor, leapt up. "Hey!" he shouted. "You leave—" The words were cut off as Lady Vice swung round and slashed his carotid artery, dropping him to the floor.

"Shut up," she muttered.

"Richard," Mariane gasped.

Then several shots sounded all at once. The noise was deafening and when the smoke cleared, three or four more people lay dead on the studio floor.

Lady Vice smiled at her associates. "That's the way, girls. Just leave one hostage each. Come on. Let's head up to the roof. We must get ready to meet our guests."

ALL BETS OFF

"AND THE DAY WAS GOING SO WELL," Hutchens muttered as he glanced out the passenger window and saw all the other patrol cars on the road, sirens flashing.

He picked up his radio. "I'm almost there, Palmer. Have we got a perimeter in place?"

"Building's surrounded, sir," came the reply. "We've cordoned off the area and I'm sending spotters into the surrounding buildings."

"Well done," Hutchens replied. "But keep everyone back until I get there. This'll be a hostage situation and an ugly one. And if we're not careful, this could end up worse than Graceville."

The Graceville Hospital siege had been a bad night for everyone and one Hutchens did not want to repeat.

"Got it," Palmer replied.

Hutchens flicked the radio off and thought it over. "What's Lady Vice playing at?" he murmured.

"What's that, Commissioner?" his driver asked.

"Lady Vice," Hutchens replied. "Is she planning to

kill me? Is she planning to kill the hostages?"

The driver shrugged. "No idea, sir. I'd say she just wants a heap of cash in exchange for letting her hostages go. Maybe she just wants to humiliate you. But I'm only guessing here, Commissioner."

"That's all right, Sergeant," Hutchens said.

He leaned forward, glancing through the windshield. "Looks like we're here."

The car came to a stop and he got out and jogged over to Palmer.

"Sir," Palmer nodded to him, passing him a pair of binoculars.

"Thanks, Palmer," he replied, lifting them up. "On the roof? Where?"

Palmer put a hand on the binoculars and guided Hutchens in the right direction.

"They're fanning out now," he said. "Nine women. Nine hostages."

"There would have been more than nine people in that newsroom," Hutchens said. "Ah, yeah. I see them now."

"I'd say the other people in that newsroom are dead," Palmer said.

"Lady Vice could have stunned them," Hutchens said, passing the binoculars back. "The way she stunned Mariane O'Hara before she kidnapped her from her apartment."

"Possibly," Palmer conceded, putting the binoculars away. He didn't need them now. They could see the women on the roof with their hostages clearly enough. And the building was only six storeys high anyway.

"However, Lady Vice wasn't wearing a gas mask when she appeared on the television," he added. "And I don't think she was carrying one."

Hutchens sighed. "Well, I suppose there's no point in worrying about it now. What about the rest of the building?"

"No lights," Palmer pointed out.

"No witnesses came running out to see you when you arrived?"

Palmer shook his head. "No."

"These girls are lunatics," Hutchens muttered.

"No argument here."

Hutchens put his hands on his hips and took a few paces. "All right. I'm going to need a moment to figure out just how we're going to deal with this."

"Ethan's still reading in his room," Angie said to Jason, trying to keep her voice as quiet as she could manage. "What am I going to tell him?"

"Tell him I had to get some things from the shop," Jason replied, slinging his Sentinel bag over his shoulder. "Or tell him I'm meeting a friend. He'll understand."

"All right," Angie said, with a little sigh. "But be careful."

"I won't be alone out there," Jason pointed out.

Angie frowned. "What about the Vampire? He might be protecting Lady Vice and her gang the way he protected Cupid."

Jason thought about it for a moment. "No, I shouldn't think so. If my theory's right and he was working with these girls, then they would have had a serious falling out after that night. Remember? I think these girls wanted Cupid dead. And the Vampire was probably meant to make that happen but instead, he stopped me from capturing Cupid because he found him too much fun."

"Well," Angie said, "there's a problem right there then."

This time, it was Jason's turn to frown. "What's that?"

"If the Vampire is now out for fun, then wouldn't tonight qualify?"

Jason stepped onto the street and looked left and right. Then Diane came around the corner in an unmarked patrol car and pulled to a stop in front of him.

Jason climbed in and slung his bag onto the back

seat as Diane pulled away from the curb.

"Well, this is a different way of doing it," he remarked, glancing about.

Diane shrugged. "Well, off the record, Hutchens wants all the help he can get. You've been recruited."

Jason smiled. "Great. Maybe I can pull a pay check from you guys."

"I thought you weren't in this for the money," Diane told him, with a slight smile of her own.

"Nor the thrill," Jason said. "Just trying to do my bit. Plus, Angie thinks the Vampire might show up."

Diane nodded. "I think I agree with your wife on that one. If he's gone rogue…"

"That's the way I see it," Jason said. "And if I can get the bastard this time, we could blow this case wide open."

"We could, but this is a hostage situation. Keep that in mind," Diane told him. "And that's another reason why I'm giving you a lift. Hutchens has given me a very specific assignment. I'm keeping you in check. Lady Vice and her girls are on the roof of the Fringe City Central studio. There are nine of them all up, all armed, and each of these girls has a hostage."

"What do police usually do in these cases?"

"Usually?" Diane asked. "We wait. We try to calm things down. Negotiate if that helps. But we don't go in guns blazing."

Jason frowned. "I'm not sure, but one of my stun gas canisters—"

"If you're not sure, then don't try it," Diane cut him off. "Lady Vice and her girls aren't all huddled together in one convenient corner of the roof. They're fanned out around the building, keeping a lookout on all points. And I've got to tell you something else. Hutchens is going along with this because he believes you can help but don't forget that this is all off the record and it *has to* be. If we work with you quietly and nobody knows, that's fine. But if we're seen working with you or even letting you get away with what you're doing, then we've got problems.

"The blackmail threat that Lady Vice has hinted at is one thing; it's highly doubtful she has any hard evidence to prove we've worked with you in the past. But if people see us letting you go tonight, we'll all be in big trouble."

"I beat a suitably hasty retreat last time, didn't I?" Jason reminded her. "Why are you telling me all this now?"

"Two reasons," Diane said. "The first is that since last time, you've been given that rather public endorsement from Mariane so you might get it in your head that you can throw caution to the wind now. But public goodwill will only get you so far."

"And the second reason?"

"This is a more delicate situation than last time. There are the hostages for starters. The area's more open. People now expect you to show up. And we're having a hard time keeping the other stations' reporters away. They're really clamoring for coverage apparently. With Fringe City Central's people dead or being held on the roof and FCBN effectively on ice, it's a dream opportunity for these guys."

Jason frowned. "They sound like vultures."

"You don't know the half of it," Diane told him.

She pulled into an alley and brought the car to a stop. "This is about as close as I can get you to the scene. Call me when you're ready. And *don't* let anyone on the roof see you."

"I won't," Jason replied as he got out and took out his bag. "Talk to you soon." He closed the door and scrambled up a fire escape as Diane drove away.

Hutchens watched as more of his people got into position around the building.

A man in S.W.A.T. armor jogged over to him. "What's the story, Commissioner?"

"We're holding back for the moment, Commander Welch," Hutchens replied. "The spotters these ladies are watching every approach to the building."

"Have they issued their demands yet?" Welch

asked.

Hutchens sighed. "I wish they would. They're just watching us."

"What are they waiting for?"

"That's the question, all right," Hutchens said. "Don't forget. They've got a surprise in store for us. Me specifically."

"You wearing a vest?"

Hutchens snorted and tapped his chest. "Got that covered." Then he walked over to his car and pulled out a helmet. "Got this too."

"Well, I'm sure we'd all feel a lot more comfortable if you put it on, sir," Welch said.

Hutchens did so, smiling. "I feel a lot more comfortable too. Although strictly metaphorically speaking."

Welch smiled back. "You get used to them, sir."

"I find it hard to believe," Hutchens said, "but I'll take your word for it." He glanced back at the roof and shook his head. "Just standing there. Maybe we could make this a straightforward sniper job. A sniper on each woman and synchronized shots." Then he frowned. "Unless these girls have got another pair of eyes outside the building."

Palmer came over and nodded to the S.W.A.T. man. "Commander Welch." Then he turned to Hutchens. "The spotters say they haven't moved since we arrived."

Hutchens nodded. "Yeah, I noticed that too. Can you ask them to look around the area and see if these bitches have any spotters of their own, either somewhere inside the building or in one of the ones around it?"

"I'll tell them," Palmer said, pulling out his radio and walking away.

Hutchens turned back to Welch. "I've got an idea, Commander. Do you think you and your men could break into the building from underneath? Make your own way through the stormwater drains or something? Maybe blow out a wall and get into the underground parking lot, Orion style?"

Welch frowned. "We may be able to but blasting our way in could make too much noise. Also, there are safety considerations to make as well. A misplaced blast or one that's just too big could bring the building down on top of us if we're not careful."

"I'm aware of the risks," Hutchens told him. "But do you think you could do it?"

"I'm not sure," Welch said. "Maybe."

"Talk it over with your men then and have a look down below," Hutchens told him. "But when you find a way down there, find one somewhere where Lady Vice and her friends can't see you."

"Got it," Welch replied and jogged off to talk to his

people.

Then Palmer came back. "I've relayed your instructions to the spotters, sir. They'll let us know if they find anything. But I just remembered something. When Lady Vice first reappeared after the West Avenue Bridge disaster, there were twelve ladies in her gang, including herself."

Hutchens nodded. "Right. So we're missing three. And they could be anywhere."

Then there was a tremendous crash. A thunderclap accompanied by blinding light. The ground gave way, throwing Hutchens and Palmer off their feet, and a cloud of debris scattered over the area. Dust, rubble and bodies flew through the air.

In a daze, Hutchens staggered to his feet. His body ached all over, his ears were ringing, his ankle was probably twisted and blood and dust coated his face.

He looked around at the post-apocalyptic landscape, trying to make sense of what happened.

For a moment, he couldn't remember what he was doing there. For a moment, he couldn't even remember his *name*. Then gradually, bits and pieces came back to him. Lady Vice. Hostages. Commander Welch.

He wondered whether the S.W.A.T. team had caused the blast. A miscalculation while trying to break into the underground parking lot.

But hadn't Commander Welch only just left a few

seconds earlier?

Hutchens closed his eyes for a moment. His head was throbbing. He was in pain and he was confused. He needed to concentrate.

He looked at the scene again. The nearest police barriers were gone. The open area in front of him—basically half the outside parking lot—had exploded underneath his people.

Understanding came to him with sickening horror. He was looking at the dead bodies of his officers. Thirty or forty people killed by the blast.

He heard the sound of a helicopter approaching and he remembered something else. Both of the police helicopters had been shot down by Cupid. One had been completely wrecked and the other was still being repaired.

He turned to his right and saw Palmer. "Come on, Palmer," he muttered, crouching down and putting a hand on his shoulder. "Get up."

He waited a moment.

"Palmer," he tried again, shaking him gently. Then he stood up, pulled the uncomfortable helmet off his head and let it fall.

He staggered away from the Fringe City Central studio as fast as he could, pulling out his radio. As he moved, he heard gun shots. The bullets ploughed through the rubble on either side of him.

The smoke and dust was probably obscuring him a little so Lady Vice and her friends couldn't see him but somehow, Hutchens thought they were missing him deliberately. That they were trying to unnerve him. That they were mocking him.

Wincing, he carried on, paying no heed to the shots. He was too deep in shock to feel afraid anyway.

"All units!" he shouted, his voice hoarse and strained. "Fall back!"

"Fall back!"

Diane heard the shouts and saw the dust, the smoke and the still burning fires in the scattered wreckage of police cars ahead.

"What's going on?"

For a moment, Diane wondered where the voice was coming from.

"Diane?"

She realized Jason was talking to her on the phone.

"Yeah, I'm here," she said.

"What the hell was that?"

"Lady Vice rigged the outside parking lot with explosives," Diane said, her voice hollow. "The police were standing right on top of them and they didn't even know."

"Jesus," Jason said. "How bad is it?"

"I'm almost afraid to find out," Diane told him, jogging over to what remained of the police barricades.

"Diane?"

Diane shook her head. "Jason, I'm needed here. Don't let the ladies see you." She flicked off the phone and looked around to see if any of the officers on the ground were still alive.

"Keep back, Diane!"

She whirled around as bullets shattered bits of rubble near her feet, the sound of the gunfire echoing between the buildings.

A piece of shrapnel caught her in the thigh, and she screamed and fell to the ground.

Then she saw Hutchens running over to her, keeping low to the ground.

"Diane! Stay down!" he shouted.

Diane nodded and a moment later, Hutchens was crouched over her.

"Are you shot?"

Diane shook her head and tried to sit up. "No. A bit of stray shrapnel." She winced as she looked at the bloody patch on her thigh and the sharp bit of metal embedded there. With an anguished cry that ended in a scream she pulled it out. Then she saw Hutchens' anxious expression. "I'm all right," she assured him as well as she could.

"Come on then," he said, helping her to her feet and

putting himself between her and Lady Vice's gang on the roof.

"Have you got a jacket?" Diane murmured as they staggered along.

"I've got a jacket, yeah," Hutchens said. "But they want to humiliate me, not kill me."

"Why are they *doing* all this?"

Hutchens shook his head. "Beats me," he muttered. "That helicopter's getting louder."

Diane risked a glance back. "I can see it."

Hutchens stopped and turned around. "Well, son of a bitch. It's a Fringe City Central one. Hang on."

He pulled out his radio. "Jonesy?"

"Commissioner?"

"How many girls in that helicopter?"

"Uh…" There was a slight pause. "Three, sir," Jones said with some elation.

"That's all of them accounted for then," Hutchens said. "Do they have any hostages?"

"The pilots. Otherwise I'd shoot the thing down right now and damn the consequences."

Hutchens smiled. "You'd get no flak from me. Are there enough snipers in place to hit all these bitches at once?"

"We've got the numbers," Jones said. "But I'm not sure if we've got the right angles. I'll check with my squad and get back to you."

"Don't bother with that, Jonesy," Hutchens told him. "If you can get all of them at exactly the same moment without risking the hostages, do it."

"Got it."

"Good luck. Over and out." Hutchens flicked off the radio and helped Diane back behind what was left of the barricade.

"I'm all right," she told him. "I can walk."

"You're bleeding badly there."

"It's all right," Diane said. "It'll clot up soon enough."

In the distance, they heard the wail of fire engine and ambulance sirens.

"We should be able to get to the survivors out there soon enough," Hutchens told her, nodding to the Fringe City Central studio. "Whether the snipers get them or not, these girls are about to clear out. They've had their fun."

Diane nodded. The helicopter was now hovering over the roof and slowly descending. "They're not going to get clean shots," she murmured, pointing to the roof. "The girls are taking the hostages with them."

Hutchens sighed. "I had a feeling that was going to happen. But they might still have a chance."

Then a scream cut through all the noise: the whirring rotor blades, the rumbling of fires and wailing of sirens.

"Oh my god!" Diane cried out.

From eighteen or twenty storeys up, in a building adjacent to the studio, one of the police spotters plummeted into the street.

Diane clasped her hands over her mouth in horror and looked up. Crouched behind a broken window just below the roof of the building was the Vampire.

Jason saw the whole thing from the top of the building behind Diane.

"I've got you now, you son of a bitch," he muttered. He ran to the ledge and fired a grappling hook at the top of the other building. It was an extremely stupid thing to do, he realized once he'd passed the point of no return, swinging out twenty storeys above the street. However, he didn't have time to set up the double-ended grappling hook and slide across safely if he wanted to reach the Vampire before he flew off.

Recoiling the grappling hook cable as he swung across to his target, he tried to compensate somewhat for his forward momentum so he wouldn't smash face first into the building and break every bone in his body. Then twisting his weight to the side as well and pulling down, he changed his trajectory enough to bring him straight at the Vampire.

The Vampire looked ready to take a swing at Jason

as he came in but seeing the speed at which his adversary was coming towards him, he changed his mind and tried to launch his glider.

The late reaction gave Jason the extra second he needed and soaring in on the end of his grappling cable, he landed a heavy kick on the side of the Vampire's head and knocked him off his perch.

However, the Vampire being the athletic and agile man he was, managed to gain some forward momentum in his fall, set up his glider and soar over to the building Jason had just come from.

Jason watched as the Vampire smashed a window and started to climb in. Then, hot on his heels, Jason fired one end of his double-ended grappling hook into the building he was on and one end into the other building. He then released and retracted his first grappling hook and slid across on his makeshift flying fox.

The whole floor was dark. Jason flicked a light switch and nothing happened. Not that he expected anything; it was pretty clear this part of the building was being renovated.

A bit of noise from the chaos on the street could be heard through the broken window behind him where the Vampire had come in but the building itself was eerily quiet. And the Vampire was nowhere to be seen.

Jason got a better look at his surroundings. He didn't use the infra-red function on his visor yet. His eyes were adjusting and he didn't want to wreck his night vision. But it was clear that most of the walls had been taken out up here so what he was looking at was largely open space, lots of support pillars and the odd wall here and there. He then got the feeling that the Vampire hadn't gone far at all. This floor was perfect for a game of hide and seek and the Vampire was probably watching him, looking for his opportunity to either make another run for it or...

A flash of silver against a shadowy blur of cloth was his only warning.

Jason stepped aside as the Vampire lunged, then he grabbed him by the wrist and flung him into the nearest pillar.

"You just couldn't stay away," Jason said, "could you?"

"You think you can beat me?" the Vampire asked, his voice hoarse and raspy from exertion.

"I think I can kick the shit out of you, you little bitch," Jason told him. Somehow, it felt almost therapeutic putting the guy in his place.

The physical mask was still in place but the mystery, the nightmare, had been dissipated, revealing an egotistical prick who was tough and agile but little else. He was pathetic.

The Vampire circled him slowly. Jason noticed that he limped a bit in one leg. Somehow he'd injured himself with all his aerial acrobatics.

Then Jason realized that his best bet was if the Vampire thought he stood a fighting chance. Moving slowly, he tried to position himself between the Vampire and the nearest window.

The Vampire made another lunge at him. Jason leapt out of the way and watched as his opponent turned around again.

Jason also noticed now that the Vampire was holding back to protect his folded glider.

"Why don't you give up now?" he asked him. "You're only embarrassing yourself."

"Tough words," the Vampire replied, his voice laced with contempt. "Why don't you come and get me?"

Jason reached towards his belt, his movements almost imperceptible in the diminished light. "All right."

Then he threw something at the Vampire's face, a small canister that shattered with a cloud of gas. It probably wouldn't penetrate the Vampire's mask but it didn't have to. The important thing was that it threw him off edge.

The Vampire stepped back a few paces, waving his

arms to ward off the stuff, while Jason circled around behind a pillar.

But the Vampire didn't wait for the ambush. When he'd recovered his balance, he ran for the broken window he'd come through, strapping the struts of his glider to his wrists, and leaping into the open air again.

"Son of a—!" Jason muttered and took off after him. He reached the broken window at a run, crouching as he came to the ledge to slow his momentum. Then he looked out, saw the Vampire, raised his grappling hook and tried to make lightning strike twice.

The hook tangled around the back of the Vampire's glider this time. Then once again, Jason swung out into empty air like a pendulum, coming up beneath his quarry. He recoiled the cable mid-swing to compensate for his forward momentum. This time though, he wasn't careening towards a collision with a row of glass windows. The Vampire was losing height and Jason was going down with him. And they were coming down close to the Fringe City Central studio.

Very close in fact. They were gliding a handful of feet over it.

Jason readied another grappling hook and looked back, ready to fire it at an antenna he'd spotted once he was level with it. That would bring him to a safe landing with the Vampire behind him.

And bruised and battered on the roof of a six storey

network studio, with the police no doubt on their way up, it was doubtful the Vampire would get away again.

Jason eyed the antenna, raising the second grappling hook.

Any moment now.

Then a lone gunshot rang through the streets, echoing around the amphitheatre of the buildings.

"Oh no!" Diane cried, watching the scene on the roof unfold.

One of the snipers had shot the Vampire, while Jason was dangling beneath him on a grappling hook cable.

The shot knocked the Vampire off his trajectory and sent him rolling him to the right, partially folding his glider in the process. Then both he and Jason fell, crashing into the roof and out of sight. It was a four or five foot fall for Jason, easily enough for him to break his neck or crack his skull. But even if he didn't kill himself, he was still going to be hurt.

This was what Diane had feared all along. What Angie had feared. What Commissioner Hutchens and the mayor had feared.

In the best case scenario, if Jason survived, he would still be lying incapacitated on the roof of the Fringe City Central studio in his Sentinel gear, with police on the stairwell already right below him.

The public goodwill that Jason had generated towards to his alter ego only went so far. If the police had the opportunity to bring him in and they didn't take it, if they bent the rules for him, then the legal teams representing every criminal misfit who came through the system would have a field day in court and the flood gates would open.

In the best case scenario, if Jason was still alive, they were going to have to bring him in.

RESURRECTION

AMONG THE ASHES

DIANE STEPPED OVER TO THE COMMISSIONER'S side.

"Eric," she murmured.

Hutchens hung his head and sighed. "I'm sorry, Diane."

"Don't give me that," Diane told him. "We owe Jason Harding a lot. And I'm not going to see him hauled off to prison if there's a way out of it."

"There *isn't* any way out of it," Hutchens told her. "I can't personally vouch for every last officer on that stairwell. When they come out onto the roof and see the Sentinel lying there... if I tell them we're all going to turn a blind eye to this..." He shook his head. "There's no way out, Diane."

"Tell them to wait," Diane said.

Hutchens looked at her with a weary expression. "What good will that do?"

"It'll give me time," Diane told him. "It'll give him time. Come on, Eric. If you don't want to do this for Jason, then do it for me."

Hutchens sighed and pulled out his radio. "Diane, I'll do it for *both* of you." He flicked the radio on. "Stair team. This is Hutchens. Hold your position a moment."

"What are we waiting for, Commissioner?"

"Lady Vice left a nasty surprise in the outside parking lot," Hutchens said. "She may have left another one on the roof. Where are you now?"

"Just below the newsroom, sir."

"All right. Check that out first and see if there are any survivors. But keep off the roof until I can get the spotters to give me the all clear. Five... ten minutes at the most. I'll get back to you."

"Thanks, Eric," Diane called over her shoulder as she ran towards the building.

Jason opened his eyes. He wondered what had woken him up. It was still dark and he felt terrible for some reason. And he had a very nasty headache. If there was a part of him that didn't ache right then, he couldn't think what it was.

He frowned. He was on a hard surface and he was dressed... in his Sentinel gear, he now remembered. Then it all came back to him and the thing that had woken him up was the vibration of a mangled phone on his belt.

He pulled it off with some effort and pushed it

towards his head. "Diane?"

"Oh, thank god you're alive! Jason, you've got to get off the roof. Can you move? I'm coming up."

"Where?" Jason managed. He heard the clanging on metal ringing louder and louder in his ears and Diane lunged onto the roof, breathless, having just sprinted up the six flights of stairs that made up the rear fire escape. She stopped by the Vampire and detached Jason's grappling hook from his glider, figuring out how to use the release trigger on the grappling hook gun.

Then she came over to Jason and crouched down beside him, putting her hand on his shoulder. "Jason, listen to me very carefully. I'm going to try to get you down the fire escape. Do you think you have any spinal injuries? It's important."

"I feel like hell," Jason told her. "But I don't think I've got a broken back."

"Come on then." Diane leaned down and slid an arm under him. "Hold onto my shoulder."

Jason slumped his other arm over Diane's back and tried to hold on as Diane brought him to his feet.

"You're hurt," he exclaimed, seeing the matted blood on the side of her leg.

"You're worse," she countered as they reached the fire escape. "Okay, no talking. Easy does it."

Jason couldn't really stand and his legs dragged

over the metal stairs as Diane walked in front of him, taking the bulk of his weight on her shoulders. It was exhausting for her too but she mustered every hidden reserve of strength she had.

As she neared the bottom of the stairs, she heard the sounds of men on the roof. Hutchens had bought them all the time he could. Then, as she brought Jason onto the street below, her heart sank.

Swerving around the corner and coming straight for her was an unmarked patrol car. And there she was with the Sentinel holding onto her.

But as the car came to a stop, she understood.

"Eric?" she asked as Hutchens leapt out.

"I'm heading up there to assist my people on the roof," he told her with a conspiratorial grin.

"What about the spotters? Could any of them have seen us?" Diane asked.

"I called them down," Hutchens said. "Told them I needed everyone I could for the clean-up. They'll be out front helping the medics and the fire brigade in a few minutes if they're not already."

Diane nodded and smiled, although tears were now streaming down her cheeks. "Thanks, Eric," she managed.

Hutchens brushed a couple of the tears away. "Don't mention it." He opened the back door, put Jason inside the car then handed Diane the keys.

"Better get going."

Diane nodded and climbed into the car, while Hutchens lunged up the fire escape to make up for lost time.

"All right," he said as he emerged onto the roof. He walked over to a group of his officers who were huddled around a prone figure.

"Is this the Vampire?" he asked.

"Yeah," one of them replied. "We've got him."

"And is he alive?"

The officer shrugged. "That's what we're trying to find out. It's kind of hard with all this junk and the fright mask and whatnot."

"What about the Sentinel?" Hutchens asked. "Was he here? I thought he was swinging around below this guy."

"He must have got away before we got here," the man said. "There's no sign of him."

And there'll be no sign either, Hutchens thought to himself as he helped the officers remove the Vampire's glider and 'inadvertently' brushed away the dust impressions where Diane had dragged Jason to safety.

Then he watched as a man removed the Vampire's mask and gloves. The mask was pretty badly scuffed and the red light surrounding the left side of the goggles was broken.

The man under the mask appeared to be in pretty bad shape but Hutchens still held his breath while an officer checked his vital signs.

"He's alive," the officer said.

"Good," Hutchens replied, pulling out the radio. "Hopefully, we can get him to a hospital and keep him that way. I'd like to have a few words with him when he wakes up."

Diane pulled herself up onto the roof. It wasn't easy. She was beginning to feel the exhaustion of the night take its toll. And she realized she'd been hurt more badly than she'd thought. However, there was nothing for it now. Everyone else was busy clearing the wreckage, looking for survivors and helping the paramedics and the fire brigade.

She shook her head. It was like a scaled-down repeat of the West Avenue Bridge tragedy.

And Lady Vice had taken Mariane O'Hara and eight other hostages somewhere in a helicopter, she remembered. She guessed a bunch of people were looking for them too. All in all, it had been a very rough evening. And the night was still young.

Then Diane saw what she was looking for. The bag in which Jason kept his regular clothes.

Opening it up, she pulled the clothes out and rubbed them in the gravel on the roof. Jason probably wouldn't like it when she gave them back to him but she was about to take him to the hospital and his clothes had to convey the impression that he'd been injured in the bomb blasts. It was the only cover story that would work. Some guy who was just a little too close to the Fringe City Central studio. Wrong place. Wrong time.

With a groan, she lugged the bag over her shoulder and made the painful climb back down to the alleyway.

Thankfully, she'd picked it well. No one was around.

And Diane noticed something else while she was down there. Eight years ago, leaving Jason incapacitated and alone in the back of a car in an alleyway like this one would have been a good way to get him killed. But these days, it wasn't a problem.

The mobs were gone. The gangs were gone and so were the backyard brothels. And while the dealers were still around here and there, they were slowly but surely disappearing as well.

The city was better than it had been. Much better. They weren't hemmed in by corruption on all sides while too many criminals to count ran wild. It was only a small handful of people trying to ruin it for everyone and the police just had to bring them in.

And tonight, they had gotten one. One of the three. Cupid, Lady Vice and the Vampire. That just left two.

Diane opened the car door and gave Jason a little smile.

Jason managed a meek smile in return. "What's that?"

Diane chuckled and shook her head. "I remember once, you said something about your mysterious figure-of-the-night persona not working with me. And I seemed to be taking away every last shred of the mystery."

Jason nodded. "Ah…"

"And I doubt you can get yourself out of that costume and dress yourself again, right?"

"My very last shred of mystery," Jason said with a theatrical sigh. "Better not tell Angie."

"Believe me, Jason," Diane said as they started the awkward but necessary process, "you look like a battered corpse right now. I don't think Angie's going to worry too much about me catching a glimpse."

Ten minutes later, Jason was dressed in regular clothes, sitting in the front with the seat reclined while Diane drove them to the hospital. Glancing at her leg briefly, she realized she ought to check *herself* in too. But she had another errand to run before she could do that. And this would be the hardest one of the night.

. . .

The Fringe City Central helicopter came down on the helipad, its rotor blades slowing. In the back of the aircraft, Lady Vice wrapped a coil of rope around Mariane O'Hara's wrists, tying them together behind her back. The other hostages were being bound in a similar fashion.

As the rotors stopped, the pilots had their hands tied behind their backs as well.

"Blindfold them," Lady Vice said.

Mariane sighed as the cloth was wrapped around her face and a knot was tied behind her head, enveloping her in darkness. It seemed like such a pointless precaution.

"Thank you for your cooperation, ladies and gentlemen," Lady Vice told them. "My girls and I are leaving now but don't worry. The police—or at least the police who are still standing—will be combing the city for this helicopter. They'll find you soon enough. Enjoy the rest of your evening."

Mariane wanted to fight back, to lash out against this crazed woman who seemed insistent on personally terrorizing *her*, but she kept silent. And, as she heard Lady Vice and her gang exiting the helicopter and making their way over the roof, she was glad she did.

The ordeal would be over soon enough.

. . .

Angie came down onto the street to meet Diane at the car. She'd been crying.

Diane stood beside the car waiting for her.

At first, Angie said nothing. She reached over and held Diane in a tight embrace, sobbing on her shoulder.

Diane patted her on her back. "It's all right, Angie. He'll be all right."

"He nearly died," Angie said, the words coming out in strangled sobs. "I nearly lost him."

"He nearly had a quite *a lot* of problems," Diane said. "But now all he's got is some bad bruising and mild concussion. The doctors don't think there's any internal damage and he hasn't broken any bones."

Angie nodded, letting Diane go, her gaze down on the street. When she looked back up again, she was more composed. "So when do you think he'll be home?"

"It may be a few days," Diane said. "Tell Ethan he slipped on the sidewalk and had a bit of a bad fall. Maybe bring him to the hospital tomorrow to see him even. It'd do Jason some good."

Angie smiled through her tears and nodded again. "That's a good idea. Thanks, Diane. For everything."

"It's all right," Diane told her. "Oh. And also, go

easy on him when he recovers. He did everything right. He had everything under control."

"He did?"

"He did," Diane said. "He was just about to capture the Vampire himself. He was moments away from it really. But unfortunately, one of our more trigger happy officers thought our only chance was to take a shot at the Vampire right then and there."

"I see."

"Try not to be angry at the guy though," Diane said. "He made a difficult decision under a lot of pressure and he didn't have much time to think it over."

Angie sighed. "You're right." Then her eyes widened. "You're hurt too!"

Diane looked down at her leg. "Yeah. But it's not too bad."

"Are you serious?" Angie asked, crouching down and looking at the wound. "I can't believe you drove Jason to the hospital and came all the way here."

Diane knew she was right. She'd already been worried about how she'd get herself back to the hospital to get her leg looked at. The exhaustion of the evening was really kicking in and she realized as the pain in her leg worsened that she'd been practically high on adrenaline the entire time.

"Give me the keys," Angie told her.

"What?"

"Give me the keys and sit on the passenger side."

"But Ethan... Jason's gear..." Diane murmured.

"Ethan's fast asleep. I'm sure I can leave him for a couple of hours under the circumstances. And I'll take Jason's gear in now and be right down."

"But how will you get home again?" Diane asked.

Angie pulled Jason's bag off the backseat. "I'll use the subway," she replied. "Go on. Get in. I'll be back down in a minute."

Diane nodded and slumped into the passenger seat. It was still in the reclined position that Jason had left it in. Diane was grateful then for Angie's quick thinking. She had come to the end of her reserves.

Angie was back in no time and soon she was driving to the hospital. Diane closed her eyes and slept on the way.

The next day, a bit after eleven, Hutchens ambled into the mayor's office and slumped down in a chair. Alison St. Claire sat next to him. Her desk was on the far side of the room.

She handed him a glass of cold water. Somehow, she thought that would go down better than a coffee right then.

She looked at him for a little bit and sighed. "How are you holding up, Eric? Did you get any sleep last night?"

"A little," Hutchens said. "Not enough."

"I was sorry when you told me about Palmer."

Hutchens smiled a little. "Well, as it turned out, Lady Luck pulled a punch there. I thought he was gone but when the medics got there, they found faint vital signs. Apparently, he's just badly concussed and eventually, he'll be a walking, talking human being again." The smile faded and Hutchens shrugged. "Eventually."

"Well, that's something, right?" St. Claire said.

"Yeah," Hutchens conceded. "It's something."

"Where were the bombs by the way?"

Hutchens sighed. "They were just under the handful of cars that were still in the parking lot. I should have figured out that Lady Vice had planted some sort of trap out there. I just wasn't thinking. And there are thirty eight police officers who are dead right now because I wasn't thinking."

"Eric," St. Claire told him. "This is not on your head."

"Well, it sure doesn't feel that way. I haven't done anything right. These upstarts who want to ruin everything and drag the city back into the pits... They've been running rings around me. I haven't made a single shred of progress in tracking them down. I failed to stop Cupid twice. Lady Vice has gotten away again. And we didn't even catch the Vampire. We just stole the capture from Jason and badly injured him in the process."

St. Claire made a face. "Ah... about that. Are you absolutely sure your cover up was clean?"

Hutchens nodded. "Positive. At the most, it's possible some people saw Diane drag Jason off the roof of the studio. You know, if they were in any of those office buildings at the time and looking right at the roof of the Fringe City Central studio when it happened. But from a distance of several hundred feet, Diane could have been anybody."

St. Claire nodded. "Just making sure. And let's see. What else? The hostages you found in the helicopter are all safe and sound?"

"Yes."

"Okay."

They were both quiet for a moment. Then Hutchens stirred. "I don't know, Alison. Isn't it time we called in outside help? I know I've made that deal with you so I can't hand in my resignation just yet—much as I want to—but there'd be no shame in bringing in the FBI or the National Guard, would there?"

"No shame in it," St. Claire said, her tone now quite serious. "But a lot of risk. If you thought the open invitation Lady Vice sent out to the scumbags of the country was bad, just imagine the message we'd send out if the National Guard were in town. It'd be as clear a message as any that we're incapable of maintaining any semblance of law and order here. And then the dam would really burst. They'd be coming in from all round if that got out."

Hutchens shrugged. "We *are* incapable of maintaining law and order."

"That's not true," St. Claire said. "We can get through this. There are just a handful of bad apples in the cart and we've got to find them. And we will. And if Jason's theory that the Vampire was working with Lady Vice is correct, then we should have a lead on her and her gang when he wakes up. And as for Cupid, he can't resist telling us where he'll be. He'll push his luck too hard sooner or later and you'll get him too. I predict a month. Six months at the most and all of this will be behind us. Fringe City will be a wonderful place to live again and we'll emerge stronger than before because we *didn't* call in the National Guard. Because we overcame our difficulties ourselves."

Hutchens sat up in his chair and looked at St. Claire with newfound admiration. "You're right, Alison." He sighed. "Thank you."

St. Claire shrugged. "It's the truth. Now, tonight, I want you to get on the TV and make a statement. We've got the Vampire and we're about to turn this thing around. We're going to bring Fringe City back."

Hutchens nodded and climbed to his feet. "You found a station that's still allowed to operate and hasn't had half its producers murdered?"

"I've found one," St. Claire told him. "Yes."

"All right," Hutchens said. "I'll do it."

He turned to leave and stopped.

"Actually, while I'm here," he said, turning back to St. Claire, "there's something I've been wondering about."

"What's that?"

"This business with the CCTV cameras," Hutchens said. "A bit of extra surveillance around the city could really help us out right now."

"I know," St. Claire said, frowning. "However, I'm a little suspicious about the timing of Ken Doyle's calls for more surveillance and Citisafe Security Systems' attempts to secure a contract with the council to plaster the whole city with surveillance cameras... and how nicely these things coincide with this sudden and *almost* irrational string of violent crimes."

Hutchens looked at St. Claire in wonder.

"I'd never even thought of the Citisafe angle," he admitted.

"Yes, well don't go thinking about it too much just yet," St. Claire said. "These people have some pretty serious legal representation and the last thing we need right now is a slew of libel lawsuits."

"Yeah, I know," Hutchens said. "Still..." He shook his head. "But Ken Doyle must be loaded. What could possibly be *in* it for him?"

St. Claire shrugged. "I'd say he's probably just not loaded enough for his liking. You know what these kinds of people are like. They have a big house and ten million in the bank. Ninety-nine percent of the world's population would give their right arm for even fraction of what they have. But they're not satisfied. They want a hundred million or five hundred. They can never have enough."

Hutchens nodded. "And if he had ten million in the bank or thereabouts, he could easily buy a few small timers to carry out his scheme. A few hundred thousand up front and a few hundred more when the job's finished, just to keep them on and make sure they don't run off. Yeah, I can see that."

"But remember this is only a theory. We're going to need some more to go on before you go and arrest this guy."

"Well," Hutchens said, "we'll see what the Vampire says when he wakes up."

St. Claire frowned. "If he cooperates. He's facing life imprisonment surely. What kind of deal can we possibly offer him?"

Hutchens smiled. "Solitary confinement if he chooses *not* to help. But anyway, what you were saying earlier is that Ken Doyle's possible involvement with Citisafe Security Systems is the reason why you're not rushing through any big CCTV contracts."

"Right," St. Claire said. "Because if I'm right about what Mr. Doyle's up to and I authorize any big contracts right now, we could be looking at a lot of problems down the line. And I don't know for sure that Citisafe Security Systems is the group Mr. Doyle's dealing with. So at the moment, I'm wary about pushing through a big contract with *any* of them. Because if a security systems company is behind this and they get a council contract out of their little scheme, then we will have effectively bankrolled Lady Vice and the Vampire. And *that*, Commissioner, is what's holding me back."

St. Claire then relinquished somewhat. "Maybe after all this is over, we can install a handful of cameras here and there and have a bit of surveillance about the place. In moderation. Actually, I think it would be quite a good idea. But I don't want to make any decisions about that while mass murderers and their employers stand to gain a fortune from it."

George Hines stepped into the Outreach Center. His wife Sonya looked up from some paperwork on her desk. "Hey honey. Where have you been?"

"Leadensway," George said. "I was just asking around to see whether the little problems we were having there had cleared up any."

"And had they?"

"Yeah," George said, sitting down next to his wife. "So I think those dealers were tied up in that business with that Caldwell character."

Sonya nodded, sensing a change in her husband's mood. She knew what was on his mind.

"The guy Jason brought in," she said. "Even though that's not the official story."

"Yeah," George said.

"He'll be all right," Sonya assured him. "Gwendolyn talked to Diane this morning."

"Diane?" George asked. "She's in the hospital too."

Sonya patted him on the arm. "And she'll be all right as well. Don't worry."

Just then, Gwendolyn came in from the back door. "Hey, George. You're here."

"Yeah. I'm here."

"It's good to see you. I've got to run a small errand for Diane and then I'm going to go and see her and Jason at the hospital. Do you think you two can hold the fort while I'm gone?"

George glanced at the door and the crowds of people who weren't pouring in. They heard the warble of a pigeon outside.

He turned back to Gwendolyn and smiled. "I think we'll manage. Oh, when you see those two, tell them we're all thinking of them here at Outreach. Claudia rang up this morning as well. She asked whether there's anything we can do and she suggested that we can use some of the budget to cover their hospital bills if we need to."

Gwendolyn nodded. "That's a nice gesture."

"It's the least we can do, right?" George pointed out. "And if we provide blanket aid to all the victims from last night, no one will notice."

"Well, Jason and Diane were injured at the scene last night too," Gwendolyn agreed.

"Exactly."

Gwendolyn then glanced at the papers on Sonya's desk and saw the notes on the budget, the check book and the lists of victims and families, hospital addresses and contact numbers.

"Ah, you're already on it," she said.

Sonya smiled. "We don't waste time *here*. When duty calls…"

Gwendolyn smiled back. "True." Then a thought struck her. "Did Claudia mention anything about running another appeal? All this recent disaster relief is putting one big dent in the budget."

Sonya tapped her forehead with her pen. "We're already on that too. We've got some advertising slots on the TV for the next few days and there should be some print ads in the papers tomorrow. We'll run them till Saturday."

"Wow," Gwendolyn said. "You two work fast. And you did all this while I was discussing that other errand with Diane? I feel like a third wheel. You can run the whole show without me."

"You're not a third wheel," Sonya told her. She grinned. "You're… moral support."

Gwendolyn laughed. "Thanks. But anyway, that's great that you got everything up and running so quickly. But if there are any jobs left over that I can take care of, let me know."

"You've got a job," Sonya reminded her. "You're going to run that errand for Diane and then you're going to head on over to the hospital and tell her and Jason that we're all thinking of them."

Gwendolyn smiled. "Thanks, Sonya. All right. I suppose I'd better get going. See you two later."

Dr. John Carter took his usual seat opposite Derek Bradley. However, this was not going to be one of their usual meetings.

"I'm afraid I've got a little bit of bad news for you," John said. "Commander Felding—Diane—isn't going to be able to make it today."

Derek frowned. "Is she okay?"

"She's fine, she's fine," John insisted, raising a hand. "But she's been injured in the line of duty and she's recuperating in the hospital at the moment."

"I see," Derek said.

"She caught a piece of shrapnel in her leg when someone was taking shots at her."

"Who was taking shots at her?"

"Lady Vice or one of her girls," John said. "Her gang set a trap for the police force last night. Things got... Things got very rough. A lot of police officers were killed. Thirty-nine. Thirty-eight killed by Lady Vice and her gang. One killed by the Vampire."

"The Vampire?" Derek asked.

John passed him his newspapers. "Here. You can read all about it for yourself. I might get some coffee from the vending machine and give you a moment to catch up. Also, Gwendolyn Fletcher's going to be here shortly."

"Gwendolyn?"

"She's not authorized to make the decisions Diane can, of course, but she'll bring you up to speed on what's going on." John smiled. "They want you out of here, Derek." He nodded over the trees behind him. "They want you out *there*."

Derek smiled too. "What about that nurse I'm in love with?"

John paused. "You haven't mentioned her for a while."

"Well, now that I might be leaving this place, I'm beginning to realize how much I'm going to miss her."

"You could always visit," John suggested, "and tell her how much you appreciated everything she did for you over the years."

Derek nodded. "I might."

"You should," John said, getting up. "It'll do you good. And I'm saying this as your friend, not your psychologist."

Derek looked at him in surprise. "You really consider us friends?"

John smiled. "I think I've known you long enough to earn that right, haven't I?"

Derek nodded. "You have. By the way, don't buy your coffee from the vending machine. Get one from the little cafeteria inside. And get me one too. And maybe one for Gwendolyn."

"That's what friends are for?" John asked, his smile still in place.

Derek smiled too. "Damn straight."

Once John left, Derek read through the main article in the first paper. He read quickly for the most part but slowed down when he reached a certain line.

"'However, the Sentinel had disappeared from the scene by the time police arrived'," he read aloud.

He put the paper down for a moment. "After falling on the roof no less," he said to himself and smiled. "The police like you, don't they? You don't kill every kid who made a dumb decision and you don't get innocent nurses shot in the crossfire."

"You could learn a thing or two from that," came a voice from behind him.

Derek looked up in surprise. Gwendolyn Fletcher sat down across from him.

"The receptionist said I could come straight through," she said by way of explanation for the suddenness of her appearance. "John's not here?"

"He's getting some coffee for us all," Derek said. "I guess he timed it to give us some time alone." He shook his head. "I must be really out of it this morning. I can't remember the last time someone sneaked up on me."

"Oh well. I'm sure when you're fully alert, you're not as easy to surprise."

"Well, I hope not," Derek replied. "Otherwise, I'd be no good to you."

Gwendolyn smiled. "No good to Diane," she reminded him. "I'm just the messenger."

Derek nodded. "Right. And what's the message?"

"We understand you've had a change of heart," Gwendolyn told him. "Dr. Carter contacted Diane yesterday to say he thinks you're ready to be discharged. Diane wants to wait a little longer until she's ready to welcome you back to the outside world."

Derek raised his eyebrows. "A parole officer?"

"A liaison," Gwendolyn corrected him. "And I'm going to be a liaison as well. Your representative from Outreach."

"And what are you going to do?"

"Help you integrate yourself back into society. Assist you with housing and getting a day job. Checking up on you from time to time."

Derek nodded. "And what am I going to do?"

"Well, Diane doesn't want to put any obligations on you," Gwendolyn said. "But she thinks you want to help put an end to this urban terrorism that's going on at the moment. Is she right about that?"

"I want to help. But what kind of help will she accept? Am I going to be a consultant or does she want a nicer version of Orion out there? Orion version 2?"

"Right now," Gwendolyn told him, "that's seriously on the cards."

Jason leaned back as the nurse wheeled him into the cafeteria.

"Here you go," the man said, positioning him in front of the large window where he could look at the city in front of him. "When you want to go back and have a lie down, press this," he added, gesturing to a caller on the side of the wheelchair.

Jason nodded. "Thanks."

The man smiled and left.

Jason groaned after he was gone. "Man. I'm a cripple."

"Not for long," came a familiar voice from behind him.

Jason would have turned around if it had been less difficult but he needn't have bothered.

Diane was a little more mobile than he was and was able to wheel up beside him.

She grinned. "Look at us. Two of a kind."

"Yay us," Jason said.

"And we're bunkies now," Diane told him. "I managed to arrange for us to share a room. Didn't fancy spending a week surrounded by strangers."

"Me neither. So a week?"

"Yeah," Diane said. "I should be out by the end of the week. That's what they said. You too, right? You're just waiting for all the bruising to go down, aren't you?"

"They were checking my internal organs today," Jason told her. "Making sure they weren't porridge. And they've been running checks to see if I suffered any brain damage."

Diane smiled. "Eight years too late for that."

Jason smiled back. "Very probably true."

"How's your headache this morning?"

"Not too bad. I feel more exhausted than anything else. But then again, I'm doped up on pain killers. Wonderful things. I wonder if they might give me a lifetime supply before I check out."

"I wouldn't bet on it," Diane told him. She looked over her shoulder and gave him a little grin. "Well, well. It looks like you've got visitors."

Sure enough, Angie and Ethan were crossing the cafeteria, Ethan running ahead of his mother.

"Steady honey," Angie told him. "Dad's not..."

The words of caution came too late however as Ethan had already climbed onto the wheelchair and given Jason a big hug.

Jason groaned a little bit but he didn't bear his son any malice for the slight discomfort his enthusiastic greeting had given him. With a broad grin, he hugged him right back. "Hey, Ethan. My little guy."

"Are you okay, Dad?" Ethan asked.

"I'm okay," Jason told him.

"But you can't walk."

"I can walk," Jason said, brushing his hair a little. "It's just a little hard at the moment because I'm a bit sore."

"That's right," Angie said, lifting Ethan off his father. "Which is why you need to let Dad have a little space." She smiled at Diane. "Hi, Diane."

"Mrs. Felding!" Ethan exclaimed in surprise. "You're hurt too. Did you fall on the sidewalk as well?"

"I twisted my leg accidentally," Diane lied. "A few days ago. Then this morning, I found out your dad was here and I thought 'what a coincidence'."

"What a coincidence," Ethan repeated, smiling. "Is the wheelchair fun?"

"Lots of fun," Diane told him. "But not worth twisting your leg over."

Ethan laughed. "Okay. I'll be careful, Mrs. Felding."

Diane chuckled. "I'm glad to hear it."

Ethan turned to Angie. "Mom, can I have a look out the window over there?"

"Sure," Angie said, patting him on the shoulder. "But don't lean too close to it. That makes Mommy nervous."

"I won't," Ethan promised and lied, running to the other end of the cafeteria and climbing up on a lounge to see what he could see from there.

"So are you going to be all right?" Angie asked Jason once he was out of earshot. "You're sure?"

"I'm sure," Jason told her. "I'm bruised. Dazed. Sore all over and I had one hell of a headache before the doctors doped me up on painkillers but I should feel better and better. At the moment, I'm comfortably numb."

Angie leaned forward and kissed him. "You're too courageous for your own good sometimes, Jason."

Jason smiled. "Courage has nothing to do with it. It was sheer idiocy for the most part. I get away with it most of the time but last night, I was just unlucky. That's all."

Another familiar face appeared.

"Gwendolyn's here," Angie said, waving to their friend as she walked on over.

"I came to see how our two valiant convalescents were doing," Gwendolyn said.

She gave Angie a big hug. "Hey, Angie. You holding up all right?"

Angie smiled. "All things considered with this thrill seeking husband of mine. I think I know how the spouses of K2 climbers feel."

"Like marrying a partner who's more likely to be around in ten years' time?" Gwendolyn asked.

Angie laughed. "Yeah, something like that."

Gwendolyn chuckled and gave Jason a light slap on the shoulder. "Hey, stud. That was quite a show you put on last night." She then turned to Diane. "And how are *you* holding up after all that excitement?"

"I've been better," Diane admitted. "But I'm doing pretty well. How did your little trip go this morning?"

"Good," Gwendolyn said with a little nod. "Very

good. We're making progress. I think when you get out of here, we'll be ready to move onto the next stage."

Angie looked at them with a puzzled expression. "What's all this?"

Jason smiled and put a hand on her arm. "I'll tell you about it later, honey. It's a little pet project these two have been working on."

Angie frowned at him. "Sounds like you're in it too."

"Oh, purely as a spectator," Jason said.

"Actually," Diane interjected, "you might be able to help out."

"How's that?" Jason asked.

"With supplies." Diane glanced around to check there was no one close by and then she continued. "Grappling hooks," she murmured. "We've got everything else we need. Can your friend in Boston help?"

Jason shook his head. "I think he's too far away. However, I know someone else who can help who's a little closer to home."

Commissioner Hutchens was also at a hospital. But not the same one. In fact, he was at Graceville, which was not a place in his list of fond memories. And the little room he was in right then was not exactly bursting with cheer either.

He looked at the man lying on the hospital bed and glanced at all the tubes and wires about the place. Things he didn't understand, except at a very basic level. And at that basic level, they told him that the man in front of him was *not* in good shape.

He stepped out of the room with the doctor.

"So," he said once they were out in the corridor, "is this bastard going to make it, you think?"

"He's in a stable condition," the doctor said. "He's not going to die on us in the next twenty-four hours or anything." She paused before continuing. "As for recovery, it's a little too early to say. There were a lot of minor bone fractures, and his skull was cracked. But that doesn't necessarily mean he's sustained any serious brain damage. But it might be a little while before we can make any reliable predictions. However, I'll keep you posted as often as I can."

Hutchens smiled and shook her hand. "Thanks, doctor."

There was a rumble of thunder outside the window and then a tapping started that grew steadily into a dramatic overture, beginning a night of steady rain.

"It's raining," Jason said, as someone *always* has to say this.

"I noticed," Diane said, concentrating as she moved a bishop.

The TV was on in the background too but they had turned it down. There didn't appear to be anything good on yet but they occasionally scrolled through the channels to see if that was likely to change.

"Hey," Jason asked, "if I can get my pawn to the end of the board, it becomes a queen, right?"

"Well, yeah..." Diane told him. "But that's a pretty big 'if' there. Or didn't you notice this pawn?" She indicated one of her pieces. "And why did you think I left my rook here?"

"I never really thought about it," Jason said. "Uh... can you move that pawn on the black square in the center one square forward?"

Diane smiled and made the move. Jason could move the pawn himself but sitting up and leaning forward was still a bit of a strain. Needless to say, he wasn't going to go swinging around on grappling hook cables for the next day or two.

"Anyway," Diane said, moving another piece and taking Jason's remaining bishop off the board, "the fact that you never really thought about what my rook was doing there is the main reason why I'm going to take your king in five or six moves and you won't even realize what happened."

"How's that? With the rook?"

"Maybe with the rook. Probably with my bishop. It depends on how everything plays out. But you'll see. Five or six moves. Because the thing is, it's not enough to just think out your own strategy. You've got to try to work out what your opponent's strategy is. And you've got to be prepared to adjust your own. Have a back-up plan."

"Sounds like a nice parallel for some of your police work," Jason remarked.

"It is."

"By the way, how come Mark and the kids didn't come to visit you today?"

"Oh, I told Mark to stay at home," Diane said. "Coming here with Caroline would be one thing. Coming here with just Elizabeth... well, you know how toddlers are. It'd be a bit more difficult but not impossible. However, coming here with both of them? It'd be too much."

"That makes sense," Jason said. "Pity though. It would have been nice to see them. I haven't seen Caroline and Elizabeth in ages. Ethan misses them too."

"Well, we'll have to arrange another outing in the park sometime," Diane said. Then she frowned and reached for the remote. "What the hell?" she muttered.

"What?" Jason asked, looking up. "Oh."

A still image filled the screen. A glowing blue bow,

on a black background with an arrow on its string.

Diane turned up the volume.

"Good evening, Fringe City. I decided to wait a respectable amount of time before addressing you once more. I am not without sensitivities, unlike a certain egotist who shall remain nameless."

Once again, the still image remained in place, with the rich voice its only accompaniment.

"When I first made myself known to you all, I told you that I had but four targets. Two are now dead. Two remain. And the rules remain as well. One bullet. One attempt, come what may.

"For this reign of terror that has taken hold of this fair city, that the mayor has allowed on her watch, there are several to blame. And if my shots ring true, then they will pay.

"Mike Evans should have taken a stand against airing the footage that played to the egos of the killers who terrorize us and induced mindless fear in the hearts of Fringe City.

"Charles Faulkner should have acted sooner against the network behind Evans, the fools at the Fringe City Broadcasting Network who started it all, by giving a failed congressman of no consequence a public platform from which he could incite the underworld of this city to further acts of violence.

"And it is on this former congressman that I have now set my sights. If you are listening to me, Ken Doyle, you are my third target and I am coming for you now. *Nine p.m., Mr. Doyle, on the hour. And if my shot rings true, then an hour is the measure of the life that remains to you."*

"That's different," Jason remarked.

"Poor Eric," Diane said, shaking her head. "He's not getting a break. These people... Cupid and Lady Vice... they're running him into the ground. There'll be nothing left." She was quiet for a moment, gazing at the floor. Then she turned to Jason. "And there's something else too. In each of Cupid's messages, he's mentioned the next target, the one he's going to go after once he's taken his shot at the present target. He mentioned Charles in the message to Mike Evans. He mentioned Ken Doyle in the message to Charles."

Jason nodded. "And he mentioned the mayor in this one."

With a groan, Hutchens got off the couch. "You're a real prick, Cupid, you know that?" He picked up his keys, looking back at his wife Sandra. "Sorry, honey."

Sandra nodded. "Go on, Eric. Be careful."

Hutchens sighed. "I will."

Soon, he was in the car and on the move.

"You're running out of tricks, Cupid," he muttered to himself. "Now, you're just giving negligible warning and not even playing your own game properly."

He flicked on the police radio. "This is Hutchens. Who's there?"

"Mitchell, sir."

"Mitchell, it's nice to meet you," Hutchens said. "You're going to be my right hand man tonight, you lucky fellow. Now, I need to know exactly where Ken Doyle is right now. I'm going to stay on this frequency. You make the calls and let me know as soon as you've found out. If you can, tell him to stay where he is until we can get there."

"Yes, sir," Mitchell said. He left the radio on, picked up a phone and dialed.

"You've reached the office of Mr. Ken Doyle," a woman's voice said. "Our opening hours are…"

Mitchell put that phone on speaker just in case anyone was there to pick up and looked up another number, which he dialed on a second phone.

"Ken Doyle."

"Mr. Doyle, this is Sergeant Mitchell from the Fringe City Police Department. For your safety, I need to know your exact whereabouts. You've been targeted by Cupid and he's taking his shot at nine p.m."

"Jesus," Doyle said. "That's in fifty minutes."

"It'll be in less than that before you know it, Mr. Doyle. Your exact location. Please."

"I'm in traffic," Doyle said. "Ah, Queens Avenue. Ah… a lot of traffic actually. The rain's really holding things up."

"Are you driving yourself tonight or are you with a chauffeur?"

"Um, tonight I've got a chauffeur. We're heading for Monroe Hall to see a musical."

"Don't hang up, Mr. Doyle," Mitchell said. "I'm going to talk directly to the commissioner and get back to you." He put the phone on speaker, hung up the first one and turned back to the radio. "He's in a limo on Queens Avenue," he told Hutchens, "heading for Monroe Hall."

"Queens Avenue at this time of night?" Hutchens said. "Jesus. And our remaining chopper's still being repaired too."

"What should we do?"

"Hold on a second, Mitchell," Hutchens said. "I'm thinking."

"Sorry."

"No, it's all right. If he's heading for Monroe Hall, then we'll try to get a few units out along Seventh Avenue. Send a S.W.A.T. van too. Then when we get there, we can throw Doyle into the back. I'd like to see Cupid try to get his one shot through *that*. And the first officers on the scene can block Queens and divert all traffic north down Seventh and out of our hair. I'm heading to Queens now."

Doyle listened as Mitchell outlined the plan.

"Sit tight for now, Mr. Doyle. And when you get to Seventh, tell your chauffer to pull over and wait."

"All right," Doyle said. The call ended and Doyle took a nervous breath.

"What's the time?" he asked the chauffer.

"Eight twenty," came the reply from the front of the limousine.

"Jesus," Doyle said. "All that talking took ten minutes."

"Try to relax, Mr. Doyle," his chauffer told him. "The police will be here soon."

"The police will be at Seventh soon," Doyle corrected him. "We're only just past Third."

"The traffic's moving."

"Yeah, that's easy for you to say. You're not the one who's been targeted."

"It's moving," the chauffer repeated.

"Not fast enough," Doyle muttered, glancing out the windows as they crawled along. The rain was really pouring down now.

"We've got forty minutes," the chauffer reminded him. "That's more than enough time to drive four blocks, even at the rate this traffic's moving. Try to relax, Mr. Doyle."

"I'm trying," Doyle told him. "Believe me."

"Convoy's on its way," Mitchell said.

"Good work," Hutchens replied. "If I'm in the right part of town, and I think I am, I should be right behind it. You got a S.W.A.T. van?"

"Yes, sir."

"Good. Leave the radio on. I may need you later."

"We're only at Fourth," Doyle exclaimed. "Fourth! It must have been fifteen minutes since we passed Third."

"Ten," the chauffer corrected. "About ten."

"So what's the time? Eight forty?"

"Eight thirty-two."

"We'll never make it to Seventh. Maybe we should take a right at Fourth and get the hell out of here."

"I think that's a dangerous idea, Mr. Doyle," the chauffer said. "The police can't protect you if they don't know where you are."

"But we have to assume that Cupid's close by and he's watching," Doyle said. "And we can assume that he's factored in the traffic. Probably the weather too. So most likely he's positioned himself somewhere up on one of the buildings overlooking the street. So if we head off down a side street, there's no way he'll be able to catch up in time for his nine o'clock deadline."

The chauffer considered this. "What if you're wrong?"

"Well, if I sit here, I'm a dead man," Doyle countered. "Unless this thing has bullet proof windows. But if we go down Fourth, then at least I'll have a fighting chance."

"The traffic on Queens is practically at a standstill. It's total gridlock."

Hutchens sighed. He was almost there now and judging by what he could see on Seventh, things were not looking good. He glanced at the time.

Eight thirty-nine… eight forty.

He wasn't worried for Ken Doyle's sake. He couldn't stand the guy and the mayor's theory about him seemed right on the money. But Hutchens was still agitated. For one thing, if Doyle really was behind the new Lady Vice and the Vampire, then he wanted him alive so the bastard could stand trial. But more than that, he was sick of Cupid always coming out on top.

"No sign of that limousine?" he asked.

"Not yet, sir," the officer on the radio replied. "We've sent spotters into the buildings on each side of the street. They'll let us know where it is as soon as they've found it."

"All right," Hutchens said. "And is the rain the main thing that's holding everything up or is there a breakdown somewhere?"

"Don't know. But if there is, the spotters'll let us know."

"Then that's all we can do for now," Hutchens said. "Keep clearing that traffic. I'm almost there."

About two hundred yards west of Sixth Avenue, there was a hold up. A car had rolled out of a small alley onto the road and was blocking the lane.

The two drivers stuck immediately behind it got out.

"Is there anyone in that thing at all?" one of them asked.

"It doesn't look like it," the other replied, shaking his head. "It looks like some idiot didn't leave the handbrake on." He leaned over the window. "Jesus, I can't see a damn thing in this rain."

"Tell me about it," the first man agreed. "Man, I'm

drenched already."

"Yeah," the other man said, wiping at the window and trying to look inside the car. "That's odd. The handbrake *is* on."

He leaned under the car. Although it was night, there was plenty of light from headlights and nearby stores and it reflected off all the water on the asphalt as well.

The man saw a large blackened hole under the body of the car.

"Have you got a cell phone?" he asked the other driver.

"Yeah," the man replied. "Why?"

"Because we should report this."

Hutchens checked the time again. "Eight forty-seven," he muttered. "This is not looking good."

He hesitated before he opened the door. The rain was hissing down, pummeling everything in sight and in a moment, that would include him. However, getting soaking wet was really the least of his problems right then.

He climbed out of the car, got drenched, took a moment to acclimatize himself to this and then he jogged over to his officers, who were sheltering under the entrance of a small specialty store.

"An emporium?" Hutchens said, looking at the sign. "We're up market now."

Huddling under the entrance and trying to kick the excess water out of his shoes, he turned to his officers. "All right. Where are we at now?"

"That limousine still hasn't passed Fifth," one of them said. "And there's more. The traffic coming this way? The reason it's so slow is because Cupid blocked up the right lane."

"What? How did he do that?"

"An empty car rolled into the lane and the drivers behind it called us because it looked suspicious," the officer told him. "So Perez commandeered some guy's bike and went down to have a look."

"Good thinking," Hutchens said.

"Yeah," the officer agreed. "Well, anyway, he took a look and got back to us just before. The brake line had been blown with a small timed explosive."

Hutchens nodded. "Right. And who would do that?"

"Exactly."

"Has Perez still got that bike?" Hutchens asked.

"Yeah. He's still down at Sixth with that car."

"Why? We can move it later."

"The brakes are off so he's trying to push it into the alley," the officer said.

"Never mind that," Hutchens said. "If he's at Sixth

and he's got a bike, he's the only one here who has a snowball's chance in hell of getting to Doyle before nine o'clock." He waved his hand. "Here. Give me that radio."

The officer handed it over, flicking it on as he did.

Hutchens held it up. "Perez?"

"Lewis?"

"No. It's Hutchens. Listen up. Forget that car for a moment and jump on that bike of yours."

"Okay."

"Then ride like hell down the street until you reach Doyle. Get him out of the limo. Smash the window and drag him out if you have to. Then try to get him under cover. Break into a shop and throw him behind something heavy. I don't know. Up to you. But I'll take responsibility for everything."

"All right, sir."

"Good luck, Perez."

Ken Doyle was starting to hyperventilate. "Oh my god. I've got to get out of here. What's the time? Eight fifty-five? Eight fifty-six?"

"It's eight forty-nine," the chauffer said, his voice calm. "Why don't you lie on the floor and get down low if you're worried?"

Doyle shook his head. "No. No. He'll get me. He'll

get me. I'm going to make a run for it."

"Why don't you wait a minute, Mr. Doyle?" the chauffer suggested. "There's a policeman coming along now... On a bicycle, no less. Genius."

There was something odd about those last few words.

"Wait a minute..." Doyle started.

The chauffer slid across his seat.

"What are you doing?" Doyle cried out. "You're not Atkins."

The driver turned around and gave him a smile. A man considerably younger and more athletic in his appearance than his regular chauffer. Doyle realized then that he had hardly shared a word with Atkins. If he had, then he would have known much sooner what was wrong.

The imposter opened the front passenger door, holding it slightly ajar. He waited a moment and then he kicked it open fully, smashing it into the knees of the police officer who had just ridden up to the car.

He then leapt out of the car and as the officer got up and tried to take a lunge at him, the man kicked his legs out from under him, pulled out a handheld automatic and shot him. Then he stood back and waved the weapon at the other people on the sidewalk.

With his free hand, the imposter opened the back passenger door and smiled at the lone occupant inside the vehicle.

"Good evening, Mr. Doyle. I'm Cupid, as I'm sure you've guessed. For your information, the clock has just ticked over to eight fifty, which still leaves you a good ten minutes if you want to make a run for it. In fact, I'll give you a minute head start."

Doyle leapt out of the limousine and ran the rest of the way to Fifth, turned right and kept going. He collided with three young women hurrying the other way. They'd just got out of a taxi and were trying to get out of the rain. He knocked two of them down on their backs. The third shouted after him but he ignored her.

He then slipped in a puddle. His legs slid out from under him and he landed on the pavement, scraping his wrist.

However, he pushed himself straight back up and kept going. Up ahead, there was an alley to his right that he weaved into without slowing down. He then reached a fire escape on the side of an old three storey building, climbed it as fast as he could and scrambled onto the roof.

There were a few protrusions here and there. Extraction fans. A rooftop stairwell entrance. But Ken Doyle ignored them and pressed on, jumping onto an adjoining building and running to the far end of it. He hid behind a skylight and took a few moments to get his breath back.

Then he looked at his wrist watch, wiping the rain drops off the glass to see it better. Eight fifty-nine.

"Well," came a voice from behind him. "That was fun, wasn't it?"

Ken Doyle whirled around but he never saw Cupid. The bullet got him first.

His watch read nine o'clock.

"Not his most public kill," Hutchens said as he looked at the body.

Lewis, the officer he'd spoken to earlier, frowned. "I don't know. A lot of people saw the chase. Man, he's cocky. Was the Specter ever as bold as this?"

Hutchens shook his head. "The Specter was timid compared to this guy." He put a hand on Lewis' shoulder. "I'm sorry about Perez, Lewis. That... It wasn't right."

The next morning, Hutchens visited the mayor's office... again. As she had before, St. Claire scheduled it late in the morning so Hutchens could have a chance to get some sleep. And once again, Hutchens still hadn't had enough.

He knew that if he wanted, St. Claire would have a

glass of cold water ready for him or have a nice hot cup of coffee sent up. But since that might take one or even *two* minutes, he got a coffee from the cafe in the lobby on the way up. Then when he finished that, he could have a glass of cold water. And after that, he could have another coffee. Then, he might just about feel like a living breathing person again.

As he entered the office, without knocking, he saw Devan Fletcher inside.

"Ah huh," he said by way of greeting. "I see you've been welcomed to our little club. Believe me, it's not as fun as you think." He turned to the mayor. "Morning, Alison. Can I resign now?"

"Hang in there, Eric," St. Claire said, getting up and guiding him to a seat. "Come on. Sit down before you fall down."

"Yeah, all right," Hutchens grunted, slumping into his seat. He looked around, wondering where to put his now empty coffee container.

St. Claire smiled and took it from him. She put it in the wastepaper basket by her desk.

"You need another one?" she asked him.

Hutchens sighed. "You know me."

"Quite well now," St. Claire said. She picked up the phone and asked for coffee to be sent up. Then she handed Hutchens a glass of cold water to keep him going for the time-being.

They relaxed for a little bit and then after the cups of coffee had been brought up, they got started.

"I noticed the networks didn't air your statement last night," St. Claire said.

"None of them?" Hutchens asked.

"None of them."

"That's amazing. They all used their brains for once."

"Yes."

"Well, that's something," Hutchens said. "Can you imagine how stupid I'd look if I'd appeared on the TV telling everyone we've got everything under control right after Cupid dropped that bombshell on us?"

"There's a lesson in that for you too, Eric," St. Claire pointed out. "People do actually do the right thing sometimes. Do you want to talk about last night?"

"Not particularly," Hutchens said. "But I can tell you what we've found out. First up, the announcement was pre-recorded and the hijacking of the airwaves was either timed or done by remote."

"Any idea how he's been doing this?"

"We find cables that have been interfered with here and there but it's hard to pinpoint exactly what he's tampered with. And he's a sneaky prick. He cleans up after himself pretty quickly."

"Cocky too," Devan said, feeling that he had to add *something* to the conversation.

HAMISH SPIERS

"And what else?" St. Claire asked.

"Doyle's chauffer was found dead in the garage under his office. Doyle's personal assistant... ah... Samantha Bennett, I think her name is. She found the chauffer this morning. Poor kid. And the rest I think you know. We found out that Cupid scaled the front of a shop on Queens Avenue and used the roofs of the buildings straightaway. He must have watched Doyle from up there while he was trying to get away or he may have guessed where he was running to in order to cut him off. But that's about it."

St. Claire nodded. "All right. Well, that's it for Cupid then for the moment. Then let's talk about—"

"Wait a moment," Hutchens said.

"What is it?"

Hutchens sighed. "That's not it for Cupid. In every message, he always mentions the target he's going to come after next. And in his message to Ken Doyle, he mentioned you, Alison."

St. Claire was quiet for a moment. Then she shrugged. "Well, we'll cross that bridge when we come to it."

For a little bit, Hutchens didn't know quite how to react. In the end, he gave up on looking for the right words and waved a hand in a gesture of defeat. "Okay."

"All right," St. Claire said. "Now, let's talk about the

370

Vampire. What can you tell me there?"

"He's still unconscious but stable," Hutchens said. "The doctors think he might wake up in a day or so and then we can talk to him. He hasn't suffered brain damage... or so they say anyway. And... oh, right. We've also identified him."

"Anyone we might know?" St. Claire asked.

Hutchens shook his head. "No, he's just a small timer. He's done prison time before for assault. His record shows he was good at sports in school and basically nothing else. He was also a bit of an adrenaline junkie, we think. Or whoever wrote the original report thought. But that would fit, given his love of leaping off buildings and urban hang gliding. And we're in the process of checking his bank accounts for suspicious payments."

St. Claire nodded. "That's pretty impressive actually. You've all done good work."

Hutchens shrugged. "It's about the only thing we *have* done right recently."

"You've got to go easier on yourself, Eric," St. Claire said. She turned to Devan. "And now, this is where you come in, Devan. When the Vampire wakes up..."

She glanced back at Hutchens. "What's his name?"

"Does it matter?"

"I guess it doesn't really," St. Claire conceded. She turned back to Devan. "Anyway, when the Vampire wakes up, we're going to want to get as much information out of him as we can. So what we're looking at is a deal whereby he spends his time in prison in a regular cell if he helps us or in solitary if he doesn't. Possibly, this means we threaten him with more charges than we actually end up using against him. Does that sound workable to you?"

Devan nodded. "Yeah. I think it might involve telling this guy a big lie, as I can't really dictate the terms of his accommodation in prison but if you think it'll work..."

"I think he's too stupid to know that," Hutchens said. "Of course it'll work."

"Well," Devan said, "it's worth a try at any rate."

St. Claire smiled. "Good. Then that's settled."

The man known to most of Fringe City as the Vampire woke up two days later.

"He's quite capable of coherent conversation," the doctor told Hutchens when he and Devan arrived at the hospital. "Although he's not particularly good company."

"Well, with any luck, he'll be well enough soon to stand trial and then we can lock him away," Hutchens told her.

"That may be a little while longer," the doctor said,

"but, yes, he's definitely on the mend now."

She opened the door. "You can have half an hour with him if you need it."

Hutchens nodded. "Thanks."

"Hopefully, we don't need anywhere near that long," Hutchens said to Devan as the doctor left. Then, bracing himself, he led the younger man into the room.

The convalescent was in a slightly reclined position and he was held in place with secure straps. There'd be no aerial acrobatics for him today.

Hutchens gave him a big grin. "Morning, sunshine. You know who I am?"

"The tooth fairy?" the man grunted.

"You're a funny son of a bitch, aren't you?" Hutchens said. "I'm Commissioner Hutchens and I'm the head of the police department here in Fringe City." He gestured to Devan. "And this here is Devan Fletcher. He's the acting District Attorney here. That's sort of like a lawyer, except he works for the city rather than any old asshole who's got money."

The man on the hospital bed scowled. "You're a funny man yourself."

"Thank you," Hutchens said. "Now, I asked Mr. Fletcher here to give me an idea of what kind of charges you'll be looking at when you go on trial. I thought you might be interested."

He pulled out a piece of paper. "So, first up, we've

got four counts of murder in the first degree, with one of those being the killing of a police officer. We think we might also charge you with assault against a police officer there as well while we're at it. Next, we've got—"

"I didn't murder the girls," the man said.

Hutchens lowered the paper and looked at him. "Oh. Well, that's odd because the whole city saw some footage of you leaving the apartment of one of the victims."

"That's *all* I did," the man said. "That was a publicity stunt to make people scared. The guy who hired me gave me all the gear, I gave him some design input and he paid me some money to go to that girl's apartment and do that stunt. That's all."

"Interesting," Hutchens said. "Then who killed those girls?"

"That stuck up bitch who's prancing around as Lady Vice. And she was more directly involved with whatever scheme it was the guy who hired us was planning. So if you're going to ask me about that, then don't bother."

Hutchens shrugged. "Fair enough. Although, if that was all you were hired to do, then why the hell did you do all those other stupid things? Because if it was just that one publicity stunt, you might have got away with just five to ten years. But since that time..."

"Five to ten years?"

"Oh well, I'm guessing here," Hutchens said, not looking at Devan. "But that publicity stunt makes you an accessory to the murder of those three girls because it helped provide cover for the actual culprit. Also, since it was deliberately designed to mislead us, you'd be charged with interfering with a major police investigation. But still, even then, you'd have a chance of at least spending the *second* half of your life out of prison. Whereas now…"

He looked at his piece of paper again. "Well, first of all, you protected Cupid the night Charles Faulkner was murdered. Whether or not you were working with him, that makes you an accessory to murder. Then you showed up at the siege with Lady Vice and threw a police officer out of a high-rise building for absolutely no discernible reason. So that's unprovoked assault, assault on a police officer and first degree murder of a police officer."

He sighed. "I don't know what they'll do with you, to be honest. I think you're looking at a lifetime behind bars no matter what happens. But you may well be looking at a lifetime behind bars in solitary confinement as well."

The man looked very pale and it wasn't due to his injuries or fatigue.

"What if I help the police now?"

Hutchens frowned. "What could you possibly have

to offer that could help us *now*? You can't bring those three girls back. Or Charles Faulkner. Or that officer."

"I can tell you the name of the guy who hired me."

Hutchens waited a few seconds before replying. He didn't want to come across as too eager in case he gave the man second thoughts.

"Well, I suppose that's something," he said at last. "Who is he then?"

"Ken Doyle."

"The former congressman?"

The man shrugged. "Maybe. I don't know who he is. I never even met the prick."

"Then how did you know you were working for him?"

"The lady acting Lady Vice told me. She contacted me and arranged the payments. Two hundred grand before the job and two hundred after. Then she transferred another two hundred grand to kill Cupid."

"She paid you to kill him?" Hutchens asked. "Then why didn't you?"

The man shrugged. "I don't know. Mainly because I like Cupid's style and I don't like the lady's. She and her friends treated me like shit. Besides, with six hundred grand in the bank, I didn't really need her any more anyway."

"Well, that makes sense, I suppose," Hutchens said. "Now, what was the lady's name?"

The man shook his head. "I don't know. She never told me. I just call her 'the bitch'."

Hutchens rolled his eyes and glanced back at Devan, who shrugged. Then he pulled out a form and a pen.

"Do you want to make an official statement about all of this?" he asked. "Because if you do, then Mr. Fletcher here may be willing to drop some of those charges I mentioned. It may make the difference between a regular cell and solitary."

"Yeah," the man said. "I can give you a statement."

The nightmare was now well and truly unmasked.

"You were right, Alison."

St. Claire gestured for Hutchens to sit and then joined him.

"Ken Doyle?"

"We checked the amounts in that bank account," Hutchens told her. "The three separate payments of two hundred thousand. They were paid out of an intermediary account that's now closed. It was a business account, belonging to an entirely fabricated corporation. Ken Doyle set it up. He put money in it for the new Lady Vice to use for her own purposes and to pay his vampire stuntman."

"Clearly, he trusted his Lady Vice more than his

vampire," St. Claire remarked.

"That's not hard to believe. His 'vampire' probably doesn't have the mental wherewithal to buy a bus pass."

St. Claire nodded. Then she reached back and pulled a newspaper off her desk. She gazed at the front page for a moment before showing it to Hutchens.

"A front page eulogy for Mr. Doyle," she explained, "praising him for all the wonderful things he's done. The city mourns the passing of this wonderful human being and all that."

Hutchens absorbed this in silence.

St. Claire put the paper back on her desk. "I guess we'll never know exactly what he was up to with his scheme. He was probably after big millions in exchange for securing a council contract for a security systems company. The crime wave would either persuade me—or a replacement—to make the contract or make the city demand one. But we'll probably never know for sure."

She gazed down at the floor for a moment and looked back at Hutchens. "But whatever he was up to, he was responsible for a lot of senseless deaths. Those girls. Their families. The victims Lady Vice killed publicly. Possibly those thirty-eight officers Lady Vice killed the other night—"

Hutchens shook his head. "No, I don't think that

was his plan."

"You don't?"

"No. If you want to know what I think, I think the new Lady Vice and her friends have gone rogue as well. Remember when we thought she was trying to blackmail all of us?"

"Yes."

"I think I've worked it out now. The CCTV camera contract. She was going to contact us quietly once she'd stirred up enough panic. Then she'd threaten to blow the lid on what we all did eight years ago unless you made that contract. Then I guess Doyle would give her one last payment once the deal was secured. But the account he'd opened for her was closed, right?"

St. Claire frowned. "Right. Charles…"

"Exactly. When Charles was shot, Doyle probably called the whole thing off. And with Cupid running loose, I guess he thought there was enough panic to drive public demand for those CCTV cameras anyway."

"But if the current Lady Vice was working with Doyle, she probably knew everything he did about what happened eight years ago," St. Claire said. "Or at least she probably knew everything he supposed happened."

"Yeah, I would assume that too."

"So why wouldn't she try to blackmail us for her

own ends? For money?"

"Because unlike you approving a big contract with a CCTV camera company," Hutchens said, "which would be all Doyle needed, she'd actually have to *collect* her blackmail money. It'd be a hard thing for her to pull off without giving us a lead on her. But you raise a good point by mentioning money. She's probably going to want a lot more before she's done."

"So she's going to roll with her new persona and make her own schemes."

"Right," Hutchens said. "Because since she and her friends have put so much on the line for Doyle's scheme, she'll need to pull off one or two more big heists to make it worth it. Enough for her and her friends to disappear and live on an island somewhere."

"So," St. Claire said, "we haven't seen the last of her, then?"

"No."

St. Claire sighed. "Oh well. I guess she's another bridge we'll have to cross with Cupid. Still, the Vampire's been taken out of the picture. And the original orchestrator of all this idiocy is dead so it's two down, two to go."

"Halfway there," Hutchens agreed.

St. Claire smiled. "And *you* wanted to resign. Shame on you. You see? We're getting there. We're going to come out on top in the end."

"I sure hope so."

"Have a little faith, Eric," St. Claire told him. "Now... I think we went off on a bit of tangent there. I want to get back to Doyle for a moment."

Hutchens shrugged. "He's dead. I would have liked to have seen him in court but now that I've had a bit of time to think it over, I can't say I'm too sorry he's dead. The man killed. He ruined families. He terrorized the entire city and tried to undo everything we've all worked to achieve here. And all for a bit of cash. They don't get lower than that."

"I agree," St. Claire said. "But that's not what I was going to ask you about. Since you've been personally affected by so much of the senseless killing Doyle orchestrated, I wanted to ask you what you think we should tell the press. If anything."

Hutchens didn't answer at first. Then he sighed. "Say nothing."

St. Claire nodded.

Hutchens looked at her with tear-glazed eyes. "That man orchestrated the murder of his own niece, remember? The Vampire's very first victim. Probably to make sure that no one would ever suspect he was involved with all of this. Now, I've never met his brother but can you imagine the pain that would bring him if he found out who had *really* killed his daughter?" He shook his head. "There's no point in going public with the truth. All it would do is hurt more people. And I think enough people have been hurt as it is."

"And these papers praising him as some kind of beacon of humanity?" St. Claire asked.

"Who gives a damn? He's just as dead either way."

HOPE

Mariane o'hara took her seat at the news desk and took a breath. Tonight, Fringe City Central was going back on the air.

There'd been considerable refurbishments made to the studio and the armed security guards by the doors were fairly hard to miss. And getting back on their feet so quickly after that terrible night was bold. Deliberately so, in fact. But they had a message to send and just because they were being bold didn't mean they were throwing caution to the wind.

Mariane turned to the new anchor, David.

"Are you all right?" she asked him.

"Me?" he asked, with a timid smile. "I'm all right. But what about you?"

Mariane smiled back. "Me? I'm fine. Actually, I'm really fine."

"All right, we're ready to go!" the producer called.

Mariane turned back to the camera.

"On in three... two..." The producer mouthed the last number and then the 'On Air' sign lit up.

"Good evening," Mariane said. "And welcome to the news at six here on Fringe City Central. I'm Mariane O'Hara and here with us tonight, taking over from our dear and much missed friend Richard Henderson, is David Hall, who we'd like to welcome to the team tonight."

David nodded to the camera. "Good evening."

The camera switched back to Mariane. "Tonight is a special broadcast. Our first since the tragedy almost a week ago, in which eleven people here at Fringe City Central were killed, and a further thirty-nine people, all dedicated men and women of the Fringe City Police Department, lost their lives as well.

"Everyone here at the network would like to pass on our most sincere thanks to all of you for the wonderful support you have given us and the many letters we have received throughout the past week. It has meant a lot to all of us."

She paused before she continued. "We have now, all of us here in Fringe City, been given something of a reprieve from the meaningless violence that has so recently taken hold over our city. And we have been given one of the greatest gifts of all. Hope.

"The apprehension of the Vampire on the night of Lady Vice's terrorist attack was a major accomplishment. However, it is only now that we can appreciate just how much of a breakthrough it really was. With the identity of this man revealed, investigations into both his and Lady Vice's crimes have been opened wide up and we now know a large part of the story behind the baffling wave of crime that struck this city.

"Lady Vice and the Vampire worked in tandem to create widespread fear and paranoia, to create a breakdown in law and order for their own ends. Initially, the Vampire was an accomplice. Lady Vice murdered the women who were believed to be the Vampire's victims, by releasing poisonous gases into the victims' rooms while they slept. She then set up the bizarre crime scenes that initially threw off the police and everyone else. And the man we know as the Vampire was simply hired to create the now infamous piece of footage that was aired on the Fringe City Broadcasting Network.

"Subsequently, however, the Vampire used his specialized equipment, notably an advanced folding glider, and went on what was effectively a crime spree joy ride which was finally brought to an end by the efforts of the police and the Sentinel.

"And with these details now known to us, we can rest assured that there will be no more Vampire murders and that only two things remain for us to ensure the safety of our city and an optimistic future for us all: the apprehension of Lady Vice and her gang and the apprehension of Cupid. And now that the police have a small lead on Lady Vice and that Cupid is rapidly running out of tricks, these two goals may be accomplished sooner than we all think."

She smiled at the camera. "And I have a personal message for Lady Vice. If you're watching, I've just enrolled in a wonderful self defense class and one of my bodyguards used to work in the special services. Just so you know."

She turned to her new partner. "David."

David smiled too and turned to the camera. "And in other news, reconstruction of the West Avenue Bridge is currently ahead of schedule. The chief engineer of the project..."

"Jason?"

Jason turned the TV down and leaned back in his bed, letting out a sigh.

"Hey," Diane said. "We already knew all this."

"I know," Jason said. "But hearing it all officially summed up like that seems to make it feel... I don't know. More real or something."

Diane watched him for a few moments. "Are you thinking of Kaori Tanaka?"

Jason nodded. "The man who orchestrated her murder's dead. And I suppose, love or loathe Cupid,

Doyle got what he deserved. And that idiot who was playing the Vampire's going to be locked away for the rest of his miserable little life. But... Lady Vice and her girls are the ones who actually killed Kaori and the others. And they're still out there." He frowned. "And I know Cupid's got nothing to do with Kaori. But he killed Charles. And I want to bring him in too."

Diane reached over and squeezed his hand. "We will. Tomorrow, we're going home. You can have a nice rest with Angie and the kids while you get your strength back. And I'm going to see a man who might be able to help us."

Hutchens picked up the file that had been left on his desk and smiled to himself. "So... how's the money trail going this morning?"

When he looked inside however, there was nothing there about accounts. It was a notarized copy of a contract. A very impressive contract.

He scrolled through it, reading aloud as he came across a certain section. "... Mr. Ken Jonathan Doyle to the sum of twelve million U.S. dollars upon confirmation of a suitable contract—no less than a sum of fifty million U.S. dollars with the Fringe City council."

He put the paper down for a moment. "Twelve

million? He ruined my city for twelve million?" He shook his head. "Son of a bitch. I'm glad he's dead."

He looked at the bottom of the contract. "Citisafe Security Systems. Well, it looks like *someone* won't be getting a council contract anytime soon."

Then he read the note that had come with the thing. "… found the original document in a hidden safe in Mr. Doyle's home. We have made a number of notarized copies and have lodged several with the appropriate bodies, while keeping several other copies here for…"

He read the rest in silence and put the file away.

"Morning, Commissioner."

Hutchens looked up in surprise. "Palmer?"

Palmer beamed. "In the flesh."

Hutchens climbed to his feet and shook his friend's hand. "Gene Palmer. It's sure good to see you back on your feet. But out already? Shouldn't you be resting?"

"It's been a week, Eric," Palmer replied, dropping his usual formality.

Hutchens shrugged. "Hm. I guess it has been. Well, I tell you, seeing you back from the dead, standing here on this sunny morning… I feel like we're finally turning this thing around."

"That's what they're saying," Palmer agreed, sitting down in front of Hutchens' desk.

"Coffee?" Hutchens offered.

"Love one."

Hutchens poured two cups. Then handing one to his friend and taking the other, he sat down and they talked.

"So, what's the current strategy with Lady Vice and Cupid?" Palmer asked. "Are we going to wait for them to show themselves again or do you think we can track them down?"

Hutchens took a sip of his drink. "Well, there's nothing we can do about Cupid at the moment," he said, putting the cup down. "We've got no idea where he disappears to between shows. But when he teleports down to Earth from the mother ship again, we'll deal with him. And Lady Vice... well, the bank account lead didn't give us anything really. She had the necessary details to access it but she didn't set it up. And I've still got people looking at Doyle's other accounts, of course, but so far it hasn't been the breakthrough I was hoping for. So, for the moment at least, it's the same deal for Lady Vice as it is for Cupid. We're just waiting for them to show themselves again."

"Why wouldn't Lady Vice go to ground?" Palmer asked. "I've read the official reports. The ones that weren't in the papers. I know about Doyle. If he's not paying her and her gang any more, then why should she continue the charade?"

"Well, there was no reason for her last stunt either,"

Hutchens pointed out. "That bank account had already been closed by then. I'd say that she enjoys the attention somewhat and that tells me we'll probably see her again for that reason alone. However, I also think she's going to want to pull off one last heist. Something to retire on. Something for the books."

Palmer gazed at him. "You know," he said. "I think you've got an ace up your sleeve you're not telling me about. You say we're waiting but that seems like the official line to me. And there's a bit of a twinkle in your eye."

Hutchens smiled. "A twinkle in my eye?"

"What are you really up to?"

"Well," Hutchens said, "we've been friends for years, Palmer, so I suppose I can trust you to keep this to yourself. But before we talk about it, why don't you lock the door?"

Jason and Diane stepped out onto the sidewalk and took in the morning sun.

"Well, here we are," Diane said. "Back in the world of the living."

"Good to be here," Jason agreed. He looked to his right. "The bus stops are down there. Although it might be nice to stretch our legs for a bit. I'm sure there are some more bus stops in the neighborhood."

"Maybe," Diane said. "Or we could get a taxi. Actually, I don't really feel like a long bus trip home."

"Yeah," Jason agreed. "Come to think of it, I don't really feel like taking the bus either. Oh well. Let's go for a walk and hail a cab when we've had enough."

"Sounds good," Diane said. "But it'll have to be a short walk. I've got an important appointment today."

Jason nodded. "Right. Actually, I might arrange one as well."

"I thought you were going to have a rest at home."

"Oh, I am," Jason said. "But remember..." He lowered his voice. "Grappling hooks and cables."

"Ah," Diane said. "Right."

Just then, a girl coming up the path on a bicycle saw them and came to stop. "Jason!"

Jason smiled, recognizing the girl at once. "Hi, Ji Eun. What a surprise seeing you here."

"I was going for a ride to the river," Ji Eun replied.

"I see. You're looking very well. You seem much better than you were last time."

"I'm... ah," Ji Eun said, smiling as she tried to think of a particular phrase. "I'm 'holding up'."

"I'm really glad, Ji Eun," Jason told her. He turned to Diane. "Ji Eun's one of my students. She was a friend of Kaori Tanaka."

Diane nodded. "Ah." She turned to Ji Eun. "I'm really sorry about your friend."

"Me too," Ji Eun said. Then she smiled. "Ah. I know you. You're Diane Reilly. I saw your photo in the paper."

"Actually, I'm Diane Fletcher now," Diane said, "but I *was* Diane Reilly before." She frowned. "You saw me in the paper? I haven't been in the paper recently, have I?"

"Oh, this was an old paper in the library," Ji Eun said. "Kaori and I looked at old papers to help us write about Lady Vice."

Diane exchanged a glance with Jason. She remembered what Kaori had written about Lady Vice. She remembered it well. And if Ji Eun was as good at joining dots as Kaori had been, and she had now seen her with Jason...

"Wow, Jason," Ji Eun said. "How do you know Diane?"

"Oh, we're old friends," Jason said. "We used to be neighbors."

Nice recovery, Diane thought to herself. But she wondered whether it would stop Ji Eun from working certain things out. The girl seemed pretty bright.

Ji Eun extended her hand and smiled again. "It's nice to meet you, Diane."

Diane smiled back, shaking her hand. "It's nice to meet you too, Ji Eun."

"I have to go now," Ji Eun said. "But it was very

nice to see you."

"It was very nice to see you too," Jason told her. "Take care of yourself."

"I will," Ji Eun told him. "You too."

Derek Bradley shook Dr. John Carter's hand.

"Well, Dr. Carter," he said. "John. I guess this is it."

"Yeah," John said. "You're heading back into the outside world. You sure dragged out the time it took to get you there though."

Derek chuckled. "Well, thanks for waiting it out and not giving up on me years ago. You probably should have though. For your own well-being."

John smiled. "Probably. But I'm glad I didn't. Look after yourself, Derek."

"You too, John."

Derek walked over to the car and climbed into the back.

"Well, well," Diane said. "Rehabilitated. Ready to be reintegrated into society. How does it feel?"

"To tell you the truth," Derek admitted, "I think I'm going to miss the institute. I haven't cooked a meal at home for so long, I don't think I'd know how any more."

"It'll come back. And don't forget that Gwendolyn and her friends at Outreach are going to help you get settled back into everyday life."

"I haven't forgotten," Derek said. "But at the moment, I'm not really worried about that. First of all, I've got a debt to pay. And I intend to pay it."

Jason dialed and waited.

"Hello."

"Scott? It's Jason."

"Jason," Scott Wilson said. "It's been quite a while. Is everything all right?"

"If by everything, you're referring to a few things you may have seen on TV," Jason said, "then everything's fine... now."

"All your equipment in working order? Anything you need repaired?"

"I need some more grappling hooks," Jason said.

He was originally planning to say he needed some grappling hooks replaced but that was a lie, whereas this, while omitting some key facts, was technically true.

"Would you like longer cables than before by any chance?" Scott asked. "You know, on account of a few things I may or may not have seen on TV."

"If you can and they won't snap, then—"

"They won't snap," Scott told him. "Trust me."

"Sorry," Jason said. "No offence meant."

"None taken. I understand why you might want the assurance. Anyway, I won't push the limits. I know about elevator cables and the cables used in bridge suspension and the ones you're using are neither. So I'm not going to try to test the limit of what I think's possible. But I can make you longer cables than the ones you were using. How many do you want?"

"Four."

"Four?"

"Four," Jason said. "If you can. I'd like some spares."

"No problem. I'll have them ready for you as soon as I can."

"Also, I'd like one or two more double-ended grappling hooks. You know the ones?"

"I know them. They won't be a problem either."

"Thanks, Scott."

"Anything else?"

"Yeah. If I run over some of the stun gas canisters, could you make a few more?"

"I can make some," Scott said. "You don't need to bring any over though. Geoffrey left me the specs."

"He did?"

"Yeah. He prepared for all eventualities with *you*. He also left me lists of material and information on where to find it quickly."

"That's impressive," Jason said. "I'll have to thank

him for that."

"You should," Scott said.

"And thank you too."

"No problem. All right, I've got to go. See you, Jason."

"Bye, Scott."

Jason hung up and went inside to see Angie and Ethan.

Now, he could relax.

"Derek Bradley," Hutchens said, standing up as Derek and Diane came through the door. "Welcome to the team," he said, shaking the man's hand. "Now as to what has happened between us in the past, I want you to know that I don't dwell on these things. Diane says I can trust you and her word's good enough for me. So we'll let bygones be bygones."

"Thank you, Commissioner," Derek replied. "However, for myself, I do need to dwell on the past a little. Now that I'm seeing things a little more clearly, I want to make up for it. That's part of the reason I'm here."

"And the rest of the reason?"

"I want to bring in Lady Vice's gang," Derek said. "And I want to stop Cupid before he kills the mayor."

"You figured that one too, did you?"

"Cupid's not exactly subtle," Derek pointed out. "But let's talk about Lady Vice first. If we can get her out of the way quickly, then we can concentrate on Cupid. Give him the attention he deserves."

"That sounds good to me," Hutchens said, gesturing for him and Diane to sit down as he sat behind his desk. "Diane says you may have some fresh ideas there so let's talk shop."

"There are a few possible leads as I see it," Derek said. "Nothing certain of course. But I'll go through them with you anyway. First of all, it's possible, though not likely, that Lady Vice and her gang went no further than the building they landed that stolen helicopter on. So one thing you may want to consider is a floor by floor search of it, investigating the apartments of everyone who lives there for any incriminating evidence."

"That would take a lot of time."

"Remind me to tell you how I found the Specter one day."

Hutchens smiled and nodded. "Fair enough. What's next on your list?"

"Get lists of female graduates from chemistry related schools in all the universities in the city, going back at least twenty-five years."

"You think this new Lady Vice could be rising fifty, do you?"

Derek shrugged. "It's a possibility. Despite the common male preoccupation with youth, I've seen some very fetching older women over the years. We shouldn't rule out the possibility that our suspects are at the older end of the spectrum."

"All right. And then?"

"Then cross reference the names with residential records, looking for anyone from the lists who happen to live in the neighborhoods between Mariane O'Hara's place of residence and the location where that drug dealer was abducted, the one she killed during that interview on FCBN."

"I liked the *first* idea better," Hutchens exclaimed.

"You could set up a program to automate that process," Derek said. "I'm no I.T. expert but I could probably write a program myself that would do the trick."

"Okay. And the reason you're interested in chemistry graduates?"

"The stun gas that was used on Mariane O'Hara," Derek said. "It wasn't stolen from Jason. It wasn't obtained through Forensic samples provided by any of your people. These ladies figured out how to make it themselves and arrived at something so close to Jason's that it threw you all for a curve."

Hutchens didn't reply.

"So," Derek said in the silence, "chemistry major."

Hutchens nodded. As Derek outlined all these things he had failed to consider, his pride was taking something of a beating. However, he was professional enough to know his pride didn't matter right then.

"Well, that follows," he said. "Were there any other things we may have missed?"

"Possibly," Derek said. "Do you have copies of statements from Ken Doyle's various bank accounts?"

"As a matter of fact, I've got some right here in my desk," Hutchens said.

Derek nodded. "I'd like to have a look at them if I may."

Hutchens shrugged. "Sure." He pulled out a folder from his drawer and passed it over.

Derek took it without a word and began perusing its contents.

"Six hundred thousand was paid into this account here," he said, pointing one out. "The one Lady Vice used to pay the Vampire?"

Hutchens leaned over his desk and looked at it. "Yeah, that's the one."

"And *all* of that money went to the Vampire."

"Yes," Hutchens said. "So we have no idea how he paid Lady Vice."

"Yes, we do," Derek said, passing him a page from another bank statement. "Through this account that he paid one point five million into."

"That's relief funding for victims of the West Avenue Bridge disaster," Hutchens said.

"Is it?" Derek asked. "Are you sure?"

"Well, that's what my officers told me. And apparently, there are twelve signatories on the account and none of them can transfer any funds out of it without approval from the other eleven."

"Twelve," Derek said, "as in the number of women in Lady Vice's gang, if you include her as well?"

Hutchens frowned. "But wouldn't that be too obvious?"

"Only if anyone knew Ken Doyle had hired them. Until the Vampire blew everything, their operation was secure."

"Son of a bitch," Hutchens muttered.

Derek smiled. "I wouldn't get too excited yet though. If I'm right, I imagine all the money in that account has already been taken out. In numerous small *cash* withdrawals." He got up. "However, even if that's the case, there's still something else I'd like to run by you. But I think it can wait until after lunch."

Hutchens nodded. "Sure. I'll need a little time to check out that account you found anyway."

"Oh, and there's one other thing," Derek said, stopping on his way out. "I don't need this right now but at some stage, I'd like to get my gear out of whatever evidence locker it's in."

Hutchens glanced at Diane and got a small nod in return.

"Well, sure," he said. "But can I ask why?"

"Ask me after lunch," Derek replied. Then he left the office.

Diane got up to follow him, giving Hutchens a smile on the way out. "Thanks, Eric."

"This is some good fish and chips," Jason said.

"I'm glad you like it," Angie replied. She smiled at Ethan running off across the grass. "And the way Ethan gobbled lunch down, I'd say he liked it too."

"You know, Jason," she said as they watched Ethan climbing on the play fort and going down the slide, "considering how Amanda gave you that time off so you could get some rest, it seems strange that the only rest you've given yourself was a stint in the hospital."

"She didn't give me time off to have a rest," Jason said. "She gave me time off to come to terms with what happened to Kaori. And that's what I've been doing. Coming to terms with it."

"And have you?" Angie asked. "Come to terms with it?"

"I'm getting there," Jason said. "The man who orchestrated the Vampire murders is dead. I've exposed the monster everyone saw on the TV as the nobody he really is. And I know that Kaori didn't suffer. She probably never even woke up. But it's like I told Diane. The new Lady Vice and her gang, the people who actually murdered her, are still out there. And although Cupid had nothing to do with it, he killed Charles. And we need to bring him in too before we can close the book on all this."

"And what if you get yourself killed in the process?"

"It wasn't my fault I nearly got killed," Jason said. "It was a trigger happy cop."

Angie turned to him. "And what difference does that make? It could be a crazy guy with steel claws on a glove who runs around in a fright mask and an opera cloak. It could be a group of women with long nails and high powered rifles. It could be a man with a sniper's rifle who's already shown he's prepared to kill bystanders if it helps him get his targets. You don't control all the variables out there."

Jason sighed. "I know. But I need to do this. Anyway, we've nearly won. We've turned it around."

"If you say so," Angie replied. "But it seems to me that all you and the police have managed to do is bring in a decoy, make the new Lady Vice gang even more desperate than they already were and force Cupid into being less and less sporting. How much of a warning do you think he's going to give the mayor now? A minute or do you think he might give her a whole half hour? It seems to me that things are still going to get ugly again before we get through this."

Diane and Derek stepped back inside Hutchens' office and resumed their seats.

"Well," Hutchens said to Derek, "it seems you were right. The money was all withdrawn in small amounts. There was only about five or ten dollars left. Also, we found the residential addresses of the signatories and every place was cleared out. The women have gone to ground."

Derek chuckled.

Hutchens frowned. "Is there something funny about that? Because I must have missed it."

Derek waved a hand in apology. "No, no. I was just thinking about the interesting little twist here. The women behind the original Lady Vice persona are now the operators of one of the biggest charity organizations in the city. The women behind the new incarnation, the imposters, were the heads of a phony charity fund. In costume and out, they're fake."

Hutchens nodded. "Yeah, I suppose I can see that. Although, I can't say I'm in a particularly humorous mood at the moment. An hour ago, you gave me my most promising lead and it's dried up already."

"I told you not to get too excited," Derek reminded him.

"You did, yes," Hutchens said. He sighed and looked at the other man. "However, you also said you had another idea you were going to run by me."

"I did," Derek said. "A sting operation."

Hutchens frowned. "Technically not legal but go on."

"That didn't stop you eight years ago, did it?"

"So you want us to put on another show," Hutchens said, ignoring the remark.

"It worked on me," Derek said. "There's no reason to assume it wouldn't work on this new Lady Vice. All we need is a tempting target."

"A charity drive perhaps," Hutchens said. "With lots of money from the city's biggest movers and shakers being thrown around like confetti."

Derek smiled. "Exactly."

"But what if the fake Lady Vice figures out it's a trap?"

"Good," Derek said. "In fact, you should do everything to make sure she *does* think it's a trap."

"But why would she walk into it then?"

"Two reasons. First of all, the bait will be tempting enough that she'll consider it worth the risk. Second, she *has* to walk into it. Otherwise, she loses."

"Loses what?"

"Her contest with you, Commissioner," Derek said. "The one she started when she killed thirty eight of your police officers. She wasn't after money that night. And she wasn't solely after kicks. She was trying to scare you, to prove that she runs the town and can do whatever she wants. That if you cross her, you'll pay a heavy price. So next time, when she holds hostages for *ransom*, she'll know you'll be more likely to cooperate."

"Because I challenged her in my public address on TV?" Hutchens asked, horrified at the idea that his own actions were what brought about the deaths of those officers.

Derek waved his hand in a dismissive gesture. "Don't worry, Commissioner. She would have waged her war on you and your department anyway. The deaths she's caused are on her hands, not yours."

Hutchens sighed. "All right then. So we set our trap, lure her in and spring it."

"We?" Derek asked. "I don't want your officers to do anything that might put them at risk."

Hutchens frowned. "Then who will bring these ladies in?"

"Jason and I will."

"Orion and the Sentinel?"

Derek smiled again. "Actually, with this being a fresh start, I thought I might choose another name. I'm quite partial to Achilles."

. . .

Several days later, Jason met Scott Wilson outside the university.

"Well," Scott said, handing over a small bag, "here you are. As promised."

"Thanks, Scott," Jason said.

Scott smiled. "You're welcome. So… when are you planning to try all your new toys out?"

"Soon," Jason told him. "Very soon."

He then met Diane in the apartment that the police department had rented out for them to use as a rendezvous point, where they could meet up without having to worry about eavesdroppers.

It was going to be an interesting meeting. He was about to meet a former enemy of his.

Diane assured him that Derek Bradley was a changed man now and Jason trusted her judgment on the matter. But all the same, he felt a little apprehensive as he went inside. However, he had told Diane that he'd have no problem working with the man and he was committed now.

"I've got the gear," he said.

Diane nodded. "So, I see." She then gestured to the man standing on the other side of the room. "Jason, I believe you've met Derek Bradley."

Derek Bradley had incapacitated him with a painful blow before racing off to Graceville Hospital, where he had inadvertently gotten that nurse Danielle Sutherland killed.

"Yes," Jason said.

On the face of it, the plan where they would work together had seemed natural enough. However, now he was face to face with the man once known as Orion, the apprehension that Jason had felt coming into the apartment was back in full force.

Derek must have sensed this too. To put Jason at ease, he walked over and shook his hand. "It's good to be working with you, Jason. I'm sorry about what I did eight years ago. I hope with time, you'll forgive me."

"I'll have to if we're going to work together," Jason said. "But for the moment, I'm happy to let bygones be bygones."

Derek smiled. "That's what the commissioner said. All right. Bygones."

"So," Jason said, "let's go through the plan."

"Not just yet," Diane said. She rummaged through a bag and pulled out several devices. She handed one to Jason and one to Derek. "Here. Take these. Before we get started, I've acquired these police radios for our personal use. They're all tuned to the same frequency so we can all talk to each other at the same time. This will help us coordinate our efforts on the night."

"Wow," Jason said, smiling as he put the radio away. "So we're an unofficial unit now."

"That's basically right," Diane said. "And since I'm already the liaison officer for both of you and I'm not tied down to any other unit, I'm going to be heading *this* one."

"Fine with me," Jason said.

"Me too," Derek added.

"Wonderful," Diane said as they all sat down. "Now we can talk shop."

"And in other news, Outreach's triple charity drive event will commence tomorrow night as scheduled," Mariane O'Hara said, *"with the assurance of the police commissioner himself that all security precautions are in place to ensure a pleasant and enjoyable evening for everyone who chooses to come to this very worthwhile event."*

The screen cut away from the news desk to a pre-recorded statement by the commissioner.

"I'd just like to assure everyone who will be coming along to the Outreach event tomorrow evening," Hutchens said, *"that they will be under the full protection of my finest officers."* He smiled at the camera. *"And if one Lady Vice should happen to be watching this, I'd just like her to know*

that I already have spotters around the building working in shifts and plenty of officers patrolling the neighborhood, both uniformed and plain clothed. If you're planning on gate crashing our party then I can only say that I'd love to see you try."

The following evening, the night of the event, Jason took up his position on top of one of the high rises in the vicinity.

The charity drive itself was being held in a six storey building surrounded by fifteen and twenty storey ones. In many ways, it was closely reminiscent of the layout of the neighborhood surrounding the Fringe City Central studio. However, there was one important difference between that fiasco and this situation. This time, the police had gotten here first.

Commissioner Hutchens glanced at his watch then gave his officers a grin. "I think it's time to go check out the newly repaired chopper."

One of the officers looked doubtful. "Do you really think that Lady Vice and her gang will try to steal the thing? Right off our roof?"

"She's an audacious little minx," Hutchens said. "The theory we're running with here is that she thinks stealing our helicopter will give her an element of surprise and a bit of an edge when we discover the air support we were counting on is missing. Also, it'll be another great opportunity for her to pull one over me."

The officer nodded. "And if the theory's wrong?"

Hutchens shrugged. "Then we just jump in the helicopter and go to the party. No harm done. Come on. Let's go."

They headed up onto the roof where the helipad was.

Hutchens looked at the vehicle and nodded to two men in S.W.A.T. armor. "Diaz. Simmons. You're up."

The men nodded and jogged over to the helicopter. One of them flung open the door and the other threw a canister into the vehicle. It hit the floor and exploded, filling the helicopter with stun gas.

The S.W.A.T. officers were already out of its range by the time it poured out from the vehicle.

Then everyone waited until it dissipated and strolled over and had a look inside.

"Here they are," one of the officers said, "squashed behind the back seats, under some of the gear in here. Uncomfortable hiding place."

Hutchens had a look. "Five of them. All right. Let's drag them out."

The officers got to it and soon all five women were out of the vehicle and cuffed.

"This one looks like the ringleader," one of the officers remarked, pointing one of them out.

"Yeah, I think you're right," Hutchens said. "All right. Boyd. Fisher. Take them downstairs one at a time and process them. Diaz and Simmons, you can help too. Everyone else, into the chopper."

Gwendolyn Fletcher stepped up onto the stage. She remembered doing this before under similar circumstances. Except then, she and the others had been playing Lady Vice's gang. Now, they were hoping to catch another group of women doing the same thing.

She looked over the crowd of people who filled the hall and frowned. Then she glanced at Devan, standing off to the side of the stage.

He walked over to her.

"Where's the mayor?" she murmured. "I thought she was going to be here."

"I'm not sure," Devan told her. "But I don't think we should wait for her. The sooner we get this going, the better."

Gwendolyn nodded. "Right."

She picked up the microphone as Devan walked away. "Ladies and gentlemen, on behalf of myself and everyone at Outreach, I'd like to welcome you all here tonight. We're so glad to see so many of you here with us and we thank each and every one of you for coming.

"Unlike most events like this one, we're actually running several drives at once. You can choose to support the one of your choice or all of them if you wish. We are running a drive over *here* to help fund the rebuilding of the West Avenue Bridge. And over here, we are raising money for the families of the brave police officers who were killed in the Fringe City Central studio siege. And over *here...*"

"Alice? Are you in position?"

The woman holding the handheld radio was sweating, the radio shaking in her trembling hand.

A gloved hand covered the radio for a moment.

"Say your line, Alice," the man behind her suggested.

"Yes. There's a police spotter one floor down, thirty yards to your right."

"I'm on him."

Alice switched off the radio.

"Well done," the man behind her said.

Alice didn't reply. She raised her binoculars again and watched the building across from her, on the far side of the smaller one where the Outreach charity drive was being held. Where her associate made her way to where she believed a police spotter was waiting.

The woman got down to the lower floor and then disappeared. Someone had taken her out. And the attack had been very quick.

Alice lowered the binoculars.

"That's one," the man behind her said. "And with you, that's two. So ten more to go. And how many were planning to steal the newly repaired police helicopter?"

"Why do you think we're planning to steal the police helicopter?" Alice asked.

"Because you and your friends are predictable. And you think silly old Hutchens won't think to look for any of you in a vehicle that's supposedly one of his."

"Go to hell," Alice muttered, brushing away a tear.

"Oh, are you sad because your little killing spree's coming to an end? You had it coming, Alice."

They then heard the noise of the helicopter approaching.

Something smashed on the floor near Alice and she collapsed where she was, overcome by stun gas.

"Nice meeting you, Alice," Derek said as he moved away.

· · ·

Hutchens grinned at the helicopter pilot.

"I guess this was probably when Lady Vice and her friends were planning to get the jump on us," he shouted cheerfully.

"I guess so," the pilot replied. "Do you want to take this thing down now?"

"Not yet," Hutchens replied. "Let's circle around the neighborhood for a while."

Jason looked down below. There was another woman leaning out a window looking for police spotters.

In one hand, Jason was holding onto his grappling hook gun. In the other, he readied a stun gas canister.

Then, releasing the grappling hook cable, he rappelled down the building and smashed the canister in front of the woman as he passed her.

He then looked up and was a little startled. For a moment, it seemed as though the unconscious woman was going to fall out of the building. However, it was only for a moment and, as Jason watched her, she slumped back inside.

Jason recoiled the cable, rocketing back up.

"Got another one."

Derek nodded. "Good work. I just got one too. That

makes four between us. Also, Diane's just got off the radio to Hutchens and she said they got five in the helicopter."

"So I heard," Jason said. "Three to go."

"Three to go," Derek said. "And I've just spotted another one."

He flicked off the radio, fired his grappling hook onto a building protrusion close to level with his current position. Then he swung down to an open balcony below, his feet landing in the small of a woman's back and knocking her to the ground.

The woman fumbled around for the automatic weapon she'd been carrying but Derek threw a stun gas canister in front of her before she could reach it.

He flicked on his radio again. "Got her. Two left. Diane?"

"I can't see anyone from my position," she replied.

"Don't worry," Jason said. "I've found them."

As Jason watched, the two last members of the gang were trying to scale the outside of the building Gwendolyn and the others were in. They didn't have any specialized equipment. Just a lot of sheer nerve.

Firing his double-ended grappling hook several times to slide between buildings, he went around to the far side of the target building before he moved in so the women couldn't see him.

Then he rappelled down the building he was on until he was level with the roof of the place. Once he was in position, he used his double-ended grappling hook again to slide across.

Smiling at the ease at which he and the others had got the drop on the Lady Vice imposters, he waited for the women to climb onto the roof. He didn't want to scare them while they were still climbing in case they fell. So he watched and waited and, when they were on the roof and safely on their feet, he walked over to them.

"Hello," he said.

The two women whirled around. One of them screamed as well but the cry was cut off when the stun gas took effect.

Jason then proceeded to the far side of the roof, staying out of range of the gas, and flicked his radio on.

"That's all of them," he said. "Let's collect them and leave them on the roof where Hutchens and his officers can find them."

"Sounds good to me," Derek replied. "Nice work, Sentinel."

Jason smiled. "You too, Achilles."

• • •

Down below in the event hall, Derek Fletcher got off his cell phone and walked over to his wife Gwendolyn, kissing her on the cheek.

"Good news, honey," he told her. "I've just got off the phone to Hutchens. All twelve members of the Lady Vice gang are in custody."

Gwendolyn smiled. "That's wonderful." She then looked at all the guests ambling around the function hall. "Well, I think this should turn out to be a very nice evening."

An hour later, Hutchens met Diane, Jason and Derek in another room of the building, with the charity drive still going on two floors above them.

The others knew that something wasn't right when they saw Hutchens. He should have been elated.

He wasn't.

"Thank you, Derek," he said. "And thank you again, Jason, too. A week ago, I would have thought it'd be impossible to bring in Lady Vice and her gang. You two made it look *easy*." He sighed. "I wish I could buy everyone a drink and celebrate but unfortunately, we've got problems. In a few minutes, I'm going to talk to my senior officers about this. But I thought I'd tell you first."

He put on a smile. "You've already worked one

miracle tonight. Perhaps you can work two."

"Cupid," Jason murmured.

Hutchens nodded. "Palmer—that's my next in command—just brought this over from the station. It arrived about an hour and a half ago."

He hit the play switch on a small combination CD/USB player.

"*Hello, Commissioner. If you're listening to this, then I assume you and your unofficial team have brought in Lady Vice and her gang. I've been watching your preparations over the past few days. They seemed well thought-out and, as I record this message, I have every confidence in your success.*

"*And I hope my confidence is not misplaced. It would be a shame if matters there tied you up and no attempt were made to prevent the death of Mayor Alison St. Claire because I've always enjoyed our cat and mouse games.*

"*You have until ten thirty to save her, Commissioner, and we're at the new West Avenue Bridge construction site. Don't be late.*"

"He's kidnapped the mayor," Hutchens said once the recording had finished.

Jason glanced at his watch. "And we've got about an hour and twenty minutes to save her."

"No one's succeeded in stopping Cupid yet," Hutchens told him and Derek. "I'm hoping you two can."

Jason slapped Derek on the shoulder. "Come on, Achilles. Let's go and work a miracle."

"Right with you, Sentinel," Derek replied.

Diane nodded to Hutchens. "I'm going as well."

"We'll be right behind you," Hutchens told her.

He then watched as the three of them left the room and took a moment to compose himself. The evening had been going so well until now.

He'd already lost one friend to Cupid. He didn't want to lose another.

ONE WAY OR ANOTHER

Diane pulled up by the east side of the river and got out of the car. The pylons of the new West Avenue Bridge on the near side were finished, as was the next pair along. A section of road passed between them, heading back into the city behind her, although it was obviously barricaded as anyone who went speeding along the unfinished bridge section would find themselves in the river.

There were lights on the bridge and along the new suspension cables. Some of them were permanent lights that would remain in place when the bridge was finished. Others were there for visibility purposes while the work was taking place.

There were also three cranes around this section of the bridge and one of them was immediately behind the near pylons. And the light was on in the crane operator's cab.

Diane opened the car door and pulled a pair of binoculars out of the glove compartment. Holding them up, she gazed at the cab but it was difficult to see anything.

She pulled out her radio. "Do you guys see the light in the crane cab?"

"*I* see it," Jason replied. "I'm magnifying the image..." He trailed off. "The mayor's in there. And she's alone."

Diane nodded and glanced at her watch. It was nine-forty, leaving fifty minutes before Cupid took his shot. Somehow, she had expected he would be standing right next to St. Claire, counting down the minutes. But now she realized how absurd that would be. Not to mention unsporting.

"He's playing with us," she said. "We have to be careful. He won't take a shot at St. Claire until ten-thirty ticks over and he'll only take one. But he won't hesitate about killing any of *us* in the meantime."

"True," Derek said. "But we still have to try to get to the mayor. At least until we can work out where Cupid is."

Listening, Jason nodded his agreement. Hopefully, Cupid was on their side of the river. And presumably, he was. With the new bridge not even half finished and no boats in sight, positioning himself on the opposite side would make it very difficult for him to take his shot. However, where he actually *was* was still anyone's guess.

Jason himself was on decent elevation now, the roof of a ten storey complex overlooking the river. The crane was on a diagonal line from him three hundred yards to his right.

There was a closer building on his right as well, a slightly larger one than the one he was on. That was where Derek was. And there were a couple of twelve storey buildings behind them. Possibly, Cupid was in one of them. But possibly, he could be anywhere.

"Derek," Diane said. "Hutchens is going to be here in a few minutes with half the police force. Maybe we should wait."

"And you think Cupid doesn't know that?" Derek countered. "He *invited* them."

"He knows about you and Jason too," Diane reminded him.

"He knows a little," Derek said. "But we might still surprise him. Besides, if he takes a shot at me, he might give himself away. Right, Sentinel?"

"Makes sense," Jason agreed.

"Good," Derek told him. "You're on lookout duty. I'm going for that crane."

Derek abseiled down the outside of the building he was on until he was level with the cab of the crane where Mayor St. Claire was being held prisoner.

He wondered how Cupid was keeping her there. Whether she was drugged, restrained or too terrified to step outside the cab and try the ladder. Any of the options would be a problem. He just hoped she wasn't cuffed to anything with something that required a key.

Oddly, although he had acquired a quite impressive skill set over the years, unlocking police handcuffs without a key was something he'd never learned.

Coming to a halt, he considered using one of the double-ended grappling hooks Jason had provided. He was glad to have them but he decided to forego it for the time-being. He already had one cable hooked on the building he was on, the one he was hanging off right then.

So getting another single hook with his free hand, he fired it at the top of the crane and recoiled the cable, while slowly releasing the other one and playing it out.

In this manner, he replicated the action of the double-ended grappling hooks and slid all the way to the crane. He then released the first hook and got a grip on the metal framework of the crane tower. And, then, he released the other.

He was right above the cab now. Then he swung himself down to the door but, as he did, a bullet struck the roof of the cab an inch above his right shoulder with a loud clang. Then another glanced off his hand

and he slipped, knocking himself against the cab and catching onto the framework below.

Jason heard the shots but he didn't see where they'd come from. Still, they now knew that Cupid was on their side of the river.

However, looking around for him was not going to work. He had to see where the shots landed. Adjusting his visor's binocular setting, he zoomed in on Derek.

There was another shot. This hit Derek in the back. While his Kevlar armor took a lot of the impact, he let go of the crane with his right hand in an involuntarily spasm of agony, slipping from his perch.

He quickly grabbed the metal frame again and swung himself around between it and the bridge pylon.

Another shot rang clear in the night and shards of hot sparks struck him across his jaw.

"He's shooting down," Jason told Diane over the radio. "I'm going to check out the buildings behind me."

"Be careful," Diane told him.

Then the sounds of sirens wailing and a swirl of red

and blue lights signaled the arrival of the cavalry.

"The police are here," Diane said.

Jason fired a grappling hook at the roof of the building behind him. "So I noticed."

He tugged on the cable to check that the hook was lodged, then he recoiled the cable and shot up towards the night sky.

There was another shot. He felt a blow to his shoulder.

Cupid had shot at *him*.

Getting a hand free, Jason pulled out another grappling hook, fired it at the far end of the building, released the first hook and swung out in an arc to his left and scrambled onto the rooftop corner of the building.

He waited a moment but Cupid didn't fire again. He glanced back at Derek.

Derek pulled himself around to the far side of the crane, where he'd be much harder for Cupid to hit. It wasn't the best cover available. Crane towers weren't solid all the way through like a good concrete building but it was better than nothing.

He then tried to pull his way back up to the cab… and fumbled. The metal was covered in grease.

Terror wasn't an emotion Derek was overly familiar

with but he felt it then. Terror and regret.

Again and again, he tried to catch onto the crane but it was no use. He was falling too fast now. He tried to pry a grappling hook off his belt but his gloves were now so covered in the grease, it was impossible.

Jason fired his grappling hook at the crane, lodging it on the counter balance jib behind the cab.

He'd actually been aiming for the hoisting jib on the other side but there was no time for a second shot. He swung down like a pendulum, the air rushing past him. Then throwing his weight forward under the grappling hook gun and twisting to his left, he sailed out behind the crane, readying another hook.

With his eyes never leaving Derek, he fired, the propulsion of the hook greater than Derek's fall.

For a painful split second Jason watched to see whether the hook would catch his new partner. There was a fraction of time—the tiniest moment—where it looked as though the hook had missed. But then, with a sudden jerk on the end of the cable, it caught onto Derek's leg.

Jason swung back under the counter balance jib of the crane with Derek dangling a hundred feet or so beneath him and breathed a sigh of relief. All the practice he'd had chasing the Vampire around had paid off.

Hutchens jogged over to Diane. "Who was that? Jason?"

"Derek fell off the crane," Diane said. "Jason swung over there. I think he was trying to save him."

"And did he?"

Diane pressed her lips together and drew in a sharp breath. "I don't know. But Mayor St. Claire's up in that crane by herself." She gestured to some buildings behind her. "And Cupid was up there taking shots at Derek when he tried to get to her."

Hutchens nodded. "Right. I'll send a S.W.A.T. team up."

He jogged back to the line of cars and armored vans that had just pulled up.

Diane raised her binoculars again and saw Derek swinging underneath Jason.

Then there was another shot.

Jason nearly let go of both grappling hooks at once from the shock of the impact.

He let out a cry and got his grip back on the grappling hook gun that was the effective lifeline to Derek. He'd nearly dropped him.

He groaned in pain. He'd been hit in the back. As it had for Derek, the Kevlar suit had saved him but it hadn't absorbed all the impact.

"Let me go!" Derek called out to him. "Uncoil!"

Jason nodded and released the cable, lowering Derek. Then he realized he was lowering him into the river. The crane was right on the edge of it.

Another shot rang overhead.

Jason looked up but he wasn't sure what Cupid was shooting at now.

Suddenly, his arm shot back as the weight on the end of the cable disappeared. He looked down in horror and saw Derek plunge into the water and disappear. In a Kevlar armored suit.

Jason recoiled the cable but didn't put away the grappling hook gun. Spinning around, he tried to see what Cupid was up to. Which was difficult when the man was nowhere in sight.

Another shot hit something up above and Jason fell with a stomach heaving drop. His hook had slipped.

He fired the other grappling hook at the hoisting jib of the crane. He felt it lodge and then he swung across to the completed section of the bridge, landing just below the nearest pylon on what would be a pedestrian promenade when the bridge was finished. He released the hook and recoiled it. And he recoiled the one that had failed as well. He looked at it in disbelief. It hadn't been dislodged. It had been mangled. Cupid, from a distance of three or four hundred yards most likely, had shot his hook and very nearly killed him in the process.

"Son of a bitch," he muttered when he got his breath back.

Then he remembered Derek. He leaned over the side of the bridge and looked down at the river's edge.

He watched the dark water for a handful of moments until he finally saw something. A drenched figure, without a helmet, gloves, chest armor or boots dragged himself out of the water and lay panting on the river's edge.

Eight years ago, Derek Bradley was certainly not on Jason's list of people he gave a damn about but right then, he was very relieved to see he was okay.

He took another breath and looked at the time. It was nine fifty-three, leaving him and the police thirty seven minutes. It was amazing, he thought in an offhand manner, that after all the mad aerobatics, his watch still worked.

He flicked on his radio again. "Diane?"

"What's going on?" she asked. She sounded upset.

"Cupid greased the far side of the crane," a third voice cut in.

"Derek?" Diane exclaimed.

"Yeah, I'm in one piece," he replied. "Thanks to

Jason and no thanks to our trigger happy friend up in the buildings. And I'm afraid I'm out of the fight. I left most of my gear in the river."

"It's up to me then, I suppose," Jason said.

"Wait, Jason," Diane started. "Hutchens said—"

Derek cut her off. "Diane. You may want to tell the commissioner about the grease. If Cupid's greased one side, he's probably greased the ladders as well. I'd say he got everything very nicely set up before he invited us here."

"Yeah, we're playing on his home turf all right," Diane muttered. "Thanks, Derek. I'll tell Hutchens. And Jason?"

"Yeah?" Jason replied.

"Be very careful."

"Got it," Jason said and he flicked the radio off. He fired a grappling hook at the top of the pylon above him. Then recoiling the cable, he sailed up and scrambled onto it, getting a look at the buildings there. Keeping his grip on the grappling hook gun in case Cupid took another shot at him, he switched on his visor's binocular view, magnified everything a little and scanned the buildings more carefully.

However, as hard as he looked, he couldn't see any sign of Cupid. And there were no more shots either.

"Prick's gone to ground," he muttered.

He turned around and realized he was in line with

the cab where St. Claire was. He magnified his view and looked inside. She was there, slumped over in a chair. For a moment, he thought she was dead but a very slight but regular expansion and contraction of her shoulders told him she was breathing.

He flicked the radio on again. "Diane. I can see St. Claire. She's sleeping in the crane cab. I think she's been drugged."

"Any sign of Cupid?" Diane asked.

"No," Jason replied. "Cupid's gone very quiet. Listen. I'm right in front of the crane arm leading over to St. Claire. I can reach her."

"Yeah, well remember what happened to Derek," Diane pointed out.

Jason switched the binocular view off and smiled. "I think I'll be just fine. I know what Cupid planted here."

"What?"

"There's a row of several wires across the crane arm and they go underneath it. I'd say they're hooked up to explosives and if anyone puts their foot on them, the end of the crane arm will break off underneath them, dropping them like a rock."

"You have a plan?"

"I have a double-ended grappling hook," Jason said. "And Cupid might not know about it."

"A double-ended grappling hook?"

"That's right. And it's awesome."

He looked down below. There were several groups of police officers converging on the crane.

"You've got teams moving in?" he asked Diane.

"Yes. What's the problem?"

"The problem? The problem is that Cupid's rigged this entire place up with traps. His turf, remember?"

"Yeah, Derek said the ladders on the crane might be greased," Diane reminded him. "You worry about you."

Jason shook his head. "No, no. I know he said that—and that's probably right—but there might be traps on the ground."

Then, that very moment, there was an eruption of bright light. A thick wall of impenetrable flames surrounded the base of the crane, preventing the police from closing in on it.

"It seems you were right, Jason," Diane said. "I just saw a flare. Cupid must have covered the area around the crane with oil and he's just set it alight."

Jason frowned. "You saw a flare? Where?"

There was a pause at the other end. "I think it came from under the bridge. Derek?"

"I saw him," Derek joined in. "Just briefly. In the scaffolding under the bridge."

"Moving in," Jason muttered. He looked at the time again. Nine fifty-eight.

"Where did those five minutes go?" he said to himself.

"What?" Diane asked.

"Nothing," Jason said. He pulled out a double-ended grappling hook. "I'm moving in. Sentinel out."

He flicked the radio off again, fired one grappling hook into the pylon, tugged on the cable to check it had lodged properly and fired another just above the cab of the crane.

It was perfect, a horizontal line between him and St. Claire. He recoiled the one cable, while uncoiling the other, and soared over the crane arm until he reached the cab.

A shot rang nearby and shattered the glass of the cab just beside his neck. Ignoring it, Jason released the grappling hooks and swung inside.

Cupid didn't shoot again.

For a moment, Jason wondered why. But only for a moment.

"Oh, shit," he muttered.

Hutchens moved over to Diane. "He's in the cab."

Diane nodded. "Yes."

"What's he waiting for?"

Diane shook her head. "I don't know."

Then the radio came alive with a bit of static and she

heard Jason's voice again.

"I can't move her, Diane."

"Okay. Talk me through the problem. What's going on?"

"It looks like there are some explosives here," Jason told her. "Three sticks, like the ones you see in movies sometimes. And they're wired to... I don't know. A trigger? A detonator? It's under her thigh. It looks as though her weight on it is keeping the explosives from going off."

"Could be," Diane agreed.

"I don't know what to do," Jason said.

"Sit tight. I'm thinking."

Then Derek's voice cut into the conversation. "I know a bit about disabling explosives."

"I could send one of my men up there," Hutchens said. "Hell, I'd go up there myself if I have to. I'm tired of other people dying."

Diane shook her head. "But *how* would you or men get up there?"

"How's *Derek* going to get up there?" Hutchens muttered when they were out of earshot of the other officers.

"I think he salvaged one grappling hook after his fall in the river," Diane replied.

They jogged past some construction vehicles and found Derek crouching in the shadows by the side of the river.

"Diane says you can get up there," Hutchens told him. "Can you?"

Derek nodded. "I've got a plan. But I'm going to need some armor."

Hutchens nodded back. "Right. Wait here." He sprinted through the construction area, past the still burning fires around the crane and disappeared into the crowds of police.

"He can sure move," Diane remarked to Derek. "I had no idea he was that fast."

Derek smiled. "Yeah. He can move all right."

Diane saw more red lights approaching. The fire brigade had arrived and one large engine was coming towards the crane, its ladder raised.

"Good idea," she said.

The truck stopped in front of the crane and the ladder came to a rest a quarter of the way up the tower. Then police officers scrambled onto the vehicle and made their way up.

"A pity we can't use the helicopter though," Diane said.

"True," Derek agreed. "But it makes sense. Cupid's

shot it down before. He could do it again."

Then just as quickly as he had left, Hutchens returned, jogging towards them with a S.W.A.T. vest and a helmet.

"Here," he said, slinging them at Derek's feet.

"Thanks," Derek said, putting the vest on first and then the helmet. He got out his radio and glanced at the top of the crane.

At that moment, a heavy rain began to fall. Derek, Diane and Hutchens were drenched in seconds.

"It was pouring down the last time Cupid pulled off one of these stunts too," Hutchens said, looking up and squinting at the cab of the crane. "It's kind of hard to see up there."

"If it makes it hard for us, it might make it hard for Cupid too," Derek pointed out.

"One can only hope," Hutchens said.

Derek smiled and turned on his radio. "Achilles to Sentinel. Can you see me?"

"Not well but I see you."

"Fire a grappling hook towards the ground as far as it will go. Don't worry if it doesn't go all the way."

"All right," Jason replied.

Derek saw him emerge from the cab and fire the hook. It was hard to see it as it came down with the rain but he saw it again when it stopped about twelve yards above him.

Derek pulled out his one remaining grappling hook and aimed. This was going to be tricky. And now there was a bit of wind blowing Jason's grappling hook around too. However, he just had to concentrate. That was all.

He fired, recoiling the hook instantly to stop it shooting far past the mark but it came straight back without catching onto the other one.

He tried again without success.

Then Derek had another idea. He left the cable uncoiled, picked up the hook from the ground and, swirling it around, flung it up and pulled down sharply.

This time, it caught Jason's hook. He gave the cable a tug to make sure it held. Then he gave Diane and Hutchens a smile.

"Nice work, cowboy," Hutchens said.

"Thanks, commissioner," Derek replied. "Wish me luck."

"Good luck."

Jason slid his end of the cable around a metal protrusion in the cab. Then, using it as a makeshift pulley, he recoiled it, lifting Derek clear off the ground and hauling him up towards him, while the rain sprayed off his back.

"Ten oh-four," Diane said, watching as he disappeared inside the cab with Jason. "Not much time left."

Hutchens' expression was grim. "I know."

"All yours," Jason said, stepping aside as Derek climbed into the cab.

Derek crouched down and inspected the wires and the explosives.

"Nothing fancy here," he said. "These are just three small sticks of dynamite. But they're enough."

"Can you disable the detonator?"

"I think I can," Derek replied. "I did some stuff like this when I was with the Navy SEALs. Once in the field." He frowned. "Usually with more equipment though, I have to admit. Right now, I'd kill for a pair of pliers."

He then studied the grappling hook he'd used to get up there. "This might help though."

"Can *I* do anything?" Jason asked.

Derek nodded. "Yeah. Stay out of the way. Look for Cupid or something."

Jason nodded. "Got it."

"I don't mean any offence," Derek told him as he set to work. "It's just that disarming detonators is tricky and I need to concentrate. So don't take it the wrong way. You've impressed me tonight, Jason. You've not only saved my life but I've seen what you're capable of and it's more than I thought. More than you'd probably think yourself, I'd imagine. Eight years ago, I said some things to you that... Well, they were things I shouldn't have said. Let's put it that way. But if I told you that you didn't have what it takes to do what you do, then I was dead wrong." He chuckled and shook his head. "I tell you, I wouldn't want to be the criminal who got on *your* wrong side."

Jason smiled. "Thanks, Derek."

Jason then stepped outside the cab and looked down. The rain was torrential now, drenching everyone, and it was very hard to see. The only dry place right then appeared to be the scaffolding under the bridge. His train of thought slid to a halt. When Cupid had fired the flare that triggered the fire trap around the crane, that's where Derek said it had come from.

Jason pulled out his radio and flicked it on. "Diane?"

"Is everything all right?"

"Up here? Derek's trying to disarm the detonator now. But what's the news on Cupid? I just remembered Derek said that flare he fired came from under the bridge."

"Yeah, we remember," Diane replied. "Hutchens sent a S.W.A.T. team to check it out. But um... getting there is a little tricky."

"More traps?"

"Yeah. At the easiest places to get onto the scaffolding. Also there are some rigged explosives along the completed road and promenade sections."

Jason shook his head. "Cupid's gone to town tonight, hasn't he?"

"His last hurrah. Yeah. Quite the party."

Jason looked at his watch. "It's thirteen past. We're running out of time."

"I know."

"And it may take Derek a while to disarm that detonator. Damn it. We've *got* to get Cupid. I'll try to get down there myself."

"Don't do anything stupid."

"I think that ship has sailed, Diane."

Diane shook her head and looked at the organized chaos around her. The fires around the crane had died out after a sustained effort from the rain, although it had taken a while with the oil fuelling them. Meanwhile, a number of officers had scrambled up the ladder of the fire engine onto the crane tower and had stopped about halfway up. As Derek had predicted, the ladders *were* greased. And last she heard, while the S.W.A.T. team was making some progress getting to the end of the completed section of the bridge and the scaffolding underneath, they weren't getting there fast enough.

"Diane?"

She held up her radio. "How's it going up there?"

"I've disarmed the detonator," Derek told her. "The mayor's safe for the moment."

Diane breathed a sigh of relief. "First good news I've heard all night."

She looked up at the crane, shielding her eyes from the rain.

"You turned off the cab light," she said.

"I don't want to make things any easier for Cupid than necessary," Derek replied. "And while we're on the subject, tell the idiot with the search light to get it off the crane, switch the damn thing off or point it at the scaffolding under the bridge and try to blind Cupid."

"Got it," Diane replied, jogging over to the idiot in question.

"Oh. And Jason's in the scaffolding under the bridge."

"I know."

"What's the time?"

Diane checked her watch and did a double-take. "Ten twenty-four."

"All right. I'm going to keep the mayor up here and

shield her," Derek said. "Hopefully, my S.W.A.T. vest will slow the bullet even if it doesn't save me."

"Derek..."

"Forget it, Diane. I've got a debt to pay. I'm paying it. Anyway, I can't risk lowering her down. Not now. Just get that search light off the crane."

Diane nodded. "Will do. Hang in there."

"That's the plan."

Jason looked around. The scaffolding under the bridge was largely shielded from the swirl of blue and red lights on the river's edge and the thundering rain, and he was searching the far end of the temporary framework overhanging the river. About a hundred yards away from the bank and all the madness that was going on there.

He checked the time. Ten twenty-eight.

There were two minutes left and no one had seen Cupid.

He wondered whether he should get off the scaffolding and see if he was climbing up the suspension cables but the police spotters were no doubt watching up there already.

Then he saw something right on the edge of the scaffolding, where it jutted out over the river.

Jason jogged over and found an oxygen tank of the

kind used for scuba diving. And next to it was a coil of rope and a pair of diving fins.

"Found your escape route, Cupid," he said.

"Very clever," came a voice from behind him. "Shall I shoot you now or would you rather turn round and see the bullet?"

Jason smiled to himself. "You might give your position away."

"The police already know I'm here somewhere. One more shot won't change that. The Sentinel? Or is it Achilles? Men in Kevlar costumes all look the same to me."

"That's funny," Jason said, still smiling. He had formed his plan now. However, he couldn't help himself. He just *had* to wait for Cupid to resume talking. The man had a very rich and commanding voice but it was clearly something of a liability for him. He enjoyed listening to himself just a bit too much.

"Yes. Well…"

Jason lunged forward, scooping up the oxygen tank and in the same movement, he leapt off the edge of the scaffolding and fell towards the river.

He twisted around, fired a grappling hook at the scaffolding and swung back under the bridge, throwing the oxygen tank onto the river's edge. And as he sailed back up on his arc, he fired another grappling hook at the scaffolding above, released the first hook and hauled himself back up under the bridge.

Then he sprinted to the end of the scaffolding. Cupid would be taking his shot at any moment. Then Jason saw him, standing on the edge of a platform, wearing a black wet suit, and with his gun aimed at the cab on top of the crane, all irritation at losing his oxygen tank forgotten.

As he closed in, Jason curled his hand into a fist and slammed it into the side of Cupid's jaw as hard as he could.

There was a thunderclap in the night. Cupid's shot. For the tiniest fraction of a second, Jason wondered whether he had arrived too late. But Cupid's arm had flung out when he'd hit him and the shot, wherever the bullet had ended up, had gone wide.

Jason then kicked Cupid in the chest for good measure, knocking him to the ground and throwing his gun out of his hands. Then he grabbed it and flung it into the river.

"That was your shot, Cupid," he said. "And you missed."

Cupid rolled to his feet and wiped some blood from the side of his mouth. "Good for the mayor," he muttered. "Bad for you."

Then he lunged at Jason.

Right then, Jason wished Derek were there. Derek was the fighter. The man with the navy SEAL expertise and the heightened physical strength. Whereas he just wanted to be home reading a bedtime story to Ethan or watching a late night movie with Angie.

But he was there and Derek wasn't.

He stepped back as Cupid took a swing and then he hit him again while he was off balance. Cupid took another swing. Jason ducked back and kicked him in the kneecap. Then he dived to the ground and kicked Cupid's legs out from under him.

Cupid groaned as he got to his feet.

"What the hell's your problem?" he cried. "The killings are over. And you got Lady Vice and the Vampire. You've won."

"You have to face the music, Cupid," Jason said. "This is the way it's got to be."

"I showed the people of Fringe City the people responsible for the madness," Cupid shot back. "I taught them a lesson they'll never forget."

Jason kicked him in the chest, knocking him over again. Cupid stood up with a little more effort this time.

"No, you didn't," Jason told him. "You just wanted your moment in the sun."

"I think you're confusing me with Lady Vice."

Jason shook his head. "Kaori Tanaka," he murmured.

Cupid looked at him in bewilderment. "I have no

idea who you're talking about."

"Of course you don't," Jason told him. "That would imply you care about people."

Cupid took another swing at him. Jason caught his wrist, grabbed his free hand and head butted him. He let go of his wrists as Cupid staggered back, letting him stagger more, and kicked him to the ground again.

Cupid let out another groan as he landed. He was shaky on his feet when he climbed up this time and his breathing was heavy and labored.

"I hated the people responsible for that girl's death," Jason said. "More than I think I've hated anyone. But you? You're just as bad as them. You looked at all the pain, all the fear, all the suffering and all the grief in the city and used it to have a few moments of glory. You didn't just pour oil on a burning man. You stuck a knife in and threw a grenade."

Cupid raised his hands in a placating gesture. "Listen…"

Jason kicked him to the ground yet again.

"This feels good actually," he confessed. "A bit of cathartic release." He looked down at Cupid. "No. *You* listen. Before I turn in for the night, I'm handing you over to the authorities. And we can do it the easy way or the hard way."

Cupid staggered to his feet. He was now standing

on the very edge of the scaffolding over the river.

He smiled. "I'm sorry to disappoint you... *Sentinel*." Then he leapt off.

Jason didn't even think. He'd had so much practice at this recently that in that moment, it became second nature. He fired his grappling hook and it caught Cupid by the ankle.

He walked along the outside of the scaffolding, hanging onto Cupid until he reached the river's edge. Then he pulled out his radio.

"Diane?"

"You got him?"

Jason smiled. "Of course I got him. This is me we're talking about here. Are you ready to bring him in?"

"We're right below you."

Jason uncoiled the cable a little more and released the hook. Cupid fell about two yards to the ground in the middle of a circle of officers, and was cuffed a moment later.

"He's all yours," Jason said. "Sentinel out."

He flicked off the radio. It was time to go. Since Angie hadn't known about Cupid kidnapping the mayor, she would have expected him home an hour ago.

· · ·

Hutchens walked over to Cupid to see him for himself just once before his officers took him away.

"I don't know what you were trying to prove, Cupid," he told him, "but a string of premeditated killings is a first class ticket to life imprisonment."

Cupid drew himself up and regarded Hutchens with a firm gaze. "I was not trying to prove anything, Commissioner. I was—"

"I don't give a damn what you were doing, you son of a bitch," Hutchens cut him off. He turned to his officers. "Take him away, guys."

Diane found Derek sitting some distance away from all the excitement.

"We did it," she said.

Derek nodded. "Yeah. We did it."

They sat in silence for several long moments.

"Thank you, Derek," Diane said at last.

Derek shrugged. "I have a debt to pay. I'm paying it off." A pensive gaze crossed his features. "You know, when I slipped on the grease and I fell, I was terrified for a moment but after that, I felt this strange sense of calm. I felt that maybe if I had fallen into the river, it would clear the debt. That by giving my life, I could pay it off completely. That maybe that was what was needed."

Diane shook her head. "You can do far more good for the city alive than dead, Derek. You're not the man I profiled eight years ago."

Derek smiled. "You profiled me?"

"Yeah. To build up a picture of the man we were looking for. Jason helped me."

"You really had it in for me then."

Diane smiled back. "You'd better believe we did."

"And now?"

Diane shrugged. "We needed you. And as I said, you've changed. You're not the same man any more. You earned your second chance."

"So what happens now?"

"You move into the flat that Gwendolyn found for you. You get settled back into everyday life. Find yourself a job probably. Things like that."

Derek nodded. "I think I'd like to have another try at getting into the police force."

"That might suit you quite well now," Diane agreed. "Provided you don't fail your psych test again."

She looked up at the stars and sighed contentedly. "However, I think things'll turn out a little differently this time around."

. . .

A little later, Jason arrived home.

"You're late," Angie said. "You said you had this all planned down to the wire." She frowned. "And you look like hell."

Jason smiled. "Long night. Bit of a rough one too."

"What happened? You said it would go like clockwork. You promised you had everything under control."

"It *did* go like clockwork," Jason said. "We got Lady Vice and her girls without a bit of trouble. The only problem was that while we were doing that, Cupid was kidnapping the mayor. Then we got one of his messages telling us that she had until ten-thirty to live."

"Oh my god."

"Relax," Jason said. "She's fine. And we got him."

"You mean to tell me you're late because you were bringing in Cupid as well?"

Jason nodded. "Yep. I'm sure you can hear all about it on the news in the morning. But at the moment, I just want to have a shower, check on Ethan and go to sleep."

Angie kissed him. "I thought you might want to do that." Then she squeezed his hand. "So it's over now?"

Jason smiled. "It's over. I think I'll sleep in tomorrow. And you can tell Amanda that I'm ready to come back to work."

Angie smiled. "I'll tell her after the vacation. And since you don't need to go swinging around skyscrapers any more, you could do with a vacation too."

"Yeah," Jason agreed. "That sounds good."

THE BREAK OF DAY

Alison St. Claire popped the headache pills into her mouth, took a sip of water and gulped them down. She then had a longer drink of water, put her glass down and closed her eyes. Then she took a few breaths, opened them again, and sat down.

"How's your head this morning?" Hutchens asked her.

St. Claire smiled. "Ask me this afternoon. But I feel a bit better now than I did when I woke up."

"Do you remember much from last night?"

St. Claire shook her head. "Not really. From what I hear, it sounds like it was quite the party." She looked serious for a moment. "I understand Jason and Derek saved my life. I'd like to thank them if I could."

"I know," Hutchens said. "But it's probably not the best idea. You know. Unofficial liaisons. Off the record and all of that. However, I'm sure I can pass on the message."

"Thank you, Eric." For a moment, St. Claire was quiet but then she smiled again. "Well, we persevered.

We made it through and now Fringe City can continue down the road with a bright, happy future."

"Yeah," Hutchens agreed. "It's actually become a rather nice place to live. I saw one of our new parks on the way here this morning. It's beautiful. And I think one of these days, I should check out the new museum."

"Oh, you haven't been? You should definitely go. Take Sandra one day."

Hutchens smiled. "All right. I will."

"So... do you still want to resign?"

Hutchens hesitated. "Well, honestly? Yes. But for different reasons now."

"I think I understand," St. Claire said. "Finishing on a high note? Time to move on? Looking forward to enjoying life for a change?"

"Yeah," Hutchens said. "Something like that."

"... a night in which not only the Lady Vice gang was brought in but Cupid as well, ending this chapter of Fringe City's journey.

"And as I saw the sun shining through my window this morning, I had to admit that right now, I'm feeling very optimistic. The future looks bright again. For Fringe City Central, on this special morning edition, this is Mariane O'Hara. So long."

Gwendolyn smiled and flicked the television off.

"I guess that makes it official," Sonya said.

Beside them, Devan smiled and shook his head. "There's no doubt about it. Lady Vice and Cupid were the only ones holding this city back and now they're well and truly out of the way."

"You don't expect the prosecution case to be particularly difficult?" Gwendolyn asked him with a smile.

"I've had difficult cases before," Devan said. "I doubt these will rank among them. How did the charity drives go last night, by the way?"

"Brilliant," George said, coming through the door and beaming from ear to ear. "Let's just say that Outreach won't have any funding problems for quite a while."

Sonya smiled wistfully. "I wonder, with the bright future ahead, whether the city will still *need* Outreach in a year or two."

"That's an optimistic thought," Gwendolyn said. "The realist in me thinks we'll be needed for a while yet. However, my inner optimist thinks it might not be on quite the same scale."

"That's something," Sonya said.

"It's *a lot*," Gwendolyn replied.

. . .

Dr. John Carter smiled at his visitor. "Derek? This is a bit of a surprise. I didn't expect to see you back so soon."

"It's good to see you, John," Derek said. "I just wanted to stop by and say hello. Also, I thought I'd tell you I'm thinking of becoming a police officer."

"Well, that's great. It's a line of work that's right up your alley, I'd say."

"Yes, that's what I thought," Derek agreed. "You know, I have to say when I first left this place, I felt a little apprehensive."

John nodded. "That's understandable. You were here for several years. It was home."

"Yeah," Derek said. "But now I think I'll be all right out there." He nodded over his shoulder. "Out in the big wide world."

"I think you'll do just fine."

"Why are you checking your e-mail now?" Angie asked.

"Oh, I was just reading about my exploits last night," Jason told her. "Then I thought, while I was at it, I may as well." He frowned. "Hang on."

"What is it?"

"I've got one from Ji Eun."

Jason read the message.

Dear Jason,

I want to say thank you for everything. When Kaori died, knowing that other people out there felt the same way I did helped me a lot. I knew that I was not alone and that other people cared. You showed me that.

Now, I realize that you did a lot more too. I will never forget your kindness or your courage. And I want to let you know that your secret is safe with me. Is that the right expression? I can't express my feelings in English completely but I want you to know that I will always be grateful to you.

I hope that now you can have a wonderful vacation and I look forward to seeing you again when you come back to school.

Thank you for everything.

Ji Eun

"Well?" Angie asked.

Jason smiled and typed a reply. Then he hit send, logged out of his e-mail account and closed down the computer.

"It's a long story," he replied, putting his arm around her and giving her a short but tender kiss. "But it has a happy ending."

Angie smiled and pulled him closer. "Well, that's good to hear. Come on. Let's go to the park. I think Diane and her kids are already there."

Jason nodded. "Right. Ethan? You coming?"

"Coming!" Ethan called out, running towards them. Jason let go of Angie and crouched down, bracing himself for the impact. However, he was still knocked off his feet as his son crashed into him and gave him a big hug.

Jason brushed a hand through his hair and hugged him back, grinning. "That's my boy."

Ethan gave him an odd look, but a kind one. "You look... happier today, Dad."

Jason swallowed. For a moment, he was so overcome with emotion, so overcome with love for his little family, that he couldn't speak.

"I *am* happier today, Ethan," he said when he found his voice again. "It's a beautiful morning."